DEATHBOOK

Books by Stefán Máni

<u>Iceland:</u>
Skipid
Odadahraun
Nautid
Svartigaldur
  (Grímsson Series)
Krysuvik (Grímsson Series)
Adventa (Grímsson Series)
Horfnar (Grímsson Series)
Daudabokin
  (Grímsson Series)
Hyldypi (Grímsson Series)
Husid (Grímsson Series)
Feigd (Grímsson Series)
Grimmd (Grímsson Series)

<u>USA:</u>
The Ritual (Grímsson Series)
Deathbook (Grímsson Series)
Dust in the Wind
  (Grímsson Series)

<u>Australia:</u>
The Ship

<u>France:</u>
Noir Océan
Noir Karma
Présages (Grímsson Series)

<u>Germany:</u>
Das Schiff
Der Stier und das Madchen
In Schwarzen Spiegeln
  (Grímsson Series)

<u>Denmark:</u>
Skibet
Ödeland

<u>Sweden:</u>
Skeppet

<u>Poland:</u>
Statek

<u>Italy:</u>
Nero Oceano

DEATHBOOK

BY STEFÁN MÁNI

Grimmson Series
Translated by Philip Roughton

Deathbook

This book is published on behalf of the author by the Ethan Ellenberg Literary Agency.
The audiobook was published by arrangement with Stefán Máni, care of the Ethan Ellenberg Literary Agency, and was produced in 2022 by TANTOR Media, Incorporated, a division of Recorded Books, which hold the copyright thereto. Performed by Ulf Bjorklund.

You can reach the author at:
Website: stefanmani.is

BORGARNES

Summer
A Heartstring Breaks

The music's rhythm is like a rapid heartbeat. The savings bank manager's house stands at the top of the slope and is full of people—full of drunk people. Oddur runs the fingers of his left hand through his dark, curly hair. In his right he holds a warm can of beer. He's dressed in a vintage bomber jacket, white shirt, tight jeans, and new sneakers. He feels a bit awkward, as he knows very few of the people at the party. Not even all of those who came from Reykjavík. His schoolmates Patrekur and Bragi are here somewhere. They probably consider themselves his friends, but Oddur knows that that friendship will last at most until their matriculation exam; they're just too different. That is, he's too different from them. Of the partygoers from Borgarnes, he knows only the wild child Eva and her cousin Áslaug. Like him, Eva goes to Hamrahlíð Junior College, whereas Áslaug …

Where is she, anyway? Oddur sips his lukewarm beer distractedly. He elbows his way through the crowded living room, trying to spot his girlfriend, the sixteen-year-old

Áslaug, whom he met at a school dance that winter. The party is at her place, in the big house belonging to one of the most powerful men in town. The home is lavish, but is primarily old-fashioned, retro—like the scene of a nostalgic advertisement. Shouts and laughter come from the spacious kitchen. Oddur assumes that his friends are holding some sort of drinking contest there. A contest that will doubtless end in disaster, as usual. He himself isn't much of a party animal and has actually started dreading the next three weeks. He should be looking forward to them, being young and free and all that, but he just isn't the type to feel the need to cut loose or let his hair down, and regrets having allowed himself to give in to the pressure from his friends, who probably only needed a third person to bring down the costs of accommodation. But, now it´s happening and it's too late to cancel, besides the fact that …

"Hi!"

Suddenly, Áslaug appears. She throws her arms around Oddur and plants a wet kiss on him. He laughs and hugs her clumsily.

"Are you drunk?"

She giggles, narrows one eye and holds up her thumb and index finger, leaving a tiny space between them. "Just a little. Just thiiiiiis little."

Oddur smiles faintly. Áslaug is very cute, with platinum-blonde hair, straight teeth, and blue eyes—and she's wearing a short, blue summer dress. But her drunkenness is making her seem childish. Technically, she is a child—underage, in any case—but she doesn't look like it at all. Now, it's as if she's closer to being around confirmation age than anything else.

"Your friends are slamming tequila," she says with a giggle. "I had one or two shots. Or five, I don't remember."

Idiots, Oddur thinks. He's a bit irritated, without knowing exactly with whom or what. Maybe with everyone and everything. It was a mistake to come to this party. But here he is, all the same. That can't be changed, and anyway, he needs to *talk things over* with Áslaug, whether he likes it or not.

Isn't it best just getting it over with?

"Listen," says Oddur. "Can we go somewhere private?"

"You naughty boy!" says Áslaug, before kissing him again. "Can't wait, huh? Did you bring condoms?"

"Easy there." He squeezes out a smile to hide his irritation. "I was thinking more along the lines of us going outside. Away from this noise. Maybe walk around the block or something. Cool down a bit, huh?"

"Oh, Romeo—oh, Romeo!" Áslaug warbles, then laughs like a little girl. Maybe because she *is* a little girl. "All right, a walk *it is*. I'll just let Rut know. Otherwise, she'll be worried."

"I'll wait outside," says Oddur. He goes out into the summer night, while she runs up the carpeted stairs to the upper floor.

Rut's room is at the far end of the hallway. Áslaug walks past the bathroom, her own room, and their father's bedroom. Then she knocks on her twin sister's door before opening it.

"Are you asleep?" asks Áslaug.

"In this ruckus?" Rut asks coldly. She's sitting by the window in her wheelchair, with a woolen blanket over her legs. Next to her, a brass telescope stands mounted on a tripod.

"Oh, sorry," says Áslaug. "But it's not like there are *always* parties here. How long has it been since Dad left us home alone? Half a year? More?"

"I know," mutters Rut as she looks out the window, from which she has a view over the town on the spit and out to Borgarfjörður, where the Hvítá river and the salt sea merge and the evening sun shines on the water's billowing surface—a blood-red sun that barely sets before it counts in a new day.

Áslaug and Rut bear little resemblance, as they´re not identical twins. Rut is dark-haired and sharper-featured than her sister, heavy-browed with a stubby nose and a serious look. Her hair is rather short and coarse, tuftier than the golden mane that adorns Áslaug. Rut is skinny and pale, with small breasts and bony limbs. In the minds of their peers, Áslaug is a stereotypical carefree blonde, eternally bubbly and smiling, whereas Rut is the silent, temperamental drama queen.

"I just wanted to let you know that Oddur and I are going out for some fresh air," says Áslaug.

"You're going to leave me here?" asks Rut indignantly. "Alone? With this riffraff?"

"Chillax," says Áslaug. "We won't be long. Besides, you're not alone. Hannes is here, Jónas and Edda and the girls—half our class!"

Rut scoffs. "They may be *your* friends, but they're not mine. Stupid idiots, if you ask me."

"Don't be so negative," says Áslaug.

"I'm not negative, just realistic," Rut mutters. "And then what? Is Oddur going to stay the night? Will I be alone tomorrow, too?"

"He'll probably stay," says Áslaug. "But tomorrow is reserved for you, my dear. Then I'll tell you about everything that happened tonight. Who kissed whom, who slept with whom, who broke up and who started going together—gossip, secrets, the whole shebang!"

"Just as well," says Rut, with a greedy gleam in her eyes.

"Any-who," warbles Áslaug. "Is there anything I can do for you before I'm out of here?"

Rut shakes her head. "Just don't be out long."

"Of course not." Áslaug hugs her sister and kisses her on the head. "Love you! See you soon!"

"Don't let him knock you up," says Rut teasingly.

"Come on!" says Áslaug with a laugh.

Rut grins.

Oddur finishes his beer, crumples the can, and tosses it into the trash bin standing at the top corner of the paved driveway to the savings bank manager's double garage. The driveway is full of visitors' cars, as is the street fronting the house. He looks at his phone to see what time it is—twenty minutes to twelve. Outside, there's a pleasant half-light, and it's between ten and fifteen degrees Celsius. From inside the house comes the slightly muffled sound of music and voices, and then the front door opens. But it isn't Áslaug who appears on the front-door step, as Oddur was hoping, but the madcap Bragi, in an unbuttoned shirt, with sweat-matted hair and a rascally grin on his face.

"Oddur! The key!" barks Bragi, like an excited dog. He's tall, stocky, with a black mop of hair and three-day-old stubble. Bragi is a year older than his classmates; he didn't pass his exams the year before Oddur and Patrekur started at their school.

"The car key?" asks Oddur in surprise. The three of them had gone up to Borgarnes in Patrekur's BMW, and

Patrekur had asked Oddur to hold onto the key to make sure that Bragi didn't drive drunk that night.

"Quick! I need some'n—we're gonna play Bean Boozled!" says Bragi, laughing devilishly.

"What?" Oddur frowns as he fishes the car key out of his trouser pocket, remembering the bad-tasting *jelly beans* that made him retch at his birthday party in middle school. "Isn't that just something for kids?"

"No." Bragi winks at him, takes the key and unlocks the car. "Not if you replace the jelly beans with vitamins and ecstasy!"

"Are you crazy?" asks Oddur.

"Hey now, hey now," says Bragi. He opens the glove compartment and takes out a dented Bean Boozled box. "We can't chug beer all night, can we? Plus, it was Eva's idea, not mine. So …"

Bragi shrugs his shoulders—the very picture of innocence. He slams the car door shut and tosses the key to Oddur, who knows it doesn't matter what he says or does—no one could keep Bragi under control in the mood he's in.

"But be careful, okay?" he says, just to say something.

"Of course, heh heh!" says Bragi as he shoots back into the house like a bat out of hell. At the door he meets Áslaug, who just manages to move aside before he knocks her over.

"What's he on?" she asks with a laugh.

"Good question," says Oddur, sighing.

They walk together through the quiet town, down the slope and out to the spit. All that can be heard is the chirping of birds and their own footsteps. They're holding hands, but are silent and seem almost embarrassed. Oddur feels awkward because he doesn't know how to say what he wants to say, Áslaug because she's both drunk and in love, which is a complicated, toxic mix—her head's too messed up for her to think clearly, or even to walk normally, which is taking her all of her concentration to do. Every time she wavers, she giggles stupidly and squeezes Oddur's hand.

"I think I had one shot too many," she says.

"I guess so," he says dryly.

They approach the arched bridge that connects the islet on which the town stands and Brákarey Island, where the district museum is located and several industrial companies operate. Under the concrete bridge, turbulent seawater flows through Brákarsund Strait. Rocky banks line both sides of the bridge.

"Here's where she swam," says Áslaug dreamily, as they walk out onto the bridge.

"Who?" Oddur asks distractedly.

"The slave Þorgerður Brák." Áslaug stops in the middle of the bridge, glances over her shoulder and smiles faintly. "She was trying to get away from her master, the villain Skallagrímur, who threw a big rock at the innocent girl and sank her to the bottom of the sea. Everyone in Borgarnes knows the story."

"Of course," mutters Oddur.

"You're so quiet," says Áslaug. She stands on tiptoe in order to give her boyfriend a kiss, but starts when he turns away. "What's wrong?"

"Wrong?" he asks in surprise. "Nothing, really. But … listen. We need to talk."

"Oh, God …" Áslaug pales. "Are you breaking up with me? No!"

"Look …" Oddur sighs heavily, shrugs. "It's a bit complicated, isn't it? You live here, I live in Reykjavík, and I'm going to Ibiza with the boys, too."

"Yes, but only for three weeks!" says Áslaug agitatedly. "It'll go by so quickly. Then comes September, when Rut and I will start at HJC. We'll be living in Eva's apartment. Then we'll be in the same school, you and I!"

"For one year, yes," Oddur admits reluctantly. "But ..."

"But what?" Áslaug asks with tears in her eyes. "Will it be embarrassing for you to have a freshman girlfriend? Is that the problem?"

"No, of course not," mutters Oddur, but of course that's *exactly* the problem. He would be made fun of at school. "But then I'll be going to the university, and then ..."

"And then what?" Áslaug wipes tears from the corners of her eyes. "Then I'll just be a high-school kid, but you a great *scholar*, huh?"

"No, just ..." Not knowing how to handle this, Oddur throws up his hands. "We're just not in the same place in life, you see?"

"But we're *together*," she says, terribly upset. "We're a *couple*, and we'll be in the *same* city—and in the *same* school. How much more *together* can two people be? I thought that ...!"

"Thought what?" he asks, shaken. What was she going to say? That he would be her husband? That they would get married? Be together forever?

"Nothing, forget it," she answers; the very picture of desperation. "But you can't be serious! We're so good together. We have so much in common. We've both had to deal with loss, you know. Your parents, my mom."

"Those aren't exactly comparable," mutters Oddur. His parents died in a car accident, whereas her mother slit her own wrists in a bathtub.

"Damn, you're lame," says Áslaug in a broken voice. "I thought you loved me."

"I never said that," he mumbles.

Áslaug's mood darkens, as if the light inside her goes out. "You don't love me?"

Oddur shakes his head. "I'm sorry if you misunderstood me."

"Sorry?" Áslaug turns away and looks with empty eyes at the restless waters of Borgarfjörður and at Mount Hafnarfjall beyond the fjord, bathed in the dark-red light of the midnight sun. "The only thing you're sorry about is having to deal with getting rid of me. I'm just a toy that you're tired of. You're selfish and have no feelings."

"Come on," says Oddur. He tries to touch Áslaug, but now it's she who shies away.

"Go," she says coldly. "Get lost."

Is she still standing on the bridge? Oddur walks quickly back into town, without looking over his shoulder. He strides up the empty streets, heading diagonally up the slope to the bank manager's house, where the dance music is still playing. Oddur tries to shake off his bad feelings about the breakup, but Áslaug's final words echo in his mind, pierce his heart like an icicle. But what did he expect? He probably deserved it. He should never have been with her in the first place. It's awful to have to break up with someone. Absolutely fucking awful.

If he meets a girl in Ibiza, he's *not* going to …

Oddur is startled by loud screaming and shrieking. Is the party really getting out of hand? But the commotion coming from the brightly lit house isn't the typical screaming of excited teenagers, but cries of some sort of distress or terror. Then the music stops.

From a distance comes the wailing of a siren. What the heck is going on?

Oddur starts running. The partygoers stream out the door of the bank manager's house and either disappear into the summer night or gather in small groups outside. Lights come on in the nearby houses and a neighbor or two appears in a window or doorway.

"Is she dead?"

"What happened?"

"Where's the ambulance?

"The cops are on the way!"

"Let's get out of here!"

The voices sound like the noisy screeching of birds. Oddur pushes through the crowd of people at the front door and rushes into the house. There's no one in the living room, but something is going on in the kitchen. He pushes a piss-drunk teenager aside and shoves his way through the door. There are eight or nine people in the kitchen, including three young men whom Oddur doesn't remember having seen before. Locals, he guesses; around twenty years old, maybe older. Two of them have cornered Bragi and Patrekur in a corner of the kitchen, while the third attempts to press and breathe life into an unconscious girl lying on the floor, pale and spasmodic.

"Eva," groans Oddur, and then a light goes on in his head. The ecstasy. She has overdosed or something. He looks up at his friends, who are stiff with fear but also so doped-up that they hardly know their own names.

"Let go of me," says Patrekur, practically in tears.

"Shut up, bastard!" says the one holding him tightly.

"Come on!" pleads the one trying to revive Eva. He's a red-haired, chubby boy in a tank top.

"Oh, God," wails a girl.

Bragi makes eye contact with Oddur and signals him by nodding his head slightly to the side. Oddur follows the signal and quickly realizes what Bragi means. On the kitchen counter, next to a toaster and bread box, is the Bean Boozled box, half-open, giving a glimpse of the pills in it.

Fuck, thinks Oddur, and then he looks again at Bragi, whose eyes are wide open in utter despair.

A chill runs down Oddur's spine. Bragi is asking him to get rid of the box, make it disappear. He's asking him to destroy important evidence.

"The cops are here!" someone shouts.

"She's not breathing," groans the red-haired boy, throwing up his hands in surrender.

"No!" screams Patrekur, desperately.

Bragi stares at Oddur and forms the word *now* with his lips. At the same moment, two uniformed police officers appear.

Oddur breaks into a cold sweat. What should he do? Help his friends? Or make them his enemies?

"Out of the way!" shouts one of the policemen, while the other immediately starts CPR on Eva. Those gathered in the kitchen start moving, giving Oddur his opportunity. He steps quickly over to the kitchen counter, closes the box of ecstasy pills, hides it behind his back and sticks it under his waistband. Then he pulls his shirt and jacket over the bulge.

"Everyone out, but don't go far!" orders the policeman. "We need statements from everyone who was here tonight!"

Oddur doesn't hesitate. He hurries outside, where a third policeman is waiting, taking down the names of those who leave the house. Oddur inches his way toward the home's trash bin and manages to rid himself of the box without anyone noticing. Moments later, the policeman turns to him.

"Name, phone number and address?"

"Oddur Bjarnason," he answers, hoarse from stress. "My number is …"

He stops when an ambulance comes tearing up, lights flashing and siren wailing. Just as the driver shuts off the siren, a loud scream is heard from inside the house, so anguished and desperate that it's as if the screamer's heart has been torn out. The hair on Oddur's neck rises, literally. He realizes that Eva is probably dead. At the same time, it's as if everything grows cold and dark. As if the summer has also given up the ghost.

Almost five hours later, a white BMW emerges from the southern end of the Hvalfjörður tunnel, on its way to Reykjavík—out of darkness and into a bright morning. Oddur is behind the wheel, he being the only one of the three friends who tested fit to drive following the taking of witness statements at the police station in Borgarnes. Patrekur is sitting in the passenger seat, with Bragi by himself in the back. They're downcast, and the atmosphere in the car is heavy. None of them has spoken a word for quite some time.

"Is there any beer in the trunk?" asks Bragi.

Patrekur shakes his head.

"How can you think of beer now?" asks Oddur indignantly.

"Because I'm sobering up," mutters Bragi grouchily.

"It's about time," murmurs Oddur annoyedly.

"Will we be charged?" Patrekur asks anxiously.

"For what?" Bragi asks in return. "It was an accident. She just took something and died. We know nothing about it. You didn't spill the beans, did you?"

"No," says Patrekur. "I said I knew nothing."

"Good thing," grunts Bragi. "Good thing too that they didn't take blood samples from us. They would probably have found the same substance they might find in her."

Oddur flushes with anger. "Her? Her name was Eva! How about showing a little respect, huh? Are you a psychopath, or what?"

Bragi snorts.

"Yeah, man," says Patrekur in a choked-up voice. "This isn't a joke, see? Do you think I want to go to jail?"

Oddur shakes his head. "All you guys think about is yourselves! What about Eva? Do you even care about her?"

"No," whispers Patrekur.

"Listen, Mr. Holier-Than-Thou," says Bragi. "What did you do with the box of pills?"

"I just made it disappear," Oddur answers.

"Good thing," mutters Bragi.

"Fucking bullshit, man," Patrekur says softly.

"Yeah," says Oddur. He grips the steering wheel and stares at the road, so empty inside that he could just as well be a lifeless doll.

"It was just an accident," says Bragi. "Accidents happen, unfortunately. But life goes on. We're going to Ibiza to have fun. When we come back, this will all be forgotten."

"I'm in no mood for Ibiza now," says Patrekur. "Not anymore."

"That makes two of us," says Oddur.

Bragi leans forward, grinding his teeth in anger. "We're *going* to Ibiza. No ifs, ands or buts. We *need* to get away. Period."

"Yeah, maybe," Patrekur says hopelessly.

Oddur sighs heavily. He feels most like breaking down and crying. Stopping the car, getting out and wandering off somewhere. But he's too empty, too tired—too numb and weak. He hardly has the energy to breathe, let alone do anything else.

Reykjavík

Autumn
Challenge

The person who came up with the idea of tearing down walls to create an open office space, only to divide it into countless small squares with movable partitions, must have been a scoundrel or an idiot, thinks Hörður Grímsson as a black thundercloud sails through his mind and shoots bolts of lightning into his nervous system. He feels like a cow in a stall as he sits hunched on a worn chair at a desk that's both small and inconvenient in shape, typing a report on the grimy keyboard of a computer that's as much of a dinosaur as the policeman working on it.

Hörður is in his thirties, a giant of a man, heavy-browed and long-limbed. His hair is rust-red and just over shoulder-length, his pale face is rough-hewn and covered with red bristle, and his eyes are emerald green, deep and intelligent. His lips are thick, his hands large, and his back wide. He's a Westfjords man through-and-through, born and raised in Súðavík, under the mountain that spat an avalanche over the village and snatched from him both his parents and his siblings. He's unsociable, moody, and hauntingly clairvoyant. Ever since he was a young man at sea, shadows from beyond have appeared to him from time to time. Harbingers in the form of a black haze—the death shadows of doomed people.

Hörður almost always dresses in a black shirt, black trousers, and black combat boots. In one corner of his cubicle wall hangs the black leather coat that he bought on impulse a few years ago but that is now practically inseparable from its owner. Fully decked-out, the red-haired giant looks more like a Gothic cathedral than a detective in the Criminal Investigation Department of the Reykjavík Police.

He rolls his shoulders and continues to type on the keyboard with two fingers. His final report on a serious assault and battery case is gradually taking its definitive shape. An ugly case involving amphetamines and bladed weapons. Deep wounds, a great deal of blood—cruelty and stupidity.

"Hörður?"

The red-haired giant grunts, finishes the sentence that he had started, and looks up inquiringly. The person who addressed him is one of his colleagues in the department, Benedikt Vagnsson. Benedikt has a receding hairline and glasses, and is usually wearing a checkered jacket with leather patches on the elbows. He's a friendly guy who looks more like a teacher than a cop.

"Axel wants to have a word with you," says Benedikt.

"Okay, thanks," says Hörður, before continuing his typing.

"I wouldn't make him wait," says Benedikt in a low voice before disappearing.

"Well then," mutters Hörður. He saves the document, gets to his feet and cracks his neck before walking over to the western end of the Cave, the unofficial name for the department's open workspace. There, he knocks on a closed door before opening it onto his boss's office, which, in contrast to the bright and airless cave, is comfortably lit and air-conditioned, as well as being carpeted and furnished with finely crafted hardwood furniture.

What might old Steppenwolf want from him? Hörður is in his fourth year in this department and a lot of things have happened in that time, to say the least. To start with, he was a kind of assistant or advisor in connection with the investigation of the murder of a member of parliament, after which he was appointed to a temporary position as a detective. He nearly blew his big chance when he took on a foreign villain of the worst sort, but managed to turn defense into offense and finally got a long-desired permanent position. But after a certain *incident* at the Smáralind mall just before Christmas the year before, he lost his gun license for an indefinite period. As if that weren't enough, he was *shifted in position*, simply exiled to the boondocks while things settled down in the City of Fear. But that was all behind—he would think. Hörður is richer for the experience and feels that he has proven himself a worthy member of the prestigious Criminal Investigation Department.

But maybe his boss feels differently?

"You wanted a word with me?" he asks from the doorway, as hesitant as a naughty boy at the threshold of the principal's office.

"Come in; shut the door behind you." Axel M. Axelsson is sitting at the other end of the office, behind an authoritative desk, with documents in front of him and green table lamps to both sides. He is wide-faced and big-boned, bald and tanned, dressed in a classic English suit with a folded handkerchief in his breast pocket, and wearing a gold tie clip and cufflinks.

"Have a seat."

Hörður obeys like a dog, scurrying over the soft carpet and sitting down in one of the two chairs in front of the desk. He has sat there many times before, usually while being chewed out, but now and then being given fatherly advice—even a pat on the back in the form of a polite compliment. What awaits him now?

Axel leafs through the documents, then looks up and takes off his glasses. "As you know, certain demands are made on those who hold the position of detective in the Criminal Investigation Department of the Police Force in Reykjavík. Demands concerning work experience, education, and physical strength. And detectives are required to attend courses and lectures regularly, both within and outside of the department, etcetera."

"Yes, of course," says Hörður as he runs over the list in his mind. He thinks he can tick most of the boxes, apart from having actually skipped one or two lectures, but only because he was busy with important investigative work.

"There are two things I wanted to talk to you about." Axel puts on his glasses again and takes a sheet of paper from the pile of documents.

"Two things?" asks the red-haired giant in surprise.

"On the one hand, you still have to have your annual physical," says Steppenwolf, "and on the other hand, you've repeatedly tried to avoid the fitness test that *everyone* who intends to work for this department must pass."

"Yes, that," groans Hörður.

"Exactly," says Axel, with a stern expression. "According to my records, you haven't taken a fitness test since Police

Academy. Is that right? And you barely drooled your way through it!"

"Well, I'd just gotten over the flu and ..."

"You mean a hangover?" Axel interjects.

"And, and ..." sputters Hörður, his face now red with embarrassment. "Listen, in connection with the physical, I completely forgot to make ..."

Axel interrupts. "Make what? A pizza? You were sent notice of your appointment for the physical and you didn't show up! You don't make any appointments here, Hörður Grímsson! You just show up where and when you're told to show up."

Hörður clears his throat. "Yes, I ... of course. But I had a bit of a cold and ..."

"Excuses?" barks Axel. "Is that all you have, excuses? What am I supposed to do with them? Print them out and frame them?"

"No, no," Hörður mutters, like a beaten dog.

"Are you hiding something from me?" asks Axel in a fatherly tone, but with a stern expression. "Are you afraid you won't pass your physical?"

Hörður shakes his head. "Not at all. I just ... skipped it."

Axel scoffs. "But the fitness test? Do you ever exercise? Do you think you're in shape for the fitness test? It's a little more difficult for us than it is at the Police Academy."

Hörður is sweating from stress. It would be wrong to say that he'd exercised in any noticeable way for more than a year—except for getting to the State Liquor Monopoly before it closed.

"When's the next fitness test?" he asks in return, to buy himself a little bit of time.

Axel flips through the files. "It's, let's see—in just over a month."

Hörður is relieved. If he pulls himself together, he should be able to get himself into decent shape in four to five weeks.

"I've never been in better shape," he says cockily. "I've lost a lot of weight, have started eating healthier and drinking less. I would undoubtedly make it onto the SWAT team if I wanted to!"

"Is that so." Axel smirks, leans back in his leather chair, and clasps his hands over his stomach.

Hörður laughs nervously. "Just kidding. Not that I'm actually thinking of applying for it. Those gray wolves there on the SWAT team are crazy monkeys. I'm more for using my brain, see."

"I see," says Axel. "But I also accept the challenge."

"Challenge?" asks Hörður in surprise.

"You're in luck—it so happens that the National Police SWAT team is holding its entrance exam for new recruits on Saturday," says Axel. "If you pass the physical part, you'll be exempt from the CID's fitness test for two years."

Hörður pales. "What?"

"Show up at 7 a.m. at Laugardalur Field," says Axel, noting this in his organizer. "Good luck! Not that you need my spiritual support, being in your best shape and all that."

THE FIRST MURDER

It's a few minutes past midnight. The night is dark, the temperature seven degrees. Patrekur is driving eastward on Suðurlandsvegur Road, out of the city toward Hellisheiði Heath. Hólmsheiði Heath is on the left, the Heiðmörk Conservation Area on the right. Patrekur is alone in the car. On the passenger seat are his phone and a USB flash drive. He drives past the Rauðhólar pseudocraters, slows down, and then turns onto the road that leads to Elliðavatn Lake. He drives along the narrow, poorly lit road with lava and pitch-darkness on both sides.

Where was he supposed to stop? Isn't this a turnout?

He drives to the shoulder of the road, puts the car in neutral and waits. Should he have his headlights on or off?

It's probably better to have them on.

Patrekur sits and waits. His throat is dry and he's somewhat nervous. Why all this secrecy? All this trouble?

He rolls down the side window. All around is silence and gloom—nothing but silence and gloom. Then a bright light suddenly shines on the road behind the car. Like a flashlight. And it moves closer.

"Hello?" calls Patrekur.

No answer.

The light draws slowly closer.

"Is that you?" asks Patrekur, his voice shrill with stress. The light moves closer. He hears the gravel crunch; faint footsteps.

The light isn't from a flashlight, but a headlamp. It's that much higher. A bright, white light that blinds him.

"Hey, would you mind not shining that right in my face?" Patrekur shades his eyes. He receives no answer, but the person who walks up to the side of the car extends his right arm. In a gloved hand is an indistinguishable object that sunders the strong light. Something oblong, open at the end.

Patrekur stiffens. Is that …?

Darkness—and then the screen flickers with tiny white dots. Someone has turned on a GoPro camera. Someone in a desolate place. It's night. The camera shakes, then moves left and right. A beam of light cuts through the darkness. The camera shows a black, empty landscape, perhaps a lava field, and the gravelly, sloping shoulder of a road.

The video is silent.

Heavy shaking, followed by the sight of a potholed road. Around a hundred meters away, a white car is parked on the shoulder, a short distance from a turnout. The car is idling, its tail lights are lit, and smoke streams from the exhaust pipe. The camera moves closer to the car, step by step.

The driver-side window lowers, revealing the head of a young, blond-haired man. He turns his head to see who it is that's walking toward the car. His mouth forms a silent word.

Hello?

The camera moves closer and closer.

The young man says something. He appears stressed, even scared. He shades his eyes.

The person walking toward the car raises his right arm. In his gloved hand is a large pistol, gray and unwieldy.

The young man, clearly startled, opens his eyes wide. A second later, the gun jerks and the camera shakes. The young man's head jerks as well; there's a gush of dark stuff inside the car and smoke obscures the view.

The camera angle lowers—the lens is now pointed straight into the car. The young man is slumped sideways, toward the passenger seat. Blood streams from his face; there's blood on the dashboard and the interior of the passenger-side window.

The young man is dead.

The camera shakes—darkness.

Fitness Test

Hörður Grímsson has often found himself in terrible trouble. He survived a deadly accident at sea and, by some miracle, escaped an avalanche. He has watched people die more often than he cares to recall. He has even stared into the void and attempted to take his own life. He has confronted evil incarnate and been punched, kicked down, and stabbed with a knife. But he has never experienced the presence of death as strongly as when he stands sweaty and short of breath at the starting line of the running track at Laugardalur Field, under a heavy sky that is as gray as a headstone.

It isn't even ten o'clock, and the red-haired giant is convinced that he won't live until noon this godforsaken Saturday in September. He's wearing shabby old running shoes and a gray sweatsuit that's two sizes too small and so wet with sweat that it appears black. His hair is matted with sweat and his face is red and swollen. He rests his trembling hands on his quivering knees and tries to catch his breath while his heart works hard to pump oxygen into his stiff muscles.

Not far from him, police officers ten years younger are chatting with each other, stretching relaxedly, and grinning in secret at the dinosaur taking the entrance exam along with them. Most, if not all of them will doubtless pass the physical part of the exam, whereas some members of that six-man group are doubtless too stupid, impetuous, or amoral to make it through the written part and the psychological assessment.

Idiots, Hörður thinks as he drinks in the cool morning air. He straightens up and looks over the green soccer field and into the empty stands on either side of it. The old national stadium, where *our boys* either crash and burn or transform into Viking-clapping heroes. Encircling the field is a regulation-sized running track that gets on the nerves of soccer fans, as it greatly increases the distance between the spectators and the players on the field.

On this burgundy-colored track, Hörður and the young idiots with dreams of joining the SWAT team have to run three kilometers at one go, and finish in under twelve minutes. On a good day, that shouldn't have posed any great problem, but as this is the fifth and final test of the day, it will be easier said than done—for the red-haired giant, at least. After taking fifteen deep knee bends with eighty kilograms on the bar, ten reps on the bench press with the same weight, and one pull-up with a twenty-five-kilogram weight on his shoulders and hanging there for a minute, he has little strength left. A two-minute plank at the end didn't help. Every one of his muscles is stiff as a board; all of his joints ache, his shortness of breath has left a taste of blood in his mouth. He feels dizzy and nauseous, and is so wiped out that he can barely stand upright, let alone do more.

"On your marks!" the examiner barks as he walks up to the starting line with a clipboard in one hand and a stopwatch in the other.

Hörður would like nothing more than to admit defeat and leave. But he's too stubborn to do so. Or too stupid; he isn't sure. Maybe he belongs on the SWAT team after all?

He limps to the back of the group and regards the wolf pack making itself ready for the race. They're no weaklings, these idiots. Stocky, and looking hard as granite. He knows some of them from police headquarters on Hverfisgata Street. Decent fellows, for sure. Just a little preoccupied with themselves. Always at the gym and guzzling protein swill day in and out.

Hörður sighs. No doubt, they'll …

"Go!" hollers the examiner, and they take off immediately. Everyone except Hörður Grímsson, who wasn't ready at all, so stiff that he can hardly move a muscle. But he just has to grin and bear it. He forces himself to start, putting one foot in front of the other, and before he knows it, his rusty joints have begun moving, his wooden muscles pulling apart and back. His heart jerks into gear and his lungs do their best.

"Jesus Christ!" Hörður cries out at the first curve. Of course, he's last by far, although the length between him and the next person has stopped growing longer. He appears to be keeping up with the others, and even to be chipping away a bit at the distance separating him from those in the lead.

He swings his arms, breathes open-mouthed, and tries to ignore the pain, the dizziness, the nausea, and the taste of blood burning his esophagus. All he does is run and run and run. He doesn't know how far he has run or how much is left. He just runs, clears his mind, and hopes that his heart won't break before he reaches the finish line.

Onward.

Farther.

Sweat trickles into his eyes. He sees nothing but a haze. He hears nothing but the whoosh of blood rushing through his head, and his heartbeat, which is like the drum solo of a death-rock song.

Onward, onward—one more step, and then another. He's going to; he tries to … he can do no more, no more.

Suddenly, it's all used up. His energy, the oxygen, his will.

He abruptly slows down, wanders around the track and then off it, falls to his knees, and hides his face in his hands. Did he cross the finish line? He's breathing so fast that he feels as if he's suffocating. The sweat is pouring down, burning hot and salty. The taste of blood is overwhelming. His heart! His heart is in pain. It's about to give up. The pain shoots up to his shoulder, out into his arm.

His heart stiffens, turns to stone.

Oh, God …

"Are you okay?"

Hörður starts in alarm. He inhales sharply through his nose and opens his eyes. He doesn't really see anything, but can smell grass. He's lying face-down on the soccer field, his arms outstretched.

He looks to the side and sees a tightly laced running shoe, blue with yellow stripes. The examiner is standing over him, looking worried. Hörður gets up halfway and clears his throat.

What happened? He isn't sure. All he knows is that he's alive. What the hell!

"I'm fine. I was just praying,' says Hörður as he gets up stiffly.

"Praying?" exclaims the examiner.

"Are Muslims banned from the SWAT team?" Hörður asks gruffly. He brushes a blade of grass off his face and spits blood.

"No, I don't think so," says the examiner.

"Just kidding," says Hörður, patting the man on the back. Then he looks around. In the distance he sees the other examinees leaving the field together.

"I have a message for you," says the examiner.

"Oh?" Hörður takes a deep breath.

"From Axel, your boss," says the examiner. "He needs you to call him at once."

Hörður exhales. "Is that so?"

The examiner nods. "There's been a murder."

"What?" Hörður is so surprised that his fatigue disappears like dew before the sun. He sets off hurriedly, almost jogging toward the exit. Then he stops and looks over his shoulder. "What was my time?"

The examiner looks at the clipboard. "11:58."

SATURDAY

Hörður Grímsson is standing on the road leading from Suðurlandsvegur Road to Elliðavatn Lake and through the Heiðmörk Nature Reserve. To his right are the Rauðhólar pseudocraters, and to his left is a grass-grown lava field, with a wooded area in the distance. Hörður is wearing his leather coat, his hair still wet after jumping into the shower following his fitness test. With a concentrated expression, he stares at the back of a white BMW 318i parked on the shoulder a hundred meters ahead of him. Around the car tiptoe white-clad members of the forensics team, armed with cameras, measuring tapes, and equipment for taking samples and fingerprints. The body is still in the driver's seat.

The road has been closed at both ends of the scene. Police cars, lights flashing, are parked across it to block access. Beyond them, curious passersby are gathering, as well as photographers and other members of the media.

"Vultures," mutters Hörður. In his mind, he goes over the details of the case. Around nine o'clock, the National Emergency Number received a call from someone named Gunnar, who was on his way up to Heiðmörk to go jogging. He drove past the white BMW and looked through its windows, then called 112 and told the respondent that there was a *dead man in a car at Rauðhólar.* As it turned out, he was right. The car is covered with dew, indicating that it has been standing there at the roadside for several hours, at least since early this morning. The car is registered to eighteen-year-old Patrekur Jónsson, who still lives with his parents in the Fossvogur neighborhood. It must be considered likely that this body is him. Patrekur was a student at Hamrahlíð Junior College—HJC. He appears to have been shot in the face by a powerful firearm at short-range.

A brutal murder, to put it mildly.

Hörður stands there looking, but without focusing on anything in particular. On the one hand, he's waiting for the forensics team to complete its precision work, but on the other, and perhaps most importantly, he's pondering and *taking in* the details of the scene, *reading* what he sees—and what he doesn't see. He closes his eyes, pulls a notepad from his inner coat pocket and writes down a few thoughts.

"What's the situation?"

Hörður sticks the notepad back in his pocket before answering Axel M. Axelsson, who suddenly appears next to him, wearing a trench coat and fedora hat.

"It isn't pretty," replies the red-haired giant. "Looks like an execution. It appears as if the victim had arranged to meet the perpetrator. The way the car is parked suggests this, and it's pretty doubtful that he was just driving around here in the middle of the night. He stops at the side of the road and lowers his window. The perpetrator shoots him as he's sitting there. They probably knew each other. At least there are no signs of a struggle, and it appears as if the deceased had nothing to fear from the person who approached the car."

Axel sighs. "That's awful! Maybe the kid owed money or something? But he doesn't have a criminal record, and the

Drug Unit doesn't recognize the name. Any clues here at the scene?"

Hörður nods. "There are a few things that I need to take a closer look at. Maybe we could meet with the forensics team at the first opportunity?"

"No question," says Axel. "Benedikt is working on fact-finding and the like. He has already contacted the deceased's telephone company. If the victim arranged to meet someone, we might find evidence of it in the records. Phone calls or messages."

"Don't we need a court order to access such data?" asks Hörður.

"We'll do what we need to do," Axel replies. "I just hope it goes as quickly and smoothly as possible. The media will be all over us. Murders are rare, fortunately. But when they do occur, the media goes too far. Television stations, newspapers, and web media—everyone wants to the first to break the story, preferably ten times a day. Clickbait on top of clickbait. It takes a great deal of energy to keep the newshounds at bay and spoon-feed them stuff at the same time."

"Speaking of which." Hörður glances over his shoulder, at the media army gathered at the roadblock. "I'd be grateful if someone besides me could handle that aspect of the investigation, as I can't see press conferences being part of the work awaiting me. An investigation like this one requires focus and precision. It's more important at this point for us to keep calm and make no mistakes, rather than hasten the investigation just to have something to tell the media."

"I agree, and that's why I assigned you to this case," says old Steppenwolf. "I'll deal with the newshounds, while you do whatever's needed. It's far better having no answers to journalists' questions for a few days than to have to answer for a faulty investigation after a few weeks or months—even in court."

Hörður is so flattered at his boss's words that he gets a lump in his throat. "Thanks for the vote of confidence."

"You're welcome," Axel says dryly. "Just don't make me regret having entrusted this to you."

Hörður feels as if he's been punched in the stomach. "No, I …"

"Keep me informed," says Axel, before heading back toward the roadblock.

Hörður sighs. He'll probably never get used to the tactics of his department head, who seems unable to praise his subordinates without immediately pouring cold water on their pride. He tries to regroup, but his ego has taken a painful hit.

Does Axel trust him or not?

He's prevented from sinking himself deeper into doubts about his own excellence when a strange sound disturbs his train of thought—a heavy buzzing reminiscent of a giant bee. What the hell is this?

Hörður looks up toward the place that the buzzing or rushing noise seems to be coming from. At first he sees nothing, but then something dark shoots through the leaden sky, high above his head.

A drone!

Goddamn newshounds are determined to get their photos of the murder scene, no matter what anyone says. Hörður curses them in silence, and then hurries toward the white BMW. He's going to ask the forensics team to cover the car before it ends up on the front page of some media outlet.

It's Saturday night and Oddur is alone at home in his single-family house in westside Reykjavík. But instead of having a party or inviting friends to play a video game, he's just watching TV with the curtains drawn over his windows. He isn't in the mood for fun, having dropped out of contact with all his old friends and had enough of his new ones. His parents are at their summer cottage in Kjós. Of course, Dr. Albert and Mrs. Jónína aren't his real parents, and he hasn't called them Mom and Dad since around his confirmation. When Oddur was less than two years old, his natural parents died in a car accident in Portugal, where they were on vacation. Oddur was being looked after at home in Iceland by his father's sister, Jónína—Aunt Nína. After the tragedy, Dr. Albert and Jónína, who were childless, adopted the orphaned boy. At the time, they were nearly fifty, and could therefore have been a little boy's grandparents more so than his parents. Now they were approaching retirement age. Oddur loves them, of course, but has never really looked at them as his parents or experienced them as such. He grew up with affection, luxury, and a certain distance between them and him. He has always had everything he needed, but at the same time, lacked something he can't put his finger on.

His life feels empty, somehow.

Dr. Albert had attended Reykjavík Junior College in his day, and therefore considered it self-evident and natural that his foster son follow in his footsteps. Oddur, however, applied to and was accepted at Hamrahlíð Junior College, where all the artsy, left-wing kids went—sons and daughters of the bourgeoisie. He really couldn't imagine doing something just to please his stepfather, without knowing exactly why. He had nothing against Reykjavík Junior College, per se, and wasn't particularly excited about Hamrahlíð Junior College.

His choice had greatly disappointed Dr. Albert. So much so that Oddur soon regretted having turned against him and his expectations. What's more, Hamrahlíð JC didn't turn out to be as interesting a school as he had expected. Mainly because he didn't find the courses challenging enough, but he also didn't fit in there. Oddur was a Reykjavík JC kid by nature, old-fashioned and ambitious; he just hadn't realized it until it was too late.

The only friends he'd made at HJC were Patrekur and Bragi. The reasons that they chose to go there were the same for both of them. Neither had good enough grades to get into the Commercial College, the mecca of the nouveau riche. But they were Commercial College types, through-and-through. Loud, energetic, and attention-seeking, always organizing things and mainly having money, clothes, girls, and partying on their minds. Why they sought Oddur's friendship was a mystery to him. Unless they were enamored of his alleged affluence—the designer clothes, the house on Grímshagi Street, and the fame of his foster father, who owned and operated a successful pharmaceutical company. Maybe not the biggest one in the country, but very cutting edge and respected outside the country. At the very least, the two made an effort to get Oddur to hang out with them, and since he wasn't interested in joining either the choir or the school quiz team, he basically had nothing against hanging out with them instead of always being alone.

That was then.

Now he prefers being alone, even though he is in fact lonely and doesn't feel all that well. But it's also precisely because of Patrekur and Bragi that he feels as if he has a black stain on his soul. He can't stop thinking about the incident at the party in Borgarnes last summer. Eva's death was a terrible shock, even though he didn't like her very much. Of course, when any young person dies in such a horrible and stupid way, it's endlessly sad. Besides the fact that she wouldn't have died if Bragi hadn't gone and gotten that damn ecstasy from the car. What an ass he can be—thoughtless and selfish.

And then the trip to Ibiza was little more than a nightmare, at least for Oddur, who had no interest in being wasted for three weeks. But there was actually nothing else to do on the island of the brain-dead but get wasted. It was possible to sunbathe during the day, swim in the sea, and that sort of thing. But the evenings were empty and endless and there was no way to kill time with two idiots without drinking, and drinking even more. Patrekur seemed to have a good time, but Bragi was completely uncontrollable and unbearable the entire time. His head was full of ideas that were all either dangerous or stupid, if not both. Among other things, they hung out and slept with girls who were incredibly reckless, if not downright dubious. Sex, drugs, and all sorts of shit. Oddur didn't like that kind of crap, but grinned and bore it. On the one hand, so as not to wind up at odds with his friends—he was stuck with them, naturally—and on the other, to forget about what had happened with Áslaug quickly and for good. Breaking up with her hadn't been easy, and she seemed to have taken it badly. At first, he felt awful about it, but then his guilt gradually faded away, luckily. He just wasn't ready for a serious relationship. He still hasn't run into Áslaug at school, but *when* it happens, because it *will* inevitably happen, he'll apologize to her for his behavior. Surely, she'll forgive him.

Maybe they can even have a cup of coffee together, just *for old times' sake?* Hopefully. It sucks to hurt people or to have them as enemies, more or less. Bad karma and all that.

Oddur makes a sandwich and takes a beer from the fridge. He glances over the home's DVD collection in search of something he hasn't watched a million times. Like most of the younger generation, he's stopped watching TV in a linear manner, but in general, he finds it more enjoyable watching DVDs than streaming movies or TV shows from the Internet. You're more insulated watching a DVD. You can shut off the Internet, cut all connections with the outside world and feel completely secure.

He's still looking for the perfect movie when his phone rings. The name of the person he least wants to hear from or meet appears on the screen:

Bragi

Oddur turns down the volume of the ring tone and lets the phone keep ringing on silent. What does this idiot want now? To get some drugs? Go to a party? Fly to Abu Dhabi, one way? Bragi hangs up. But then sends a message:

Call me, asshole. It's important!

Oddur sighs. As soon as Bragi has had one beer, *everything* is important. Then he *has to* do this or *say* that and *get there* or get someone to *come here* or *get hold* of these guys or *beat up* that one or whatever else and all or nothing. The kid is, will be, and always has been completely overwhelming and unbearable.

Maybe he should just turn off his phone? Yes, in a minute. Oddur continues to look for a movie. *Taxi Driver?* The *French Connection 1* and *II?* He loves old movies, old music—the old school, when everything was ambitious, well-made, and free of glamor and pretense. Maybe a bit of an overgeneralization, but there's *something* about the nineteen sixties and seventies that's been lost in modern times. Some honesty, depth.

Oddur continues looking. He's in no hurry, and anyway, looking is often funner than finding. To look for something, to search, is to travel; to find is to stop. He runs his fingertips along the spines of the DVDs, tilting his head to read them. The house is dark and quiet.

Finally, he decides to watch *The Godfather*. The first one, or maybe even all three. They're together in a black box, with a picture of a hand holding a cross that's both a religious symbol and a marionette controller. He puts the disc in the player, plunks down on the couch and grabs the remote control.

Wasn't he going to turn off his phone? Yes. He unlocks his cell phone, but decides to give his social media apps a once-over before turning it off. Or, he doesn't really decide to do so; it's more like an involuntary habit—a bad habit, at that. Someone has added him on Facebook. Sunna Sæmundsdóttir, blonde and very cute. He looks at her profile, clicks on *see more about Sunna*. She went to Réttarholt Middle School and is now at Hamrahlíð Junior College, maybe in her first or second year? She seems a bit familiar, her name and face, but he still can't quite place her. But since she's at HJC, and clearly a real cutie, he accepts the request.

He looks through the usual apps: Instagram, Twitter, Snapchat, but sees nothing more interesting than usual. The same photos, stories, jokes, and other crap. People are and always will be unoriginal and predictable. He takes another look at Facebook, where some notifications are awaiting him. Someone commented on a post on a page that he once liked; some events that his friends have clicked "interested" in are about to begin, and his newest friend, Sunna Sæmundsdóttir, invites him to like a page called Deathbook—neither more nor less.

"Okay," says Oddur with a chuckle. He's too curious not to do anything, so he likes the page and opens it. Deathbook appears to live up to its name; the page looks to him like a gloomy place, with extremely dark images—ghosts, zombies, leafless trees, crows, the moon in clouds, and the Grim Reaper. The profile picture is of a sinister skull with a hood on its head. Next to it is the name of the page. Below it is the following identifier:

Local Service—127 followers

@Deathbook

"What is this?" mutters Oddur. He sees that a few kids from HJC have already liked the page. Maybe it's some HJC fad that he hasn't heard of. It wouldn't surprise him.

He scrolls down the page a bit. He finds no further information, just pictures and gloomy, death-related memes. One of them is a picture from a morgue, in which a corpse is lying under a sheet, with a label hanging from its big toe. In the picture are these words: "The moment … for which you were born." Another is a sinister picture of a cemetery at night. It also has a caption: "Ten out of every ten people … die of death."

"Just how *dark*?" mutters Oddur, who still has no clue as to the nature or purpose of this page that Sunna really wanted him to like. Who is she? He clicks back to Sunna Sæmundsdóttir's profile page on Facebook, but is startled when his phone rings. It's Bragi, again.

"Damn, you're a pain, man!" Oddur barks. He waits until Bragi gives up, and then hangs up. Then he turns off his phone and tosses it aside. He presses play and starts the movie. He's going to watch them all, do a *Godfather* marathon. Eat junk food and drink beer. Stay up until morning, then sleep all day until dinnertime.

Sunday

Lying on a white table in the office of the Criminal Investigation Department of the Reykjavík Police is evidence from the scene of the murder at Rauðhólar; everything from preliminary reports and countless photographs to plaster casts of footprints and tire tracks. In the middle of the table are two clear plastic Ziploc bags. One of them holds a USB flash drive, and the other, a box containing candy—the Bean Boozled game.

Standing around the table are three policemen: Hörður Grímsson and Axel M. Axelsson of the Criminal Investigation Department, and Jenný Karlsdóttir of the Forensic Services Department. Jenný is about the same age as Hörður; one or two years younger, as far as he remembers. She's very tall for a woman, at least 180 centimeters. In high- or medium heels, she's probably as much as two meters high. She has a full head of thick hair: a pitch-black, curly mane. Jenný is big-boned and fleshy, not exactly fat, but nowhere near being gangly. She's a *big* woman, in any case. But she's got style, and a commanding presence. She has large, coffee-brown eyes, an incredibly strong voice and a very strong personality to match it. Many people find her downright frightening, or at least overwhelming.

Hörður Grímsson mainly finds her attractive, and uncomfortably charming. He has a bit of a crush on her, while being terrified of her at the same time. And maybe he's frightened of her precisely because he's got a bit of a crush on her. Because what if she showed him the same sort of interest? He would be completely defenseless against such attention; would literally melt. Which would be horrendous, because he's in a relationship with a woman he loves. A short, quiet, and wonderful woman called Bíbí, who's the only woman who understands him. Or rather, puts up with him and his innumerable flaws.

Hörður looks at his watch. It's two o'clock in the afternoon. All day yesterday was spent on the investigation, as well as today, Sunday, until now. And presumably the rest of the day will be, too. Maybe he'll manage to kiss Bíbí good night before he crawls in bed and falls asleep. Not exactly the weekend Bíbí had imagined. He himself loves living for his job. But at the same time, he feels guilty about his endless absences from home, and then is always so distracted on the rare occasions that he gets to spend "quality time" with the woman he lives with that it doesn't really live up to its name. He's actually never fully present, mentally; his head is always so full of thoughts that he can't share with his beloved because they are, on the one hand, confidential, and on the other, purely horrific, and would keep her from sleeping at night.

"Right then," says Axel. "Let's start by going quickly over the case history and sharing with each other what we know. Then we can discuss conjectures and theories. Jenný, would you like to start?"

"Absolutely," says Jenný in her deep yet feminine voice. "Isn't it most natural to start with the cause of death? Of course, an autopsy hasn't been done, but the cause appears cut-and-dried. Shot in the head at close range with a powerful firearm. The bullet entered the front of the skull, through the nasal bone, and went diagonally down and to the left and out the nape of the neck to the right side of the deceased's skull. We found the bullet in the passenger seat. It's being analyzed. We think it's either a .44 or .45 caliber. My bet is a .44."

"Handgun or rifle?" asks Hörður. His mouth is so dry from stress at the presence of the tall, attractive Jenný that his voice sounds like a poor imitation of Tom Waits. His heart is pounding and his palms are sweaty.

"Good question," says Jenný. She glances into the green eyes of the red-haired giant, who blushes and looks away. "Since there are hardly any large-caliber handguns in Iceland except within our ranks, it would be easy to conclude that it was a rifle. But I certainly can't rule out the other possibility. In fact, I find it more likely."

"Why?" asks Axel.

"The deceased was shot at very close range, as I said," replies Jenný. "And there's no indication that he was afraid of the person who approached the car, let alone tried to defend himself or escape."

Axel crosses his arms. "What does that have to do with it?"

Hörður clears his throat. "Look. If the perpetrator had been carrying a rifle, he would have had a hard time hiding it from the victim. Besides the fact that he would have had a harder time swinging it up and aiming, standing as close to the car as he was."

"Exactly," says Jenný. "Thank you, Hörður."

The red-haired giant blushes again.

"What if he blinded the victim?" asks Axel. "For example, with a flashlight."

Jenný nods thoughtfully.

"So he was holding a flashlight *and* a rifle?" Hörður asks skeptically.

Axel grunts. "He could have taped the flashlight to the barrel, couldn't he?"

"It's possible," says Jenný. "But I don't think we should rule out a handgun right away. It's a real possibility."

"Which would change things," says Hörður. "The gun could certainly have come to the country illegally, but if it's registered, then it could hardly be privately owned, right?"

Axel nods. "I think that all legally registered handheld firearms in the country are under the ownership and control of the police. I don't think we should mention a handgun to anyone at this stage of the investigation."

"Of course not," says Hörður. "But I'm going to investigate this further."

"Just be careful," Axel mutters.

"Then there's the evidence from the scene," says Jenný. "It's quite interesting. First there's the USB flash drive that was in the car's passenger seat. On it were a total of eight photographs that we've printed out, as you can see. Nude photos of a woman who appears to be the same age as the deceased, probably taken during a web chat. Screenshots."

Hörður looks reflexively at one of the piles of photos on the table. The girl in the photos is slender, blonde, and very good looking. If he had to guess, he would say she was American. A typical prom-queen type. The cutest girl in her class, even the whole school. The one that all the boys have a crush on. The one who ends up going out with the stupid sports star who has a Camaro and a rich dad.

"The photos aren't exactly hard-core," says Jenný. "But they're racy enough that the girl in question wouldn't want them passed around, I would think."

Axel, looking gravely serious, nods. He has a daughter in her twenties and would break every bone in the bastard that took such photos of her. And if that same person spread them around—he can't even begin to think of what he'd do. "Extortion?"

"Why not?" says Jenný, looking at Hörður, who blushes for the third time in a few minutes.

"Hörður?" says Axel.

The red-haired giant clears his throat. "The record of calls from the deceased's telephone company indicates just that, yes."

Hörður reaches for a thin stack of papers and hands Jenný one of them. "This exchange took place earlier in the evening."

Jenný takes the sheet and skims over the text:

21:11 How much do you want for the photos?

21:13 New number?

21:14 Name the amount

21:37 100,000?

21:38 Meet me at Rauðhólar at midnight. There's a turn-out in the road. Park the car there and wait

21:48 Okay

"Couldn't be clearer," says Axel, after taking the sheet from Jenný. "And the medical examiner believes that the murder was committed between half past eleven and one at night, with a half-hour margin of error."

"The deceased didn't know the number of whoever sent the messages, as the phone was a so-called *burner*—a disposable one," says Hörður. "But he knew immediately what was going on. He had these photos and wanted to sell them. Whether it was the girl who wanted to buy them or some third party is one of the big questions. But Patrekur thought he knew who was calling, at least, even though he didn't know the number. That definitely tells us something."

"Who is the girl; do we know that?" asks Axel.

Hörður nods proudly. "The deceased's Facebook page is relatively open. You can see loads of photos and so on. I found the girl in a few photos there, taken half a year or so ago. Her name is Lísa Kristjánsdóttir, and she's also a student at Hamrahlíð Junior College; the school's principal confirmed it. I think they were a couple for a while, she and Patrekur. I'll be questioning Lísa later today, as a witness."

"Very good," says Axel.

"Where do you get a disposable phone like that?" asks Jenný.

Hörður shrugs. "The easiest way is just to order them online, from Amazon or a similar site. They're cheap phones with numbers and prepaid credit. They cost about 40 euros, I guess."

"Who is the deceased?" asks Axel. "That is, what do we know about him? Why did he need money so badly?"

"Patrekur has no criminal record and had no connection to drug dealers or anything like that," says Hörður. "The only thing I found in the system is a witness statement that he gave this summer when a girl died of a drug overdose at a party in Borgarnes. He was there with his two friends and a lot of other young people."

"A criminal case?" asks Axel.

"No, no charges," says Hörður. "At a glance, he was just a typical high-school kid. But he owned a car, which isn't a given, and seems to have bought it with his own money.

He'd had part-time jobs ever since middle school, mainly making and delivering pizzas. He didn't have many debts, and I understand from his parents that he went with his friends to Ibiza a few weeks ago. His parents were hardly in the mood for talking, actually—understandably so. But maybe the credit-card bill from the trip to Spain was higher than their son expected?"

"Maybe," mutters Axel. "But if we look at the case from the other side—who would *kill* over such photos?"

"An enraged father?" Jenný suggests. "A jealous boyfriend? Lisa herself?"

"All good and valid theories," says Hörður. "Naturally, I'll check out Lísa's background and circumstances. But somehow, I feel as if this case is more complicated than it seems—even that it isn't necessarily about these nude photos."

"Why do you say that?" asks Axel.

"There's that damn box, for example," says Hörður as he points at the packaging from the Bean Boozled game. "It was found at the scene. *Outside* of the car. On the ground below the open side window. Isn't that right, Jenný?"

She nods.

"There were no blood stains on the box," says Hörður, "which indicates that it was placed there *after* Patrekur was shot. And that the person who put it there is probably none other than the murderer."

"Otherwise, there would have been blood stains it?" asks Axel.

"Yes, very fine droplets—a fine spray," says Jenný. "When a bullet hits a victim, there's more or less an explosion and blood sprays in the direction of the shooter. There are very likely drops of blood on the gun barrel and even on the killer's clothes. We found drops on the exterior of the car door and on the rocks at the shoulder of the road, next to the box and *under* it. But not on the box itself."

Blood, blood, blood ... Hörður looks at the stack of photos of the victim's body and the car's interior. Blood splatter, splotches of brain, bone shards, blood spray, and drops of blood here and there and everywhere.

Shattered head. Gaping mouth.

Pale skin.

Clenched fingers.

Staring eyes.

"What is this box?" asks Axel.

"It's a game," says Jenný. "Like a box of chocolates, with compartments and such. But there are jelly beans in the compartments. Everyone tries some. Most have a fruity taste, but one or two are disgusting—tasting like dog food, wet wipes, old socks. It's a kind of *take it if you dare* game. But this box is empty. No jelly beans. But there's a powder residue in some of the compartments. We'll be analyzing it."

Axel nods. "I see what you mean, Hörður. This box is completely out of place. It doesn't fit."

"Exactly," says the red-haired giant. "It's bothering me, and I have the feeling that it's *supposed* to bothering me, us—that it's there to throw the investigators off."

"It could also be some kind of message," Axel suggests. "To us, to the victim ... to some third party."

Hörður nods thoughtfully. "Keen observation. I think we should keep the existence of this box to ourselves. Maybe one of the people I'm going to talk to will mention it of their own accord, or this stupid game."

"And in doing so, give themselves away?" asks Jenný.

"Possibly," says Hörður.

"I like your thinking," says Jenný, winking at the red-haired giant, who blushes once more.

"What about fingerprints?" asks Axel. "Or these plaster casts? The footprint and the tire-tread pattern?"

Jenný clears her throat. "These plaster casts are of no use unless you arrest someone. Then you can compare them with that person's footwear and/or a car that he drove on the night in question. It isn't even certain that this tire-tread pattern fits the car we're looking for, but it's more likely than not that the footprint is the perpetrator's. I would think these were Timberland hiking shoes or something similar."

"Exactly," says Axel.

"Regarding fingerprints," says Jenný, "we dusted the car's interior, the dashboard and such, and the exterior on the driver's side—around the window, the roof and the door handle. We got a lot of fingerprints, including some that were whole or nearly whole, but it has to be considered probable that most or all of them belong to the owner of the car and his friends or family. But if it so happens that the perpetrator touched the car and/or got into it that night or at some other time, it isn't at all unlikely that we have his fingerprints."

"His?" exclaims Axel.

"It's just a manner of speaking," says Jenný condescendingly. "Naturally, the perpetrator could be a woman. It's all the same to us in Forensics."

Now it's Axel who blushes. "Yes, of course. Sorry. I wasn't thinking clearly. Hörður, do you have any more questions?"

"Not really," says the red-haired giant. "Except, did the victim have anything on him that could be useful to us? Notes, keys, a wallet? I see that his clothes aren't here."

"Keen observation," says Jenný. "We're still analyzing the clothes. It's time-consuming taking blood samples from the fabric, as well as soot particles. The deceased had house keys in his pocket, his phone, a debit card, and his driver's license. And wore a delicate gold chain around his neck."

"And the car?" asks Axel.

"It's in our garage and being investigated," says Jenný. "At first glance, there's no obvious evidence in it."

Axel nods, then looks at Hörður. "So are we good here?"

Hörður mulls things over before answering. "I think so. For the time being, anyway. I'm still trying to figure it all out. Some things are obvious, others aren't. I have the feeling that not everything here is as it seems."

"Just come back as often as you need, Hörður," says Jenný. "That's what we in the Forensics Department are here for: to investigate, support, and explain. You're also welcome to give me a ring. If I'm not at work, I'm on call."

She hands him her business card—they exchange glances.

"Thank you," says Hörður, his voice hoarse with stress. "I'll do that."

An hour later, Hörður is sitting in his cubicle in the Cave, preparing to question Lísa Kristjánsdóttir. He types notes into a document on his computer, the clicking of the keyboard amplified in the otherwise empty space.

"You're no slouch," says Axel, who managed to sneak up on the detective without him noticing.

The red-haired giant stiffens in his chair and the hair stands up on the back of his neck. "Are you trying to give me a heart attack?"

Axel gives him a fatherly pat on the shoulder. "Sorry. I didn't mean to sneak up on you. You were obviously distracted."

"Just focused," mutters Hörður, half-peeved that someone managed to catch him off guard like this. He tries to remember what he was going to write next.

Wasn't it something to do with an alibi? Yes, that was it! He starts typing again, with his boss hanging over him.

"By the way, how do you like Jenný?" Axel asks unexpectedly.

"Huh?" Hörður blushes and loses his train of thought again. "Just fine. You know. Good-looking woman. Very charming."

Axel grins. "I meant professionally."

Hörður's face turns deep red, almost purple. "Yes, of course."

"She's sharp as a tack," says Axel. "Educated at Cambridge. Was the highest in her class. She's done a great job. But is certainly controversial, at least within her department."

"Oh?" asks Hörður in surprise.

Axel clicks his tongue. "Probably just jealousy. Some have suggested she got ahead just because she's a woman—the guys who've been there longer. The gender quota, you see. And apparently, she's hard to work with."

Hörður scoffs. "The only people who *aren't* hard to work with are spineless wimps and ass-kissers!"

"Tell me about it, Hörður," says Axel with a wry smile. "But I came to let you know that Lisa is here."

"Is she waiting for me in the Swimming Pool?" asks Hörður.

"That's my understanding," says Axel.

"Alone?" Hörður moves the cursor to the print icon on the screen and right-clicks.

"I think so, yes," says Axel.

Hörður gets to his feet and walks over to the printer. "Interesting."

The interrogation room of the Criminal Investigation Department is windowless and painted a peculiar turquoise color, making it look undeniably like an empty swimming pool. In the room are a simple table and three chairs, as well as recording equipment. Holding a red folder, Hörður walks in. He closes the door behind him. At the table sits an eighteen-year-old girl in a white sweatsuit and white basketball shoes. She's slender and sits hunched, with her hands in her lap. Her blonde hair is gathered and fastened with a hair tie at the back of her neck. She stares wide-eyed at the red-haired, black-clad giant. Her eyes are blue.

"Lísa Kristjánsdóttir?" Hörður asks as amicably as he can. The girl nods.

The green-eyed giant sits down across from her at the table. A loud screech is heard as he drags his chair closer to the table. "Thank you for coming. My name is Hörður Grímsson and I'm a police detective. You have the status of witness, and are here of your own free will. I just need to ask you a few questions in connection with a case that I'm investigating. You're welcome to call a lawyer or guardian, if you wish."

Lisa shakes her head, determined, but at the same time sheepish. As if she doesn't want anyone to know that she's there.

Hörður regards her carefully. Lísa is very good-looking, without putting any effort into it or it being particularly special. She was born cute and will probably always be cute. But whether that will turn out to be a blessing or a curse for her, he doesn't know.

"Do you know why I invited you here?" Hörður asks gently.

Lísa's face reddens. "Yes … no. Not really."

Hörður watches her closely. Does she know that Patrekur is dead? He doesn't think so. "You said yes, first. So you have some idea, some suspicion … right?"

Lisa takes a deep breath, blinks. Then she shrugs. "No. I'm just stressed. I don't see why I'm here."

"Very well," says Hörður. He knows that she's lying. That she's hiding something from him. He just doesn't know exactly what it is. "Tell me, how well do you know Patrekur Jónsson?"

Lísa starts. She stiffens in her chair and the redness disappears from her childish face. "Why are you asking me about him? What did he do?"

Hörður narrows his eyes. "What makes you think he did something?"

"Just because." Lisa blushes again, bites her lower lip.

Hörður snaps the elastic bands off the corners of the red folder, takes the printouts of his notes from it and looks at them. "Where were you between 9 p.m. and 2 a.m. on Friday night?"

Again, Lísa starts. "Why? What's this all about?"

"Just answer the question," says the red-haired giant.

"I was just at home," answers Lisa, somewhat rattled.

"On a Friday night?" Hörður asks skeptically. "A young girl like you? Not at a party? Or out on the town? Or maybe you had a party at your house?"

Lísa scoffs. "Not everyone is always partying, you know!"

"Okay," says Hörður. "Who was at home with you?"

"Mom, Dad and my brother," says Lisa.

"And they'll confirm that you were with them at that time?" says Hörður.

"Of course!" Lisa is irritated now. "But why do you need to know this?"

Hörður pulls out a photo from the folder. One of the nude photos that were on the USB flash drive in the passenger seat of Patrekur's car. He lays the photo on the table and pushes it over to Lisa, whose face pales in horror. "What can you tell me about this photo?"

Lísa picks up the photo and places it face-down on the table. "Where did you get it? Did he put the pictures on the Internet?"

"He who?" asks Hörður.

"Aw, Patrekur!" snaps Lisa, irritated and upset. "Weren't you asking about him before?"

"Did he threaten to do so?" asks Hörður. "Put these photos on the Internet?"

"Yes, or ..." Lísa sighs heavily and crosses her slender arms. "He didn't mean it, I think. He was just fucking with my head. Letting me know that he had me in his power, something like that. But he's no idiot, you know. Bragi would be more likely to do something like that. It's also all Bragi's idea, to get pictures like those of girls. He's put such pictures out there, on web pages and the like. He's the one who's an idiot, not Patrekur."

Hörður looks at his notes. "Who is Bragi?"

"Unnsteinsson, a friend of Patrekur," mutters Lisa. "I can't believe that Patrekur would have put the pictures on the Internet!"

Hörður writes down the name. "Nobody posted them online."

"Oh? Then what?" asks Lisa, confused.

"What photos are these?" Hörður asks in return. "Who took them? And when?"

"It was in February," says Lísa. "We were together, Patrekur and I. Nothing serious, but still. Then I went on a ski trip to Austria with my family. Patrekur and I Skyped in the evenings. We were flirting and such. He made me strip for him, and all kinds of stuff. What I didn't know was that he was taking screenshots the whole time. These are them."

"And then?" asks Hörður.

Lisa shrugs. "We broke up. No drama, just, you know. It wasn't fun anymore. Shortly afterwards, I heard about the pictures through Bragi. I lost it and asked Patrekur for them but he refused, saying he wanted to keep them. Then we slept together after the spring exams, unexpectedly. It just happened; we were drunk. The next day I asked him again for the pictures and he got really pissed off, asked if I'd slept with him just so I could get the pictures, you know. We argued and blah, blah."

"And then?" Hörður asks again.

Lísa clears her throat. "Then he got in touch this summer, just before he went to Spain with his friends. Asked me to come to see him, you know."

"No, I don't know," says Hörður.

"To sleep together," says Lísa irritably.

"Okay," says Hörður.

"I said no, I didn't want that hold-me-let-me-go-bullshit," says Lísa. "Then he threatened to put the pictures on the Internet."

"Go on," says Hörður.

Lísa wipes a tear from the corner of her eye. "He basically forced me to sleep with him. It was awful. I felt really bad afterwards. He'd been my boyfriend and all that, but it didn't change anything. I didn't want to, you understand?"

Hörður nods. "Were you mad at him?"

"Yes," says Lísa, on the verge of tears. "Very much. But you know. Time flies. You just go on with your life. I actually stopped being mad at him, I guess. But now I'm really confused. I mean, why do you have the pictures?"

Hörður thinks about it, before deciding to lay his cards on the table. "Patrekur is dead."

"What?" Lisa jerks as if he'd run an electric current through her chair. Her surprise is genuine.

"He was murdered," Hörður adds.

"No," Lisa whimpers. Her whole body trembles as if she's about to go into shock. She blinks, throws her hands over her mouth, and howls like a wounded animal. Patrekur was her schoolmate and boyfriend for a time, but still, Hörður feels as if her reaction is exaggerated. It's as if Lísa imagines that *she* killed the boy.

"Are you okay?" Hörður asks in a fatherly tone. "Do you want me to call a doctor?"

Lisa shakes her head. She's pale and still trembling. It's been a long time since Hörður has seen anyone so upset.

"Is there something you're not telling me?" he asks.

"No," whispers Lisa.

"Very well," says Hörður. "But it appears that the murder of Patrekur has something to do with these photos. He received a text message offering him money for them. He arranged a meeting with someone and had the photos with him. They were found next to the body, on a flash drive. The person who murdered him didn't take them."

Lísa sits there stiffly, listening, but Hörður doesn't know whether she hears him or understands what he's saying.

"I have to ask," he says politely. "Did you send him that message or do you know if someone sent him a message of that sort? Have you or anyone close to you tried to buy the photos?"

Lisa shakes her head. "Not at all."

"Your father? Anyone?" asks Hörður.

"No," whispers Lisa. "Nobody knows about this. Just some girlfriends of mine, and of course Patrekur's friends. No one in the family. Dad wouldn't do anything like that, either—absolutely not!"

Hörður nods. Naturally, he'd looked up her father. Kristján is around fifty, an ichthyologist working at the Directorate of Fisheries. A university-educated office bloke who has never gotten as much as one speeding ticket and doesn't have a gun license. And Lísa's brother Lárus is only twelve years old, a seventh-grade student.

"I had to ask," he says.

"Oh, God!" groans Lisa. She's still trembling, but her face is now closer to being green than gray.

"Do you need to throw up, or ...?" Hörður asks hesitantly.

"Maybe. No, I don't know," whimpers Lisa. She obviously feels very bad. Physically as well as mentally.

Does she blame herself for Patrekur's death?

"I'm going to let you go, my friend," says Hörður. "But if there's anything, anything at all, that might be of use to us in the investigation, then I ask you to tell it to me now; don't hold back. No matter what it is."

Lisa shakes her head. "I don't know anything. Nothing!"

"Suit yourself," says Hörður, who is sure that the girl knows something she doesn't want or dare to talk about. He looks at his notes, and then remembers the box from the jelly beans game. "Listen, tell me, did you and Patrekur play games, sometimes?"

Lísa is baffled. "What games?"

Hörður shrugs. "Just, board games or whatever. You know, Monopoly or that sort of thing. Boxes with stuff and instructions."

Lísa throws up her hands. "What are you talking about?"

"I don't know, to be honest," mutters Hörður, somewhat sheepishly. "That's all for now. But we'll talk again."

Monday

Oddur had a very hard time getting up that morning, as he'd managed to turn night into day in the space of one weekend. He'd gone to bed around 2 a.m., but didn't fall asleep until around four. So when the alarm clock on his phone rang at half past seven, he'd slept for three and a half hours, at most—and probably only three.

Fuck …

He hit the snooze button a few times, then jumped in the shower and skipped breakfast. Then he called for a taxi, because wasn't sure he could make the bus. Nor did he really feel like walking to the bus stop in the dark and cold.

The taxi pulls up to the main entrance of Hamrahlíð Junior College, a dark-gray, low-rise building that's more reminiscent of a gloomy, rocky hill than a prestigious educational institution. And the institution's prestige is actually rather limited. Few people brag about having gone to HJC.

Oddur uses a credit card to pay the driver, before stepping out of the taxi's warmth. He slings his backpack onto his shoulder and strides up the sidewalk, a little late for his first-period class. His hair is still wet after his shower. He looks down and sees that he ought to have given himself more time to polish his shoes.

As he enters the spacious lobby, he notices that there are students everywhere. But they aren't rushing to class;

instead, they're standing there in little clusters, whispering to each other.

What's going on? Oddur had headed straight for the room he was supposed to be in almost two minutes ago, but now he slows down, stops, and looks around in surprise. Isn't it an ordinary school day? Did he miss an e-mail? Why is everyone so serious?

Suddenly, the loudspeaker screeches, and the principal's familiar voice breaks the silence. *"Dear students. I would like to ask you to leave your classrooms and gather in the auditorium. I'll address you there. At the end of my talk, we will spend a few moments together before you return home. Classes have been canceled for today."*

"*What* is going on?" Oddur asks himself. He follows the stream of students heading toward the auditorium. The whispering starts again, but some of the students stop talking as he approaches, elbow the person next to them and make vague gestures, glancing askance at him.

Oddur is starting to feel strange, as if he's dreaming. Are they looking at *him*, talking about him? Or has he grown paranoid?

"Hey!"

Oddur starts in alarm and loses his balance when someone grabs him forcefully by the upper arm and pulls him around halfway. His backpack slides off his shoulder and falls to the floor.

It's Bragi, of course.

"What's wrong with you, man?" asks Oddur, straightening his hair before reaching for his backpack. But he can't get it, because Bragi grabs the lapel of his jacket with both hands, yanks him and shoves him against the nearest wall.

"What's wrong with me?" Bragi hisses through clenched teeth. He splutters with rage and stares at Oddur with a gleam of madness in his eyes. "What's wrong with *you*, you idiot? Not answering your phone. Not responding to messages! Who do you think you are?"

"Whoa! Easy!" Oddur tries to free himself, but Bragi is both bigger and stronger. He slams Oddur into the wall again before letting him go—so hard that the nape of his neck smacks into the hard concrete.

"Fuck," howls Oddur. He feels his neck and then looks at his fingers, as if expecting to see blood. "Are you trying to kill me?"

"Watch what you say!" Bragi hisses. Oddur has never seen him so worked up. "Don't you know what happened, you piece of shit?"

"No," groans Oddur. "I don't know."

Bragi inhales through his distended nostrils. "Patrekur is dead."

Oddur is taken aback. "What's that? How?"

"He was killed," Bragi hisses. "Shot in the head. Executed!"

"Huh?" Oddur blinks. "What? Who ...? Are you sure?"

"Of course I'm fucking sure!" says Bragi. "What do you think the principal is going to say, you fool? Patrekur's dad called me yesterday. To ask if I knew anything. Apparently, Patti went up to Heiðmörk on Friday night to meet someone. He was murdered! Then I called you. Why didn't you answer?"

"I ..." Oddur's mouth is so dry that he can barely speak. "I just didn't have my phone on me."

"Bullshit," hisses Bragi. "You've been avoiding us since we came home from Spain. You think you're better than us. Too fine, too good. Just admit it!"

Oddur sweats and sees spots of light before his eyes. "No, no, I just …"

"You just what?" growls Bragi, with a menacing expression. "You'd better watch your step. That's what you should do. I'm sure the police will talk to us, Patrekur's closest friends. They probably want to know what we know and what we don't."

"I don't know anything," says Oddur.

"No. You know nothing in your idiotic head," says Bragi. "But if they ask you about what happened in Borgarnes, you'd better not say anything stupid. Is that understood?"

Oddur pales. "Why should they ask us about that?"

"Because it connects us," says Bragi. "We were there, all three of us. We gave statements."

"I see," says Oddur. "But you don't think that what happened there is connected to what happened to Patrekur?"

Bragi blinks, thinks this over. "I certainly hope not. But if it is, then don't start telling them some bullshit."

Oddur shakes his head. "Come on. Of course not."

"You'd better not," growls Bragi, before storming away. Not in the direction of the auditorium, but the exit.

"Moron," mutters Oddur, his voice trembling with emotion. He adjusts his lapel and shirt collar, then glances around. The hallway is empty, or nearly so. Standing at the corner by the cafeteria is a skinny boy with a crewcut and round glasses, dressed in army pants and a denim jacket. He's clearly been watching Oddur and Bragi, but when Oddur sets eyes on him, he looks furtively away and acts awkward.

"What are you staring at, fresher?" Oddur barks. He hasn't seen this pipsqueak before, and therefore assumes he's a new student.

"Nothing," replies the skinny kid in a tremulous, mousy voice before disappearing.

"Fucking loser," mutters Oddur. He picks up his backpack from the floor and slings it over his shoulder. He's halfway to the exit when his phone rings. He stops, looks at the phone and gets a knot in his stomach.

444-1000—isn't that the police?

Hörður and Axel are sitting at the long table in the spacious operations room in the innermost part of the Criminal Investigation Department, both with cups of freshly brewed coffee and the former with a portion of the files on the case in front of him. At the top center of the whiteboard at the end of the room, Hörður has written the name of the deceased. Extending from the name are several lines that end with the names of friends, close relatives, and one ex-girlfriend.

"The first morning meeting, huh?" says Axel, sipping his coffee.

Hörður nods. "And probably not the last."

"No closer?" asks Axel.

"No," says Hörður, "but that doesn't mean anything. I'm still evaluating the circumstances and evidence from the scene and putting things together. The person who did this organized it well. This is definitely a case of criminal intent. The perpetrator made few or no mistakes. In order to catch him, I need to work in the same way. Organized, and unhurried. It'll take patience."

Axel nods, both sympathetically and concernedly.

Hörður heaves a sigh. "No need to remind me about the pressure from the prosecutor, the media, and the relatives of the murdered man. I'm quite conscious of all of it. But I need time and understanding. As soon as we start rushing things, we make mistakes. One mistake leads to another, and the house of cards collapses."

"I know, I know," mutters Axel, before pointing at some photographs that Hörður has on the table in front of him. The photos are passport-size, all of young people. "Tell me about these photos."

Hörður takes a sip of his black coffee. "Of course. This is the deceased, Patrekur Jónsson. I think it's important to view him as a person of flesh and blood and not just a name or lifeless body at the scene of a murder. The same with others connected to him and/or his circle. It's sometimes said that you can't see the forest for the trees. Which is perfectly valid. But before I go any further, I want to get to know all the trees in the forest. I don't want to know just their names, but to recognize them by sight. Get a feel for them. So that I see not just a forest, but identifiable individuals."

"I understand," says Axel.

"These are the deceased's closest friends," says Hörður, pushing two of the photos forward. "Bragi Unnsteinsson and Oddur Bjarnason. All three of them were at a party in Borgarnes this summer, where a young girl died after taking some type of drug. This girl here, Eva Andrésdóttir. Her father, Andrés Aðalsteinsson, is chief of police in Borgarnes. I'm going to head west in the next few days and chat with him and maybe some of the young people who were at the party."

"A possible connection?" asks Axel.

Hörður shrugs. "Who knows? I'll question Bragi and Oddur afterwards, as witnesses. Something could possibly come out of it. They both go to Hamrahlíð Junior College, like Patrekur. I know that classes there were cancelled today."

Axel nods.

"This is Lísa Kristjánsdóttir," says Hörður, sliding the picture of her forward. "Patrekur's ex-girlfriend. The one in the nude photos, which seem to be connected to the case in one way or another. I'm not sure Lisa herself is involved. But she could be. She knows *something*, of that I'm convinced."

"What about the firearm?" asks Axel.

"I'm leaning toward it having been a handgun," says Hörður. He looks for and finds a printed list among the other case files. "Rifles of that caliber are rare. There are fifty-seven legally registered .44 caliber pistols in the country, all owned by the police force or police officers, eight of them with special collectors' licenses. "There are a few handguns registered to pest-control companies and competitive marksmen, but most if not all of them are of a smaller caliber."

"You don't imagine that a policeman shot the boy, do you?" asks Axel skeptically.

"I'm just putting facts on the table for you," answers Hörður, "and not imagining one thing or another. There are a lot of unregistered guns in this country, both old weapons and ones that have been smuggled in. I don't think it unlikely that the murder weapon was smuggled into the country, either by a gun enthusiast or a criminal gang."

"It's not hard to believe, yes," says Axel.

"But one of those who has a collector's license for a .44 caliber pistol is the chief of police in Borgarnes," says Hörður. "The aforementioned Andrés Aðalsteinsson."

"The father of the girl who died?" asks Axel.

Hörður nods.

Axel gives a low whistle. "That's got to be considered a strange coincidence."

After his phone conversation with the deep-voiced police-man, Oddur decided to walk down to Hverfisgata Street. The caller asked Oddur to meet him in half an hour. He couldn't imagine hanging out at the empty school or waiting for a bus, and if he took a taxi, he would be at the station far too soon. So he buttoned up his cashmere coat and set off. The call upset him, as well. Why do the police want to talk to him? A walk in cold weather might help him calm his nerves.

He heads down to Miklabraut Road, crosses it, and then takes a diagonal course over Miklatún Park, from the southeast to the northwest corner. Miklatún is one of the largest green spaces in the capital. A large, square area of lawns, footpaths, trees, and bushes that could be the equivalent of New York City's Central Park, but definitely isn't, neither in terms of size, beauty, nor popularity. Miklatún is really no more than its name—a "big field"—which is underused and underappreciated, since there's almost nothing in it.

Oddur, however, slows down instinctively as he walks through the desolate-seeming park, then looks over his shoulder. He's alone there, apart from some busying himself with something by the trees near Lönguhlíð Street. Oddur takes a deep breath. It's good to get away from the traffic and its pollution and the narrow residential streets. The good thing about parks like this is that they have a calming effect on the mind. Oddur has done a lot of traveling with his foster parents over the years and has visited many historic and beautiful parks, from the aforementioned Central Park to the Luxembourg Gardens in Paris and Versailles itself. Despite the fame and beauty of those gardens, however, he simply couldn't enjoy them, perhaps precisely because of the pressure that their fame and renowned beauty put on the experience. If something was wonderful in advance, it was practically doomed to disappoint him. In any case, Oddur always thought he should feel different when he saw or experienced something famous and important. But a garden is of course always just a garden and a church just a church. And although remarkable events had once taken place at the Brandenburg Gate in Berlin or at the Place de la République in Paris, they were long past, and the square was just a spacious roundabout and the gate just like any other gate, despite its size.

Oddur stops in the middle of Miklatún and looks up at the gray sky. Can he experience real emotions? Is it normal to be hardly ever impressed by one thing or another? Or always to get tired of everything?

He isn't sure. He's never been anyone other than himself and therefore has nothing with which to compare. But sometimes he feels as if others experience the world differently than he does. People can become dumbstruck with admiration for buildings, works of art and poetry, or fall head-over-heels in love with another person. He definitely has a taste for beautiful design and really appreciates good movies, and he's certainly gotten crushes on girls. But he has very rarely been head-over-heels captivated with anything. And his attraction to a girl never lasts long enough for any real relationship to form.

Should he be worried about this? Oddur heaves a sigh. He doesn't know the answer. Maybe he doesn't want to know. He looks at his watch, then sets off walking again. In any case, he decides not to worry about it for now. His friend is dead and the police want to talk to him.

He doesn't feel well. He also feels sorry for Patrekur's closest relatives, and is worried about all of this. It would therefore be quite a stretch to call him emotionless. He's just not as impressionable as some, that's all.

Oddur leaves the park and takes Rauðarárstígur Street northward. He's approaching the Hlemmur bus station when his phone rings. He gets a bad taste in his mouth, stops and looks at the screen. It's Bragi.

He dares do nothing but answer.

"Yes?"

"When are you supposed to go see the police?"

Oddur looks at his watch. "Just now, in about ten minutes. I'm right outside the station, actually."

"I have to be there right after you. Watch what you say."

Oddur throws up his hands. "Watch what? I don't know what happened to Patti!"

"We don't know what they're going to ask. I'm just telling you to be careful. Don't mention dope or give them any bullshit."

"No, yes—of course not," mutters Oddur.

"Do you have an alibi? Where were you when Patti was killed?"

"I didn't kill him!" says Oddur agitatedly. "I don't even know when it happened!"

"Calm down, man. It was on Friday, during the night. I think around midnight, though I'm not exactly sure. I was downtown with the guys from Árbær. You can say you were with us, no problem. I mean, maybe the cops think we had something to do with it, you never know."

"What bullshit, man," says Oddur, his voice hoarse with stress. "Why should they think that?"

"How should I know, huh?"

"I've got nothing to hide," says Oddur.

"That's good. But meet me outside the station afterwards, okay?"

"Why?" asks Oddur.

"Wait for me. Period!" Bragi hangs up.

"Idiot," Oddur mumbles, before sticking the phone in his pocket and walking off. At the intersection at Hlemmur, he looks to both sides before running across at a red light. The police station is across the street, big and dreary-looking. The entrance is on the east side, opposite the old gas station. Oddur glances around before trotting up the stairs and opening the door to the lobby.

Oddur looks at his watch. He's sitting alone in a windowless room, waiting, his head aching from stress. The woman in reception had asked a policeman to take him to the *swimming pool*. Whether this turquoise room was the pool, he didn't know, but here is where he was left.

He hears footsteps echoing in the corridor, then the squeaking of hinges when someone pushes open the door. A black-clad giant so big that he has to lower his head as he enters the room. The giant is coarse-looking and pale, with tousled red hair and green, moody eyes. He has a folder in one hand and something that looks like a shoebox under his other arm.

"Oddur?" he asks in a deep voice.

"Yes," he replies.

The giant lays the folder and the box on the table before sitting down. "My name is Hörður Grímsson and I'm a police detective. We talked on the phone earlier."

"Yes, right," says Oddur. He feels so bad in the presence of the giant that he has difficulty breathing.

"As I told you then," says the giant, "I'm investigating the murder of your friend Patrekur."

Oddur nods.

"What do you know about it?" The giant opens the folder, takes a blank sheet of paper from it and writes something on it with a ballpoint pen.

"Nothing," says Oddur. "Nothing at all. I only heard about it this morning when I got to school."

"How did you hear about it?" asks the giant.

"My friend told me," says Oddur. "That Patti was dead, that he'd been killed."

"What friend is that?" The giant holds his pen over the sheet of paper, ready to write down the reply.

"Bragi," answers Oddur. "Bragi Unnsteinsson. He was actually a good friend of Patti's. I didn't meet them until I started at HJC. We spent a lot of time together, but not anymore. I haven't seen them in weeks."

"Not since Spain, or what?" asks the giant.

"Something like that," says Oddur.

"Did something happen there?" asks the giant. "In Spain?"

Oddur shakes his head. "No, nothing."

"So why haven't you seen these friends of yours since you came home?" asks the giant.

"Just because," says Oddur in a shrill voice. "We'd hung out so much together. Gotten a bit tired of each other, see. And as I said, the two of them had known each other for a long time. Maybe I didn't really fit into their friendship."

The giant nods, as if he understands this completely. "Where were you last Friday, from 10 p.m. until 2 a.m.?"

Oddur swallows. "Just home alone. My parents went to their summer cottage on Friday afternoon. I was just at home chilling all weekend. Watched a little TV on Friday but went to bed quite early. Fell asleep around midnight, probably, maybe half past one."

"Is there anyone who can confirm that?" asks the giant.

"No," says Oddur.

The giant nods as he writes something down. "Nothing happened in Spain, you say, but something did happen in Borgarnes shortly before you left, right?"

Oddur stiffens. "Yes."

"Tell me about it," says the giant.

"A girl died there, at a party," says Oddur in a low voice. "Eva Andrésdóttir. She was at HJC. There were a few of us there from HJC, as well as kids from Borgarnes and maybe elsewhere. She went into cardiac arrest, Eva. Apparently, she took some drugs."

"Did you witness it?" asks the giant.

Oddur shakes his head. "I went out to get some fresh air. Was away for maybe twenty minutes, half an hour. When I came back, Eva was lying on the kitchen floor and someone was trying to revive her."

"You didn't see her take drugs?" asks the giant.

"No," Oddur replies, blushing.

"And you don't know what drugs she took, or what?" asks the giant.

Oddur flushes. "No."

The giant looks pensively at the box on the table. "I'm going to show you something, but you've got to promise not to tell anyone about it. Understood?"

Oddur nods.

The giant opens the box, and from it takes a smaller box inside a Ziploc bag. The smaller box is marked Bean Boozled, front and back.

Oddur's heart starts pounding. Is it the box from the party? The one he threw in the trash? How can that be?

The giant pays careful attention to his reactions. "You've seen this before, haven't you?"

Oddur takes a deep breath and tries to think clearly. What should he say? "I've seen *this kind* of box before. I've played this game, if that's what you mean."

"Have you ever had this game?" asks the giant.

Oddur shakes his head.

"Has anyone you know had this game?" asks the giant.

Oddur hesitates, but then nods. "Bragi."

The giant grunts. "If this was the game that belonged to your friend Bragi, would I find your fingerprints on it?"

Oddur feels weak from stress and discomfort. His hands are trembling and he's dizzy. "I don't know. Maybe. As I said, I've played it with Bragi and Patti and others."

"Very well," says the giant. "We'll call it a day … for now. You'll be escorted from here down to the basement, where an officer will take your fingerprints. You're under no obligation to comply with my request. But if you refuse, I'll demand that you be arrested on suspicion of being an accessory to murder. Which would mean custody for up to a week."

Oddur hesitates on the sidewalk in front of the police station, at the corner of the old gas station. He wants to get as far as possible away from this dreary building, to hurry home to safety and warmth—to a hot bath. He looks at the fingers of his right hand, whose fingertips are all smudged with black ink. The officer who brought him down to the basement had taken his hand and pressed each of his fingers, one after another, onto a wet ink pad and then onto the appropriate box on a special sheet of paper. He'd felt like a spineless tool in the hands of a faceless representative of the system. Like a character in a book by Kafka.

Like a man who is guilty without having done anything—as far as he knows.

Oddur looks at his watch again. How long will Bragi be? He's been waiting for a little over fifteen minutes. He himself was in the belly of the beast for around twenty-five minutes.

How awful would it be to end up in jail? To be sent to an institution and only be allowed out again after many, many years? He wouldn't be able to handle it; that much he knows.

"Hi."

Oddur is startled by someone addressing him. Someone who must have been hanging around the old gas station. Some shrill-voiced runt in army pants and a denim jacket.

"You, again," says Oddur, recognizing the fresher who'd been eavesdropping on his conversation with Bragi earlier that morning. The fresher with a silly knitted cap, black and white with dangling ear flaps with braided yarn hanging from them—a kind of Inca hat that's nothing but a fashion accident.

"Sorry. I didn't mean to startle you," says the fresher in his tinny voice.

"What the hell are you doing here? Were you following me?" asks Oddur. The fresher reminds him of the unbearable kid from the movie *About a Boy*, which is based on the book by the same name by Nick Hornby. He can hardly believe that this pipsqueak is of junior-college age. But freshers are just children, of course.

"No, I was being questioned," says the fresher.

"Why?" asks Oddur.

"I'm from Borgarnes," says the fresher. "I was at the party, you know."

Oddur stares at him. "You were? I don't remember you."

The fresher smiles awkwardly. "No one ever remembers me."

"And?" Oddur asks anxiously. "What did they want to know?"

The fresher shrugs his slender shoulders. "Just, whether I'd seen anything. If I knew anything."

"And?" Oddur asks again.

"I don't think I was able to help them much," says the fresher.

"Is that so," says Oddur. "Anyway, I don't know how what happened in Borgarnes could be related to the death of my friend."

The fresher shrugs. "Unless someone were taking revenge."

Oddur gets a knot in his stomach. "Revenge for what? No one forced Eve to do what she did. Or is that what they think, maybe?"

"Maybe. But …" The fresher stops mid-sentence, stiffens and looks behind Oddur. "I have to go now. Bye."

The fresher hurries back to the gas station and disappears around its corner.

"But …?" Oddur calls after him, before throwing up his hands.

"Who was that?"

"Fuck!" says Oddur, being startled again. Bragi had walked right up to him without him noticing. "Do you want to give me a heart attack? First the fresher, then you."

"What fresher?" Bragi asks gruffly. "Who was that?"

"I don't know," replies Oddur. "But he was at the party in Borgarnes. The police were talking to him, too. But he said that he had nothing to tell them."

"Just as well," says Bragi, before poking Oddur hard in the chest. "But what did *you* say to them, Judas!?"

"Judas?" exclaims Oddur, rattled. "Nothing! What do you mean, man? I *know* nothing and I told them nothing!"

"You know what happened in Borgarnes," growls Bragi, with a menacing expression.

"Do you think that's related?" asks Oddur. "That's what the fresher thought. That what happened to Patti might have been revenge."

Bragi snorts. "Why does the cop have my Bean Boozled box? The box you were supposed to *get rid of.* Which you *said* you'd gotten rid of!"

Oddur swallows. "I don't know. I threw the box in the trash. They didn't find it then; otherwise they would have asked us about it. I don't understand how they could have it now."

"You just threw it in the nearest trash bin? Are you an idiot?" Bragi asks angrily. "How could I have trusted you! And now some lunatic has killed Patti! You know Eva's dad is a cop, don't you?"

"Yes, or ..." Oddur stammers. "I'd forgotten that."

Bragi pokes Oddur's chest again, harder this time. "If anyone is taking revenge for Eva's death, I hope that person kills *you* next."

"Me?" Oddur whines.

"Yes, you!" barks Bragi. "Or maybe you're helping the killer? Did you keep the box instead of getting rid of it? Maybe it's you that's taking revenge?"

"No, I ..." stammers Oddur.

Bragi shoves him hard. "Just watch what you say. Watch your step. Otherwise, you'll have me to deal with, you spoiled idiot!"

"Stupid bastard," Oddur whispers irritably as he watches Bragi march off like a soldier on his way to battle.

Oddur is so upset that he notices neither the fresher, who was watching everything from the shadow of the gas station, nor the red-haired giant standing at a window on the fourth floor of the police station, looking down.

Oddur is sitting with his foster parents at the dinner table of their home on Grímshagi Street, pale, distracted, and lacking any appetite. Dinner is always at seven o'clock, on the dot. On Mondays, it's always fish. This time, Mrs. Jónína serves oven-baked trout with asparagus and sweet-potato mash. The radio is on and tuned, as always, to Channel 1—the news.

The murder of Patrekur is still the first news story in all the media. Understandably, of course, but Oddur has a knot in his stomach and a buzzing in his ears. Misery pours over him like dense darkness.

"*... who was a student at Hamrahlíð Junior College, where classes were canceled today due to this tragedy. Later this week, a memorial service will be held for the deceased Patrekur, so that his classmates can ...*"

Oddur looks alternately at Albert and Jónína, who are hunched over their plates and appear to be completely disconnected from the world around them. Aren't they listening? Or do they simply not care?

"*The police in Reykjavík still decline to discuss the case with the media, but according to the newsroom's sources, no one has been arrested in connection with the murder.*"

"So awful to hear," Mrs. Jónína suddenly mutters.

Oddur is all eyes and ears.

"What is?" mutters Dr. Albert.

"Oh, the news," says Mrs. Jónína apologetically.

"Good fish," mutters Dr. Albert.

"Yes, isn't it?" says Mrs. Jónína proudly. "The Melabúð store never fails."

Oddur rolls his eyes, then lays his napkin on the table and gets up. "Thanks for dinner."

"You're not going to eat any more?" asks Mrs. Jónína.

"I don't have much of an appetite," Oddur replies. He smiles apologetically and leaves. He goes straight to his room on the top floor, shuts the door behind him, and unlocks his phone.

Social media is alight with comments on the murder case, everything from expressions of sadness, grief, or anger to self-appointed policemen exchanging conspiracy theories and rumors. Oddur tries to ignore most of the bullshit, likes a few tribute posts, and replies "maybe" to an invitation to attend a memorial service being held by the student union in collaboration with the school administration and a priest. Maybe he'll go, and maybe not.

Oddur sees that he has some unread messages, including several from Bragi, two from girls asking if Patrekur was his friend, and one from the page that he liked the day before—Deathbook. What *is* this and why is this death thing sending him a message?

First, he opens a message from Bragi:

I still don't understand why the pigs have you-know-what that you-know-who was supposed to get rid of ... If you're screwing me over you rat then just get rid of me immediately or otherwise I'll get rid of you!!

Is this a death threat, or …? Oddur's mouth goes dry and his heart starts beating fast. Why won't Bragi leave him alone? The damn idiot. Should he tell the cops about this?

He sighs. No, then of course they'd want to know what Bragi is talking about. That would just make things worse.

Oddur decides to try to forget Bragi's lunacy for the moment. He turns his attention to the message from Deathbook—whatever or whoever that is. Its profile picture in Messenger is a skull in a black hood, just barely revealing the empty eye sockets. The message turns out to be a simple question:

Who is your number one?

"What crap is this?" Oddur mutters. He notices the green light next to the Deathbook profile picture—whoever it is, is *online*.

In return, Oddur asks:

Number one what?

Deathbook is typing, and then comes its reply: *Who is at the top of your death list?*

"Death list?" asks Oddur in surprise, before typing a question:

Which is a list of??

Deathbook: *People you want me to kill.*

Oddur scoffs. Is this a joke or …?

Are you joking?

Deathbook: *If you don't have a name for me, then I'm joking. But if there's someone making life hard for you, I'm not joking.*

Oddur shakes his head. What nutjob is this?

Who are you??

Deathbook: *Well, the man with the scythe—who else?*

"Yeah, yeah," mutters Oddur, lying there in his bed. "I just happen to be chatting with the Grim Reaper, neither more nor less."

So I can ask you to kill someone for me?

Deathbook: *Yes*

Oddur smirks. *Is this a game?*

Deathbook: *Yes*

The screen of Oddur's phone illuminates his face, and he thinks things over. This is a joke, right? What else could it be?

But what sort of joke, then? He really doesn't get it.

Deathbook: *Sometimes we need to cleanse ourselves. To rid ourselves of adversity such as negativity, hatred, and evil forces. Sometimes this adversity manifests itself in the form of a flesh-and-blood person. In such a case, we need to get rid of that person, who is a symbol of everything that works against us in life. Then we need cleansing—catharsis. I'm the one who does the cleansing.*

Oddur nods. Okay, this makes a little sense:

I understand

Deathbook: *Are you suffering adversity in your life? Who is it that is making things difficult for you today? Causing you anxiety, worry, and pain? Do you have a name?*

Oddur gets a knot in his stomach. Of course he has a name. There's only one person who fits.

If he could make Bragi Unnsteinsson disappear with a single snap of his fingers, he wouldn't hesitate to do so. His life would be better immediately. But is he going to share such thoughts with a nameless individual on social media?

No.

Oddur closes Messenger and exits Facebook. Maybe he should see what's going on on Twitter?

Hörður is sitting on the living-room sofa at home, cup of coffee in hand, watching a wildlife show hosted by David Attenborough, who, this time, is talking about big, non-flying birds. Hörður fidgets moodily, as he doesn't like big birds. Yet he isn't sure why.

"What are you watching?" asks Bíbí as she sits down next to him on the sofa. She's drinking chamomile tea from a Moomin mug, and she snuggles up to her live-in partner—the coarse giant with whom she shares her life.

"Birds," he mutters

"You don't like them, do you?" asks Bíbí. She's as unlike Hörður as can be. Short and cheerful, always smiling and with a clear, quivery voice. While he resembles an old, grumpy bear, she's more like a hummingbird fluttering around his head.

"Not such big birds, no," he mutters. "There's just something menacing about them."

"Menacing?" exclaims Bíbí. On the screen, Attenborough is crouched a short distance from an emu, which are certainly large, but seem very unlikely to attack the old TV personality.

Hörður grunts. "There's just something unnatural about them. Maybe because they walk on two legs, like humans. Then there are those big eyes. It's as if they *know* something. Or are plotting something. I just don't trust them."

Bíbí laughs her titillating laughter and pats him on the thigh. "You're very special, did you know that?"

"Oh, yeah?" Hörður smiles faintly. "I just want little birds. Passerines that say *bí-bí*. And are even called Bíbí."

"You're such a gem." She kisses him on the cheek and cuddles him closer. "If you're not too tired later, now's a good time—if you know what I mean."

"Is that so," says Hörður, trying not to sound as skeptical and exhausted as he really is. Not physically exhausted, but mentally. They've been *trying*, as it's called.

Or, she's been trying. He's more or less just been playing along—*doing his part* and hoping at the same time that nothing happens because he's not sure that he's ready for such a package. Their shared life is also starting to revolve around this—around her menstrual cycle and timing and methods and nutrition and goodness knows what else—which of course kills all romance. Sex between them is no longer passionate and intimate, but something that needs to be done to achieve something else. What used to be a wild, passionate fusion has now become a calculated obligation.

But then nothing happens, which makes him feel guilty because he of course believes that nothing happens because he doesn't want anything to happen. Then he sees the disappointment in Bíbí's eyes, holding yet another negative pregnancy test, and he feels like he's the worst scumbag on earth.

Which he might be …

"Is everything okay?" she asks. "Your whole body stiffened up."

"Yes, of course," he says. "Just fatigue. Muscle cramps. Stress from work."

"I understand," says Bíbí. "Would you like to take a long, hot bath? With scented salts and lather? Then I could massage you and …"

She stops when his phone starts ringing.

"Sorry," Hörður mutters as he fishes the phone out of his shirt pocket. He looks at the screen, and feels a bit faint as he does. It's Jenný. He called her from his car on his way home to the Grafarvogur district, but she didn't answer. He'd actually hoped that she wouldn't call back.

"It's work," says Hörður before answering. "Yes?"

"It's Jenný. Do you have time to talk?"

"Sure," says Hörður. Upon hearing her deep voice, he flushes and his heart beats so fast in his chest that it hurts. "Is there anything new?"

"Yes and no. We've finished analyzing the fingerprints. We found one or two things there; it's just a question of how much we can read into the results. But the chemical analysis of the residue from the box just came in."

"And?" asks Hörður.

"Some of the powder residue contains substances that are found in common types of ecstasy pills, among other things. Some of it, though, seems to be ordinary vitamins, such as C and B."

"Ecstasy pills?" exclaims Hörður.

"Maybe you can drop by here tomorrow? I'll be at the lab in Grafarholt. The car is there. The victim's BMW."

"I'll do that," says Hörður.

"Great. See you then."

Hörður hangs up, and then wipes a drop of sweat from his forehead.

"Your face is bright red," says Bíbí.

"Is it?" he says.

"Who was that?" she asks.

"No one special," he mutters. "The Forensics Department. They're working day and night on the investigation."

"I see," Bíbí says dryly.

Hörður tries to calm his heartbeat by taking a deep breath. He leans back on the sofa and turns his attention to the TV screen, where some lions are chasing a young ostrich, which they then catch and kill.

Borgarnes

Autumn
Tuesday

"Morning meeting number two," says Axel, with dead seriousness. He and Hörður are sitting at the long table in the spacious operations room in the innermost part of the Criminal Investigation Department, both with cups of freshly brewed coffee in front of them and the latter with some of the case files as well, including photos of three young male residents of Borgarfjörður. To the right of the whiteboard, next to the name of the murdered man, Hörður has written *Borgarnes—party*. Below it are a few names.

"Tell me about our next steps," says Axel, before taking a sip of his coffee.

"I haven't ruled out the possibility that the murder of Patrekur is related to what happened in Borgarnes this summer," says the red-haired giant. "On the 10th of July, several young people who met at Hamrahlíð Junior College, as well as a number of other young people from the town, gathered at the home of Áslaug Ellertsdóttir, who had finished middle school in the spring. A 17-year-old girl, the hostess's niece, died after ingesting drugs, probably ecstasy. This is all noted in the local police reports on the death—reports that are lacking in many respects, as is the investigation in general. I suspect that the ecstasy pills were in the box found at the scene of the murder. I'm going to meet Jenný later to find out what Forensics has uncovered. Then I'm going to go out west to talk to the father of the girl who died, as well as some of the kids who were at the party. Maybe one of them saw the box or the ecstasy pills."

"The chief of police?" asks Axel. "Andrés. The one who owns the handgun?"

Hörður nods.

"You don't think he shot the boy, do you?" asks Axel skeptically. "Isn't he in his sixties? He's been on the police force for over forty years. I looked him up yesterday. A spotless career."

"No one is above suspicion, not even police chiefs in their sixties," says Hörður. "But Andrés has a forty-year-old son named Heiðar. He could have taken his father's gun and used it to avenge his sister's death."

Axel nods. "I find that a more plausible theory."

"Maybe," says Hörður. "Let's not forget the message that Patrekur received. He was lured to Rauðhólar by someone who knew about the nude photos. I doubt that anyone outside that group of junior-college kids had such knowledge."

Axel sighs. "Still, it isn't out of the question?"

"I'm sure I'll come a little closer after my visit to Borgarnes," says Hörður. "But I don't envisage finding the culprit there. There's something about this murder that bothers me. It just seems so thought-out and mechanical—so *cold*. More like an execution than a violent crime of passion."

"Which means?" asks Axel.

Hörður sips his coffee thoughtfully. "The killer didn't know the deceased personally. Or is completely unscrupulous. What I fear most is that he'll kill again."

"Why do you say that?" asks Axel.

"I don't know." Hörður shrugs. "The killer left that box on the scene. As if he's trying to tell us something, or mislead us—as if he's playing a game."

"Fine," says Axel. "But what can you tell me about those young people you've talked to?"

Hörður fidgets. "I doubt that Lísa Kristjánsdóttir is directly involved in the murder, but there's something she's not telling me. I also doubt that the nude photos of her are the reason for the murder, but they're connected to it; I just don't know how, exactly. Oddur Bjarnason doesn't have a solid alibi, but I can't say that he's a probable perpetrator. A privileged brat who wears designer clothes and a gold watch. But he might know something. I'll be talking more to him. Bragi Unnsteinsson, on the other hand, is a rather unreliable character, temperamental and possibly on the psychopathic side. He apparently collected nude photos of girls and used them against them. He has acquaintances in Árbær who have been arrested with small amounts of drugs on them. He admitted to having one of those boxes—a Bean Boozled game."

"Does he have an alibi?" asks Axel.

"Yes," says Hörður. "He was out partying with his friends. Several witnesses have confirmed it. But footage from surveillance cameras will prove it one way or the other. We'll know very soon."

Axel grunts. "So you don't have any suspects in your sights?"

Hörður shakes his head. "But it's slowly coming along. These kids know something that they aren't telling me. One of them will surely give in, sooner or later. It's all a matter of patience. There will be a memorial service for Patrekur at HJC tomorrow. I'm going to be a fly on the wall there, with the principal's permission. It'll be interesting to see who shows up, and maybe who doesn't show up. Maybe I'll find out something today, out west."

"Why do you think they're hiding something from you?" asks Axel.

"It's just a hunch," says Hörður. "Young people are strange creatures who put their own interests above everything else. These kids are preoccupied with vain things like the opinions of others, popularity and the like."

"These are strange times," says Axel. "I remember the days when teenagers kept diaries and feared nothing more than that someone would read them and their deepest secrets would be revealed to everyone. Today, kids put all their secrets straight onto social media and are only worried about not getting enough likes."

"Good point," says Hörður. "But I also witnessed an interesting scene yesterday, here on the sidewalk in front of the station."

"Oh?"

Hörður nods. "I'd finished taking statements from Oddur and Bragi. I went up to the cafeteria, got a cup of coffee and strolled over to the window, as usual. Then I see Oddur talking to another guy, a skinny boy. It was probably half an hour since Oddur was done here, so he seems to have lingered outside. Maybe waiting for Bragi, who then shows up. Then, the thin kid disappears, but Bragi seems to give Oddur an earful. It was as if he was scolding him, or threatening him."

"I see," says Axel. "Who was the third one? The skinny kid?"

"I'm going to find out," says the red-haired giant.

"We don't have all the time in the world," says Axel with fatherly seriousness.

"I know, I know," says Hörður, a little irritated. "But there's no point in pressing forward when we have so little to go on."

Axel heaves a sigh. "Maybe I should bring in reinforcements? There are actually only two of you working on this at the moment: you and Jenný. She in the lab and you in the field."

Hörður gets butterflies in his stomach when Axel says "you and Jenný." "There's no need at the moment. Benedikt has been helping with fact finding and other computer work, besides handling the phone calls and so on."

"You've got to be careful not to hog the stage," says Axel. "Don't let your ego get in the way."

"My ego?" Hörður exclaims, surprised. If he told his boss how much he doubted himself and his own excellence, Axel would probably demote him all the way down to a parking enforcement officer.

"There's a lot of pressure on us, and it's very uncomfortable having no answers," says Axel. "I don't know how much you follow the media, but there's hardly anyone talking or writing about anything these days but the murder of Patrekur. But as long as the *police decline to comment on the case,* a void is formed that both reporters and the general public fill with speculation and gossip."

Hörður scoffs. "I don't follow the media reports on the case, and I'm not about to start now. My role is to investigate, not feed the media. You can add people to the team if you want, but that will just mean spending more time in meetings, doing more supervision, report writing, and coordination of operations."

"Fine," says Axel. "We'll just press on. For the time being."

The first class this morning is English. One of the classes that they all have together: Oddur, Bragi, and Patrekur. But Oddur had stopped sitting with them in the back row. He moved forward two rows, and there he sits now, trying to focus on what the teacher is writing on the board. The atmosphere at school is oppressive—a strange mixture of sadness and tension. Sadness because a student was murdered. Tension because the murderer is still at large.

The empty desk next to Bragi works like a magnet. No one in the room can withstand the temptation to glance at it from time to time, not even the teacher. He looks there every time he addresses the class—even he is in the power of the screaming absence emanating from that unremarkable desk.

But Patrekur's desk isn't the only empty one in the classroom. Oddur notices that Lísa, the ex-girlfriend of the deceased, isn't present. She probably called in sick. Has maybe had a nervous breakdown or something. Oddur really regrets not having called in sick himself. Maybe he'll do that tomorrow?

He nods, as if to agree to his own idea. But then he remembers that damn memorial service. Doesn't he have to go to it? Yes; anything else would likely be inappropriate.

Suddenly, Oddur scratches the back of his neck, as if he's got lice or something. He stops scratching but looks over his shoulder, because he has the feeling that someone is staring at him. And lo and behold. Bragi is sitting hunched by the window, staring at him with a malicious gleam in his bloodshot eyes—and then he drags his index finger across his neck.

Hörður drives up Ártúnsbrekka Hill. In his mind, he has already set off for the west, but he still has to stop to see Jenný in Grafarholt. The Forensic Services Department is moving from Hverfisgata to a brand-new building on Vínlandsleið Road. Hörður drives up around the building, which is set against a hill, and parks his SUV at the eastern side of the upper floor, next to a wide sectional door with a smaller, standard door in the middle. He steps out onto the asphalt parking lot, adjusts the collar of his leather coat, and slides his fingers through his shock of hair before ringing an unmarked doorbell.

The door opens and Jenný appears in the doorway—in all her glory. She's wearing a white lab coat over jeans and a shirt, and has a hairnet on her head and plastic covers over her Dr. Martens shoes. "Hi! Come in."

"Thanks." Hörður flushes just to see and hear her. He lowers his head as he strides over the threshold. Behind the bay door is a space the size of a double garage. In the middle of it is Patrekur's white BMW, its doors open, and more or less covered in fingerprint powder. A member of the forensics team is stooped over the back seat, running the nozzle of a special vacuum cleaner back and forth over it.

"Ebbi is collecting hair, flakes of skin, and anything else that can hide in such upholstery," says Jenný.

"Do you think the murderer got into the car?" asks Hörður.

"We can't rule out any possibilities, of course," says Jenný. "It's unlikely that the perpetrator got into the car that night, simply because he didn't *need* to. But that doesn't mean that he definitely didn't get into the car, in addition to the fact that he may have been in the car at some point earlier, not least if he knew the victim. And since we have these theoretical possibilities, we're studying the car high and low, because it's very inconvenient being wise in hindsight."

"Of course; silly question on my part," mutters Hörður.

"But beyond that, of course, we're just taking the opportunity to put what we've learned into practice," says Jenný, winking at the red-haired giant. "It's not every day that we get to investigate a whole car."

"I see," says Hörður, blushing.

"Anyway, I was just about to take a coffee break," says Jenný. "Would you like to join me?"

"Oh, sure," says Hörður, despite the fact that the combination of no breakfast and downing so much coffee is giving him heart palpitations. He follows Jenný out and into the changing room, where she takes off her lab coat, hair net, and shoe covers. Her jeans fit her tightly and her black cotton shirt is stretched over her huge breasts.

"It's always good to get that hairnet off," says Jenný as she shakes her black mane.

When Hörður catches the scent of her hair conditioner, he feels a bit giddy.

Jenný opens another door. "Here's the break room."

Hörður sits down at a table by the window, while Jenný pours two cups of coffee. "Milk or sugar?"

"Black," says the red-haired giant.

"Like your conscience?" asks Jenný, winking at him again. She hands him his coffee and takes a seat.

Hörður's face reddens. It's definitely a bit exciting to have a secret crush on someone, but also embarrassing. He feels vulnerable in Jenný's presence, defenseless against her charms.

"You're not wearing a ring," she says casually. "But I understand that you have a wife?"

Hörður stiffens. "Huh? Yes … or. I live with a woman, yes. But we aren't married or anything like that."

Jenný laughs. "I'm just teasing you. Relax. It's not as if we're on a date or anything."

"Yeah, exactly." Hörður's heart is beating so fast that his chest aches.

"Too bad," Jenný mutters, as if distracted.

Hörður's eyes widen questioningly. Too bad what? Does she want to go out with him? He decides to change the subject. "What came out of the fingerprint analysis, by the way?"

Jenný smiles teasingly and sips her sweet café au lait before answering. "We found fingerprints from both Oddur and Bragi inside the car. On the dashboard and the back of one of the front seats. Which is natural, because they were friends and hung out together. We also found other finger-prints but don't know whose they are. A lot of different peo-ple have been in that car, no doubt."

"Yes, no doubt," says Hörður. "Anything else?"

"Gunpowder residue, blood—as we expected," says Jenný. "But the meatiest thing was in the Bean Boozled box."

"Oh yeah?" Hörður says excitedly.

"There were traces of powder in the compartments, as you recall," says Jenný. "Some of it turned out to be vitamins, either C or B12. But some held traces of methylenedioxymethamphetamine."

"MDMA?" exclaims Hörður.

Jenný nods. "Ecstasy, in tablets or crystalline form. I guess this game has been *updated*, you know, to make it more exciting."

Hörður whistles softly. "I'm heading up to Borgarnes. A girl at a party there this summer died of a drug overdose. Patrekur, Oddur, and Bragi were there."

"An interesting coincidence," says Jenný.

"Exactly," says Hörður. "And Bragi has already admitted to having had such a box. Were fingerprints found on it?"

"No, in fact," says Jenný. "Not a single one. Which must be considered very peculiar, if not downright suspicious."

Hörður nods, distracted. "Someone wiped off the box. Probably to remove their own fingerprints. Maybe the same person who left the box by the car."

"The murderer?" Jenný asks.

"Very likely," says Hörður.

They look each other in the eye. She smiles but he blushes and looks away.

During his free periods between classes, Oddur habitually goes to the school library, where can he always find a quiet corner for reading. But after the incident with Bragi in English class, he's both too restless to read and feels somewhat claustrophobic. Bragi's presence has become so overwhelming and uncomfortable that he can't even imagine being in the same building as him, let alone in the same room. And if Bragi were to go looking for him, he would start in the library. So Oddur decides to get some fresh air.

He goes out the school's back door, wraps a scarf around his neck, and meanders along the grassy crag after which the hillside is named. He knows as little as Bragi how the Bean Boozled box ended up in the hands of the police. But Bragi seems to think that it has something to do with Oddur; that *he* brought the box to the police. Why should he have done that?

Oddur sighs. Of course it's impossible to understand Bragi's way of thinking, let alone argue with him about anything. The guy's head is so messed up that it's ridiculous.

He ambles eastward, hopping from rock to rock and letting his mind wander. Should he send Lisa a message? Ask how she's doing and all that? She's probably suffering. But she's cute, too—very cute.

Oddur takes out his phone and opens the messaging app. Would he send her a message if she *wasn't* cute?

Maybe. But probably not.

So, might he be hitting on her more than expressing his sympathy for her? He isn't sure.

Maybe it's a little of each?

He taps in a message, deletes it—taps in another, edits it a bit, and reads it over.

Hi, Lisa. I don't know how you're feeling. But I know it will pass. Hang in there. Hugs, Oddur.

Is that okay? He thinks so—and then just sends it.

Hörður drives along the foot of Mount Hafnarfjall on his way to Borgarnes, visible across the fjord. He's leaning back in the leather seat, steering with the fingers of one hand. His black SUV rushes along effortlessly at just over a hundred kilometers per hour. The heather and scrub are now in their autumn colors, yellow, red, and brown. Colors that remind Hörður of the masterpiece *October Rust* by Type O Negative. The band's frontman, the depressed Gothic giant Peter Steele, once came to Iceland, alone and without letting anyone know. Peter is very interested in Iceland and sometimes says that he's of Icelandic descent, which is either wishful thinking or a conscious lie. He says that he's going to move to Iceland one day and settle in a hut in the woods. Which is of course sheer fantasy, as there are no real woods in the country, let alone with log cabins in them, just summer cottages surrounded by scrub and lava rocks. But if Peter is serious about coming, then Hörður would offer him his house in Súðavík. His childhood home—*Future.*

How cool would that be?

Hörður drives over the Borgarfjörður bridge, enters the town and parks his SUV at Hyrnan, the largest gas station of three at the end of the bridge. The town of Borgarnes is like one big service station. Countless people stop here every day, but none for long. Gas, food, bathroom, goodbye. He steps onto the asphalt and stretches. Before going to see the town's police chief, he is first going to interview three men in their twenties who were at the party that summer. He asked them to meet him at Hyrnan at noon.

He hopes that they're here.

Hörður walks in through the automatic door and looks around the gas station, which is in fact an entire service center with a cafeteria, a convenience store and souvenir shop, etc., as he tries to recall the names of those he's going to meet. Gísli, Eiríkur, Helgi? Probably not.

He does, however, think he sees the young men, sitting together at a window table, eating fast food. There are three of them, all of a similar age, countryside types, and clearly waiting for someone—gawking at the entrance like dogs waiting for their master. One of them is wearing a wool sweater, another a fleece jacket marked Olís, and the third a coverall marked Vírnet. Naturally, they noticed the red-haired giant when he walked in, but probably had preconceived notions about what police detectives from Reykjavík look like. They keep glancing at the door, in any case.

Hörður buys a cup of coffee and a cruller before heading over to them. "Do you mind if I sit down?"

The young men look at each other in surprise, but none of them answers the question. Hörður sits down, smiles at them, and bites into his cruller.

"Are *you* the cop?" asks the man in the Olís jacket.

Hörður nods. Then he asks them about the fateful night. They say that they'd been out cruising around. There had been little going on, actually nothing but the party at the home of the savings bank manager. They drove by a few times but didn't go in until they heard some girls there start screaming.

"Not friends of ours."

"We were never invited to parties there."

"Those kids were snobs."

Hörður nods sympathetically. "But what did you see when you went in?"

They describe the scene to the best of their ability. Eva was lying on the kitchen floor; one of the guys from Reykjavík was attempting to give her first aid. The other two were arguing, or shouting at the other one. There was a big commotion. They asked what was going on. The Reykjavík guys all went on the defensive; one of them gave them a bunch of crap. Someone said something about drugs.

"Who said something about drugs?" asks Hörður.

They don't remember; shrug their shoulders.

"I tried to help Eva," says the one in the Vírnet coverall. "I pushed the other guy away and started CPR, which I learned in Search and Rescue."

"Was Eva a friend of yours?" asks Hörður.

They shake their heads. "Not a friend, no."

"I held onto the big guy," says the one in the fleece jacket. "His name is Bragi. He's the one who had the drugs."

"We held onto him until the police arrived," says the one in the Olís jacket.

"How do you know the drugs were his?" asks Hörður.

They shrug, look at each other.

"Did you see drugs?" asks Hörður. He lifts his coffee to take a sip, but stops. He's already had way too much coffee.

They shake their heads.

"We heard afterwards that they were his, Bragi's," says the one in the wool sweater.

Hörður pulls a photo from his coat pocket. "Did you see this box in the house? Maybe in the kitchen?"

They take a close look at the photo.

"What does it say? Bean … Booz?"

"I don't think so."

"No. What is that?"

Hörður sighs heavily, puts the photo back in his pocket. It's half past twelve. The chief of police said that he would be at home at lunchtime. "Just one more question, boys. Where does Andrés, the police chief, live?"

"Do you mind if I ask you a few questions?" says Hörður. He's sitting at the kitchen table at the home of the chief of police, who lives in an old two-story single-family house on a green, quiet street near the swimming pool. The weather report is being read over the radio, and the aroma of fried fish hangs in the air. The police chief had warmed up leftovers for lunch and finished eating before the red-haired giant knocked on the door.

"Of course," says Andrés. He hands Hörður a pot of hot coffee. "But I don't really see how I can help you."

"Thanks," says Hörður. He sweats at the thought of drinking more coffee, but he has to accept it—anything else would be rude.

Andrés sits down opposite him at the table. He has thinning hair and a gray, weary-looking complexion, with bags under his eyes. "My wife has gone back to work. Otherwise, she would no doubt have made crepes for you."

Hörður smiles faintly. "Coffee is all I need."

"You're investigating the murder of the boy, aren't you?" says Andrés.

Hörður nods. "They were here this summer, the deceased and two of his friends. At a party where a girl died. Eva, your daughter."

The police chief's mood darkens. "I remembered his name. Statements were taken from most if not all of those who were at the party. But the two cases aren't related?"

"I don't know … maybe," says Hörður. "Tell me, why were no blood samples taken from any of the guests? For example, the ones who came from Reykjavík. To find out who took drugs and who didn't. And why wasn't a better search for the drugs carried out? Nothing was found at the scene, was there?"

Andrés groans, as it isn't easy for him to discuss this. "It was a hectic night. A lot of things went wrong, maybe everything. Mistakes were made, that much is certain. No, no drugs were found and no one was charged with anything. It was a tragedy, that's what it was."

"There's no denying it." Hörður clears his throat. "But one of the possibilities I'm exploring is whether someone might possibly have been taking revenge for your daughter's death. What do you think about that?"

Andrés is surprised. "Who should that be?"

Hörður shrugs. "A close relative or friend. You, your son … I don't know."

Andrés's temper flares, but he keeps his composure. "What's with these accusations?"

"I've got to ask; you must understand that," says Hörður. "Being a policeman yourself."

"Yes, maybe." Andrés takes a deep breath. "But I didn't shoot the boy. I would never do such a thing. And my son lives in Norway."

"Very well," says Hörður. "Does anyone else come to mind?"

Andrés shakes his head. "No one would take revenge for Eva's death. She wasn't that popular."

"No?" asks Hörður in surprise.

"No," says Andrés, in a choked-up voice. "She was always in trouble, the dear. Unruly. Difficult, as they say."

"I see," says Hörður. "But there's something else. You own a handgun of the same caliber as the one Patrekur was shot with."

Andrés's eyes widen in surprise. "A .44 caliber? That's unusual."

"I know," says Hörður. "Which is why I'm asking these uncomfortable questions."

"I'll be damned," mutters Andrés. "But he wasn't shot with *my* gun, that much is certain."

"What makes you say that?" asks Hörður.

"What makes me?" Andrés asks irritably. "Well, it's always in its place. Locked in a drawer in my desk. I clean it twice a year, at my desk. Apart from that, it's in the drawer. It doesn't go far."

"When was the last time you saw it?" asks Hörður.

"The fourth of July," Andrés replies without hesitation.

"How can you be so sure?" asks Hörður.

Andrés smirks. "I clean the gun on the US Independence Day and on the Savior's birthday. *That's why* I can be sure."

"Very well," says Hörður. "How about showing me the firearm?"

"If you insist." The police chief gets to his feet and Hörður follows him into the hall, then up a carpeted staircase.

Hanging on the wall of the hallway upstairs are a number of photographs, many of them of the deceased Eva.

"It's here." Andrés opens the door to his study and turns on the light. The curtains are drawn over the windows and the air in the room is heavy. On one wall hangs the American flag. The police chief sits down at his desk. He opens a shallow drawer in the middle of it and takes out a small key covered by stationery.

"You keep the key there?" asks Hörður.

"Maybe not quite by the book," says Andrés, "but no one has any business here anyway."

"Maybe," says Hörður.

"And the gun is here," says the chief. He sticks the key in the keyhole of a locked drawer at the top right of the desk. There's a soft click, and he pulls out the drawer. At its bottom are a green felt liner and an empty packet of cartridges.

Nothing else.

Andrés's face pales. "I don't understand this. The gun *was* here. It's *always* here!"

"But it's not here," says Hörður gravely. "It hasn't been here for some time, because it was used to murder Patrekur Jónsson."

The chief opens the drawer all the way, as if he doesn't believe his own eyes. His hands are trembling. "Who could have taken the gun?"

"You said you cleaned it on the fourth of July," says Hörður, taking out his notepad. "Your daughter died on the tenth of July. You must have had a number of visitors here in the days following her death?"

Andrés shrugs. "Yes and no. The priest came, and my wife's friends. Our son Heiðar came from Norway. He stayed a week."

"Any more?" asks Hörður. "Think carefully."

The chief sighs. "I don't know … I don't remember. My brother came—the savings bank manager."

"Your brother *and* the savings bank manager?" asks Hörður.

"No," says Andrés. "My brother is the savings bank manager."

"I see." Hörður makes a note of this. Didn't the boys at Hyrnan say that the party had been at the home of the savings bank manager? Was the party at his house, your brother's?"

The chief nods sadly. "He was abroad, but left his daughters alone at home. And then all this happened. It was a double trauma, a real family tragedy. They came here on the Monday night following. Of course, my wife and I could very well have gone to see them. But … my wife was in a terrible shock …"

"Your daughter died in your brother's kitchen," says Hörður somewhat distractedly, writing something in his notepad.

Andrés nods again.

Hörður clears his throat. "So they came here, your brother and his wife?"

"No," says the chief. "My brother is a widower. His wife, Guðrún, took her own life many years ago. He came here with his daughter Rut. My young niece."

"How old is she?" asks Hörður.

"Sixteen, I think," Andrés mutters.

"Could either of them have taken the gun?" asks Hörður. "At least in theory?"

The police chief shakes his head. "Actually, my niece excused herself to go to the bathroom. But she's in a wheelchair. Neither of them came up here. No one come up here except my wife and I."

Hörður clicks his tongue, and then points at the empty drawer. "But that doesn't seem to stand up to scrutiny, does it?"

"No," says Andrés weakly. "Probably not. But *theoretically*, anyone could have taken the damn gun. Our house is never locked, you see."

Hörður, on his way back to Reykjavík, drives out of the southern end of the Hvalfjörður tunnel. As far as he can tell, his day's work hasn't yielded anything. He still doesn't know who the killer is, although he is fairly certain of what the murder weapon was. Which is a step in the right direction.

It appears as if there's a direct connection between the murder of Patrekur and the death of Eva Andrésdóttir—that the murder was carried out in revenge. But who is the ruthless avenger? And why was Patrekur murdered, and not …?

Hörður loses his train of thought when a light on his SUV's dashboard comes on. It's the low-fuel light—he forgot to fill the tank before leaving the capital. No big deal at all. From experience, he knows he can drive up to fifty kilometers with the light lit.

A few raindrops hit the windshield. Hörður switches on the wipers. As far as he recalls, it's supposed to be raining over the next few days, more or less.

Oddur is lying in bed in his room listening to music. He reads Lísa's reply for the hundredth time:

Thanks—you're cute

His heart warms and he can't help but smile. Does he have some guilt about feeling so good, so soon after his friend was found murdered? Yes, a little—but life goes on. And they were never *such* good of friends, he and Patrekur.

Reykjavík

Autumn
Wednesday

"So we know what the murder weapon was?" asks Axel. He and Hörður are sitting alone in the operations room early in the morning, just as they've done the last few days.

"Yes, I believe so." Hörður pushes a photo across the table. "Here's a photo of a comparable weapon. A .44 caliber Smith & Wesson police revolver. Six shots. A heavy piece of work."

"It was taken from a locked drawer at Andrés' house?" asks Axel.

Hörður nods. "Along with a pack of bullets."

"Was the forensics team going to go out west today?" asks Axel.

"Yes," replies Hörður. "To look for fingerprints and other clues. But I'm not optimistic that anything will come of it."

"No, maybe not," mutters Axel. "But this narrows the circle a bit, doesn't it? If we assume that Eva didn't have a boyfriend or close friends from the capital, then the murderer must be from Borgarnes or be closely connected to someone from there. Only a select few knew about the gun in that drawer."

Hörður nods thoughtfully. "What I have the hardest time understanding is why Patrekur was killed. If someone were avenging the death of Eva Andrésdóttir, there's no evidence to suggest that Patrekur had that death on his conscience. After all, he himself thought that he was going to sell Lísa Kristjánsdóttir the nude photos that he took of her. But Lisa doesn't appear to be implicated in this crime. It just doesn't make sense."

"No," Axel says wearily. "It doesn't."

"It's most likely that the drugs that killed Eva were Bragi Unnsteinsson's," says Hörður. "Bragi is also the one most likely a perpetrator of some sort, of all the young people on my list. But it wasn't he who was shot—nor was he the one who did the shooting. His alibi is solid."

Axel looks at the whiteboard, glances over its names. "Just to speculate; where would we be if Bragi *were* the killer?"

"Very well." Hörður clears his throat. "In that case, we would doubtless have a connection to Eva's death. They attend a party with drugs brought by Bragi. The girl dies. The boys hide the drugs or get rid of them; make a narrow escape, so to speak. But they've got a death on their consciences. Eva's death ties them together ... but can also divide them. Bragi is tough, but Patrekur feels miserable about it. He feels the need to confess, to ease his conscience. He tells Bragi that it's best for them to step forward and tell the truth. Bragi loses it."

Axel nods. "It could have happened like this."

"But it probably didn't," says Hörður.

"No," says Axel, frowning.

"Something is missing from the picture!" Hörður throws up his hands in despair. "Whether it's a person or a fact, evidence or something else. *Something* is missing. We see ripples on the surface, but we don't know what rock was thrown into the water."

"Or who threw it," Axel adds.

"Right," says Hörður in semi-surrender. "But the memorial service is today. I'm hoping someone there loses their cool—says something, does something, I don't know. But at some point, the culprit will make a mistake. No one is perfect. No one can keep a poker face forever—no one but a sphinx made of stone."

"Still, time is on his side, not ours," Axel reminds his colleague.

"I think those kids hold the answers," says Hörður stubbornly. "And I *will* find them."

Oddur, among a large number of other students, heads toward the auditorium. The atmosphere in the school is heavy and solemn. Most of the students walk in silence, others whisper or speak in low tones. Many stop whispering when they see Oddur, or nod to him—giving him attention and respect solely for having hung out with the deceased. Some of them probably even envy him the connection. Death grants fifteen minutes of fame.

Oddur picks up his pace. He feels as if he's a participant in some sort of charade and regrets having coming to school. Of course, not everyone remembers Patrekur, and even fewer knew him personally. But when someone dies in dramatic fashion in a microenvironment, everyone wants a part in the play that starts spontaneously, preferably a role on the big stage. Everyone imagines that they remember the deceased, and those who don't claim to have known him will cling to those who do, whether they're exaggerating or lying or not. The girls had had crushes on him, the boys had chatted with him at the last dance or during their free periods, and every single mouth in the school smacks its lips over one of the countless rumors about Patrekur and the reason why he was killed.

"He was a coke-head."

"He owed money."

"He was messing around with a criminal's girlfriend."

"He was selling drugs."

Idiots! Oddur is pissed off, but tries to stay calm. He elbows his way into the auditorium, which is filling quickly, and tries to find an empty seat, preferably next to someone he knows, and not least, as far from Bragi as possible. The seats at the back fill first; not everyone is comfortable sitting in front of the stage. On it sits the principal, the teachers, and a priest clad in black, with a white collar. In the middle of the stage is podium with a microphone on top. In front of the podium, to one side, is a vase holding a flower bouquet, and to the other, a large framed photograph of Patrekur, with a mourning ribbon over one corner.

Oddur doesn't see Bragi anywhere, but it looks to him as if Lísa is sitting by herself in the third row from the front, left side. Should he?

Why not?

He hurries down the aisle to Lísa's row and makes his way over to her. She looks up and gives him a quick smile. She's as white as paper and is trembling as if cold.

"Hi," Oddur whispers as he sits down next to her.

"Thanks." Lísa grabs one of his hands and squeezes hard, like a child afraid of losing his parent.

"You're welcome," Oddur whispers, without being sure what she was thanking him for. Probably just for sitting by her. And he's glad that he did.

When the principal goes to the podium and taps the microphone with his finger, the babble in the auditorium dies down.

"Hello? Is this on? Dear students. We are gathered here today to remember Patrekur Jónsson, who …"

As the principal says the boy's name, Lísa utters a half-stifled cry, as if she'd been stabbed in the heart. She throws her hands over her mouth, squeezes Oddur's hand even harder and bursts into tears. She rocks forward and back in her seat as the tears roll down her bloodless cheeks, biting her thumb at the same time to stifle her sobs.

A murmur runs through the auditorium; all eyes turn to her and the principal hesitates. But then he goes on, introducing the priest to the audience.

"I'm sorry," groans Lísa through her sobbing.

"No need to apologize," says Oddur. He pulls a handkerchief out of his coat pocket and hands it to her, then kisses her on the top of her head and hugs her. Lísa cuddles up to him as if she's eight years old again and he's the rock in her life.

The priest steps up to the podium.

Oddur glances around him, checking to see if everyone is staring at them. It doesn't appear so—any longer—but from across the aisle, one row behind, eyes stare at him, full of contempt and hatred. Oddur hurriedly looks away, but the poisonous gaze manages to freeze him to the depths of his soul and make him feel sick.

Bragi has certainly made his presence known.

Oddur tries to swallow, but it's as if he has a potato stuck in his throat. Why can't Bragi leave him alone? What has he done to deserve this hatred?

Outside, it's pouring rain, as was forecast. Hörður runs his fingers through his wet shock of hair and inhales a raindrop up his nose. He keeps as low a profile as possible. He arrived early, unbuttoned his wet leather coat, and sat down in the back row of the auditorium, to the right. The students who arrived first were surprised to see him, as none of them recognized this red-haired, black-clad giant. But as the auditorium filled, the students' reactions became more subdued, and finally no one took any notice of him.

He just sat quietly and waited, and then frowned and tried to remember what it was he was going to do *before* he went to HJC. Yes, exactly—fill his car's tank. He'll just do it after the service.

When Lísa Kristjánsdóttir entered the auditorium, she didn't notice him, being surrounded as he was by students in the darkened corner. Nor did she look around much, but just slunk down the aisle and sat down by herself in an empty row very near the front. Patrekur's death had clearly hit her hard.

Lisa sat there by herself until Oddur joined her. Hörður watched their every move. As did Bragi. He'd arrived shortly after Oddur and found an empty seat a few rows in front of Hörður.

When Oddur hugged Lísa, it was as if Bragi got an electric shock. He rose halfway from his seat and looked as if he were going to fly straight across the auditorium and tear them apart. Then Oddur spotted him and was startled. It was as if Bragi had given him an invisible slap ...

Hörður fidgets in his seat, like an excited spectator at a sports competition, having witnessed quite a show that he is convinced has something to do with the case he's investigating. The tension between Bragi and Oddur is palpable—electric—and it's as if Lísa is the reason for their conflict.

A love triangle? Is that what all this is about? Hörður can hardly believe it, but sometimes the answers are just as simple as the questions are complicated. But whether the murder of Patrekur was a crime of passion or not, it's clear that his ex is connected to it in one way or another. The girl in the nude photos.

The auditorium is silent as the representative of the National Church of Iceland starts speaking. Apart from the sounds of a few people clearing their throats, a pin could have been heard dropping. The priest is gray and pallid, both frail and respectable. He stands behind the pulpit, glances over the audience and speaks about loss, sorrow, living and dying. His voice is deep and warm.

"… when we see divinity reflected in the eyes of a newborn baby, it's as if eternity opens like a flower in our hearts—we are filled with love practically to bursting. But when the God who gives changes into the God who takes, our hearts cool, curtains close over our eyes, and our thoughts darken. We become sad, angry, and we lose faith. Or do we?"

When the priest says *like a flower*, Hörður's attention focuses on the bouquet in front of the podium. The flowers are lilies; large, white, and cloying. They're truly reminiscent of death: pale as bloodless flesh, drooping powerlessly, their smell sweet and suffocating and reminiscent of decay.

Hörður feels slightly nauseated. It's hot in the auditorium—hot and cramped. The priest's voice penetrates his head and the smell of the lilies lies like a slimy blanket over his respiratory organs. He hears a buzz and the hair rises on the back of his neck. He feels a chill, perhaps from the rain.

Is he getting sick or ...?

Hörður doesn't realize what's happening until he sees the shadow, and then it's as if someone splashes cold water on him. He has experienced all of this many times before, but the *symptoms* still manage to creep up on him. To the right of the priest, from Hörður's point of view, a black haze gradually forms—a horizontal death-shadow that hovers a few centimeters above the stage and seems to stare into the auditorium.

Hörður's heart skips a beat, like an animal that claws are clamping down on. He can't breathe, his whole body stiffens, and he gapes like a fish on dry land. All he hears is a buzz, as if from an untuned radio, and all he sees is the cursed death-shadow—a harbinger of doom.

Then it's as if *something* lets go of him. He hears the priest speaking, his heart beats, and his lungs fill with air—and at the same time, the shadow dissolves into nothing. It disappears into the other dimension, the world beyond.

Hörður stands up so abruptly and clumsily that his chair overturns. He raises his hands high and shouts across the auditorium: "Look out, Reverend—look out! Death is among us!"

The priest stops. The shout echoes throughout the auditorium, and is replaced by a murmur and staring eyes.

Hörður stands there looking awkward as the drawn-out seconds pass, one after the other. It appears that there is no looming danger. No one tries to kill anyone and no one drops dead. He lowers his arms, clears his throat, and mutters an apology as he rights his chair and sits down. Some people giggle, others whisper, and before long a few have started laughing.

The priest knocks on the podium. "Silence, dear children—may I have silence?"

Hörður hides his face in his hands. What's going on? Didn't he see the shadow? Was no one doomed to die?

Or did he prevent something bad from happening?

As soon as the ceremony ends, Oddur gets to his feet. He half-pulls Lísa out of her seat, wanting to get out of there as quickly as possible, away—as far from Bragi as he can. Fortunately, Lisa allows him to take charge. She's too confused to have an opinion on anything. Oddur puts his arm around her and together they hurry out of the auditorium, through the chattering crowd and into the corridor.

"Are you going to class?" asks Lisa.

"I don't know. Are you?" Oddur looks over his shoulder. He doesn't see Bragi anywhere, but spots the policeman who questioned him, the red-haired giant who nearly turned the memorial service into a farce. He's hovering at the entrance to the auditorium, looking sheepish.

"I'm going home," says Lisa. "I don't feel well at all."

"Let's go, then," says Oddur. He takes out his phone and taps in a number as they head toward the main entrance. "I'm calling a taxi. It's pouring rain."

"All right," says Lisa.

They walk out of the school and wait together for the taxi under the eaves at the entrance. The rain pours down like a waterfall. Lísa shivers. Oddur hugs her and kisses her on her wet head.

The door opens and Bragi appears next to them. "What do you two think you're doing?"

Oddur stops hugging Lísa. "What?"

Bragi walks quickly over to Oddur and shoves him, pushing him nearly out from under the eaves into the rain. "First, Patrekur is killed. Then all of a sudden, the cops show up with my box. And now it's like you're starting up with Patrekur's girlfriend—when he was your friend! Or maybe you never were his friend?"

"Ex-girlfriend," says Oddur, rattled. The rain wets his hair and forms beads on the shoulders of his cashmere coat. "They broke up long ago."

"Don't be splitting hairs, you loser," growls Bragi. "You leave the girlfriends of your friends alone, period!"

"Bragi, don't ..." says Lisa, on the verge of tears. She's still standing under the eaves, and pulls her coat tighter around herself. "We're just friends, really!"

"You heard what she said," says Oddur, who sincerely hopes that Lísa didn't mean it. They're not *just* friends, are they?

"Leave her be," Bragi hisses, poking Oddur in the chest with his index finger. "Or you'll be sorry, loser! Or should I say murderer?"

"What are you ...?" Oddur asks, but stops when Bragi shoves him again, so hard that he nearly falls over.

"Traitor!" Bragi growls, before storming back into the school.

Hörður feels a bit regretful following the incident at the memorial service. He doesn't understand what happened ... or *didn't* happen, rather. He saw the shadow; he's sure of it. But no one died. Not yet, at least. Unless it was someone who wasn't in the auditorium, but elsewhere in the building.

Could that be?

He blinks, looks around. The auditorium is emptying out and the stage is empty. Oddur and Lísa are gone, as is Bragi.

Hörður's head clears and he hurries out to the corridor. The students stream in both directions, probably going to their classes. He looks to both sides but doesn't see the young people he came to surveil.

Maybe they've gone to class. But they could also be on their way home.

He walks toward the main entrance, heavy of step and distracted. He can still smell the lilies—a cloyingly sweet scent that reminds him of decay. He still feels the presence of death. He *was* in the auditorium, the black one. His shadow had appeared on the stage.

The flickering shadow of the Grim Reaper …

Hörður walks through the lobby, out the door and practically runs into Bragi Unnsteinsson, who is on his way in. Hörður stops abruptly and tries to grab Bragi by the shoulder, but the latter, dripping wet, deftly avoids him.

"Can I have a word with you?" asks the policeman.

"I'm late to class," the young man snaps, before disappearing into the school.

"Hey!" calls out Hörður. He feels like running after the boy, knocking him down and handcuffing him. But he has no justifiable reason to do so, and would probably get into trouble if he let his temper get the better of him.

Instead, he just snorts and rolls his shoulders in order to shake off his irritation. At the same moment, a taxi drives up to the school and stops where two young people are waiting on the sidewalk. It looks to Hörður as if it's Oddur and Lísa.

"Hello, hello!" calls the red-haired giant.

The young people look over their shoulders. Oddur has already opened the taxi's back door, but they wait before getting in. The icy rain hammers on the roof of the car.

"Hello," says Hörður. He buttons his coat and turns up his collar. "Are you in a hurry?"

Oddur shrugs and puts his arms around Lísa, who is pale and sickly looking. Her blonde hair clings to her cheeks. "Lisa isn't feeling well. It was hard on her. The service."

"I see, I see," mutters Hörður. "But what did Bragi want from you? He seems very upset."

Oddur sighs heavily, looks away. "He's just half-crazy or something."

"Oh?" asks Hörður. "Is he harassing you? The both of you?"

Oddur shrugs his shoulders, and the rain runs in thin streams down his wool coat. "Yes and no. He's just like that. Everyone is either with him or against him. In his mind, I'm against him—and I'm made to pay the price for it."

"Why does he think you're against him?" Hörður asks as he brushes a wet lock of hair from his face.

"Just because," says Oddur, clearly impatient, seeing as how they're soaked and the taxi's meter is running. "Because I don't want to hang out with him anymore, you know."

The cold rain forms puddles and streams.

Hörður nods thoughtfully. Then he turns his attention to Lisa. "He doesn't want you two to be together?"

Lísa blushes. "Yeah, something like that."

Oddur smiles a crooked smile.

"You were waiting for Bragi following your questioning at Hverfisgata. You two spoke together on the sidewalk in front of the police station," says Hörður. "Why?"

Now it's Oddur who blushes. "He asked me to. He's really paranoid about what happened to Patrekur. He wanted to know what I said and so on."

"What you said about what?" asks Hörður.

Oddur thinks things over before answering. "He found it strange that the box should have been there at the murder scene. The Bean Boozled game."

"Why?" asks Hörður. "Was the box yours?"

Oddur reddens and blinks. "No."

Hörður grunts and straightens his back. He towers over them like a black-clad, green-eyed lighthouse. "There's something you're not telling me. Something you both aren't telling me."

"Not at all." Oddur shakes his head and looks at Lísa, who hesitates and looks down at the stream of water at her feet, before shaking her head as well.

"Very well." Hörður unbuttons the top buttons of his coat and takes two business cards from the inside pocket. He shudders as cold drops trickle down his back. "But if there's something you want to tell me, something you remember or think might be relevant to the investigation, call me. In full confidentiality, I promise. Okay?"

"Of course, no question." Oddur takes both of the business cards before motioning to Lísa to take a seat in the back of the taxi ahead of him. He then sits down next to her and shuts the door behind him. Finally, he leans forward and says something to the driver.

Hörður stands at the curb with his hands in his coat pockets, looking with a serious expression into the taxi. The rain hits his leather coat and runs down to his shoes. Isn't he forgetting something? Wasn't there something he was going to ask Oddur?

The young people in the vehicle's back seat act as if they don't see him outside it. Finally, the car drives off, and it's as if a heavy load is removed from their shoulders. The red-haired giant's presence was clearly disconcerting to them.

Why?

Suddenly he remembers …

"Hey, hello!" yells Hörður. He runs after the taxi and knocks on its roof. The car stops abruptly and Oddur rolls down the window.

"What?" Oddur asks as Hörður bends like an ogre down to the open window.

"It wasn't just Bragi you spoke to outside the police station," says the red-haired giant, "but another young man, as well. A skinny boy. Who was it, and what did he want from you?"

"Why don't you just ask him?" Oddur asks in return as he points out the window toward the school.

Hörður follows his gesture. In the rain, the school building looks more like a black medieval castle. And lo and behold. At the foot of the castle wall, on the eastern side of the imaginary drawbridge, stands the boy whom the red-haired giant had been asking about.

The boy's eyes open wide and he glances furtively to both sides, like a robber caught in the act.

"You!" Hörður calls, and the boy freezes in his tracks. Oddur rolls up his window and asks the driver to go.

"What do you want from me?" the boy asks as Hörður approaches him. He looks with a frightened expression at the rain-soaked giant towering over him, pale and rough-hewn, with dark locks of hair hanging down his face.

"I'm a police detective," says Hörður. "Who are you, might I ask?"

"Haukur," says the boy, in a high-pitched voice. "A reporter for the school's newspaper."

"Reporter, yes," Hörður says as he takes the measure of the boy. He's wearing the same clothes as he was outside the police station—a denim jacket, army pants, and white running shoes. He has a silly looking knitted cap on his head, and round steel-frame glasses on his stubby nose. His head is conspicuously oval and his face childish. Haukur isn't exactly masculine. He's like the peace-loving Gandhi as a teenager. Kind of a vegan-type, probably gay or just asexual.

"What's your last name?" asks the red-haired giant.

"What is this about?" Haukur asks in return. "Why are you talking to me?"

"What were you doing outside the police station on Monday morning?" Hörður then asks. He pulls out his notepad and pen, opens the notepad and tries to shelter the pages from the rain.

Haukur shrugs. "As I said, I'm a reporter working on a little summary of Patrekur's murder for our newspaper, *The Newssheet*. I just wanted to know what Oddur had to say. What the police had been asking him about and so on."

Hörður scoffs and writes something down. "Investigative reporter?"

Haukur smiles apologetically. "Maybe. Or, well, that's what I want to be. But it isn't as easy as I thought."

"Don't be poking your nose into matters that don't concern you," Hörður advises him. "The police are in charge of investigating the case. Reporters just get in the way and tend to be detrimental to our investigations."

"Don't you need accountability, like everyone else?" Haukur asks. "You know, the Fourth Estate."

Hörður closes his notepad. "First of all, you're just a kid. And secondly, I don't need any damn accountability. What I need is to be left in peace to do my job …"

"Excuse me!" says someone behind the red-haired giant.

Hörður turns around. It's the old gray-haired priest who addressed the students in the auditorium. He's standing there in a light-colored trench coat, under a black umbrella, smoking a cigarette.

"Do you have a minute?" asks the reverend, smiling at the policeman.

"Yes, just a moment," says Hörður, before turning back to the diminutive Haukur. "Where were we?"

"You were talking about being left alone to do your job," says Haukur.

"Yes, exactly," Hörður mutters as he reaches into his coat pocket for a business card, which turns out to be half wet. "Here's my number. Don't be snooping around, but if you *do* find anything that might be useful to my investigation of the case, call me *before* you write anything or doing something stupid. Okay?"

Haukur takes the limp, damp card. "Yes, great. Awesome—thanks! I'll give Áslaug your number, too. She's the editor. We'll definitely be in touch!"

"Yeah, okay—*whatever*," says Hörður, who immediately regrets having given this scrawny fellow his phone number. "But don't call just to call, and *stop* snooping, huh?"

"Okay." Haukur smiles idiotically, and then runs to the entrance and disappears into the school.

What a strange boy! Hörður shakes his head and sighs before turning back to the reverend, who is standing there smoking beneath his umbrella and smiling a typical priestly smile, a sort of gentle but half-awkward, kindly smile that reminds the red-haired giant of the ashamed look made by a shitting dog.

"What is this silly grin on everyone's face today?" Hörður asks gruffly. "Is the rain that fun? Or were you smoking something illegal?"

"Just a Prince," says the sergeant, taking a drag on his cigarette.

"Prince, huh?" Hörður rolls his shoulders. Damn, he could go for one of those right now!

The priest pulls out the pack and shakes a cigarette out of it. "Go on. We only live once."

Hörður opens his eyes wide in inquisitive surprise, then accepts the cigarette and sticks it in his mouth. "First of all, can you read people's minds? And secondly, aren't you supposed to preach moderation and proclaim eternal life?"

"Maybe." The priest lifts his umbrella for Hörður to get under, too, and then lights the red-haired giant's cigarette.

"Thanks," mutters Hörður. He takes a drag from the cigarette, inhales the smoke and groans with pleasure.

"But … no." The priest smiles faintly. "Addiction literally shone from your eyes. Regarding your question, we live only once in this body, in this earthly existence. There are no addictions in heaven, so … and besides, we harm no one by smoking. No one but ourselves."

"This is cursed poison," says Hörður, blowing smoke out of his nostrils. "A wonderful poison, but poison nonetheless."

"Yes, yes." The priest drops the stub of his cigarette onto the ground and steps on it. "But I wasn't going to talk to you about addiction, but about what happened at the memorial service earlier. Your strange shouting."

Hörður nods. "That's what I guessed."

"Death is among us?" says the priest in an inquiring tone. The raindrops fall on the umbrella over them, creating a rapid but pleasant drum beat.

"I'm Catholic, though more or less irreligious," says Hörður. "But I was brought up in belief in the holy sacrament, God and the devil—light and darkness. Man is a puppet of these forces. We walk either in the way of light or the way of darkness. Evildoers are under the power of the prince of darkness. And where evil reigns, death is never far away. And death was with us today. It appeared to me on the stage, to your left, in the form of a black haze."

The priest stares in obvious perplexity at the red-haired giant. "Are you ... clairvoyant?"

Hörður shrugs. "I'm just telling you what I saw."

"And what does it mean?" asks the priest. "Your vision, or whatever it was?"

"I thought that someone would die, there and then." Hörður coughs. He feels dizzy from the nicotine, but takes one more drag before tossing away the half-smoked cigarette. "Now, though, I don't know what to think. But I'm afraid that something bad is going to happen. That this won't be the last memorial service here at this school."

"I don't know what to say ... or think," mutters the priest. "But I really hope it was just a hallucination ... a figment of your imagination."

"I hope so, too." Hörður smiles a crooked smile. "But there's *something* out there. Something evil that's lurking in the shadows."

"Have you ever seen such a …?" The priest stops in the middle of his question when the policeman's phone starts ringing.

Hörður fishes the ringing phone from his pocket and wipes the haze off the screen. "Sorry. It's my boss. I have to answer it."

"No problem," says the priest.

"Hello," says Hörður as he answers the phone. He walks out from under the cover of the umbrella and to the parking lot where he parked his black SUV.

The priest watches him walk away.

"You've seen that sort of thing before, haven't you?" asks Axel M. Axelsson in a fatherly tone, yet not without the skeptical air of a down-to-earth intellectual. The two of them are sitting in the operations room, he and Hörður Grímsson. The principal of Hamrahlíð Junior College had called Axel to tell him about the *incident* in the auditorium—to *lodge a complaint* about the detective whom Axel had convinced him to allow to attend the memorial service, in the *interests of the investigation*. The principal hadn't quite understood what interests the policeman had been looking after when he got up and shouted something about death, like the worst sort of mental patient. Axel couldn't easily answer that, so he immediately called the red-haired giant into his office.

"Yes, yes," Hörður admits grudgingly. He feels awful, sitting there in front of his boss like a naughty schoolboy in front of the principal. First of all, the incident was highly embarrassing. Secondly, he finds it very difficult to talk about his clairvoyance or whatever it is that he has, let alone try to explain *it* to ordinary people.

"I vaguely remember you mentioning it," says Axel somewhat awkwardly, as he himself has a very hard time believing in phenomena such as dreams and omens. "The black mirrors case, right?"

Hörður nods. What his boss doesn't know is that the red-haired giant's clairvoyance has played a part in all of his murder investigations. If he wasn't clairvoyant, he probably wouldn't be a cop. At least not a police detective.

Axel heaves a sigh. "Of course, I don't know what came over you there at the school. But according to the principal's description, it was rather … unfortunate. Can you explain it in any more detail?"

"Actually, no," mutters Hörður. "But I think someone is doomed to die. Someone at the school. Probably a student, without my knowing it for sure. Whoever it is could be dead as we speak. But whenever it happens, it will happen, and it won't be an accident, but a carefully planned, malicious deed. A murder."

"Like the murder of Patrekur?" asks Axel.

Hörður nods. "Same person. New victim."

Axel shrugs. "Do you know who it will be?"

Hörður shakes his head. "But I would like us to keep watch on the three youngsters. Oddur, Bragi and Lísa."

Axel sighs. "How can I justify something like that? And even if I got the authorization for it, the manpower and funding, can you imagine the wave of fear that would sweep through the school community? The police believe that the murderer will strike again, and is therefore going to safeguard three students out of what? Three hundred? Five hundred? And we're not just talking about HJC!"

"Couldn't it be without the knowledge of those parties?" asks Hörður. "Just a general security measure?"

"Are you joking?" asks Axel, shocked. "Or are you suggesting that we spy on members of the public? Without authorization or any real reason?"

Hörður's face reddens. "Not spy on, just monitor. One of them could be the perpetrator."

"We have to follow the rules," says Axel heavily. "We've made the mistake of *monitoring* suspicious individuals too closely, and been slapped with restraining orders."

"I understand," mutters Hörður. "But since I'm working on a murder case, I get unlimited overtime, right?"

"Yes, and?" asks Axel suspiciously.

Hörður shrugs his shoulders obstinately. "There's nothing stopping me from parking my car wherever I like, at any time of day or night. I wouldn't be monitoring anything, just thinking."

Axel grunts like a bear. "Who are you going to be following?

Oddur is propped up on his elbow in bed, chatting with Lísa on the phone. The window curtains are drawn and the only light in the room comes from a green lava lamp on the nightstand.

"Thanks again for taking me home this morning. It was very sweet of you."

Oddur warms up inside; he's crazy about Lísa. "My pleasure."

"But what's gotten into Bragi?"

Oddur gets a knot in his stomach. Why did she have to mention him? "I don't know. His head's just messed up."

He has hardly spoken the words when his phone beeps. Someone has sent him a message.

"I know."

Oddur removes the phone from his ear and glances at the screen. On it is a Messenger chat head with which he's very familiar. Of all people, it's Bragi who has sent him the message.

His heart begins pounding and his mouth goes dry.

"Are you there?"

Oddur holds the warm phone to his ear again. "Yes, of course."

"Can you meet me soon? I need to tell you something."

"Yes, of course," says Oddur, cheering up again. "Tell me what?"

"It's an absolute secret. I can't really talk about it, but … but I have to share it with someone before I lose my mind or something."

"Okay," says Oddur. He senses that what she's going to tell him is very important. What can it be?

"Can I trust you?"

"Of course," he says. "Yes. Absolutely 100 percent."

"Good. We will be in touch."

"Okay."

"Bye."

"Bye."

As soon as Lísa has hung up, Oddur opens the message from Bragi. He *wants* to wait to do so, just to lie down on the pillow and think about Lisa and the fact that they're going to meet—that she's going to entrust him with a secret. But he *has to* know what message that idiot Bragi sent him. Otherwise, he won't be able to relax and clear his head.

The message is much more disturbing than he could have imagined. An MMS. An unclear photo from their trip to Ibiza. Oddur remembers pretty much nothing about that night, as he was plastered. But there he is, naked in bed with some girls, taking one of them from behind while another girl watches. Bragi had invited them to their hotel to party. Two Swedish hippie girls. They had slept with them, all three of them. And Bragi had obviously taken photos. Which is just like him.

Below the picture is a flickering ellipsis. Bragi is writing something. Then the text appears:

Stop meeting Lisa or I'll send her this picture too

No! Oddur feels a terrible chill. What a fucking asshole that kid can be. Why is he acting like this?

Should he answer? What can he say?

Oddur sighs heavily. He's numb and confused. Finally, when something good happens in his life, something exciting, that bastard has to go and wreck it …

"I hate that miserable fucker," says Oddur, on the verge of tears. Is he going to start crying because of this? Maybe. Unless he pukes first. Either way, he feels sick—with hatred.

Suddenly, another message pops up. But it isn't from Bragi—it's from the mysterious Deathbook:

Do you have a name for me?

Oddur grits his teeth. Of course he has a name. It's painted with red in the sky and echoes in his mind. He asks in return:

It won't go any farther?!

Deathbook: *Just between us. 100 percent confident*

Oddur thinks it over—hesitates—but then goes for it. What does he have to lose?

Bragi Unnsteinsson

Deathbook: *Received. Your wish is my desire*

Okay? Feeling half-bewildered, Oddur clears his throat.

What happens now?

Deathbook: *Catharsis …*

Mental cleansing, huh? Oddur needs something like that. But how is that cleansing supposed to take place?

"The world is full of idiots," Oddur mutters as he sets his phone to silent and closes his eyes.

ANOTHER MURDER

After sending Oddur the photo and the text message, Bragi decides to go for a swim to try to blow off some steam and relax, hopefully. He's angry, sad, and confused. Sad because of the death of his best friend. Angry at Oddur because of the box that had been found at the murder scene—the box that he said he'd gotten rid of. And then there was Oddur's hitting on Lísa—completely tactless and disgusting. How big of a loser can a person be?

But first and foremost, Bragi is confused. His best friend was *murdered*—shot with a gun. Who killed him and why? He doubts that Oddur has any direct connection to the deed—he's too much of a wuss for that. But why was that fucking box there, then?

The whole deal makes Bragi feel incredibly uneasy. It's disturbing knowing that Patrekur's murderer is out there somewhere. The box has something to do with what happened in Borgarnes. Could someone be taking revenge for that?

If so, is he in any danger?

All of it is fucking with Bragi's head. He has no idea what's going on. He doesn't trust Oddur and feels both powerless and fearful, feelings that are screwing with his psyche. He feels like beating the crap out of someone, preferably Oddur. Screaming until his lungs burst. Or drowning himself in booze and drugs, until his brain fries and he drifts into oblivion …

But first, he's going to go for a swim. As a child and teenager, he did competitive swimming. The Árbær Swimming Pool is within walking distance of his parents' house. He finds a free lane, dives into the pool's deep end and relishes the silence, the weight of the water and its clarity. Then he starts swimming freestyle, powerfully, first one kilometer and then another, until he can't go on. Then he goes to the hottest hot tub and stretches his tired muscles as the cold raindrops massage his head and shoulders. Finally, he relaxes in the steam room and the medium-hot hot tub, alternating several times between the two.

Going swimming was a good idea. He feels a little better. Not much, but a little.

It's still raining. Hörður is sitting in his SUV in a large parking lot between two apartment buildings in Hraunbær. The car's engine is idling, but its headlights are off. He's been sitting there since six o'clock, when Bragi returned home from his swim. The raindrops tap lightly on the car's roof and stream down the windshield. The radio is on and tuned to the BBC World Service; Hörður listens with one ear to the news commentary and various reports while watching the main entrance of the apartment building on the right, a four-story, blue-and-white painted U-shaped building with an unpretentious yard. The other apartment buildings on the street are all in the same soulless ghetto style.

Bragi doesn't own a car, but his parents have an old gray Subaru parked in a marked space a short distance from the apartment building's main entrance. Each apartment has its own specially marked parking space on the lot outside the entrance. At the back of the building is a basement door, leading directly to the yard. But since Hörður can't monitor both doors at once, he has chosen to watch the front door. Unnsteinn, Bragi's father, is a bricklayer. He drives a van that's nowhere to be seen. His wife Halla, Bragi's mother, works at the Health Clinic at the Mjódd Shopping Center. She returned home in the Subaru around fifty minutes ago, bringing with her two Nettó shopping bags.

Hörður sighs, then takes a sip of coffee from a travel mug that he bought at a 10-11 convenience store. He frowns, as the coffee is both cold and bitter. In a bag lying on the passenger seat are a roast-beef sandwich, a Prince Polo chocolate wafer, and a bottle of orange Gatorade.

Wasn't he going to call Bíbí? Yes. He unlocks his phone, opens the list of contacts in his address book and calls his live-in partner. The Bluetooth system mutes the radio, and Bíbí's voice is heard over the SUV's speakers.

"Hi hi! Are you on your way home? I have a lasagna in the oven."

Hörður grimaces; he loves lasagna. "No, unfortunately. I'm stuck working. I have no idea when I'll be free. Maybe not until sometime tonight."

"Oh, that sucks. Maybe you can warm up leftovers when you get home? There'll definitely be plenty for you."

"I'll do that, thanks," he says. "I'll be careful not to wake you up if I come home really late."

"No, just wake me up. I see so little of you these days. Besides, now's a good time for me, you know."

"I know." Hörður rolls his eyes. He's on the verge of asking *isn't it enough having lasagna in the oven,* but has the sense not to. "See you sooner or later. Bye until then."

"Bye, darling."

Hörður hangs up by pressing a button on the steering wheel. He's peeved about missing the Italian dish, which would no doubt be served with an oil-soaked salad and warm garlic bread. But at the same time, he's glad to get a little break from all this ovulation and pregnancy-sex that has permeated their relationship these past months.

A baby, huh? Just the thought of it makes him feel a bit anxious. Not only does he make it out to be even more work than it is, having to feed and clothe and raise a screaming infant who will be helpless and needy for years, he also doesn't understand how any sane person can think of bringing a child into the world as it is, with all its wars and natural disasters—to add one more soul to the billions that already live on the blue planet and are on the cusp of destroying it.

What future are the parents of the twenty-first century offering their progeny? None, in the opinion of the red-haired giant. At best, a black one.

Hörður fidgets in the leather seat. He's been sitting there for so long that his body has started to ache. And now he has to pee. Maybe he should have skipped the coffee? He could just as well chug his Gatorade and pee in the bottle, but then he would just have to pee again and the bottle would be full …

He loses his train of thought when a white van is driven into a space on the parking lot, not far from the apartment building's main entrance. The van is marked with the name and logo of a bricklaying contractor. Out of it steps a robust-looking man in gray work clothes; presumably Bragi's father. He goes into the building, and the lights in the stairwell come on.

Hörður opens his notepad and writes down this information: who came and at what time. Not that he thinks it will make a difference. But one never knows. Besides, he has nothing better to do than to note such things. And *if* something happens, then it will all make a difference.

He puts down the book and sighs. On the radio, a BBC presenter is recalling the historic event when a whale of a rare species strayed up the River Thames and couldn't find its way back out. Videos of the whale were featured in newscasts all over the world. Rescuers managed to capture the whale and hoist it onto a barge that was supposed to transport it back to the sea, but the wounded and exhausted whale gave up the ghost before they could achieve their goal.

After dinner, Bragi goes to his room as usual. There, he generally listens to music, plays video games, or hangs out on the phone or computer. Tonight, though, he's too restless to concentrate on any one thing. His parents had listened to the news while eating, as usual, and it was one report after another on Patrekur's murder, although there was no news of the investigation—yet again.

"Who could have *done* this?" asked his mother, in a tone blending maternal duty and anxiety.

"And why can't they find him?" added his father, looking at the same time at Bragi, who had lost his appetite. He is nearly overwhelmed with grief, but doesn't know how to handle it or process it or whatever else it is that people do in such situations. Instead of crying or asking for help or discussing his feelings, irritability and anger just flare up in him time and time again.

"Why are you looking at me?" he'd snapped at the dinner table." "*I* didn't kill him!"

His parents were taken aback, as if he'd given them an electric shock. Then they looked at each other, dumbfounded and confused. Bragi had apologized, gotten up and left. His anger had quickly abated, and was replaced by pangs of guilt. Why had he acted like that? Had *they* done anything to him? Then his guilt made him irritated again. Don't they understand how bad he feels? Can't they show him some consideration and turn off the damn news? Isn't it enough that he's grieving? Does he also have to suffer because of his parents' stupidity?

Bragi grits his teeth in anger. He clearly should have swum five kilometers—or fifty. He's literally exploding, like a volcano. He's very irritated, not only in his thoughts and nerves, but literally in his flesh and bones. It's an irritation that he has experienced before, and because of that, he knows that Patrekur's death is neither the beginning nor the end of this intolerable emotional state. Simply put, he's suffering because his body needs drugs.

He's in fucking withdrawal!

Bragi snorts, then switches on his laptop and opens the browser. Some weed would calm him down a bit. Morphine would help him relax and sleep. But what he wants most is cocaine. To fire up his ego, and at the same time get rid of his fear and anxiety, to feel as if he's the king and that everyone else is just a pawn.

He opens Facebook in order to check the underworld dealer pages that he usually buys from, such as Green Elf, Bling Bling, and The Fixer, but gets a little distracted when he sees that his inbox is full of messages. So he starts by looking at them. Most of the messages are from old friends and acquaintances who won't shut up about the death of Patrekur, who was his only real fucking friend. Death has a strong pull, and now everyone and their grandma wants to be friends with Bragi, who despises such ass kissing.

But one message captures his undivided attention, being in entirely different tone. It's from a dealer he liked relatively recently—7th Heaven. Some girl sent him an invitation to like the page, as he recalls. At the moment, he doesn't remember who it was, but she'd sent him a friend request shortly before and he'd accepted it because she was so cute. Silja? Sandra?

It doesn't matter. He'd bought weed through that page once, and gotten an excellent product for a very good price. The only downside was that this person was either a complete beginner or badly paranoid. He didn't want to meet his customer, and instead, Bragi had to leave money in an envelope (who uses envelopes?) in a certain place and then pick up the weed in another place—it had been taped to a tree branch in Miklatún Park. The Green Elf used similar methods, but was classier.

He opens the message from 7th Heaven:

Mega-week:

Marley 3k

Elvis 3k 3pcs

Flash 4k

Andes 14k

Mega-week, like the ones advertised by Domino's Pizza. Pretty good. Bragi smiles faintly—for the first time in a long time. But he has definitely seen better prices, except maybe for coke. Fourteen thousand for a gram of Andes Mountains coke is below market price, way below. Question of whether it's just some rubbish?

He types on the keyboard, hits *enter.*

Good andes? Don't lie to me!

While Bragi waits for an answer, he goes over his financial situation—he has almost forty thousand in cash. Which is pretty sad. He makes a few mental calculations. If he gets the guy to sell him two grams of coke at twenty-five thousand, he'll have thirteen thousand left. For that, he could possibly get five grams of weed (Marley) or fifteen ecstasy pills (Elvis), if the dealer will give him a volume discount. If so, he would sell the old ones at an inflated price to some fresher, and in that way get a few thousand krónur back.

He can make good money on such deals, but maybe he should just start refinishing cars again in the evenings and on weekends? It pays well, cash-in-hand, but is just such damn hard work. It sucks to be broke and …

His laptop beeps. 7th Heaven has answered.

Top product. Crystalline snow.

Bragi almost licks his lips. Crack cocaine. He's got to get some! He calculates fast, pumped up by a little greed, and types faster than he thinks.

I'll take 2gr Andes + 6gr Marley, 38k cash take or leave.

He exhales hard, as if he's been running. This counter-offer *has to be* accepted! Then he'll re-sell the weed at six thousand per gram, which will give him thirty-six thousand, meaning that he'll actually be getting the coke for two thousand krónur, which is nothing! If it happens, he'll buy more off this fool, preferably at a lower price, and let the ball roll on and on and on …

The computer beeps.

Ok

Yes! Bragi lifts his clenched fists over his head and opens his mouth wide, but avoids screaming with joy. His heart beats faster and he sweats with excitement. He sends a message back.

Where and when? I'm game now.

Bragi gets to his feet, puts on his leather jacket, and paces the room as he waits for an answer.

Come on!

Hörður is sitting in his black SUV, waiting. It's thirteen minutes past eleven. His lower back aches and he has to pee. The rain knocks on the roof and streams down the windows, the radio hums at low volume, and the heater blows warm air. He sighs, shakes his head, and tries to change his position a little.

How long should he wait? Until midnight? Longer?

He's eaten his sandwich and the chocolate wafer and is half done with the Gatorade. What he needs is cigarettes. It's impossible to do nothing for a long time without smoking; that's just how it is. But he quit smoking, of course. He grunts moodily. Maybe he should always carry a pack on him, just in case? For situations like these. Sometimes not smoking is simply unbearable. There's just something about smoking. Opening a new pack, breathing in the aroma of the tobacco. Lighting the first cigarette of the day, sucking in the bitter smoke and feeling how …

What light is this? Hörður squints. It's half dark in the car, but a little light on the dashboard is glowing. He just hadn't noticed it before because the steering wheel overshadowed it. Is one of his headlights out, or …

No! The hair rises on the back of the red-haired giant's neck. It's the damn fuel light! It's been on since he left Borgarnes. How far has he driven since then? He isn't sure, but there's hardly much gas left in the tank. He just hopes it's *enough*. The needle of the fuel gauge is alarmingly close to zero, but there could easily be up to ten liters left in the tank.

Or what? Yes, sure, couldn't there be? Hörður curses himself in silence. Should he go and fill the tank? He wouldn't be away very long. But what if Bragi comes out at exactly the same time? It could easily happen.

"It'll be all right," mutters Hörður. "It *has to* be all right."

Still, he could call someone and ask that person to bring him a can of gas, couldn't he? Yes, but who? Not Bíbí. She's angry enough about him being almost never home these days. Asking her to help him be away from home even longer would really be pressing his luck. He isn't going to call Axel, either. Old Steppenwolf isn't going to find out that he forgot to fill his SUV's tank. What about Þóra? Isn't she still in Tenerife with her girlfriend? Yes, he thinks so.

Hörður heaves a sigh. Just to do something, he scrolls through the most recent calls on his phone. He stops at one name, and his mouth goes dry and he gets butterflies in his stomach. Should he call Jenný?

Maybe. Or not. Why not?

Before he knows it, he has pressed the green handset symbol. The Bluetooth system takes over and the ringing sounds throughout the car. He feels a rush of heat. What is he doing? Shouldn't he just hang up? Yes. He looks at the steering wheel, trying to find the right button. It was just rashness, a mistake …

"Hi, cutie!"

Cutie? Him? Hörður stiffens, is dumbfounded.

"Are you there?"

He clears his throat. "Are you busy?"

Bragi shuts his laptop, switches off his bedroom light, and goes downstairs. It's dark in the hall and the living room. He expected to find his parents watching TV, but apparently, they'd gone to bed. He himself had been watching TV shows and YouTube videos for three hours, filling the time since that drug-dealer freak said that he couldn't meet him until half past eleven.

But, better late than never. Naturally, he'd checked a few more dealer pages but no one else was offering cocaine at fourteen thousand krónur per gram. The next cheapest was eighteen thousand per gram. So …

Bragi sneaks into the vestibule, puts on shoes and finds the car keys in his mother's coat pocket, then slips out onto the landing and shuts the apartment door behind him. He jogs down the stairs and opens the door onto the darkness and the rain.

Hörður looks out through his wet windshield as he speaks to Jený through the hands-free system.

"I was on my way to bed. I'm wearing only a nightgown. How about you?" Her voice is low and seductive, deep and warm.

"Still working," says Hörður, trying not to think about the person in a nightgown on the other end of the line. "If it can be called work. Just sitting in my SUV, watching an apartment building in Hraunbær."

"A stakeout?"

He smiles faintly. "Yes, I guess so."

"And what, you're bored? Is that why you called?"

"Yes … or …" He looks at the fuel gauge and the lit indicator.

"I could also come and keep you company. I live in the Sel neighborhood, not far from where you are."

Hörður swallows—carnal impulses spread through him. How would *that* turn out? Probably just one way. "It's just, you see … I didn't really know who I could call. I'm almost out of gas."

Jenný laughs. "How embarrassing?"

"Well," says Hörður, miffed and hurt. "Everyone can forget these sorts of things. But since the murderer is at large, such otherwise innocent mistakes could bite me pretty hard in the ass. I'm monitoring a possible perpetrator, but he could just as well be the next victim."

"I see. I can meet you in about fifteen minutes. I just need to pop on some clothes and stop at a gas station. Where exactly are you?"

"Great, thanks! I'm …" Hörður stops when a light comes on in the apartment building's stairwell, and shortly afterward, someone opens the front door. A young man, tall and dark-haired, wearing black trousers and a black leather jacket.

It's Bragi.

"You were saying?"

"He's just come out," says Hörður in a low voice. He watches Bragi run to his parents' Subaru, unlock it, and get behind the wheel.

"The one you're keeping an eye on?"

"Yes." The red-haired giant's heart pounds in his chest. Bragi drives off, out of the parking lot and in the direction of Bæjarháls Road. "He's driving away. I've got to follow him."

"Fuck! I'll call you as soon as I've gotten the gas, okay?"

"Okay, thanks." Hörður hangs up, puts the car in gear, switches on its headlights and wipers and follows Bragi, who drives through a roundabout and turns west. The red-haired giant maintains a bit of distance between them. There are few people out and about at this time of day, making it more difficult than otherwise to follow a car without its driver becoming aware of it. But the reduced visibility because of the rain helps a bit.

Bragi slows down at the lights at Höfðabakki Road. He's clearly going to go straight on, rather than take a right down to Vesturlandsvegur Road or a left into the Breiðholt subdivision. Hörður drives slowly toward the intersection. When the lights finally turn green, he's only a few meters behind the Subaru. Bragi crosses Höfðabakki toward Ártúnsholt and immediately turns right down a sloping street called Straumur.

"Where is he going?" mutters Hörður. He stays about two hundred meters behind Bragi's car, following it through the heavy rain. The Subaru disappears now and then in the rain and twilight, and then the brake lights come on for a few seconds before Bragi turns again to the right, this time heading under Vesturlandsvegur and north along Breiðhöfði Road. Hörður gives the SUV a bit more gas, but slows down again when he sees Bragi stop at a red light at the intersection at Bíldshöfði Road. The Höfðabakki area comprises nothing but companies, mainly repair shops and various service companies, but also factories, car dealerships, and detailers, as well as a few restaurants. Breiðhöfði Road crosses it from south to north.

When the lights turn green, Bragi hits the gas and drives fast down the empty street. Hörður also steps on it, but makes sure not to follow the Subaru too closely. Red brake lights illuminate the darkness of the night, and then Bragi turns right again, this time onto Stórhöfði Road, which runs along the edge of the Höfðabakki area, crossing it from east to west. When Hörður comes to the intersection, he sees Bragi slow down again and turn left, down Svarthöfði Road, which runs in a steep arc down to Sævarhöfði Road.

Just as Hörður turns onto Stórhöfði, Bragi disappears from his sight. Hörður steps on it again in order to narrow the gap a little before he too turns down the slope. But he has barely pressed on the accelerator when the engine starts to hiccup. Hörður grinds his teeth and grips the steering wheel harder.

"No, no! Not now!" he shouts in despair. But the engine keeps hiccupping; the SUV limps and gives up—it's out of gas.

Hörður sits there as if paralyzed. He can't believe this has happened. The silence is maddening.

His heart is pounding and his blood pressure could probably split his head in two. Two questions sit on his shoulders like Óðinn's ravens and croak in his ears.

What should he do? What *can* he do?

Hörður steps out of his SUV into the cold rain. To his right are cold-looking industrial buildings, to his left is nothing but darkness and gloom. The sky is black, the rainwater forms a stream at the curb, flowing toward the nearest drain.

The red-haired giant curses under his breath, then brushes a rain-soaked clump of hair from his pale face. Should he call the station and ask the dispatch officer to request all units to be on the alert for a gray Subaru? He wrote down its license-plate number in his notepad. He could say that the driver is suspected of driving under the influence or something like that.

Yes, he'll do that, just in case. He picks up his cell phone and unlocks it. Bragi is probably just on his way to a date or something but …

Hörður hasn't started entering the dispatcher's number when his phone rings. It's Jenný. He wipes a raindrop off the phone's screen before answering.

"I'm stopped—out of gas."

"Tell me where you're."

He does.

"I'm on my way."

Hörður hangs up. His mouth goes dry and he feels completely awkward—again. It's night, and Jenný is on her way to meet him. What does that mean? He doesn't know, but is both excited and nervous.

The rain is pouring down. Hörður shudders. He's about to get back into his SUV, but stops when two flashes illuminate the darkness somewhere farther down toward the bay. Lightning? Can it be?

He listens, waits for the thunder. All he hears is a faint echo of what could be distant thunder, but also something completely different. He watches, listens, waits.

But all he sees is darkness. All he hears is the murmur of the rain and the gurgle of the streams that it forms.

Hörður isn't at home, but in the bathroom of a woman not his own.

What am I thinking?" He looks into his eyes in the mirror, after washing his hands and splashing his face with water. The question is good and valid, but he doesn't know the answer to it. Or doesn't want to know.

He heaves a sigh, not understanding himself. After having poured the fuel that Jenný brought into his SUV, he smelled like a petrol bomb and his fingers burned, since he'd spilled the volatile liquid over his hands. Then she'd practically demanded that he follow her back to her place so that he could wash off. For some reason, he'd agreed to the idea, yet without fully understanding why. Couldn't he just as well have driven to Grafarvogur as to the Sel neighborhood?

Yes, of course. But it's as if he's powerless against the charms of this hefty member of the Forensics Department—against the crippling allure of the fleshy Jenný Karlsdóttir. Anyway, he followed her home in the rain. And now here he was, in her bathroom. At midnight.

Is she trying to get him into bed with her? He isn't sure, but he sweats and feels slightly dizzy at the thought, which is both exciting and horrifying. Exciting because he wants to. Horrifying because he doesn't want to cheat on Bíbí. He's not the type who does such things.

Or what? Hörður stares into his own eyes. But maybe Jenný didn't have any such thing on her mind. Maybe she was just worried that the gas was burning his skin, which it certainly did. Nor is it as if she'd dolled herself up for him or anything like that. She got out of her car wearing no makeup, dressed in baggy sportswear, and holding onto a can of gasoline. Not exactly like a *femme fatale* from an old *noir* film. Still, he'd gotten butterflies. The fact that she didn't even appear to be trying to be sexy had been very provocative to the red-haired giant.

Hörður shakes his head as if to ward off all carnal thoughts. Then he looks around. The bathroom in Hörður's Grafarvogur home is always clean and tidy, because Bíbí keeps it that way. At Jenný's, there are things all over the place, like after an earthquake. The shelf above the sink is covered with cosmetics, hair ties with strands of hair on them, cheap jewelry, and who knows what. The sink itself is grimy with toothpaste and soap, and the trash can underneath it is overflowing with stuff he doesn't want to know about. On the floor are puddles and piles of towels and clothing, including dirty underwear. The shower cubicle is half full of shampoo bottles and its drain is clogged with hair.

Hörður retches slightly. Could he really kiss a woman who lets things get like this? She's clearly a total slob.

He's startled by a knock on the door.

"You okay in there, big guy?" Jenný asks in her deep voice.

He clears his throat. "Yes, just a second."

Hörður splashes more cold water in his face, then dries it with a dirty towel before opening the bathroom door. "I guess it's best that I get going …"

He stops—or rather, becomes paralyzed—when he sees Jenný standing outside the door. She's wearing only a thin-as-can-be silk nightgown, not even tied at the waist. Her breasts are right there before his eyes, huge and shapely, their nipples standing erect. Then there are her wide hips and soft belly; her thighs are no small things, and he catches a glimpse of black curly hair between them.

"Do you see anything you like?" she asks in a deep, seductive voice.

Hörður blinks. Jenný has put on lip gloss. Her lips glisten like cherries. She stares at him with her mouth half open and a sensual gleam in her eyes. He swallows, frozen in his tracks, but his heart is beating so fast that his chest aches.

"Take me," whispers the seductress. Then she grabs his shirt, pulls him closer and gives him a wet kiss. At first, he's like a statue of himself, a lifeless tree trunk, but as her tongue breaks its way through his defenses, his resistance collapses like a house of cards. He closes his eyes, embraces her, and kisses her back.

Hörður is terribly excited. She's so big! No matter where he moves his hands, they find flesh everywhere—a whole lot of warm, soft female flesh that he wants to squeeze, kiss, bite and …

"Come with me!" Jenný tears herself from his arms and pulls him behind her toward the bedroom.

Hörður obeys, tearing off his clothes at the same time and tossing them here and there. In her bedroom, countless candles burn on the shelves and furniture around a double bed. The bedclothes are black; over the headboard hangs a red painting reminiscent of an ocean of fire. Jenný lets her nightgown fall to the floor, and then she sits down on the edge of the bed and impatiently waits for her giant lover to draw near.

Which he does, in all his grandeur.

Hörður dreams that his phone is ringing. But he can't reach it, because he's trapped in a dark, cold dungeon, chained to a gloomy stone wall. The phone rings in the distance, in an empty room full of books up in the castle's living quarters. The book room is huge but empty. The ringing echoes through the castle, which stands on a hill above a forest, under steep, jagged mountains.

Outside, wolves howl; an owl flies silently through the darkness. The wind whispers in the leaves of the trees.

Answer, answer, answer …

"I'm stuck. I can't reach it," mutters the red-haired giant in his fitful, nightmare-haunted sleep. He tosses and turns, moves his eyelids.

Finally, he wakes with a start. The phone!

Hörður jumps naked out of bed. Under the thick duvet, Jenný mumbles something. It's pitch-black in the bedroom. He gropes his way out, bumping his shoulder into the door frame, and wanders, drunk with sleep, into the hallway. A faint light from the light poles comes in through the kitchen windows. His clothes are scattered over the parquet.

He hurries toward the vestibule, where his phone is ringing inside his leather coat.

He pats the damp leather, finds his phone in one of the coat's pockets and fishes it out. Could it be Bíbí? Guilt gnaws at the roots of his heart. What was he thinking?

Hörður looks at the screen. Axel? His stomach tightens.

"Yes?" he asks hoarsely.

"Another murder."

"Oh, no," whispers the red-haired giant, as guilt devours his entire heart in one gulp.

Thursday

It's six o'clock in the morning. It's still raining, but not as hard as during the night. The sky is black and turbulent, the earth is wet and there are puddles everywhere. The rain is unceasing, the droplets as cold as they are many.

Hörður Grímsson's rusty red hair is sopping wet and clings to his bloodless, sleep-deprived face. The rainwater trickles in thin streams down his leather coat, soaks his trousers, runs over his shoes and forms puddles at his feet. It runs under the neckline of his shirt, as well, making him shudder. He stands there unmoving with his collar turned up and his hands in his pockets, staring with green eyes at a new murder scene, frowning and deeply pensive.

The company Björgun Ltd. has been in operation for many years on the reclaimed land at Sævarhöfði, near the mouth of Grafarvogur and the estuary of the Elliðaá river, at the foot of the steep banks of the industrial area at Höfðabakki. It's a big company, specializing in dredging projects in harbor areas and at sea and doing mineral extraction from the seabed of Kollafjörður Fjord, Faxaflói Bay, and Hvalfjörður Fjord. The company's premises off of Sævarhöfði Road are considerably large. They are entered by driving through an open gate a short distance from the intersection with Svarthöfði Road. Directly ahead upon entering is a low-rise office building, large piles of gravel on the right and a gravel lot and other buildings on the left, including some sort of garage. On the gravel lot, near the road, are huge connected concrete towers under which heavy trucks can be driven—old concrete silos that fell out of use long ago.

Parked between the silos and the garage is a sedan, a gray Subaru that the red-haired giant knows by sight. A white tent has been erected over the car to protect it from the rain and the zoom lenses of newspaper photographers. Inside the tent work white-clad members of the Forensics Department, in addition to the medical examiner, who performs a simple examination on the body and then, based on his findings, tries his best to determine both the cause and time of death.

After arriving on the scene, Hörður peeked into the car through its open side window. Bragi had been murdered, like his friend Patrekur. Shot in the head and stomach from close range with a powerful handgun—most likely a .44 caliber Smith & Wesson. He'd pitched forward, and the body was leaning forward and to the side. Splotches of blood and brains cover the inside of the passenger door, as well as part of the dashboard and windshield.

The sight is horrific, to say the least.

"*Copy-paste?*" asks Axel M. Axelsson, who appears next to the red-haired giant. He's wearing his English wool coat and a matching wide-brimmed fedora hat.

Hörður nods. "More or less."

Axel clicks his tongue. "As you predicted, huh? I should have put more stock in what you said. One is always wiser in hindsight."

"It was I who screwed up, not you," says Hörður in a broken voice. "If I hadn't forgotten to get gas, then ..."

Feeling horrendous, he sighs heavily.

"That's enough of that!" says old Steppenwolf firmly. "Everyone can make mistakes, and most of us do so now and then. It's called being human. You asked me for backup—don't forget that. You wanted to monitor certain young people, including Bragi. Don't forget that either. If I had done as you asked me, we wouldn't be standing here."

"But you couldn't agree to my request, could you?" Hörður asks listlessly.

Axel rolls his shoulders. "It would have posed a certain professional risk. If we had managed to prevent the murder, no one would have said anything. But if it hadn't worked, I would probably have already had to resign."

"Exactly," mutters Hörður. The media would have chewed up and spit out the chief. The man who clearly knew that certain young people were in mortal danger but didn't tell them about it, much less protect them from it. It would have been a public execution, nothing less. Professional malfeasance, utter humiliation.

"*Shit happens*," Axel says bitterly.

Hörður looks aside, up into the darkness above the rocky bank looming over Sævarhöfði. "I was going to call the station after my SUV ran out of gas, but I didn't. To request backup. I thought about reporting drunk driving or something like that, to have all officers on duty keep an eye out for the car. But ..."

He shrugs, looking hopeless.

"It wouldn't have changed anything, would it?" asks Axel. "The time frame was too tight. How long do you think it was from when you lost sight of the car until Bragi was murdered?"

Hörður shuts his eyes. He envisions the two flashes that he thought were lightning. They had been the flares of a gun firing. And the echo that he heard was the gunshots, not thunder in the distance.

"Three, four minutes, at most," he finally replies. "If I had run down the slope, I could have stopped the murderer or arrested him."

"Or been shot yourself," Axel adds. "If, if and maybe. Stop this speculation. It's useless."

Like me, adds the red-haired giant in his mind. They stand there for a moment in the rain, silent as mourners at a funeral.

Hörður kicks mud off his shoes before getting into his cold SUV. He starts the powerful engine, sets the heater to high and the fan to maximum. He's drenched and shivering from the cold. A haze forms on the inside of the windows and the engine heats up slowly and poorly. The fuel light is still lit, as he put only about five liters in the tank last night.

Last night …

Hörður sits in his parked car and tries *not* to think about what happened, about what he *did*. But it's easier said than done. His head is full of images and memories of warm flesh, wet kisses, and …

His cell phone rings, startling him. Who is …? He pats his coat's damp leather, finds his phone and tries to pull it out of the narrow pocket. But everything is wet and rigid and …

"Hello? Hörður?"

He stiffens. It's Bíbí. She's speaking through the hands-free system. Did he somehow press the green button?

"Yes," he says, inhaling a cold raindrop up his nose.

"Where are you? You didn't come home yesterday?"

Hörður looks at the clock on the dashboard. It's ten minutes to seven. Bíbí has just gotten up. Alone in their double bed.

His heart sinks into the deepest darkness. What has he done?

"No," he says hoarsely. "Something … Something came up."

"Oh?"

"Yes … I …"

"You what?"

Hörður clears his throat. "Another murder was committed."

"Jesus!" She's obviously taken aback. But he can also hear that she's relieved. She expected him to say something else.

Something completely different, and worse …

"Just call me when you can. Let me know if you need anything. Luvyou!"

"Thanks, sweetie," he says. "Will do."

"It's eight o'clock," says Axel M. Axelsson, who is sitting as usual at the end of the long table in the operations room. He's wearing a cream-yellow shirt, no tie, and blue suspenders, and is tapping a fountain pen on an open minute book. "Morning meeting number … I've lost count. It doesn't matter, I'll put it in later. Our investigation has gotten much more complicated, dear colleagues. Two murders have been committed. Two brutal murders, presumably by the same perpetrator. And we're nowhere nearer a solution, unfortunately."

Old Steppenwolf glances at the red-haired giant sitting to his right.

Hörður Grímsson, looking sheepish, bows his head. His hair is still half damp and tousled, like that of a good-luck troll. Jenný Karlsdóttir is sitting opposite him at the table, straight-backed and focused. Nothing in her appearance or demeanor would suggest she had had little sleep or was upset at all by the events of the night.

Benedikt Vagnsson is sitting next to Hörður, while the medical examiner, a distinguished-looking man in his sixties, is next to Jenný.

"Let's start at the beginning." Axel puts on his glasses and runs his eyes over a memo. "The first person to come to the scene was an employee of the Security Center on his regular rounds. He'd stopped at Björgun around eleven o'clock that evening. When he returned at around two o'clock, he saw a gray Subaru on the gravel lot, parked but running. He went to the car, looked in it, and then called the Emergency Number. The security guard didn't touch anything at the scene, according to his own statement. He didn't open the car and didn't attempt resuscitation or anything of the sort because he said he'd seen that the man, that is, the deceased Bragi, was *definitely dead*, in his words."

"What's the name of this security guard?" asks Hörður.

Axel takes another look at the memo before removing his glasses again. "Hermann Brynjarsson. He's thirty-eight years old, and has worked for the Security Center for twelve years. Clean criminal record and so on."

Hörður nods. "Very well. But I'm going to request information on his movements last night and try to get it confirmed. From now on, we'll pursue all loose ends and follow every single lead, leaving no stone unturned."

"Very good!" says Axel, patting the red-haired giant on the shoulder. Looking proud of himself, Hörður straightens up and then glances at Jenný, in the hope that she'll be looking at him with admiration and love in her eyes. But she's looking at her phone, and doesn't seem to have noticed the praise he was given.

"And so, we have our professionals," says Axel, turning his attention to the medical examiner. "Let's start with the cause and estimated time of death."

"Yes, of course." The examiner clears his throat, then puts on his glasses and takes out a memo.

"Two bullets, .44 caliber," mutters Hörður. "The deceased was shot in the head at short distance, then in the abdomen. The time of death is half past eleven last night."

The examiner's eyes widen, and he looks at the memo and back at the detective. "Eh, yes. That's right. I actually have nothing to add to this. We haven't finished our analysis of the bullet that was found, but …"

The examiner shrugs.

"It's very likely of that caliber," adds Jenný, nodding at Hörður, who blushes and looks away.

"The forensics team found something at the scene, didn't it?" asks Axel.

"We sure did," says Jenný. "As you recall, a box was found next to Patrekur's car. The packaging from a game called Bean Boozled. There was some powder residue in this box, containing active ingredients found among other places in ecstasy. By the car in which Bragi was murdered, we found a small plastic bag containing three blue tablets. They're undergoing chemical analysis as we speak, but I'm sure that they're comparable to the tablets that were in the box, or are even the same tablets. But that would be impossible to prove."

"Was the bag closed?" asks Axel.

Jenný nods. "It was knotted and lying in a muddy puddle by the driver's side door, almost hidden. But the tablets were undamaged."

"Hörður?" says Axel.

"The same story," says the red-haired giant. "The murderer left the tablets at the scene, like the box. At least that's my opinion. The perpetrator is either trying to tell us something or mislead us. Either way, this is clearly important. I'll go into this aspect of the investigation in more detail later."

"Fine," says Axel, as he leafs through the files in front of him. "After the deceased's parents were notified of the crime, Forensics took all of his electronic devices for analysis. The deceased had his phone with him, but a laptop in his room was handed over to us. I have here a transcript of the communication that took place via Facebook shortly before the deceased drove from his home to a meeting with the perpetrator or perpetrators. Since the other party involved in this communication, presumably the perpetrator, has deleted his account, we don't even know what he called himself on that platform. But it had most likely been a dealer page. Here is a copy of the messages."

Axel hands each of them a copy of the document. Hörður glances over his copy:

Mega-week:

Marley 3k

Elvis 3k 3pcs

Flash 4k

Andes 14k

Good andes? Don't lie to me!

Top product. Crystalline snow

I'll take 2gr andes + 6gr Marley, 38k cash take or leave

Okay

Where and when? I'm game now

11:30 Björgun Sævarhöfði, on premises. Behind the concrete silo. I'm coming by car

Any chance earlier??

No.

Ok

"This is very similar to the method used to lure Patrekur up to Heiðmörk," says Axel. "But in this case, it was a tempting drug offer, and the communication was done via a social app, not via SMS to a phone number."

Hörður sighs. "Incredible to fall for it. So soon after his friend goes to meet some mystery person and is murdered. Where's the logic?"

"If you're addicted to coke, there is no logic," says Jenný. They look each other in the eye, she and Hörður. He feels an electric charge in his hindbrain and looks quickly elsewhere.

"It's clear as day that this person is cunning and will stop at nothing," says Axel. "Whether he's working alone or not, we don't know. But we've got to find this madman before more people die. If you thought there was a lot of media interest in this already, it'll be overwhelming now. As well as the pressure from the public, the Alþingi, and the Minister of Justice. We have a lot of work to do, but we can't expect to have much elbow room to do it, unfortunately. We've got long, hard days ahead of us, dear friends."

"What are our next steps?" Benedikt asks cautiously. "Do we have any leads or theories? Who will be running the investigation? Hörður?"

"I'll be directing it, assessing the situation as we go along, making the main decisions and requesting search warrants and court rulings if necessary, and so on," says Axel. "Hörður has been in charge of the field investigations so far and will no doubt wish to continue, isn't that so?"

Hörður swallows. "Yes, if you trust me to."

Axel hesitates, but then nods. "Now isn't the right time to start from scratch. But you'll have more help. Benedikt is hereby released from his other duties, and will work on this case exclusively. He'll be here to assist you day and night. Forensics will also be constantly on call in this case."

Jenný nods in confirmation.

"Very well," says Benedikt. "What are our next steps? Are we working on any leads or from any theories? Or just groping in the dark?"

Hörður clears his throat robustly before answering. "First, let's look at some important facts. The two victims knew each other. Patrekur and Bragi were friends; they'd known each other for some time and attended the same school. This is important. What's even more important is that the person who got them to come meet him knew them personally, and/or knew a lot about them. He knew about the nude photos that Patrekur took of Lísa Kristjánsdóttir, and that Bragi was fond of cocaine, was even addicted to it. I say *he,* but I'm not ruling out that the murderer may be female."

Hörður gets up from his seat, goes to the whiteboard and writes on it as he talks. "These facts indicate that the murderer belongs to a) Patrekur and Bragi's group of friends, b) is closely related to that group of friends or c) is a close relative of theirs or someone close to them. This narrows the circle somewhat. But not so much that the answer should be obvious. I'm convinced that the murderer is practically before our eyes. But for some reason, we can't see him. Not *yet,* at any rate."

"And then there's Borgarnes," says Benedikt, who is looking over the older scribbles on the whiteboard. "It's connected, too, isn't it?"

Hörður nods, before briefly going over what happened in the summer. The party, the ecstasy, and the death of Eva Andrésdóttir. "Here we get back to the box with the ecstasy tablets. It's very easy to conclude that someone is taking revenge for Eva's death. She's the daughter of the police chief in Borgarnes, Andrés Aðalsteinsson, who owns a .44 caliber Smith & Wesson handgun that has disappeared. I don't suspect Andrés, but our first task now is to verify his alibi for last night and confirm that his son Heiðar isn't in the country. As well as look into Andrés's close circle in search of a possible perpetrator. But it appears that Eva wasn't popular—not at all, in fact—so this theory is rather weak. But there's *something* there, damn it! And the murder weapon must be the police chief's gun; anything else would be an incredible coincidence."

Benedikt nods. "I'll look into all of this. At least to exclude the father and son. Who knows, maybe one of them is the culprit?"

"Sounds good," says Axel.

"What about that connection—the nude photos and cocaine?" Jenný asks. How should the father and son have known about them?"

Hörður shrugs. "Maybe Eva kept a diary?"

"Yes, maybe," Jenný mutters.

"I'll check it out," Benedikt says, noting this in his notepad—*Eva, diary?*

"What do you say, shall we meet here again tomorrow morning, if nothing significant happens before then?" asks Axel, before continuing without waiting for an answer.

"Forensics is working on what it found at the scene. The body will be autopsied at the first opportunity. Hörður and Benedikt will divide the work and continue the investigation. This case is both big and unique. Two young men killed with a firearm. The perpetrator entices them to meet with him in a cunning and bone-chilling way. There's little else being talked about in society but these atrocities and the media pumps out news, non-news, gossip, and pure nonsense. The pressure on us from the outside is enormous. But I want the most pressure to come from us, ourselves. This case is an acid test, a challenge." Old Steppenwolf pauses for effect. "Things are looking pretty murky, as they stand, but we must keep in mind that the clouds always break, eventually. Finally, I must remind you not to talk to the media. All inquiries should be directed to me. Understood?"

As soon as Axel ends the morning meeting, those present gather their notes and coffee cups, get up from their seats and go to work immediately. Determination shines from every face. Hörður is no exception, although his mind is much more restless than usual. Despite facing a demanding murder investigation that should occupy all his thoughts, he's having a hard time forgetting the adventures of the night or keeping his eyes off of Jenný, who pretends not to notice him.

She leaves the operations room with dramatic flair and her attractive bulk, her low-heeled shoes clicking as she hurries through the Cave toward the exit. Hörður hurries after her and catches up to her toward the end of the corridor, near the elevator.

"Jenný?" he says.

Looking surprised, she stops and waits for him.

Hörður glances over his shoulder, but the corridor is empty. Nobody's eavesdropping. "Hey … thanks for last night?"

Jený smiles faintly. "Likewise."

Hörður's mood lightens. He thought that she might be mad at him or something. He really wants to grab her, kiss her and … Instead, he clears his throat politely. "Hey, um … meet again tonight, or …?"

Jený's eyes open wide at the question. "What would your wife say if you didn't come home two nights in a row?"

With a pitiful expression, Hörður shrugs his shoulders. "I don't know. Maybe I should talk to her about it? If she throws me out, could I stay with you for a while?"

"Whoa!" Jený takes a step backward and raises her palms, as if he has tried to hand her a dead rat. "What are you talking about? Are you going to leave your wife?"

Hörður reddens, blinks. "Uh, I don't know. Is that a bad idea, or?"

"What do I know?" snaps Jený. "But don't leave her for *my* sake! I don't want to get involved in any drama. What happened yesterday was just sex, you understand? I'm not looking for a boyfriend."

Hörður feels sick with disappointment, since he thought she had fallen for him—just as he has fallen for her. "I see. No problem."

Jený gives him a motherly smile and pats him softly on the cheek. "You big lug!"

Then she marches to the elevator and presses the button.

Hörður watches her disappear into the elevator. He has a headache on top of his nausea, and a pain in his heart. How can she be so cold? He walks slowly back into the Cave, finds some strong painkillers and washes them down with old coffee.

He has work to do, but has lost all his reasoning and concentration—all his grounding.

Oddur is at school. His first two classes were Icelandic, but for the third, English, he had to change rooms. English is one of the few classes that they share: he, Lísa, and Bragi. But neither of the others is there. Oddur was relieved when he didn't see Bragi sitting in his usual place, but Lísa's absence is disappointing and a little worrisome. He'd been looking forward to seeing her, to get to see her and smile at her—to see her smile back and at the same time feel warmth in his heart and butterflies in his stomach.

But her desk is empty, just like her chair. She usually sits in the same place, diagonally in front of him. Sometimes she sweeps back her loose hair. She always puts her bag on the floor to the left of her desk. A brown leather bag with a cute YooHoo bear fastened with a plastic lock to the handle. The stuffed bear is white with a brown face and ears, big blue eyes and a striped tail, blue and gray. He finds it so endlessly sweet that Lísa has this bear on her bag, like an elementary-school kid.

She must be feeling awful. Patrekur's death clearly hit her very hard. Maybe understandable and all that, but Oddur feels jealous because of her intense, drawn-out expression of grief.

Did she love Patrekur so much? Maybe she still loves him?

When the teacher enters the room, Oddur tries to shove aside these thoughts. The teacher is a middle-aged woman, colorless and unexciting, but an excellent instructor who also speaks very beautiful Oxford English. Oddur opens his textbooks, but sees that he has forgotten to do his homework.

"Dear students," says the teacher in a high-pitched voice, instead of starting the lesson as usual.

Silence descends over the class. Oddur looks up. Dear children? What's going on? The teacher is pale and trembling, as if she's cold—or is she scared?

"Something has come up," says the teacher. "For the second time in a short time. The principal will address the school shortly. After that, everyone will go home."

She clears her throat, and then her eyes flutter toward the back of the room, to the empty seat where Bragi usually sits.

The hair rises on the back of Oddur's neck. No! He can't believe what he's thinking. But he knows it's true.

Lísa is at home alone. She called in sick, since she doesn't feel well at all—she has no appetite and a bad headache. Her mother offered to stay at home with her, but Lísa persuaded her not to. She couldn't wait for her parents to go to work. She has secrets that she really doesn't want them to discover. They *mustn't* discover them. It's enough that she's gotten herself involved in something dangerous. The last thing she wants on her conscience is something bad happening to her brother.

It would kill her!

Lísa is upstairs in bed with her laptop, partly under her duvet. Her hair is tousled and she's still wearing the clothes she slept in: pink panties and a white T-shirt that reaches down to her hips. It was Patrekur's shirt; she's been sleeping in it since they were together. The curtains are drawn over the window and the only light on is the lamp on her nightstand. She opens her browser and then Facebook. She hopes that she doesn't have any new messages. But as it turns out, there are twelve.

She swallows. Maybe they're all from her friends? But no, she doesn't get her wish. Deathbook has sent her another message. Why won't this thing leave her alone?

Lísa gets a knot of anxiety in her stomach and tears in her eyes. She hardly dares to open the message but will probably have to. She clicks on it.

The message reads:

The game continues. It's your turn. Tomorrow you´ll be sent a name. It's your subject.

Lísa wipes a tear from her cheek. What bullshit is this? She types a question:

Subject?

Deathbook replies:

The one you're going to kill. Give and take.

Lísa feels a chill. This must be a joke. Yet she knows it isn't a joke, is no *game*. Otherwise Patrekur would still be …

She yelps when her phone rings. Who the …? She looks at the screen and sees that it's Oddur. Isn't he at school?

"Hi?"

"Have you heard the news?"

She gets a knot in her stomach. "What news?"

"Are you at home?"

"Yes, what's …?" She isn't able to finish her question, because Oddur interrupts.

"I'll be there in a quarter, max."

"But …?" Lísa looks at the screen. Oddur has hung up. She hurriedly taps in a question and sends it:

"You're scaring me. I don't want to be in this game. Leave me alone, please!"

Deathbook answers:

If you do as I say, you'll have nothing to fear. In just a few days you'll be free. But if you disobey or tell anyone, you know what will happen ...

Lísa catches her breath. Yes, she knows it well. This lunatic has threatened to murder her little brother if she doesn't follow the rules.

Hörður is sitting in his cubicle in the Criminal Investigation Department when his cell phone rings. He had opened the telephone directory website *ja.is* on his computer and was about to call the main number of the Security Center to get more information about the movements of this Hermann fellow the night that Bragi was murdered.

He looks at his phone's screen but doesn't recognize the number displayed on it. It's a landline number.

"Hörður!"

"Hello, this is Áslaug." The voice is youngish, bright, and cheerful.

The name rings some bells. "Áslaug who?"

"The editor of The Newssheet.*"*

Hörður nods. The school newspaper of Hamrahlíð Junior College. Yes, right. Do you have any information for me?"

"Yes and no."

"I don't give interviews or anything like that," says Hörður firmly. "The same rules apply to all reporters."

"Do you know the story of Þorgerður Brák?"

Hörður grunts. He's fairly well read in the Icelandic sagas and actually enjoys discussing them. *Egill's Saga* is a masterpiece, although the *Saga of Gísli Súrsson* has always been his favorite. "Yes, pretty well, in fact."

"Tell me what you know," says the young editor.

Hörður clicks his tongue. "Well, she was a bondwoman … a slave of Skallagrímur Kveldúlfsson and nurse to his son Egill. She was Irish, if I remember correctly. Skallagrímur took her captive while on a Viking raid. She was also considered to 'know a lot,' that is, to be skilled in the magical arts."

"Quite good."

"Then he killed her, Skallagrímur. A foul-tempered fellow, him," says Hörður, who is on a roll. "He'd been competing against his son Egill in a game of *knattleikur*, a kind of ice-hockey of its time. The seven-year-old Egill won, which the old man took very badly. He attacked his son and might have killed him if his nurse Þorgerður hadn't stepped in and separated them. So Skallagrímur directed his anger at her. Þorgerður fled to the shore, jumped in the water, and started swimming away. She was probably trying to get over to the small island at the end of the headland named after Borg, Skallagrímur's main farm. But the chieftain, her master, tore up a big rock and threw it at her. It landed on his slave's shoulders and sunk her. The strait where she was killed is called Brákarsund after her, and the island, Brákarey."

"Indeed," says the editor, a little coldly.

"Egill wasn't too pleased with his father for that killing, as he was fond of his nursemaid," says the storyteller Hörður. "He took revenge by killing his father's favorite servant. At just seven years old!"

"Yes, yes. But remember, Hörður Grímsson, that stories like these aren't just faint letters on calfskin, but living events that echo through the centuries and still take place to this day."

"What do you mean?" asks Hörður. He straightens up, realizing that this call is probably something more than just a courtesy one.

"Women still make the mistake of trusting men. And men still sink women into the dark depths of the sea, even though they no longer use rocks—not literally, at least. But their words weigh heavily. They're even heavier than the rocks of the Saga Age."

Hörður gropes for his notepad and pen. "Let's just start over. Whose daughter are you, did you say?"

But the only answer he gets is a click when the caller hangs up. Hörður writes one word in his notepad:

Áslaug?

Then he finds the phone number that this Áslaug called from and enters it into the search box on *ja.is*.

The result is returned immediately. The girl called from the Master Baker bakery in the small Suðurver shopping center, close to HJC. Maybe she works there part-time, along with school? Hörður makes a note of this, and then calls the office of HJC and introduces himself to the woman who answers.

"The memorial service is tomorrow morning, during first period," says the woman.

"Memorial service?" asks Hörður in surprise.

"For Bragi. Isn't that what you wanted to ask about?"

"No, in fact," mutters Hörður.

"Reverend Árni asked about you, whether you would come again."

"I suppose he really wouldn't want me there," says Hörður sheepishly.

"On the contrary. He found you very interesting. He's a good man, our Reverend Árni. He's been a real support to the students during these terrible times."

"Is he meeting the kids, talking to them?" Hörður interestedly.

"He's counseling them, yes. We've set aside time for students to talk with him."

"Could I get the names of those who have gone to speak to him?" asks Hörður. He turns to a blank page in his notepad and clicks his pen.

"There's no such list. The counseling is free and anonymous. Do you have any better idea of who is behind these crimes? The papers have started talking about serial murderers! I'm just hoping the police are on their trail."

"Yes, exactly. I need information about two students," says the red-haired giant.

"Oh."

"They're not under suspicion of anything," Hörður adds.

"Which students are they?"

The red-haired giant looks in his notepad. "A boy and girl. They both work for *The Newssheet*, which is apparently the school newspaper or something like that. Haukur and Áslaug. I don't have their patronymics, but I gather she's the editor."

"Hm. There is no actual editor of the paper, only a five-member editorial board that splits up the work. And in that group, there is neither a Haukur nor an Áslaug, if I remember correctly. I have it somewhere here ..."

Hörður curses to himself. He should have gotten more information from those kids. Are they playing with him? If so, for what purpose? "Maybe you could compile a list of all the students at the school with these names and send them to me? Along with photos, preferably."

"Yes, it should be possible. Still, I would need to report it to the principal because of the new privacy laws, and ..."

"Do I need to remind you that this is a murder investigation?" Hörður asks dryly. "A double murder investigation, rather."

"No, of course not. But ... wait, here it is. No, there's no Haukur and no Áslaug on the editorial board."

"Damn," Hörður mutters irritably. "Send me the list as soon as possible."

"I'll do that. What's your e-mail address?"

Hörður tells her, then hangs up. He sighs, frowns, and rubs his temples with his fingertips. He has high blood pressure and a throbbing headache.

The investigation isn't on the right track at all, and he feels miserable.

Oddur is sitting in bed with Lísa, who cuddles up to him like a motherless child. He's wearing jeans and a button-down shirt. She's still dressed only in her panties and a t-shirt, with her feet pulled under her and her toes beneath the crumpled quilt.

"I'm glad you came," she whispers.

"It's good to be here," says Oddur hoarsely, before kissing her softly on the top of her head. He's fond of Lísa and is worried about her well-being. But he also has a crush on her, and this situation is messing a bit with his mind. He can sense that she's in need of some support; closeness, warmth and understanding. But this, being on her bed and she wearing so little, not even trousers or a bra beneath her t-shirt, is making him excited, to tell the truth. His heart beats fast, his mouth is dry, and he's self-conscious about the bulge in his jeans.

What would Lísa say if she sees that he has an erection? He's very uncomfortable about it. But he can't help it, either. That's just how his body is responding to her presence.

Oddur clears his throat. He likes the feeling of wanting Lísa, because doing so helps him forget all the horror and madness in their lives these days. Still, they probably can't avoid discussing these things. "Um, you said you needed to tell me something, when we talked last night. Something important. A secret."

"Yes," whispers Lísa, fearfully. "But now Bragi is dead as well, and I don't know if I can tell you."

Oddur gets a knot in his stomach. "This secret. Does it have to do with the deaths of Patrekur and Bragi?"

Lísa hesitates, then gives a quick nod.

"I have a secret, too," says Oddur softly. "Maybe we have the same secret?"

"I don't think so," says Lísa, on the verge of tears. "I mean, it's not your fault that Patrekur's dead, is it?"

Oddur swallows. "No, maybe not. But Bragi's death might have something to do with me. What I said, or something. I don't know."

Lísa pulls back from Oddur and looks him hard in the eye. "What do you mean?"

Oddur thinks for a moment, and then decides just to let it out. "Are you familiar at all with … Deathbook?"

Lísa cries out softly and claps her hand over her mouth. The hairs on the back of Oddur's neck stand up.

"It made me ask for Patrekur to die, this Deathbook, whatever or whoever it is," says Lísa agitatedly. "I was reluctant to name names, to play the game, but it wouldn't give up, just pressed me harder and harder and didn't quit until I gave it a name. But the weird thing is that it was like it was waiting for the *right* name the whole time. It wanted me to name Patrekur as the person …"

Oddur nods. "… you wanted dead. Same thing with me."

Lísa shudders, and says, "Then I was sent a video."

"A video?" replies Oddur in surprise.

Lísa takes a deep breath. "I saw Patrekur being murdered. Deathbook sent me a recording of it. The murderer was wearing a camera. Oh, Oddur, it was awful! I can't describe it …"

She throws herself into his arms. He pulls her in and holds her tightly.

"If I don't do as I'm told, my brother Lárus will be killed," sobs Lísa. "The same if I tell anyone about this. Which I've now gone and done."

"This won't go any farther," says Oddur reassuringly. "I'm in the same boat. We're in this together. And we'll get through this together."

"How?" she asks.

He breathes in the scent of her hair. "I don't know. But we haven't done anything wrong. Even if we wished for something, that's not a crime. We're innocent. But someone's playing games with us. We just have to find out who it is."

"Yes," she says. "But there's more. I got a message earlier. This isn't over, see."

Oddur gently releases Lísa from his embrace and looks into her tear-swollen eyes. "What message? From Deathbook?"

She nods.

"Will you tell me what it said?" he asks softly.

Lísa nods again, then sniffles and brushes a lock of hair from her face. "Afterward, I promise. Kiss me first."

"Kiss …?" asks Oddur surprisedly. His heart jumps and he feels a pleasant tingling sensation. Lísa nods for the third time. They look into each other's eyes, lean in closer, and let their lips touch.

He takes her in his arms as they lie back on the crumpled blanket. She slips her tongue into his mouth. He plays with the hair at the nape of her neck with one hand and strokes the inside of her right thigh with the other. She pulls him toward her, undoes his belt, and tugs at his shirt, popping off one button. He feels her soft breasts through her thin t-shirt.

Oddur moves his hand up her thigh, slowly, gently—his fingers inch carefully toward her pink panties. Lísa moans, opens her legs wider, and thrusts her tongue deep into his mouth.

It's a sunny and mild autumn day, the air is humid and the streets and yards are still wet after yesterday's rains. Hörður parks his black SUV in the parking lot east of Suðurver. He walks into the Master Baker and takes off his sunglasses. The bakery is spacious and smells of freshly baked bread and cakes. The warmth inside is like that of a sunny beach. Behind the protective glass of the long counter are rows of pastries, with bread on shelves on the wall behind it. At the far end of the shop, nearest to Hamrahlíð, are tables and chairs for those who choose to enjoy the delicacies there.

"Can I help?" asks an attendant in a work uniform bearing the company's logo. She's around twenty years old, maybe a little younger.

"Eh, yes," says the red-haired giant. He pulls out his ID and looks firmly into the girl's eyes as he shows it to her. "I'm with the Criminal Investigation Department. Have you been working here all day?"

The attendant is impassive. "Ever since we opened. Why?"

"Is your name Áslaug?" Hörður asks authoritatively.

"No," the girl answers bluntly.

"Okay," says Hörður. "But is there an Áslaug here?"

"No," the girl answers again.

"But someone called from here this morning." He looks in his notepad. "About ten o'clock. A woman, probably a young girl. Ring any bells?"

"Yes, I let her make a call. She said she'd lost her phone." The attendant brushes flour off her cheek. "What's going on?"

"Can you describe her to me?" asks Hörður.

The attendant shrugs. "Yeah, yeah. She was fairly small. Thin. A skinny one, you know. Small breasts and a tiny butt. Blonde, fairly long hair."

"Okay." He makes notes of all of these. "Anything else? Any distinctive features?"

"Not really," replies the attendant. "Just very ordinary, really. But her makeup was pretty lame, I guess."

"How so?" asks the red-haired giant.

"Aw, just, you know." She shrugs. "Clumsy, I don't know. And her hair was probably dyed. It was just way too blonde. Like a Barbie. But she wasn't a real Barbie; she needed a few more hours in the tanning salon for that."

Hörður heaves a sigh; he has completely lost the thread. "In other words. Skinny, rather ordinary. But lame makeup and dyed hair?"

The attendant nods, and then leans closer to the policeman. "Was she a hooker or something?"

Hörður knits his brow. "Was that *your* impression?"

"I don't know," says the girl. "Just saying. There was just something *cheap* about her, you know?"

"Yes," says Hörður, who both understands and doesn't understand. He feels as if there's something a little *odd* about all of this. As if the girl who called him didn't want to be recognized. That she'd even been wearing a disguise.

Unless the description is nothing but a fabrication?

The red-haired giant stares grimly at the attendant, who opens her brown eyes wide, making her look like a deer caught in a car's headlights.

"What?" asks the girl, panic-stricken. He sees fear in her eyes. But also innocence. If she were hiding something, she would blush, blink, and/or look away. But she does none of these things.

Hörður draws a breath in through his nostrils, and then gives a little, apologetic smile. "Nothing. I just realized that I haven't eaten anything today."

Which is true. And just as he says this, his stomach starts rumbling.

"Oh," says the girl. "Can I get you something, then?"

The red-haired giant says yes. He runs his eyes over the selection behind the glass and finally points to a raisin teacake. "One of those, and a black coffee."

Shortly afterward, he's sitting at a table by the window with a steaming cup of coffee and the fragrant teacake in front of him. He looks distractedly out the dusty window as his coffee cools and the pastry hardens. He has had practically no sleep and is so tired that he doesn't know if he'll be able to get up from the table again.

He's thinking about the investigation, which is becoming more and more complicated, forming a tangled mess that's growing bigger with each passing day instead of gradually unraveling.

He thinks of his passionate night with Jenný, and the cold splash of water he got from her in its wake. He thinks about Bíbí and the fact that he will not only have to face her soon, but will also be forced to face himself and what he has done.

Hörður sighs. What should he do? What *can* he do?

Act as if nothing is out of the ordinary? Admit his offense? Talk to her about what happened, or live in a lie? Continue living with Bíbí, or step aside?

He's feels completely numb, with a bad taste in his mouth and a hard knot in his stomach. All he knows for sure is that he has no appetite for a teacake or coffee at the moment. Unfortunately.

Oddur is standing there naked in the bathroom at Lísa's house. He's glistening with sweat and breathing shallowly, amazed and happy at once. He can hardly believe that this happened. They *did* it; they slept together. For nearly eleven minutes, he experienced bliss upon bliss and forgot about all the bad things that were going on in his life, in their *lives*. He and Lísa—they're one.

"Wow, man," Oddur says to his reflection. He'd definitely like to do this more often. Again and again, forever. Lísa is the one for him. It's out of the question that he would ever get tired of her.

He finishes washing, then dries his hands and half-erect dick. The condom went down the toilet. He knows that condoms shouldn't be flushed because they can clog the pipes, but he wasn't going to leave a used condom in a trash can at Lísa's house, was he?

Grinning, Oddur shakes his head. He turns off the light and sneaks back into Lísa's bedroom. He's going to jump straight back into bed with her, kiss her over and over and feel her warm, sweaty body. He hopes she has more condoms, because he's really in the mood to …

But as soon as he opens the bedroom door, he sees that they aren't quite on the same page in this regard. Lísa has put on sweatpants and a baggy sweater, and put her unbrushed hair in a ponytail. She's sitting cross-legged in the middle of the bed, with an open laptop in her lap.

"Hi," says Oddur shyly. He feels silly being naked while she's dressed—besides suddenly feeling as if he's been used. Did she just need a little release? And why does she have condoms? Does she do this often? And is he just another of her lovers?

Isn't she in love with him?

"I'm just checking to see if there's anything new." says Lísa, without looking up from her computer screen.

"Okay." Oddur gathers up his clothes in a hurry and starts getting dressed.

"But there's nothing, luckily," she says. "Do you have your computer with you?"

"No, just my phone," he replies.

"You can log on to Facebook on my computer," she says.

Oddur finishes dressing. "Okay."

"Would you mind handing me my bear?" says Lísa. "The one on my bag."

"No problem."

The bag is on the floor by her desk. Oddur bends down, removes the YooHoo bear from the handle and hands it to Lísa. What does she want with the bear? He's curious, but doesn't want to ask for fear that the question is stupid.

"Thanks."

"Welcome." Oddur sits down on the bed next to her and takes her laptop. On it, Facebook is open. He decides to change users and enters his e-mail address and password.

"Apparently, I'll be getting a name tomorrow." Lísa opens a zipper on the back of the bear and takes a small plastic bag out of it.

"A name?" asks Oddur in surprise.

"From Deathbook." Lísa opens the plastic bag, which contains several hand-rolled cigarettes. She sticks one of them between her lips.

"Oh?" asks Oddur in surprise. Still, he's more surprised to find out that she smokes. Or is he misunderstanding something?

Lísa nods. "Apparently, I'm supposed to kill someone. Give and take. Deathbook killed Patrekur for me. Now I've to kill someone instead or in return, or whatever it's called."

"What?" Oddur can hardly believe what he's hearing.

Lísa opens her nightstand's drawer and takes a lighter from it. "Just what I said. Otherwise, Deathbook will kill my little brother."

"I've never …" Oddur stops as Lísa lights her cigarette, and then inhales the smoke. Smoke that's as sweet as …

"Want some?" she asks, handing him the joint.

"Weed?" asks Oddur.

Lísa nods.

Oddur swallows, feeling half-stressed. They're supposed to be at school. It isn't even noon, and they've done it and are smoking dope. He knew that Lísa was what's called a "bad" girl—that is, a bit wild and such. But he didn't know that she was actually bad, in the sense of being the wrong company.

He feels that he ought to get going. But he's powerless in her presence, a spineless tool. So he accepts the joint and takes a drag. The smoke tickles and burns his throat; he nearly coughs, but manages to hold the smoke down for a few seconds.

"Thanks." He exhales and smacks his lips at the dry and bitter aftertaste. "But …? I didn't know you smoked this stuff. And do you take it to school with you?"

Lísa takes another drag. "I don't dare do anything else. Mom sometimes goes through my stuff."

"But …?" Oddur feels slightly dizzy—the weed is starting to work. "But can't she smell it?"

Lísa shrugs and exhales. "I light incense afterward and open the window. Anything?"

Oddur blinks a few times to bring his eyes into focus. The high slinks like a snake through his veins and opens like a rainbow flower in his head. He giggles. "Anything what?"

"On the computer," Lísa asks, half irritably. "On Facebook."

"Yeah, sorry." Oddur directs his flickering attention to the computer screen, opens the message and feels a chill. A new message from Deathbook awaits him. It's … "A video."

"What?"

"I got a video," whispers Oddur, hoarse from stress and smoking. He doesn't want to see this video, but before he knows it, has pressed play. It's as if his body is doing things from which his mind is detached—a numb mind that floats like a balloon high above reality.

At first, the screen is fuzzy, displaying only snow and electrical glitches. Then the electronic snow turns into a heavy rain. It's dark outside. The video is silent. Someone is walking across a gravel lot toward a gray car whose engine is running. The rain pours down. The lot is pocked with countless puddles in which the drops land. Someone is sitting in the gray car. The side window is down.

Lísa leans against Oddur. "Is that …?"

"Bragi," whispers Oddur. He's paralyzed and stares at the screen. He doesn't want to watch but he can't stop. He's frozen.

The camera is mounted on the head of the person approaching the car. The perspective is from above. Bragi squints and says something. Suddenly a gun appears. It's in the hand of the person approaching the car. Bragi's eyes open wide. The image shakes, and there's a flash of light and smoke. Bragi jerks, something dark splashes inside the car. Another flash and …

"Fuck!" Oddur shuts the laptop with a bang, then jumps out of bed and heads to the bathroom, where he throws himself on his knees and pukes into the toilet. He pukes until he screams and starts sweating.

Oh, God—oh, God!

He flushes the toilet and rinses his face with cold water. *Bragi's head exploded; brains and blood spewed out …* He's dizzy, nauseated, and so stoned that he can't think clearly. When he returns to the bedroom, he finds Lísa looking at the screen of her opened laptop.

"There's more," she says.

"What?" moans Oddur. He crawls onto the bed with her, completely drained of energy

Lísa points to the screen. Below the video is a message, similar to the one she has already received:

The game continues. It's your turn. Tomorrow you'll be sent a name. It's your subject.

"What does this mean?" Oddur asks listlessly, with the taste of puke in his mouth.

"Tomorrow we'll get the name of the person we're supposed to kill," Lísa answers coldly. "Give and take. It's a game, get it?"

"This is sick," says Oddur. "We'll go to the police, that's what we'll do. Right?"

Lísa takes a short drag from the joint. "And say what? That Patrekur and Bragi are dead because we wanted it? That we've been exchanging messages with some lunatic on the Internet for days, but want to report it *now* because we're scared?"

"Yes … or …" Oddur splutters. He doesn't want to smoke any more, but reaches for the little that's left of the joint because the high numbs his pain, suffocates it beneath a heavy leaden blanket. He takes a drag and swallows the smoke, holds it down.

"We know nothing about this person," says Lísa hopelessly. "What if he watches our every move? We go and talk to the cops, who may not even believe us, and at the same time endanger our loved ones. Do you think I want my brother killed? He's unbearable, but he's also just twelve years old."

"Of course not," Oddur says. He scratches his head; tries to think clearly. "Who sent you a request to like this page, Deathbook?"

"Some Kjartan, I recall," says Lísa. "Kjartan Atli something. I've been searching for him since this insanity started, but he's deleted his profile. He probably never existed."

Oddur nods. "Same here. Except that in my case, it was a girl. Sunna Sæmundsdóttir. She'd recently sent me a friend request. She's also deleted her profile. Unless *she* may be a he or they or who knows what."

"That's what I'm saying." Lísa takes the last drag from the joint before stubbing it out. "We don't have anything to go on. How could the police possibly find this person? This like page was probably created via a fake profile on a stolen laptop, through some free guest Wi-Fi network. And as soon as they start poking their noses into it, this same person will delete the page and make himself scarce. And we'll live in fear for the rest of our lives."

"Yes, maybe," says Oddur. "But what do we do then? Nothing? We're not going to murder anyone?"

"No, probably not," says Lísa unconvincingly. "Maybe we're just being fucked with, huh?"

Oddur hides his face in his hands. "How can you say that? My friends are dead. Someone *shot* them in the head."

"I mean, maybe it's *over*," says Lísa. "Maybe more people won't die—but we're just being fucked with."

"Why?" asks Oddur.

Lísa shrugs.

"What if we get names tomorrow?" asks Oddur. "What if we're really expected to kill other people?"

Lísa bites her lower lip. "We'll see, okay? We'll figure it out when and if it happens, huh? I can't handle any more bullshit today."

"Okay," says Oddur. "But do we agree *not* to do as this person says? Not to let him play with us. To go to the police instead of end up in jail, maybe. Right?"

Lísa hesitates, but then nods.

"Good." Oddur closes the laptop lid. He wants to close his eyes, too. But he doesn't dare. Every time he does, he sees Bragi's head explode.

Hörður is sitting like a condemned man on the living-room sofa at home, staring at the TV news without hearing or seeing any of what's happening on the screen. He actually hit *mute* as soon as another story about the murders came on, and he hasn't unmuted it yet—although it wouldn't change anything even if the sound was at the highest volume, because the red-haired giant is stuck inside his own head; tangled in a net of confused thoughts, pangs of conscience and guilt.

He'd sent Bíbí a message earlier in the day, telling her that he'd be home around dinnertime. He didn't want to go home, because he feared facing her, but he could no longer keep away from his own home, and besides, he had no other place to sleep, unless he just checked into a hotel. So he kept his word and returned home around seven, dead-tired and stressed out. Bíbí had welcomed him like the Prodigal Son from the Bible, showered him with love and kisses, and then sent him straight to a warm bubble bath while she cooked one of his favorite dishes—oven-baked lamb shank with brown sauce, mashed potatoes, and pickled red cabbage.

Everything she did was salt in the wound that burned in his heart. He'd felt like shit as he lay there in the bath, and no matter how hard and often he scrubbed his flesh, he couldn't get the filth out, because he was dirty to his soul. But he did manage to squeeze out a smile and eat a whole lamb shank without retching or giving up. He had so little appetite that even the thought of cold water made him feel ill.

"Should I bring you coffee, darling?" calls Bíbí from the kitchen. She's been tidying and washing up and has apparently made coffee, as well.

"Yes, please," replies Hörður. He doesn't really want coffee, but maybe it'll perk him up. Besides, Bíbí will have a harder time hugging and kissing him if he's holding a cup of hot coffee. Not that he doesn't find her attractive. He just knows that she wouldn't even look at him if she knew what he'd done. She would break down and cry and …

Ugh! He can't think this through to the end. Would it be better to protect her from the truth and stagger onward with his guilty conscience like a lump of iron in his belly, or tell her what happened and accept the consequences?

He doesn't know. He knows nothing in his selfish, stupid head.

"Here you go."

Hörður blinks his eyes as he starts from his own despondency. Bíbí is standing next to him, holding his cup.

"Thanks, sweetie," mutters the red-haired giant, taking the cup.

"You don't have the sound on?" asks Bíbí. She makes herself comfortable next to him on the sofa and leans into him, her man.

Hörður sips his coffee carefully. "I muted it. I don't like seeing or hearing stories about the murder case. There isn't anything to report, unfortunately, but the media doesn't let that stop them."

"People are stressed and worried, of course." Bíbí takes the remote control and turns the sound back on. "It's practically all anyone's talking about. There's a murderer on the loose, after all."

Hörður sighs. "Yes, yes."

"How's the investigation going, otherwise?" Bíbí asks gently, after a few moments. In general, she doesn't want to know anything about the dark world he moves in because of his work, but she also doesn't want to seem indifferent to the job he loves and doesn't want to live without.

"It's not going at all, damn it," Hörður answers ruefully. He has no desire whatsoever to discuss work with his live-in partner, but even so, the thought of doing so is much better than that of thinking or talking about the blessed *side step* that he took—the hot and sweaty night of sex with the tall, fleshy Jenný, the strong-voiced Valkyrie he'd desired for so long. "Two brutal murders of young men, but little or no useful evidence at the scene. At least not fingerprints or other biological samples. But these crimes seem to be connected to a particular group of friends, a party in Borgarnes, and some damn game in which people choose candy from a compartmented box, and some get ordinary candy and others some foul-tasting stuff."

"Bean Boozled?" asks Bíbí.

"Exactly," says Hörður. "But these kids replaced the candy with vitamins and ecstasy tablets."

"I see," says Bíbí. "The things they come up with. But how is this connected to the murders?"

"I'm not sure," says Hörður. "But a girl died playing this game this summer, at a party in Borgarnes. It's as if someone is taking revenge for her death. But there's just no one in the girl's closest circle who seems likely to commit such crimes, besides the fact that she definitely wasn't the type that someone might need to avenge."

"Maybe someone is playing a game?" Bibi suggests.

Hörður doesn't hear the question, because he's going over his visit to Borgarnes in his mind. Did he overlook something there? Should he have talked to the savings bank manager, as well—the brother of Andrés, the police chief? The party was held at his home. But he actually wasn't in the country at the time, and …

He blinks. Did Bíbí say something? "Who's playing a game?"

Bíbí shrugs. "The murderer? I read online that he'd lured those boys to meet him."

"Where did you read that?" Hörður asks skeptically.

"I think it was on *dv.is*," says Bíbí. "Maybe it was just speculation; I don't remember. There's so much written about the case."

A game, thinks Hörður. What if some young people are playing a horrific game in which the participants can lose their lives? So the murderer is the one controlling the game. But no one involved talks about the game because it would be breaking the rules. You talk—you die.

Friday

"The fifth morning meeting, if I'm not mistaken," says Axel M. Axelsson as he looks at his gold watch. "It's seven o'clock, everyone invited is here, and there's nothing to wait for. Let's start with Forensics."

There are four of them sitting at the long table in the operations room. Benedikt Vagnsson is next to Hörður, who glances at Jenný, sitting opposite him—the seductress who blinded him. She obviously took a shower before heading to work. Her hair is still half-damp and smells of coconut. Hörður feels ashamed just seeing her, but at the same time, feels his dick harden. His mind and flesh don't quite see eye-to-eye on this matter, any more than many others.

"Our examination of the gray Subaru is pretty much completed," she says. "Nothing unexpected or new came out of it. The fingerprints that were found belong to the family, and so on. The murdered man was shot twice with a .44 caliber handgun; we found both the bullets, which are similar to the bullet from the previous scene, where Patrekur Jónsson was discovered murdered."

"And the bag?" asks Axel. "The one with the blue tablets in it?"

"The bag itself didn't help us," says Jenný. "That is, no fingerprints or anything like that were found on it. The tablets turned out to be ecstasy. Their chemical composition is the same as in the traces of powder found in the box on the scene at Rauðhólar. In other words, both the gun and the tablets connect the two murders. Meaning that the odds of the murderer being the same are overwhelming."

Hörður grunts.

"Yes?" says Axel, who is familiar enough with the red-haired giant to know when he has something on his mind.

"Neither the murderer's fingerprints nor other biological evidence have been found at the murder scenes," says Hörður. He directs his words to Axel because he can't face Jenný. "So we don't know whether the same person was at work or not. The same weapon doesn't rule out different perpetrators. The person behind the killings is most likely the same. But that person didn't necessarily pull the trigger."

"A long shot, if you ask me," Jenný mutters. She's clearly insulted, but tries to cover it over by grinning sarcastically.

"Do you have a new theory?" asks Axel interestedly.

"Maybe," mutters Hörður. "Maybe not. I'll get into that later."

"Very well," says Axel. "Anything else from Forensics? Weren't you investigating Bragi's computer? And his phone?"

"Yes," says Jenný. "Our chief expert in the field of cyber-crime is working on that side of the two murder cases, that is, the relationship between the perpetrator and the victims. But it's time-consuming, difficult work, not least because the perpetrator has covered his tracks. The Facebook page that was used to lure Bragi down to Sævarhöfði no longer exists. We've sent an inquiry to Facebook and have also contacted Interpol, which has more experience in this area. But even if we get the IP address of the computer on which that page was created, it isn't at all certain that we'll find the computer itself. Not unless the perpetrator did the work on his own computer and on his own home network, which has to be considered unlikely. But naturally, it would be useful to know if the IP address is Icelandic or foreign."

Axel nods. "We'll just wait for the results and hope for the best. Anything else?"

"Yes." Jenný straightens up and opens a folder on the table in front of her. "I requested the autopsy report of the girl who died at the party in Borgarnes, Eva Andrésdóttir. I was hoping that someone had taken a blood sample from her and sent it in for a chemical analysis, in order to find out what drug it was that killed her. But it wasn't done until the autopsy, when the substances had decomposed to such a degree that any such analysis would have been useless. Some trace elements were found in both her blood and the blue ecstasy tablets, but not in any significant amount, so we can only assume that she took the same tablets as were found at the scene at Sævarhöfði. Unfortunately."

"Sorry to hear that," says Axel. "But you did your best. Keep it up. Benedikt, do you have anything for us?"

"Something, but not much," Benedikt replies. He puts on his glasses and pulls a memo from the inside pocket of his tweed jacket, unfolds it and looks it over. "My main task was to rule out the possibility that Eva's father Andrés or her brother Heiðar had been here in Reykjavík the night Bragi was murdered. Andrés said that he'd been at home that evening, and that his brother Ellert had stopped by. Andrés's wife, Oddbjörg Eyvindardóttir, was at a choir rehearsal. The neighbors say they saw Andrés's car in the driveway that same evening, as well as his brother's car. I spoke to the police in Akranes and then officers in Borgarnes who were on duty that evening—that precinct is in charge, among other things, of traffic enforcement on Highway One, from the mouth of the Hvalfjörður tunnel on the Akranes side and west to Mýrar. None of them noticed the police chief's pickup truck."

"The officers in Borgarnes are Andrés's subordinates, right?" asks Axel.

"That's right," says Benedikt. "Meaning it's possible to question their testimony, not least in court. But until anything else comes to light, I've got to take them at their word. And Andrés's son Heiðar is in Norway; that's confirmed."

"What's your opinion?" asks Axel.

"I consider it very unlikely that Andrés was out and about that night," says Benedikt. "Still, it isn't entirely out of the question. I've requested images from the surveillance cameras in the Hvalfjörður tunnel in order to rule out that possibility. Then there's Hvalfjörður itself, which would have added forty minutes. But as I said, the neighbors saw the brothers' cars at Andrés's house that night, until half past ten."

"Did you speak to the brother, Ellert?" asks Hörður.

Benedikt nods. "We talked on the phone, and then I looked him up in the system—a clean criminal record. He said that he and his brother had been watching television together until Andrés's wife returned from her choir rehearsal. Ellert's a widower and says that he visits his brother regularly, not least after the events of the summer."

Hörður knits his brow as he tries to recall his and Andrés's conversation at the latter's house. "Doesn't he have a disabled daughter?"

Benedikt looks at his notes. "I'm not sure. My handwritten notes are still in my briefcase. I inadvertently left it in my car."

"No problem," says Hörður. "I also have it written down somewhere."

"Maybe you want to go ahead?" says Axel to the red-haired giant. "I'm curious to hear this new theory of yours."

"A theory and not a theory," says Hörður, blushing. "In any case, I had a kind of revelation last night. A new perspective, maybe. Or …"

He clears his throat; his voice is husky from stress. What if they think that what he's about to say is complete bullshit? He really wishes he could backpedal on all of this, but it's probably too late and would only make things worse.

"Keep going," says Axel in a fatherly tone.

"It's this with the box, that game—Bean Boozled," says Hörður. "Kids and young people like to play games. They're bored with everyday life and even with reality itself. That's why kids use drugs and play video games and role-playing games. They do whatever they can to escape reality, change it and/or make it more exciting. In this case, an innocent "try-it-if-you-dare" game was transformed into an exciting drug lottery. You pick a pill that either does nothing at all or elevates you to a higher level. Does this sound about right, or what?"

Jený shrugs, while Axel and Benedikt nod.

"But anyway." Hörður clears his throat again. His pulse is racing and he has begun to sweat. "I started thinking, what if this is all one big game? By that, I mean the murder cases that we're investigating. What if someone or several people have created a game in which participants can die? A kind of Russian roulette that's played through social media. You join in due to peer pressure or thrill seeking or a promise of great reward, but when you want to back out or quit, it's too late. I don't know, maybe I'm just talking nonsense. What do you think?"

"I find this idea very, very far-fetched," says Jenný. "To put it mildly."

Hörður turns bright red.

"I don't know what to say," says Benedikt. "Sounds like you're really stretching. But do we really know what's going on with young people these days?"

"Exactly," mutters Hörður.

"All ideas and theories have a right to be heard," says Axel. "That's why we're here. To discuss facts and air our views on them. Hörður is thinking outside the box, and that's fine. But I don't quite understand this imaginary game. Are you suggesting that someone is compelling young people to murder each other?"

"I have no theories about this imaginary game." Hörður wipes beads of sweat off his forehead. "But *if*, and that of course is a big if, these young people are playing such a game, it would explain their cohesion—the *silence* that I, we, haven't been able to break. I have a strong feeling that the kids that I've talked to so far either haven't told me the truth about something or have simply lied. *Why*, I don't know. But maybe it's because they're stuck in some game that they experience as a greater reality than the reality that the rest of us, boring adults, live and work in."

"I don't know what my teenagers think or what they do online, that much is certain," says Benedikt.

"Kids their age certainly have different ideas about life and death than their elders," Jenný admits. "For example, they think that nothing will happen to them and that they'll live forever. Death is just something that happens to others."

"Exactly," says Hörður, breathing a little lighter.

Axel nods thoughtfully. "Is there anything we can do to break this alleged silence?"

"It might not be good to put too much pressure on them," says Hörður. "But since we have two unsolved murders on our hands, we can't be endlessly patient, either. I want to call Oddur and Lísa back in for questioning. But first I'm going to go to a memorial service for Bragi at HJC. Maybe I'll get a few more clues there. Among other things, I need to get hold of two kids, Haukur and Áslaug—I don't have their patronymics yet. Maybe they know something, and maybe not."

"Áslaug?" asks Benedikt in surprise. "The name rings some bells. Is that the disabled daughter, maybe?"

"What kids are these?" asks Axel.

"This Haukur has been prowling around the investigation, among other things loitering outside the police station," says Hörður. "When I spoke to him, he said he was working on a story for the school newspaper. Then this Áslaug called me, introduced herself as the editor of the same paper. She just asked me about the saga of Egill Skallagrímsson; it sounded a bit like she was pranking or teasing me."

"*Egill's Saga*," mutters Benedikt. "Borgarnes, once again."

"I then contacted the school and found out that the two don't work for the school newspaper, and probably aren't even students there," says Hörður. "At least I didn't recognize them from the photos the school sent me."

"Just some crackpots?" asks Axel.

Hörður shrugs. "Or people playing a game."

When Oddur wakes to the sound of the alarm clock on his cell phone, he's in two minds as to whether he should go to school. He lies there under his warm duvet and stares up at the half-dark ceiling. He hasn't been at home much this week, which maybe wasn't for the better, whether he likes it or not. But then he remembers the memorial service for Bragi and it's as if the light down duvet turns into solidifying concrete. There's no possible way that he would attend a memorial for a friend who was dead because he requested it. He feels guilty enough already. He would no doubt break down and confess everything, in front of the entire school, the principal and the priest.

Suddenly Oddur understands how Lísa felt at the memorial service for Patrekur. She was thinking and experiencing the same things as he is now—guilt, remorse, and shame. It's no surprise that she started crying. He doesn't know how she managed to get to her feet and leave the room. He had to support her, of course, but still.

The poor girl. Oddur sighs. He understands her better now, since they're experiencing more or less the same thing. Maybe it's no surprise that she's numbing herself by smoking weed. In fact, he himself wouldn't have anything against calming his nerves a bit and taking the edge off the anxiety that feels like an iron knot in his stomach.

Oddur unlocks his phone and opens Messenger, and then breathes a sigh of relief. No new messages from Deathbook. He writes a message to Lísa:

Are you going to school?

She answers almost immediately—she's probably in bed with her phone, like him:

No, I'm waiting for ma and pa to go to work

He asks:

Do you want me to come over?

She answers:

Yes

Oddur smiles. He's going to take a shower, and then call for a taxi. He's going to take his backpack with him so that Albert and Jónína won't suspect him of skipping school.

Outside, it's cloudy and cold, with a chilly westerly blowing. Hörður is standing by a dark-gray concrete wall next to the main entrance of Hamrahlíð Junior College. He has buttoned his coat up to his neck and turned up the collar; his hands are deep in his pockets and his expression is gloomy. The memorial service for Bragi Unnsteinsson was poorly attended, and sad in every way. Neither Oddur nor Lísa showed up, nor that Haukur who is claiming to be a reporter. Hanging over the school is a cloud of sorrow blended with suspicion and fear. Many students have called in sick, even dropped out or changed schools. The death of one student is a shock. The death of two is equivalent to a curse.

One more body and the school is doomed.

Hörður is pensive. Could someone at the school possibly be seeking revenge? For what, then? Bad grades? Hardly … He's unable to carry on pondering this, because the man he was waiting for suddenly appears. It's the priest who gave him a cigarette two days ago, after the memorial service for Patrekur.

Reverend Árni Sigfússon, wearing the same trench coat as last time, but without an umbrella.

"Here we are again," the gray-haired priest says as he lights a cigarette, before handing the pack to the policeman.

"Thanks," mutters Hörður. He accepts both a cigarette and a light, then inhales the smoke and groans with pleasure.

The priest laughs softly. "Some people smoke when they drink, others after sex. You're the first person I know who smokes only following memorial services."

Hörður nods, with a distant expression.

The priest clears his throat. "This was inappropriate, of course. I apologize."

Hörður blows smoke out his nostrils. "No apology necessary. It was actually pretty funny. I'm just not the type to laugh at jokes. Not out loud, at least."

Reverend Árni takes a drag from his cigarette, looks thoughtfully at the sky. "There were fewer here today than on Wednesday. Whatever the reason."

Hörður shrugs. "A lot of students are staying at home today, I understand. One murder may not shatter a community such as ours. But two murders clearly do. At least our cohesion is gone, for now. While the murderer is at large, the students and parents are understandably on alert."

"Yes, understandably," mutters the priest.

"Apparently, though, Bragi wasn't particularly popular," Hörður adds. "Something of a bully, as far as I understand."

Reverend Árni nods. "The principal didn't actually word it like that, but hinted at something along those lines."

Hörður, feeling a bit light-headed, puts out his cigarette. "I understand you've been supporting the students. That they were invited to look to you as a counselor or something like that."

"It's called pastoral care," says the priest. "Yes, the school sent an e-mail to all the students and suggested they get in touch with me if they feel bad or are in need of psychological support."

"And has anyone gotten in touch with you?" asks Hörður.

"Quite a few of them, yes," replies Reverend Árni. "Why?"

The policeman takes out his list of all the students named Haukur and Áslaug. There turned out to be eleven Haukurs and seven Áslaugs. Next to each name is a passport photo of that person. "Do you know any of these kids?"

The priest takes the list and glances over the names and photos. "Not at a glance, no. Are you looking for someone in particular?"

"One Haukur and one Áslaug," replies the red-haired giant. "They're not under suspicion of anything. I'm just overturning stones."

"I'll keep that in mind," says Reverend Árni.

"Please do." Hörður hands him a business card. "And if you remember something, hear something or see something—anything—then don't hesitate to contact us."

Oddur crawls back into Lísa's bed and kisses her on the mouth. Then they look into each other's eyes and giggle. He's so happy that he feels like singing and dancing. The first time had been good, but the second was nothing short of perfect. And when he came back from the bathroom after flushing the condom down the toilet, she was waiting naked for him under the covers, instead of having gotten dressed and started thinking of something else. They cuddle each other, two warm, sweaty bodies—two souls in love that merge into one irresistible bliss.

He, at least, is in love, and can only believe that she is too.

"What are you thinking about?" asks Lísa.

"About you," Oddur replies conscientiously. "And you?"

"Did you get any new messages?" she asks.

Oddur's mood dampens. "No, not since the last time I looked."

Lísa gives him a peck on the cheek, then jumps out of bed and puts on a T-shirt and underwear before grabbing her laptop, which has been charging on the floor. She sits down on the bed, crosses her legs and opens the computer. "I hardly dare look, but I can't wait any longer. Do you feel the same?"

"Yes," Oddur lies. He props himself on his elbow and pulls the duvet closer around him. He would rather delete his Facebook account and forget about this Deathbook bullshit—pretend it never happened. He just wants things to be the way they were, except with Lísa by his side. Which is ironic, since he and Lísa would probably never have become so close were it not for the murders and this damn Deathbook.

She hunches over the computer screen, which bathes her face in a blue glow.

"Anything?" he asks nervously.

Lísa shakes her head. "Maybe it's over?"

"I think so," says Oddur, hoping at the same time that it's true, even though he doesn't believe it, deep down.

"Do you want to have a look?" Lísa hands him the computer, and then goes to get her YooHoo bear.

Oddur's stomach tightens. He was hoping she'd let the dope be. He doesn't want to get high for the second day in a row, but he also knows that if she lights a joint, he'll have a hard time saying no. He wants to share *everything* with her because he dreams about them doing everything together, like real couples do.

"Anything?" Lísa unzips the zipper on the back of the bear and pulls the bag out of it.

"I'm not in yet," mutters Oddur. He types in his information and presses *enter*. Lísa sticks a joint between her lips and reaches for her lighter.

"Do you smoke weed every day?" he asks, trying not to sound angry or boring.

"No, no," says Lísa. She lights the joint and inhales the smoke. "Just if I'm stressed or bored. I only have enough for three more joints. Bragi always got it for me. I don't know what I'll do when my stash is finished."

"Okay," says Oddur, just to say something. It gets on his nerves that Bragi was her supplier. Was there something more between them, maybe? But he's also relieved that she won't have to deal with a guy like Bragi anymore. Maybe she'll just stop smoking dope?

"Anything?" asks Lísa as she inhales, before handing Oddur the joint.

"No," replies Oddur, both relieved and surprised. He's gotten so used to feeling nervous that it comes as a bit of a surprise to him when nothing bad happens. "Maybe it *is* over, huh?"

"Like I said," says Lísa, smiling her sweetest smile.

Oddur is so relieved that he laughs. Then he finally takes the joint and has a drag. He holds the smoke in, feels the active ingredients stream into his blood, and finally exhales.

The high swims along his veins and explodes like silent fireworks in his head. "Wow …"

"Yeah, wow …" Lísa takes another drag and leans into him, and they both let themselves fall backward—onto the soft bed.

They stare at the ceiling, then look into each other's eyes and giggle—stare again at the ceiling, watch it transform into an ethereal sea and floating sky.

Oddur fumbles for her hand, intertwines his fingers with hers. Their intimacy is passionate, they melt and merge like candles burning side by side. "I love you."

"What?" Lísa hands him the joint with her other hand.

"Nothing." He takes a drag, coughs, and then flies even higher.

Lísa giggles. "You're an idiot, you know?"

Oddur giggles too, but at the same time feels a slight sting in his heart. Doesn't she love him? But his high numbs the pain, smothers the doubt, and turns everything into a soft daydream. They're together, everything is good and …

"Your phone," Lísa says lazily.

"Huh?" Oddur has no idea what she's talking about, but then realizes that the carousel music that's been playing for a few moments in the background isn't a barrel organ in the hands of a monkey wearing a bellboy's costume, but the ringing of his phone. "Who is …?"

He lets go of Lísa, gets up and crawls like a lizard out of bed and fishes the phone from his cashmere coat. He thinks he recognizes the number, but isn't sure. Yes, isn't it …

"The police," he mutters. Somewhere inside him his heart starts beating faster, but he feels neither fear nor anxiety. And yet …

He answers. "Hello?"

"Oddur? This is Hörður Grímsson here. Can you come down and talk to me again at eleven o'clock? Same place as last time. Just a few questions."

"Yes … or, look …" Oddur plays with his tongue, which feels too big for his mouth. Can he leave the house? Probably not, but what happens if he … "If I can't, what then?"

"Then your position changes from being a witness to being a suspect, and I'll have you picked up."

"Yeah, okay …"

"So you'll be here at eleven o'clock, right?"

"I guess so," says Oddur. There's a click. The policeman has hung up.

Oddur looks at Lísa. "That was …"

"I heard your conversation," says Lísa, who has sat up in bed. "It's probably nothing important. He just wants to talk to you. And don't you say a word about you know what."

"No?" Oddur asks in confusion.

Lísa shakes her head. "It would just get us into trouble. Plus, it's over, remember?"

"Yeah, probably," Oddur mutters, but he's startled when Lísa's phone begins ringing.

In a darkened room, the screen of a stolen laptop illuminates a ghostly face. Pale fingers move quickly over the keyboard and the screen displays a list of nearby wireless networks, all password-secured. Low clicks are heard as the fingertips dance on the keys. A program is launched—a hack that unlocks the selected wireless network. In a few seconds, the computer is connected to the Internet. The fingers dance, the Thor browser is opened, then Facebook, and finally the Deathbook subpage.

The page's administrator cracks his knuckles before opening the message window.

Oddur steps out of the taxi in front of the police station. He doesn't feel well at all, it being neither comfortable nor wise to leave the house stoned in the middle of the day, let alone to go to police headquarters. Deep down, he's restless and nervous, but still so incredibly high that he feels a strong need to giggle. Lísa had lit incense that she claimed would wipe out the smell of weed. He decided to trust what she said, even if not wholeheartedly. She was supposed to come to the station a half an hour after him. Oddur can't imagine why they're being called back in for questioning, but he's worried that they're in some kind of trouble, even serious. For concealing important information or evidence from investigators, which they're certainly doing. Lísa, on the other hand, was convinced that the police were just groping in the dark, that they knew nothing and were therefore spinning in circles. She was also adamant that they shouldn't say anything. She made him promise to wear a poker face—to keep his mouth shut, because if he didn't, he could put her little brother's life in danger.

"I promise, I promise," Oddur mutters as he walks up the stairs, before giggling accidentally. At the reception desk on the first floor, he asks for the red-haired giant, Hörður Grímsson. After a few moments, a uniformed police officer appears and takes him to the same interrogation room as before, green-painted and windowless. There he sits and waits, so dry-mouthed and high that he has to drum with his fingertips on the table to prevent his mind from fluttering out of his body and his imagination from taking over.

When Hörður Grímsson walks into the Swimming Pool, where Oddur Bjarnason is waiting for him, the smell is the first thing he notices—a strong smell of incense that he has encountered many times before from the clothes and in the abodes of hash heads.

"Sorry to keep you waiting," says the red-haired giant, although without meaning it, because he always makes suspects wait in the spartan room just to get on their nerves and show them who's in charge.

"No problem," mutters Oddur, who is dressed as usual in high-quality, classic clothing. Hörður guesses that the creamy yellow shirt is made of a material that he hasn't heard of and cost a quarter of a workingman's monthly salary. He himself is in black, square-shooting cotton that is stiff in the morning and smells of sweat by the evening.

Hörður sits down across the table from the witness, opens a folder, and takes his notes from it, a few printouts from a computer printer. He glances into Oddur's eyes and sees that they're bloodshot, that the pupils are slightly dilated. Could be from sleepless nights and a fever. But also from smoking weed.

The policeman clears his throat and then looks over his notes, acting as if he's reading them carefully. He hums and haws, clicks his tongue, and occasionally nods, as if agreeing with what he reads. Minutes pass, and Oddur clearly feels worse and worse. He fidgets, starts sweating, and doesn't really know how to act. The silence gnaws at him, and finally, he feels compelled to break it.

"Why am I here?" he asks hoarsely.

Hörður continues to read a bit, then looks up with an empty, neutral expression. "Because I asked you to come?"

"I mean ..." When his voice wavers, Oddur clears his throat. "I already told you everything I know, which is nothing. I don't know anything! Can I get a glass of water?"

"We won't be that long," mutters the policeman.

"But I'm thirsty, anyway," Oddur says.

"I think you know something," says Hörður firmly. He puts down his notes and looks again into the eyes of the witness, who blinks and looks away. "You know something but don't want or don't dare to tell me. Which is it? Don't want or don't dare?"

Oddur swallows but doesn't answer.

"Either way, you're hindering the progress of justice," says Hörður. "And that is a crime!"

"I know nothing," whispers Oddur, pale with terror.

Hörður heaves a sigh. "Is someone threatening you? Is there some game going on that you don't dare talk about for fear of punishment? If so, then I'll see to it that this same game is stopped, and that the person responsible for the crimes I'm investigating is arrested and prosecuted."

Oddur swallows again and blinks several times, as if he's digesting what the red-haired giant has said but is having trouble understanding it fully.

Hörður leans forward over the table and props himself on his elbows. "Is someone playing with you? You and Lísa and maybe others?"

Oddur hesitates, stiffens, and squirms. He thinks it's best just to lay all the cards on the table, tell the truth and leave it to the police to unravel the nightmare that his life has become. But he promised Lísa that he would keep quiet, not do anything to put her little brother's life in danger. And he doesn't want to go back on his words—doesn't want to betray the girl he loves. Does he love her? Maybe—probably; he isn't sure. But there's *something* between them. She's important to him, and she trusts him. Which is why he shakes his head.

"No?" asks Hörður. "Are you sure?"

"No," says Oddur, wiping sweat from his forehead. "I mean yes—I'm sure. I don't know what you're talking about."

"Very well," Hörður grunts, far from satisfied. He reaches for one of the pages of notes, on which are only two names. "Let's talk about something else. I asked you before about the skinny boy who was talking to you here in the parking lot in front of the police station. The boy you pointed out to me as he stood at the wall of Hamrahlíð Junior College, in the rain after the memorial service for your friend Patrekur."

"That's right," says Oddur.

"He says his name is Haukur," says the red-haired giant. "Can you tell me anything about him?"

Oddur shakes his head. "I don't know him at all and have only spoken to him once. Out here."

"What did you two talk about?" asks Hörður.

Oddur shrugs. "I can hardly remember. He said that he'd been questioned, too. That he was at the party this summer, when Eva died. He was wondering whether Patrekur's murder was related to her death, if someone was avenging her or something like that."

Hörður grunts again. He has no idea why he didn't ask Oddur about this earlier. Who is this Haukur and why does he lie to everyone he talks to?

"You'd never seen him before?" he asks, just to say something.

Oddur shakes his head.

Hörður jots down a few notes next to Haukur's name—if that's this loser's actual name. *Says that he was at the party in Borgarnes. Thinks the murderer might be taking revenge for Eva's death. Gives false impressions. Is snooping. <u>Who is he??</u>*

"There's another name I'd like to ask you about," Hörður then says. "Another person. A girl named Áslaug."

Oddur starts, and it doesn't escape the red-haired giant's notice.

"Do you know her?" Hörður asks firmly.

Oddur clears his throat. "I know one Áslaug, at least. Or knew, rather."

"Knew?" Hörður asks gruffly. "Is she dead, or …?"

"No, not at all," Oddur says hurriedly. "But the Áslaug that I knew was my girlfriend for a short time. Nothing serious, though. Just a summer love, so to speak. Still, we were together for a few months. But we didn't see each other often. She lived in Borgarnes, see."

"In Borgarnes?" asks Hörður excitedly. Everything seemed to point back to Borgarfjörður. Does this mean something?

Oddur nods. He fidgets in his hard chair, as if he doesn't feel well. Having to recall the events of the summer certainly isn't helping. "The party was at her house. This past summer, you know. When Eva died."

"I see," says Hörður, making a note of this. He's half peeved at himself, because he should have known this. Áslaug's patronymic is Ellertsdóttir—she's the daughter of the savings bank manager. Why did he think Ellert had only one daughter?

"Does she go to HJC?" he asks, despite her name not being on the list he received.

"I think so, yes," replies Oddur. "She finished middle school this spring and was going to start there this autumn, since she'd been accepted. But I haven't seen her. Maybe she went to another school?"

Hörður is pensive. "Why should she have gone to another school?"

Oddur blushes. "To avoid running into me? I don't know."

"Why should she avoid you?" asks the red-haired giant.

Oddur, looking sheepish, shrugs his shoulders. "She really liked me. But it wasn't reciprocal. I broke up with her. She didn't take it well, I think."

"When did you see her last?" asks Hörður.

Oddur sighs. "In the summer, up in Borgarnes. The night of the party."

"The night Eva died?" asks Hörður.

Oddur nods.

"Tell me about that night," says Hörður.

Oddur fidgets again. "It was just like any other party, pretty much. But I asked Áslaug to go outside with me to get some fresh air. I was going to break up with her then, but she didn't know it. We walked down to the sea, where we talked together on some bridge."

"The Borgarfjörður bridge?" asks the policeman.

Oddur shakes his head. "Just a small bridge leading to some island."

Brákarey Island, in Brákarsund Strait, thinks Hörður. When Áslaug called him, she asked him about the story of the bondwoman Þorgerður Brák. Why?

"I see. Go on."

Oddur clears his throat. "I broke up with her, and she was really hurt. She didn't want to back to the party with me, so I went alone. When I got back to the party, Eva was unconscious. You know the rest."

Hörður grunts. "You brought the drugs that killed her, didn't you? The blue ecstasy tablets. It was your fault that she died, and now someone is taking revenge for her death, right?"

Oddur's face turns deathly pale. "It's not true."

"What's not true?" asks the red-haired giant.

"We didn't bring any drugs," says Oddur.

"So you say." Hörður grins coldly. "Maybe you're telling the truth. But I think you're lying. The murderer out there also thinks you're lying. That's why I would stay at home as much as possible, if I were you. And lock the door."

Oddur swallows. "Do you think my life is in danger?"

"No question," Hörður answers. "But you can always turn to me. I can protect you, *if* you tell me the truth. The *whole* truth."

Oddur nods, his expression distant. "I have your number."

Hörður leans back in his chair and crosses his stout arms. "We're done for now. I'll ask someone to walk you out. But mark my words. Stay at home for the next few days—lock yourself in. And remember that it's the truth that will save you, and no one and nothing else."

"Yeah, okay." Oddur stands up but feels wobbly, like a shaky old man.

Lísa is on the bus, on her way down to Hlemmur square. She took a shower, dressed in clean clothes, brushed her hair and put on makeup. She's listening to music on her phone through ear buds, chewing mint gum and staring out the window with a vacuous expression. As the bus approaches its destination, she glances at her phone and immediately feels a chill. On the screen is a chat head that she hoped she would never see again—a skull on a black background.

A new message from Deathbook.

Are you ready to receive the name of your subject?

The bus slows down, rocks like a boat at sea, and then stops at the station. Its brakes squeal and the doors open with a whoosh. The passengers get up and start trickling out.

Lísa is completely numb. She can barely breathe, let alone stand up. What should she do? Her phone rings; a new message.

Or should I send someone your brother's name?

Lísa groans, as if someone has punched her in the stomach.

"Are you getting out here?" calls the driver.

"Yes," Lísa manages to answer. She totters down the aisle and manages to get out before the driver shuts the door and drives off again. She stands half-paralyzed on the sidewalk outside of the Hlemmur bus station, looking at the police station looming across the street like the cliffs of Dover. Somewhere within its white walls, Oddur is being questioned. He'd better be keeping his word! Her heart pounds in her chest. With trembling fingers, she taps her reply onto her phone.

Send me the name

Lísa hurries across the street; she's late for her interview. As she walks past the old gas station, her phone rings again. She stiffens, but keeps walking. Does she dare look? She stops at the base of the steps leading to the police station's main entrance, pulls herself together and reads the message. Then she reads it again and again.

"No!"

The phone rings.

Confirm receipt or I'll send someone your brother's name.

A chill grips Lísa, but at the same time her eyes fill with burning tears. She sees only a haze, yet manages to send a reply.

Confirmed

"Oh, God!" She walks up the stairs and opens the door. What should she do? What a nightmare!

Lísa wipes away her tears, takes a deep breath, and states her business to the woman sitting behind the glass partition in the lobby.

"Someone will come in a moment to take you upstairs," the woman says.

"All right," whispers Lísa. She feels so bad and so unreal that it crosses her mind that she's dreaming, that this is one of those nightmares that you believe are happening until you suddenly wake up, sweaty and screaming in the darkness.

She longs to wake up. To be able to scream out in terror, and then fall back onto her soft pillow.

Oddur walks down a long corridor, accompanied by a uniformed female police officer. He's both confused and scared following his conversation with the red-haired giant. Why was he asking about Áslaug? Does she have something to do with this case? And then there was that about his life being in danger, and making sure to stay home. How real is that danger? Maybe he should have told the policeman about Deathbook and the devilish game that the administrator of that page is playing. But then he would have betrayed Lísa …

"Through here," says the police officer as she opens a door at the end of the corridor. Beyond the door is a staircase, but she presses the button for the elevator instead, as they're on the building's third floor.

Oddur relaxes his stiff shoulders and tries to breathe normally. The police are hopefully on the trail of the murderer. All he and Lísa need to do is keep calm, stay at home, and wait for the police to find and arrest the villain.

They step into the elevator, and the police officer presses 1. The elevator rattles downward.

Oddur sighs. The farther he gets from the green room and the red-haired giant, the better. He's almost more frightened of that black-clad, green-eyed troll than the face-less murderer who shot Patrekur and Bragi in the face.

Almost …

The elevator opens onto the first floor, and they head toward a locked door on an interior wall that separates the rest of the police station from the cold-looking lobby. The police officer presses a switch on the wall, the lock clicks, and the door opens.

Oddur walks briskly into the lobby, as he can't wait to get out into the open air—out into freedom. But he stops abruptly when he sees Lísa, who is standing there shuffling her feet on the tiled floor, pale and red-eyed, as if she's been crying. She's on her way to her interview, of course—he'd forgotten that.

"Lísa," he groans.

"Oh!" she calls out softly when she sees him, before throwing her hands over her mouth.

"Lísa Kristjánsdóttir," says the police officer who accompanied Oddur. The officer holds the door open and gestures to Lísa. "Come with me."

"Oddur," says Lísa as she dashes over to him and hugs him tightly. She bursts into tears and whispers sobbingly in his ear. "I love you. I love you. Remember that I love you."

"I love you too," whispers Oddur in return. Lísa releases her grip on him, squeezes out a crooked smile, and disappears through the door, which closes behind her.

What was that? thinks Oddur. He stares at the closed door, then walks out into the biting autumn weather.

Why was she crying? What drama was this? And she said she loved him, and asked him to remember it—as if she were on her deathbed or something. She who is always so mellow and …

Oddur starts when his cell phone makes a familiar sound. A new message. He has a mild anxiety attack, which then turns into a hard knot in his stomach when he sees a white skull on a black background.

Are you ready to receive the name of your subject?

Oddur feels sick. Clearly, it isn't over. Had Lísa received the same message? Is that why she was upset? Had she been given a name? Who might it …?

Another message appears.

Or should I send someone the name of your love?

Oddur stares at the screen. What? His heart begins beating faster. He taps in a question.

What do you mean?

The answer comes right away.

If you don't accept your subject, someone else will get this name: Lísa Kristjánsdottir. Do you want a name?

He's got to protect Lísa. Doesn't he? Yes. She loves him and he loves her. Oddur walks over to Hlemmur and sits down on a bench there. He feels weak and breathless, as if he'd been running. He answers.

Yes

After half a minute, the name comes.

Haukur Hansson

What? Oddur tries to think clearly. Haukur who? The one the police were asking him about? The skinny guy in the denim jacket? He taps in a question.

Who is that?

The answer comes after a few moments.

You'll find him

How? Where? Oddur hides his face in his hands. What nutjob is behind this? He pulls himself together and taps in a clear message to this anonymous individual.

I can't find a person I don't know. Leave me alone. I'm done with this game. One more message and I'm taking this to the police. Is that understood?

He sends the text and waits between hope and fear. His hands tremble like an old man's.

One minute, no answer. Two minutes, no answer. Almost three minutes, and Oddur has begun to believe that the nightmare is finally over. But then his phone lights up, startling him so much that he emits a half-stifled shout.

If you do as I say, you'll have nothing to fear. In just a few days you'll be free. But if you disobey or tell anyone, you know very well what will happen … Lísa will die.

Oddur breaks down. His throat tightens and his eyes fill with tears. Why is he being treated so badly? What has he done to deserve such a horrible thing?

It's twenty minutes past one in the afternoon. Hörður is sitting in his cubicle in the Cave and has opened a new document on his computer's word-processing program. He has three printed reports on his desk: notes from his interviews of Oddur and Lísa that morning and the notes he made when he spoke to Police Chief Andrés at his home in Borgarnes. He's going to combine the information from these three interviews into one report and see if anything new comes to light. New information, a new perspective, whatever.

He takes a sip of the coffee that he poured into his cup about fifteen minutes ago and grimaces as he swallows it. It's cold and thick as tar. He desperately wants a cigarette, but has stopped smoking, of course, and therefore doesn't have a single one, besides the fact that smoking is prohibited in this building as well as all other buildings in the western world, and no doubt elsewhere.

Hörður grunts in irritation. The world is getting worse and all that.

"Focus," he mutters to himself, then runs his eyes loosely over the papers that he has spread over his cluttered desktop. He usually starts by running loosely through reports such as these, sort of looking for keywords and contexts before reading them line by line, word for word. He prefers to understand the size and extent of the forest before entering it and looking at each tree individually.

His interview of Oddur was very interesting, for many reasons. The young man said a few things that would be worth investigating further, but what he *didn't* say was also interesting, and strengthens the red-haired giant's belief that both Oddur and Lísa aren't telling him the whole truth. His interview of Lísa was really worthless. She was very distracted and half-hysterical; according to her, she was suffering post-traumatic stress disorder due to the two murders. Hörður wasn't completely convinced, but that didn't change the fact that the girl couldn't tell him anything sensible.

Hörður types a few lines into his blank document. That skinny kid, Haukur, is still a mystery, but that Áslaug who called Hörður from the bakery at the Suðurver shopping center is possibly Áslaug Ellertsdóttir, who held the party on July 10 in Borgarnes and was for a time the girlfriend of Oddur Bjarnason, who says he broke up with her that same evening. Áslaug is the daughter of Ellert Aðalsteinsson, the savings bank manager and widower who is the brother of Andrés, the chief of police. After the death of Andrés's daughter Eva, his brother Ellert visited the couple, and with him was his daughter Rut, who is confined to a wheelchair. Since the police chief's gun was kept on the upper floor of the house, it was out of the question that anyone in a wheelchair could have gotten hold of it, even though the girl had left to go to the bathroom. All of this was stated in Andrés's testimony. But where was Áslaug that night? Why didn't she go to her uncle's with her father and sister?

The red-haired giant curses to himself. He feels as if he didn't prepare himself well enough before going up to Borgarnes. He should have asked Andrés more about this, and he should have talked to Ellert and his daughters, too. But at that point, he saw no real reason to turn Borgarnes upside down.

And yet …

Hörður gets to his feet, cracks his neck, and then goes and gets himself a new cup of coffee. Or, newer coffee, anyway. He munches a cookie, remembering at the same time that he's eaten almost nothing today. As he rinses down the cookie with the hot coffee, he suddenly realizes something, without knowing why he should do so at that particular moment. Namely, he doesn't remember reading the statements of the savings bank manager's daughters in connection with the death of Eva Andrésdóttir. Rut may not have been at home, but Áslaug held the party, and it would be more than a little strange if the police hadn't taken a statement from the party's host. Or does he just not remember having read the report?

He sits down at the computer and opens Löke, the police department's database, enters "Áslaug Ellertsdóttir" in the search window, and presses *enter*. If the girl has ever been suspected, charged, investigated, given a witness statement, or been named in any official report, it has been registered and stored in this powerful database. The result of the search causes the hair to rise on the back of Hörður Grímsson's neck.

"What the …?" he whispers. Can this be? He looks at the date, and is dumbfounded.

He gapes in amazement. How could he not know this? Did Andrés really not mention a word of this?

Hörður scrutinizes the notes he made while talking to the police chief. He comes across the following sentences, all quotes from Andrés Aðalsteinsson talking about his brother:

He was abroad but left his daughters alone at home.
Then this all happens.
It was a double trauma, a real family tragedy.

"Double trauma," Hörður mutters before gritting his teeth. He'd listened to the police chief speak, but not heard what he said. "Damn it!"

Hörður leans back in his chair and weighs and evaluates this new and unexpected information. It may change something. But can it change everything? He isn't sure. But it must make some difference. He just doesn't understand how.

Or, yes. In any case, he realizes that not everyone he has spoken to is who they say they are.

Or what?

Oddur is pacing the floor of his bedroom with his phone to his ear, waiting for Lísa to answer. He has called her seven times and sent eleven messages, but she still hasn't answered. He's so stressed that he feels as if he's losing his mind. He hangs up and sends yet another message.

Talk to me. Please. I'm losing my mind.

Oddur lies down on the bed, phone in hand, and tries to relax. He's sweaty, his hair is tousled and his thoughts rush in circles inside his airy head like frightened birds in a cage.

Lísa had been crying. She hugged him tightly and said that she loved him, as if she were about to be executed. Why was she crying? Has she also been given a name? Or has something else happened?

What?

When the phone rings, Oddur jerks as if from a jolt of electricity. He looks at the screen. It's Lísa! Finally ...

"Hi!" He sits up in bed and presses the phone so tightly to his ear that it hurts.

"Hi." The voice is sad, empty—distant.

"What's wrong?" he asks anxiously.

"Nothing. Everything. Sorry I didn't answer. It's just ..."

"I understand," he says, without understanding anything. "Thanks for calling. I was so scared. I thought something might have happened, you know."

"That someone might have killed me?" asks Lísa vacuously.

"Don't say that," whispers Oddur, his voice hoarse with stress. He waits for her to say something, but hears nothing but her breathing.

"Are you there?" he finally asks.

"Did you get a name?"

Oddur hesitates. He certainly did get a name. He's supposed to kill someone named Haukur. "Yes. What about you?"

"Yes."

Oddur is so stressed that he feels sick. Should he ask her what he's imagining? He takes a deep breath. "Is it me, by any chance?"

Lísa doesn't answer.

"Is it me?" he asks, terrified.

"Of course not."

"Okay," says Oddur, not quite convinced. "That's good. When can we meet? I miss you."

"Maybe we should take a little break? Wait until this is over."

"Maybe," says Oddur.

"You didn't say anything, did you?"

"No," says Oddur, while wishing that he had. At least then it would have been in someone else's hands. They would have been free, or at least safe. The police would protect them.

"Good. It would just have made things worse."

He swallows. "Maybe."

"Mom's just come home. I've got to go."

"But …?" Oddur stops, because Lísa has hung up. He stares in disbelief at his phone. She couldn't even say goodbye?

Hörður is still sitting at his computer, with a pain in his neck and a stitch in his lower back. He looks up Ellert Aðalsteinsson, the savings bank manager, on *ja.is*, and calls his cell-phone number, but gets only an automatic message that the phone is switched off or outside the service area. When no one answers the home-phone number, he tries calling the savings bank. He gives his name to the woman who answers and asks for the manager.

"Ellert is out of the office today. He'll be back on Monday."

"It's important that I speak to him," says Hörður. "Is he abroad?"

"He's gone salmon fishing at the Hítará river. He'll be home tonight."

"Thanks for the information." Hörður hangs up, then jots a note to himself. *Call Ellert.*

He turns back to the online telephone directory and searches for Rut Ellertsdóttir. There turn out to be three of them, one of whom is listed as living in Borgarnes. He recognizes the address from the statements taken from those who were at the party where Eva Andrésdóttir died. Rut's cell-phone number is listed. Hörður calls it, but no one answers. Maybe she's at school?

The red-haired giant has only just hung up when his cell phone rings. At first he thinks it's Rut calling back, but then sees on the screen that it's not—he doesn't recognize the cell-phone number that appears there.

"Yes?"

"Hörður Grímsson?" The voice belongs to a young woman, as far as he can hear.

"Who's asking?" he asks coldly.

"My name is Viktoría and I'm a journalist at DV. I wanted to ask you a few questions about ... "

Hörður interrupts her. "Let me stop you right away, Miss."

"Miss?"

"Aren't you a young woman?" asks Hörður, slightly bewildered. Can't he say 'Miss' anymore? He clears his throat and continues. "I won't comment on anything at this stage of the investigation. All inquiries must be directed to the head of the department, Axel M. Axelsson."

"I know, sir, but I just wanted to give you a chance to answer a few simple questions before I go up to Borgarnes and find the answers to them myself. If you answer them, then our readers will feel that the police are doing their job and are possibly on the trail of the murderer. But if I answer

them before the police do, the public's confidence in their work will decrease even more, and they didn't have much to begin with. According to a recent poll by ... "

Hörður interrupts again. "Listen to me, dear! I know you're doing your job and all that, but do you realize that by sticking your nose into things you ought not to be, you could do serious damage to our investigation of this case?"

"Listen, nutsack! I have every right to ask questions, and you know that. I'm writing a long article about the murders of the two boys, and according to my sources they were at a party in Borgarnes this summer where a young girl died from a drug overdose. I'm on my way west to talk to the locals. I'm under no obligation to tell you this, but wanted to give you in the Criminal Investigation Department a chance to comment before I finish my article and publish it."

"I see, I see," mutters Hörður. Did she call him a nutsack? He tries to assess the situation in the blink of an eye. This reporter is probably on the right track, just as he is. It's not unlikely that some answers will be found in Borgarnes. But he has the feeling that he's still a few steps ahead of the reporter. If she's heading west now, she probably won't be able to talk to the bank manager, Ellert, before he returns home from fishing. But it's not out of the question ... "When do you think you'll publish your article?"

"Hopefully on Monday."

Hörður takes a deep breath through his nose. Should he take the chance that he'll solve the case before then? Or should he try to delay her finishing the article—to stretch things out? "What do you say we talk again tomorrow or the day after? I'm sure you'll have even more questions then. Maybe we can share information?"

"That sounds good. Thanks!"

Hörður breaths slightly lighter. He's uncomfortable about having a newshound on his heels; he has enough of a workload and pressure on him already. But if all goes according to plan, he'll be able to separate the wheat from the chaff and arrest the culprit before this reporter harms the investigation.

But since when does everything go according to plan in the Criminal Investigation Department? The red-haired giant doesn't need to answer his own question. It answers itself, anyway, and backs up the answer with facts and statistics.

The answer is rarely—very, very rarely.

Hörður lifts his phone again and calls the office of Hamrahlíð Junior College. He knows the number by heart, and the voice that answers has become as familiar as the chirping of birds in the spring.

"It's Hörður from CID," he says.

"Do you have any good news?"

"Not yet, not yet," he replies wearily.

"Well. What can I do for you today?"

"I'd like you to check the student registry for me. I'm looking for a girl. Rut Ellertsdóttir."

As he waits, Hörður fiddles with a paper clip. If it were 1950, he would light a filterless cigarette with a match, and even spike his coffee with cheap whiskey from a bottle hidden in his desk drawer under a stack of pornographic magazines.

"She's a freshman, started this fall."

"Oh?" Hörður is somewhat surprised, as he's become accustomed to chasing shadows. He opens his notepad and grabs a pen. "Do you have her address?"

Hörður knocks on the door of his boss's office before opening it onto the air-conditioned, half-lit room that smells of books, expensive aftershave, and furniture polish.

"Yes?" Axel M. Axelsson looks up, takes off his reading glasses and looks inquiringly at the red-haired giant. The only light on in the office is a green-shaded, bronze reading lamp on the giant teak desk.

"Are you busy?" Hörður asks from the doorway.

"Come in and close the door behind you," replies old Steppenwolf. "I was just preparing for a press conference. I'm almost finished."

Hörður does as his boss asks. He crosses the soft carpet and sits down in one of the visitor chairs in front of the desk. Behind it, Axel leans back in a leather chair with a high back and clasps his hands over his stomach.

"What's on your mind?"

Hörður clears his throat as he tries to get comfortable in the low chair, which turns out to be as hopeless as getting into a small car. "I just wanted to give you an oral report on the state of things and our next steps."

Axel nods. "Go ahead."

Hörður looks up and to the side, like a storyteller who is about to launch into a narrative of an adventure from long ago. "I'm heading back to Borgarnes tomorrow. I overlooked a few things when I was there this past week. Nothing may come of my visit, but I still have the feeling something's there that I don't fully understand or realize—something flickering on the edge of the field of vision. Among other things, I'm going to talk to the savings bank manager, the police chief's brother. I should have done it the other day, but I didn't think it was important."

"Do you think he knows anything?" asks Axel. "Or is he on your list of suspects?"

Hörður mulls this over. "Neither, in fact. I'm more interested in his daughters; they might know something—at least one of them. Although Ellert might know something, without me thinking that he's keeping anything secret from the authorities."

"Could you be any vaguer?" says Axel reproachfully. "You're speaking almost in riddles. You know how I feel about that."

Hörður nods, with a cryptic look on his face. "You'll have to forgive me. I know you want tangible evidence and irrefutable facts. But as long as we don't know who the murderer is or what his motive is, we've got little else but ideas and guesses. We're chasing an invisible man, a villain who uses text messages and social media to mislead others, a kind of digital ghost who, however, incarnates now and then and shoots his victims at close range. Ghosts don't leave footprints. Bloodhounds don't find them. But intuition can—maybe."

"A ghost, huh?" asks Axel irritably.

Hörður shrugs. "Sorry, it's just a way of putting it. But maybe it's better to speak of a man with two faces. We know that the murderer contacts his victims through computers and phones. He also knew enough about these kids to be able to lure them to meet him in out-of-the-way places, late at night. So it has to be considered probable that he either knows the victims personally, or knows a lot about them."

He doesn't even consider it out of the question that he's seen the murderer, even spoken to him, without of course realizing that that person was also the mysterious killer—the shadow character that he's looking for. The thought is annoying, to say the least.

Axel sighs. "Yes, of course. And what? Do you think you'll find him in Borgarnes, the man with the two faces?"

"I don't know," replies the red-haired giant. "But I do know that I'm not alone in looking for him out west. A reporter woman from *DV* called me earlier, some Viktoría."

"We'll call her a journalist," says Axel in a fatherly tone.

"What?" says Hörður.

Axel sighs. "Keep going, Philip Marlowe."

The red-haired giant clears his throat. "Viktoría is on her way up to Borgarnes to talk to the locals. She knows about the party and the girl who died. Like me, she's putting two and two together."

Axel scoffs. "Can those damn newshounds really not leave us alone to do our jobs?"

Hörður shrugs. "You know how it is."

"You don't seem to be too worried about this journalist sticking her nose in," says Axel. "Why not?"

"She can certainly harm the investigation," says Hörður. "But I'm more worried about the two kids I interviewed for the second time this morning, Oddur Bjarnason and Lísa Kristjánsdóttir. They were both pretty ill-disposed, so to speak—completely stoned and clearly under great mental strain."

"On drugs?" asks Axel.

Hörður nods. "There's something that's really troubling them, besides the deaths of Patrekur and Bragi. I think they're in danger, and they know it. Maybe someone is screwing with them—threatening them or playing with them in some way. I'm sure they know something, but don't want or don't dare to talk to the police about it."

"I see," mutters Axel. "We should probably shadow them?"

"Shadow?" Hörður asks in surprise.

Axel smiles a crooked smile. "If I had taken what you said seriously the other day, we probably could have prevented Bragi's murder. I won't forget that miserable fact as long as I live. His death weighs on me like a nightmare."

"But you did take what I said seriously," says Hörður determinedly. "You wanted us to keep an eye on the young people I mentioned, but you also explained to me why you couldn't permit it—unless we kept an eye on all the students at the school."

"Yes, yes," mutters Axel, gravely. "But still, I did *nothing*, and I can't let that fact go. That's why I asked for a meeting with the Intelligence Unit the day after the murder, and yesterday I met with two of its members. Very interesting meeting, to say the least. A meeting that I should have called for earlier, because I didn't realize the technological advances that have taken place recently."

"The Intelligence Unit?" exclaims Hörður. He's starting to feel like a total greenhorn. First Axel talks about *shadowing* without explaining it further, and now there's an entire unit that the red-haired giant has never heard of.

Axel nods. "High tech."

Hörður whistles softly.

"They operate undercover," says Axel in a low voice. "And not without reason. They work only according to orders from above, and what they do can never see the light of day, let alone a well-lighted courtroom. The less we know, the better and safer it is for everyone."

"I see," says Hörður, who is all eyes and ears. "And how can they help us? What's shadowing?"

Axel clears his throat, and then leans forward on his elbows. "Shadowing is when they put so-called eyes on the home and/or workplace of the individuals that someone wants shadowed—usually it's the Drug Unit monitoring key players in organized crime. The cameras used are tiny, almost invisible, but operate both day and night. The Intelligence Unit then monitors the recordings via computers. When an individual being shadowed gets up to something, it's reported to the head of the relevant department, who then presumably makes personnel and cars available and follows the shadowed subject."

Hörður nods thoughtfully. "This is awesome. So we could have Oddur and Lísa's houses shadowed and have them followed when and if they're out and about?"

"I would have to submit a formal request first, but yes, that's how I understand it," Axel replies. "Would it be those two kids, mainly? Or would we want to shadow anyone else?"

Hörður thinks this over. He would like to monitor that Haukur, but doesn't know who he is or where he lives. And then there's …

"What about Borgarnes?" asks Axel.

Hörður blinks, having lost the thread. "You mean the police chief's home?"

Axel shrugs. "Just an idea. Maybe unnecessary?"

"Let's start with Oddur and Lísa," says Hörður. "When do you think the cameras could be in place? *The eyes,* I mean."

"Before dark, hopefully." Axel looks at his gold watch. "I have to attend a press conference later. Of course there's nothing to report, but I've got to try to stay on good terms with the media and keep the public relatively informed. I'm thinking of proposing a kind of curfew for young people in the capital area, even elsewhere. It wouldn't be a statutory curfew, but I am going to recommend that parents and guardians ensure that young people between the ages of sixteen and twenty stay at home after ten o'clock in the evening, at least for the next few days. How does that sound?"

"Sensible," says Hörður. "But maybe you should try to appeal more to the young people themselves, instead of placing the responsibility on the shoulders of their parents and guardians? Kids at that age don't want to be told what to do, besides the fact that those eighteen years and up are considered adults and therefore don't have to obey mom and dad anymore."

"You're right," Axel mutters as he makes a note of this.

"Did you hear what the police chief said?" Dr. Albert asks at the dinner table. On the radio, the news is being read, and the police press conference is the main story of the evening.

They're eating oven-baked fish, for which Oddur has no appetite. He eats a little rice just to appease Mrs. Jónína.

"Yes," replies Oddur, who had in fact been listening with only one ear. He's more worried about the threat from Deathbook than from the murder investigation. After all, he knows who the murderer is. That is, the *next* murderer. It's none other than himself. At least he's expected to kill the next victim.

Unless Lísa does so first. But he doesn't see her as a murderer. Absolutely not.

He could also say the same thing about himself. He couldn't even imagine hunting for food, let alone shooting another person to death. But if he doesn't, someone will kill Lísa.

And *that* mustn't happen …

"No young people may be outside after ten o'clock," says Dr. Albert.

"Exactly," Oddur says. He's also worried about Lísa, as she was so terribly upset when he last spoke to her, and he hasn't heard from her since. Why has she cut him off like this?

"Your phone?" says Mrs. Jónína.

"Huh?"

"Isn't your phone ringing?"

Oddur blinks and listens. Through the loud radio news, he hears a familiar ringtone. Could it be Lísa?

"Sorry," he says, practically jumping up and dashing from the table.

"What is this?" Dr. Albert says gruffly. "You might think the world was ending!"

"Now, now," says Mrs. Jónína.

Oddur runs up the carpeted stairs and goes to his room. His phone is charging on his desk. The screen displays a number he doesn't recognize—probably a foreign one, because it starts with a country code. He's so disappointed that he almost doesn't answer.

"Hello?"

"Oddur?"

"Who's asking?" he asks in return. The voice on the phone is familiar, yet not.

"Haukur."

Oddur gets a knot in his stomach. "Haukur who?"

"We spoke in front of the police station. I go to HJC."

Oddur recognizes the voice. It's is the skinny boy in the army pants, with the silly cap. But is this the same Haukur that he's supposed to kill? "What do you want?"

"I need to see you."

"Now?" Oddur sits down on the edge of his bed. He doesn't know what to think or say, what to do or not. "Why?"

"It's important."

"You can't tell me on the phone?" Oddur tries both to keep up some sort of conversation and, at the same time, to think fast and clearly. What if this Haukur is also entangled in the game that Deathbook is directing? What if he's been given a subject? What if Oddur is his subject? Is that why he wants to meet?

"It isn't safe to talk about it over the phone, believe me. Everything's being monitored."

"Who's monitoring everything?" asks Oddur.

"You've got to meet me!"

Oddur thinks things over. "Why should I trust you? You know what's going on. Two of my friends are dead."

"Aren't you and Lísa together?"

"Yes," says Oddur hesitantly. They *are* together, right? He's isn't sure about anything any longer. "Why?"

"She's in danger."

Oddur stiffens. "Lísa's in danger?"

"Can you meet me tonight?"

Oddur heaves a sigh. "Maybe. Where?"

"Don't you live in on the West Side?"

"Yes."

"Meet me at the lumpfish sheds on Ægisíða Road at ten o'clock. Can you do that?"

"There's a curfew, haven't you heard?" asks Oddur.

"You can't slip out unnoticed?"

Oddur thinks about it. He can get out of the house unnoticed; that's not a problem. But is it a good idea to meet someone late in the evening? Down by the sea? "I don't know if it's a good idea."

"What I have to say is very important. And it will save Lísa's life. That's just how it is."

Oddur gets a lump in his throat. How can he say no?

Hörður drives south down Lönguhlíð, taking note of the street signs on both sides of the wide street, and signals to turn when he comes to Drápuhlíð. He drives slowly down the street and tries to see the numbers on the gray tabby stuccoed houses, which are all much the same, two stories, basement and attic, no doubt built in the same decade of the last century, probably the fourth or fifth. Encircling the houses are small yards, fenced off with beautifully shaped concrete walls that winds, frost, and rain have taken a toll on over the years. But time isn't just a destructive force. During those same decades, moss has managed to cover the walls to a large extent, filling in cracks and holes and giving the otherwise spiritless concrete an organic and textured appearance.

When Hörður finally spies the house where Rut Ellertsdóttir is registered as living, he pulls his SUV into a vacant parking space at the curb, puts the transmission in neutral, and sits in the parked car for a while. He looks at the dark-gray house and its peaceful surroundings and thinks of everything and nothing as the car's powerful engine murmurs idles with a murmur.

The investigation isn't really going very well. Hörður has no idea who the murderer is or when he'll strike again, and then at whom. Still, he's surprisingly calm about all of it, like a hunter resting his tired bones on a riverbank after casting for fish for nearly a week without getting so much as a single nibble. But the fisherman knows that there are fish in the river. And where there are fish, those same fish will bite. It's just a matter of having patience and not giving up.

Hörður sighs, shuts off the engine and steps out of the car. He's patient, there's no denying that; although *stubborn* may be the more correct word. Yet he doesn't know how long Axel can wait for something significant to happen. Old Steppenwolf, however, seems to have faith in him, and that's what's important.

He walks in through the gate and follows a flagstone sidewalk to wide steps that lead to a splendid main door. In the yard are large, hefty trees that are beginning to shed their leaves in autumn colors—beautifully colored leaves that cover most of the lawn. To one side of the door is a bronze door phone, on which are three buttons with name tags next to them. Families live on the first and second floors, but the tag next to the top button is empty. Hörður presses it, but no one answers. He looks over his shoulder, down the steep stone steps. If he understood Chief of Police Andrés correctly, his niece, Rut, is in a wheelchair. How could she get it up these stairs? And then all the way up to the top floor?

Or does she live in the basement?

Hörður is halfway down the steps when the door opens and a woman in her forties appears in the doorway. She's wearing a dark blue coat and has a small poodle in her arms. She looks at the red-haired giant as if he were death himself, come to snatch her from earthly life.

He tries to squeeze out a friendly smile. "Excuse me. But I'm looking for the girl who lives on the top floor. Rut Ellertsdóttir. Do you know if she's home?"

"The girl? No, she hasn't been seen since this spring," says the woman.

"This spring?" Hörður doesn't understand this at all. "No, she started junior college this autumn. She's a freshman."

"There's a boy living upstairs, a student," the woman says resolutely. She's clearly on her way out but doesn't dare close the door behind her, should this formidable leather-clad man attack her. Her dog squirms restlessly and growls softly. "Sometimes a girl visits him, but she doesn't live here."

"But in the basement?" asks Hörður. "Maybe she lives there?"

"I should think not," says the woman before shushing her dog, which responds by barking loudly. "A single man lives there, an old bus driver. He's lived there since I don't know when."

"Yes, well then." Hörður lets this sink in. He smiles at the woman and heads back down the stairs. "Thanks for your help, and sorry for the inconvenience."

"You're welcome," the woman mutters. She finally closes the door, then puts down the dog.

When Hörður is halfway to the gate, he stops and turns around. The woman, who has come down the steps, stops as well, terrified. The dog barks and raises a fuss.

"The girl," says Hörður. "The one who sometimes visits the student, what does she look like?"

The woman scoffs, as if the question offends her. "She's just a girl. Thin and blonde."

"She's not in a wheelchair, is she?" he asks. "Or is disabled in any way?"

"God, no!" says the woman, as if he'd asked if she was a cannibal with a bone through her nose. "She drives around on a small motorcycle, a Vespa or whatever they're called. What kind of questions are these?"

"Nothing, forget it," says Hörður. He leaves the yard, gets back in his car, and starts the engine. The woman marches off with the dog at her heels. The red-haired giant regards the house again. The top-floor windows are dark.

If Rut doesn't live here, where does she live?

It's five minutes to ten. Oddur walks into the living room on the ground floor, where his foster parents are watching a British crime drama on television.

"I think I'll just turn in early," he says, pretending to yawn.

"All right, friend," says Dr. Albert.

"Good night," says Mrs. Jónína, without taking her eyes off the TV screen.

Oddur walks through the hall toward the stairs. But instead of going up them, he sneaks into the vestibule and grabs his coat and shoes. Then he sneaks back in and goes to unlock the back door, which once opened onto a sun deck but now leads to a greenhouse where Mrs. Jónína grows orchids. Oddur shuts the door carefully behind him, puts on his shoes and coat in the warm, humid greenhouse and finally slips out through a narrow door at its other end. The flimsy door rattles as he shuts it behind him, and tropical air and a heavy floral scent accompany him out into the dark and cold garden.

It had rained after dinner. Oddur hurries across the wet lawn and climbs over the fence separating their yard from the grassy public space between the streets Grímshagi and Lynghagi. He walks quickly along a gravel path, past a basketball court, through a playground and then along a footpath over to Lynghagi. In just a few minutes, he has come down to Ægisíða Road, where he walks west along a paved path toward the old lumpfish sheds standing in a little cluster on the otherwise empty seafront. Next to the rickety, corrugated iron sheds are three old wooden light poles that cast a feeble light on them and their surroundings.

Oddur walks along with his hands stuffed in his coat pockets and his collar folded up to his ears. The night is cold and humid, and one or two raindrops fall from the black sky. From the sea comes a heavy purl, and a car or two drives along the rainy road in front of the large single-family homes beyond it. Oddur draws hesitantly closer to the sheds, which look bedraggled and somewhat ghostly in the twilight. There's no one else out and about, except maybe rats and stray cats. There's a hint of salt in the air, mingled with the smell of seaweed and tar. Beneath his feet, the gravel crunches with each step.

Oddur stops between two sheds and looks around. His heart is pounding in his chest. Was it a hoax? Or has he fallen into a trap? "Is anyone here?"

"Yes, me." The voice is thin and weak, like a child's. A short-statured creature peeks around the corner of one of the sheds, then steps into the dim light from the light poles. It's the strange boy with the round glasses and Inca hat, who wears army pants and a denim jacket.

"Haukur?" asks Oddur.

The boy nods.

"What do you want?" Oddur asks coldly. Supposedly, he should kill this boy, and therefore doesn't want to get to know him at all. What's more, he has no reason to trust this dainty little oddball. But merely the thought of maybe having to harm this pipsqueak makes him feel sick.

Haukur looks to both sides, as if to make sure that no one is eavesdropping. "What I have to say has to do with what's been happening. You know, the death of your friends and all that."

"Yes, that's what I thought," says Oddur suspiciously.

"There's something very strange going on," says Haukur. "Or terrifying, rather. Something that quite a few people know about, but definitely not everyone. Probably not the cops. I don't know if you know what I'm talking about or not. But I think you do."

Oddur blinks. Does he mean Deathbook? "Maybe. Can you be more specific?"

Haukur nods. "I'll try. Have you been sent any messages, for example? Uncomfortable messages from someone you don't know?"

The hair rises on the back of Oddur's neck and he feels an abrupt chill. "Yes."

"Me too," Haukur whispers as he takes a step closer. "Maybe you've been given a name?"

Oddur stiffens, then nods curtly.

"Me too," says Haukur. "But I'm not going to do as I'm told."

"No?" Oddur asks in surprise.

Haukur shakes his head. "I'm not going to hell when I die. I'm going to play the one who's playing us. I'm going to break this vicious circle—and you're going to help me do it."

"Oh, am I?" Oddur asks skeptically. "And *how* am I going to do that?"

"By killing me," Haukur says firmly.

"What?" says Oddur.

"The thing is, I'm dying." Haukur takes off his hat, revealing his buzz cut. "I have cancer. The radiation therapy wasn't enough. The disease has spread to my bones. I don't have much time left to live."

"Oh …" Oddur doesn't know what to say.

"So …" Haukur shrugs, then puts his hat back on. "If I die before I'm supposed to kill my subject, then I'll be free from my obligation. And if you kill me, another participant in this bloody game, then you'll have done your part, and you'll also be free from your obligation. Then the game will be thrown off kilter and who knows, maybe it will just peter out?

"But …?" Oddur thinks this over. "But what about the person you're supposed to kill? Would he just be out of the woods?"

"Hopefully," says Haukur. "Will you tell me who you're supposed to kill?"

Oddur sighs. "I'd rather not."

"All right," says Haukur. "But maybe you can change subjects? Say you want to kill me."

Oddur smiles a crooked smile. "I can't kill you. I can't kill anyone! It's just out of the question. Forget it."

Haukur looks straight into Oddur's eyes. "The thing is, I'm supposed to kill Lísa Kristjánsdóttir."

"No," groans Oddur. "Tell me it's not true!"

"If I don't do it," says Haukur sadly, "then someone will kill my sister, and that can't happen. It *absolutely* can't happen."

"Oh, God," says Oddur, hiding his face in his hands. "What a nightmare!"

"So," says Haukur. "If you kill me, then I can't kill Lísa. She'll be safe, like my sister. As will the one you're supposed to kill; though it's not absolutely certain."

"Your name is Hansson?" Oddur asks wearily, as if he knows perfectly well that it is—which he does.

Haukur nods.

"You're my subject," says Oddur, smiling apologetically. "You're the one I'm supposed to kill."

Haukur starts in alarm, but then shrugs. "And …? So it's perfect! Can't you see?"

"Yeah, or … I don't know," mutters Oddur. He's beginning to realize how Deathbook works, how it thinks. If he doesn't kill Haukur, Haukur will be given the order to kill Lísa, and thus the threat that Lísa will be killed becomes a reality. He who kills, is safe—he who hesitates, dies. Or what? This conversation has given Oddur a headache—he doesn't feel well at all. "Still, I can't do it. I mean, how would I go about it?"

"I've given that a lot of thought, and think that we get help," says Haukur. "I think Deathbook tells us what to do and even helps us with it. That's probably how it works."

Oddur nods thoughtfully. "Yes maybe. Patrekur and Bragi were obviously lured to out-of-the-way places. Do you think Deathbook did that?"

"I think so, yes," says Haukur. "And then the person who was supposed to do the killing was sent to the same place, and the gun was probably waiting there. All you have to do is take the weapon and shoot. That's how I see it."

"Yes, that makes sense," Oddur says. He shudders and pulls his coat tighter around himself.

"So ..." Haukur takes a deep breath.

"So what?" asks Oddur. He's so cold that his teeth chatter.

"Now we wait," says Haukur in his tinny voice. "We wait and hope that you get instructions before me."

"This is insane," mutters Oddur. At that same instant, the wind suddenly starts blowing and it starts raining again. He squints and looks at the sky. The icy raindrops hit his face.

But still, this isn't insane, is it? Oddur thinks. No, insanity is arbitrary and illogical, and not at all evil in nature. Deathbook is precise, cunning, and merciless, like some devilish machinery.

THE TOWN BY THE BRIDGE

Autumn
Saturday

When Hörður Grímsson parks his black SUV at the curb in front of the savings bank manager's stately house at the top of the hill in Borgarnes, it's a quarter past ten in the morning. The weather is calm but a bit cold—the sky is reminiscent of mercury, and the turbulent waters of Borgarfjörður of molten lead; beyond the fjord looms the gloomy Mount Hafnarfjall, like a gateway to the realm of darkness and death from a story by Tolkien. The red-haired giant shuts off his car, but sits there behind the wheel regarding the house for several long moments. Here is where the party was held at which the police chief's daughter died. It was summer then, and the world was full of light, colors, and life. Now it's autumn; winter is approaching and the world is gray and wan, like an abandoned house.

Hörður had spoken to Ellert on the phone the night before. He said he would be home the next morning. Parked in the driveway in front of the garage is a newish Volvo SUV, dusty after a trip. Otherwise, there's no indication that anyone is at home. The windows are either dark or their curtains are drawn shut. In addition, the yard is unkempt, as if no one has tended it for several months—not since the beginning of July or so. It's even as if the paint on the house has faded and the woodwork has gone rotten. But the policeman knows full well that that's doubtless just his imagination. The grayish autumn weather just has that effect.

Hörður steps out of his car and breathes in the clean and healthy rural air. Borgarnes is a pretty, friendly town located in one of the most beautiful places in the country. But it's not a damn bit exciting—more like a soulless suburb than a lively small town. The red-haired giant walks up to the house, at the same time going over in his mind what he didn't know until that morning, after doing a little digging around. Ellert definitely has two daughters. Twins named Áslaug and Rut. They were both home on the night of the fateful party, but neither of them gave the police a statement. He knows why one of them didn't do so, but the other sister's silence is still a mystery to him. He has his suspicions, however.

He rings the doorbell and waits.

Several long moments pass before the householder comes to the door. Ellert Aðalsteinsson is around fifty but looks much older, more like a ghost than a man of flesh and blood. It's as if he's never been out under the bare sky, let alone when the sun is shining. His hair is gray, his eyes lackluster, and his skin like paper.

"Good morning," says the red-haired giant. "We spoke yesterday. My name is Hörður Grímsson."

"Yes, of course," Ellert says in a voice that's as fragile as the workings of an old clock. He's rather short, and so thin that it looks as if the dark suit he's wearing is hanging on a coat hanger. Hörður actually finds it rather odd that someone would be wearing a suit at home before noon on a Saturday, but the savings bank manager is probably one of those old-fashioned, formal intellectuals who always dress like gentlemen.

His boss, Axel, is one of those types. But old Steppenwolf has the aura of a man of authority and elegance.

"Come on in," says Ellert, who's more like an accountant at death's door.

"Thanks." Hörður enters a wide vestibule. Ellert closes the front door, and then asks the policeman to follow him. Hörður takes off his rough-soled shoes, but not his coat. He follows the bank manager through a spacious hall and into a large kitchen. An arched staircase leads from the hall to the upper floor.

The house is both big and luxurious, but at the same time, both very old-fashioned and in a somewhat dilapidated condition. Not that it's on the verge of collapse or pest-infested, but more as if nothing has been done for it since it was built in the middle of the last century. The flooring is worn, both the wooden floors and the thick carpets; the walls probably haven't been painted for decades, there's dust everywhere, the woodwork is dull and colorless, the silver and copper are tarnished and it looks as if about one out of three light bulbs is out.

Hörður knows that the bank manager's wife took her own life five years ago, after struggling with depression since her pregnancy with the twins. She locked herself in the bathroom with a bottle of vodka, a razor blade, and an enormous quantity of sleeping pills. He'd read this in reports on the case.

The house echoes her story. Depression can cast a long shadow over any family, infecting, poisoning, and paralyzing.

The disappearance of the afflicted person does little more than deepen the same shadow, leaving an abyss of sorrow, guilt, and regret. Not least in the case of suicide.

"I'd just started making coffee," says Ellert, half-apologetically. He pours ground coffee into the open funnel on an automatic coffee machine.

"Brilliant," says Hörður, trying to sound encouraging. Ellert appears as fragile as a porcelain vase with cracks in it, and the red-haired giant doesn't want to be the one who breaks it into pieces.

The policeman sits down at the kitchen table and looks around while the householder finishes what he's doing. According to police reports, it was here, in the kitchen, that Eva lost consciousness. She collapsed onto the floor and never got up again. Here, she gave up the ghost before being carried away on a stretcher, covered with a blanket from head to toe.

It's probably not unusual for Ellert to visit his brother, and not the other way around.

"You're investigating the murders of the boys?" says Ellert. Standing at the sink, he lets cold water flow into a glass coffeepot with a black handle.

"Exactly," Hörður answers. He looks at a pile of window envelopes on the table, next to a sugar bowl. Like others, savings bank managers also have bills come through their letter boxes. The envelopes have been opened, but the bills are still in them.

"So why are you here?" asks Ellert. He turns his back on the policeman as he carefully pours the water from the coffeepot into the coffee machine's tank.

Hörður uses the opportunity to look through the window envelopes. Most of them are from credit-card companies, and it would appear that the bank manager uses more than one credit card, even three. He takes a peek at one bill and sees withdrawals from the Bónus supermarket in the Kringlan shopping mall, the Vinnufatabúð men's clothing store and other stores in the capital area, as well as websites such as AliExpress and Amazon and high charges at the Suzuki dealership, a photo shop, and City Park Hotel. The return address on some of the envelopes is of a psychologist in Reykjavík.

"Why?" asks the red-haired giant distractedly. He folds a bill from the psychologist and sticks it inside his coat.

"A journalist called yesterday," says Ellert. He places the pot on the coffee machine's burner, beneath the funnel, and switches on the machine. "Some woman. She didn't actually reach me, but left a message with my secretary. From what I understand, she thought that these murders were possibly related to the death of my niece, my brother Andrés's daughter Eva. Do you think so too?"

Hörður clears his throat. "I'm really just trying to fill in certain gaps, that's all. I'll ask you a few questions about one thing and another. But I won't stay long or cause you any inconvenience. I'm a public servant, after all; not a newshound."

Ellert nods. "Very well. Shall we go sit in the living room?"

"As you wish." Hörður gets to his feet and follows the householder into the living room, which is half-lit, as the curtains are drawn over its windows for the most part. They sit down on a worn Chesterfield sofa, opposite a large fireplace full of soot and darkness.

"Your colleague got in touch with me," says Ellert. "His name was Benedikt, as I recall."

"That is right," says Hörður.

"He grilled me about me and my brother's activities," says Ellert sadly. "He seemed to be trying to confirm our alibis in connection with these murders. If my brother and I are among your suspects, you're hardly on the right track in your investigation."

Hörður smiles apologetically. "Naturally, we have to rule out all possibilities. Don't forget that your brother's gun is gone. And the boys were shot with weapons of the same caliber."

"Yes, that's right," Ellert mutters.

Now that he's mentioned the murder weapon and its provenance, Hörður decides to seize his opportunity. "You visited your brother and his wife shortly after the fateful night, you and your daughter Rut—right?"

Ellert nods. "Yes, we did. Grief can unite families."

It can also divide them, Hörður adds in his mind.

"Your daughter Rut is confined to a wheelchair, isn't she?" asks the policeman. "I noticed that there was a kind of lifting apparatus attached to the railing of the stairs in the hall here."

"Yes and no," Ellert replies. "She had a nervous breakdown following her mother's death. For a while, she was completely bedridden, but then was able to move her upper body. She was confined to a wheelchair for a long time, but has slowly been recovering."

"So she isn't paralyzed?" asks Hörður.

"No, not physically," Ellert replies. "Her spinal cord is undamaged, I mean."

Hörður clears his throat. "Where is she now?"

"In Reykjavík," Ellert replies. "She started at HJC this autumn. The plan was for the sisters to move in with their aunt Eva. My brother Andrés owns a small top-floor apartment in the Hlíðar district. He bought it when Eva started her further education."

"On Drápuhlíð Street?" asks Hörður.

Ellert nods. "That's right. Rut lives there alone."

Hörður frowns. "Are you sure? Yesterday I met a woman who lives in that house, and she said that there's a boy living on the top floor, a student. Besides, there's no real wheelchair access to that apartment."

Ellert shrugs his shoulders in semi-surrender. "Where else should she live? The stairs are no obstacle. As I said, her paralysis was mental, not physical. In fact, I think this house caused her paralysis. The memories of her mother's death, rather. In any case, she regained her strength as soon as she left home. Not overnight; slowly but surely. And that's why she doesn't want to return here. She's doubtless afraid of becoming paralyzed again."

"Do you speak to her often?" asks Hörður.

Ellert smiles faintly, even as his mood darkens. "You lose contact with kids at this age. For various reasons. And she's very busy, too. Has a lot going on."

"At school?" asks Hörður.

"At school and in her personal life," Ellert replies.

"Personal life?" asks Hörður in surprise. "Do you mean guys? Is she in a relationship, or …?"

"No, nothing like that," Ellert replies curtly, as if this comment about guys really rubs him the wrong way. "She's just been seeing a psychologist quite often. Because of her breakdown, and all that. I understand that this work is far from over. But I hardly know anything about it all. It's a private matter; all of it. I just pay the bills."

"All right." Hörður blushes, feeling ashamed at having stolen one of the man's bills. But only slightly. He doesn't always go by the book, as it's said, and has certainly gotten into trouble because of it. But more often than not, his shamelessness has given him an advantage that has made the difference between life and death at critical moments. What's more, he's about as good at restraining himself as a kid in a candy store. At best, he's impulsive and impatient—at worst, scheming and dishonest.

"I think the coffee is ready." Ellert gets up. "You'll have a cup, won't you?"

"Yes, thanks—black, no sugar," says Hörður, as he, too, gets up from the sofa. "Maybe I'll take the opportunity and use the bathroom. Where would it be?"

They walk together to the kitchen.

"There's a small guest bathroom in the hall, to the left," says Ellert. "There's a bathroom upstairs, as well."

"I'll manage," says Hörður. Ellert disappears into the kitchen but the policeman plods into the hall, then glances over his shoulder before sneaking up the stairs leading to the upper floor. Upstairs is a hallway with doors on both sides. One door is closed—the one that leads to the master bedroom and bathroom. The room that he's looking for is at the hallway's end. At the foot of a queen-sized, made bed is a folded wheelchair, which tells him that these bright quarters belong to Rut Ellertsdóttir.

Hörður steps over the threshold. The light enters through the floor-length corner window, through which is a view of the harbor area and the mouth of the Hvítá river, then Brákarey Island and the expansive Faxaflói Bay. The room has a bookshelf, desk, and chest that turns out to be locked. The bookshelf mainly holds academic books, on everything from human history and astronomy to religion, gender studies, and biology, and among the books are old trophies (soccer, basketball, track and field), framed photos (two of the sisters, one of David Beckham, and two of Tiger Woods), beautiful rocks and wood carvings (a headless, naked man). By the window is a telescope on a tripod. Hörður bends down, narrows his left eye and looks with his right through the telescope. What he sees is the arched stone bridge connecting the harbor area and Brákarey Iceland. Under the bridge, the cold sea churns.

The red-haired giant straightens up and turns his attention to what's covering the desk. It's a kind of diorama, made of cardboard and painted and decorated with glitter and small objects. The setting is a grassy headland, a blue sea, and a small island off of a black beach. On the beach stands a hideous troll. At the troll's feet is a black, sea-beaten stone the size of a walnut. But in the proportions of the artwork, the stone is more like a boulder. Behind the troll is a smaller human figure, maybe a boy—very ugly. In the channel between the land and the island, a female figure is swimming—peeking out from the blue-painted waves are the shoulders and head of a red-haired woman who stares hopelessly at the island, which never draws closer.

"Brákarsund Strait," says Ellert from the doorway.

Hörður is startled, but manages not to show it. "Exactly."

He notices a dusty label at the bottom of the artwork. *"Brákarsund" Áslaug and Rut. 5th Grade."*

"They were so fond of this, especially because they received an award for it," says Ellert proudly. "You were looking for the bathroom, weren't you?"

"Yes and no," Hörður replies. "I peeked in here and got curious, that's all."

"Oh, you don't say," Ellert mutters, looking pensive. As if he's trying to remember whether the room had been open or not.

"Do you know what's in this?" asks Hörður. With his foot, he taps the chest sitting there on the floor. As Ellert turns his attention to the locked chest, Hörður takes the opportunity to remove the stone from the artwork and stick it in his pocket. The boulder that the ogrish Skallagrímur would have lifted over his head—if the work had suddenly come to life—and thrown at the bondwoman, hitting her in the head and thereby putting an end to her escape.

"No," Ellert replies, after trying to open the chest. "It's locked and I have no idea where the key is. Why do you ask?"

Hörður shrugs. "Just curious."

Ellert looks at him suspiciously. "Shouldn't we have our coffee before it cools down?"

Hörður smiles politely. "Of course."

As they walk past the closed room, Hörður stops. "Is this the other sister's room? Áslaug's?"

Ellert nods quickly. "But you're not going in there."

Hörður grunts obstinately, but decides not to say anything that could upset the bank manager. But now that he's a bit irritated, he has a hard time restraining himself.

"Rut was at home when her cousin died," says the red-haired giant as they stroll down the stairs. "But she didn't give the police a statement. Why not?"

Ellert stops in the middle of the stairs and looks over his shoulder at the black-clad giant following him like a shadow. "First of all, she didn't see anything. She was up in her room the whole time, in her wheelchair. Second, she'd had another nervous breakdown. Not because of Eva, but …"

The bank manager's voice breaks and his eyes fill with tears.

"I understand," says Hörður. "I didn't mean to upset you. But I've got to do my job; you must understand that."

Ellert nods.

"I found Rut's phone number on *ja.is*, but she still hasn't answered any of my calls." Hörður looks up the number on his phone and reads it to Ellert. "Is this her number? Or does she have a new one, maybe?"

"That's her number," the bank manager replies. "I don't know if she has another one."

Hörður grunts moodily.

"She doesn't answer when I call her, either," Ellert says apologetically.

"I see," says the policeman. "Then I may be forced to put out a wanted notice for her. That's why I need a photo of her. Preferably a recent one, and not too small."

The sun breaks through the clouds and shines in through the large windows. Its rays are as hot as freshly brewed coffee.

"Thanks for dragging me out and perking me up. I really needed it," says Lísa, smiling at Oddur. Her loose hair is still half-damp following their swim and she smells of soap and shampoo, mingled with a faint odor of chlorine. She's wearing no makeup and is dressed in jeans, a shirt, and a boyish bomber jacket, but Oddur has never found her so beautiful, so perfect—so irresistible.

"My pleasure," says Oddur, smiling out to his ears, and they lean over the table at the same time and kiss. The kiss isn't long, but is both warm and heartfelt. Oddur gets butterflies in his stomach.

He's so enamored of her that he nearly feels sick.

"What?" she asks, half-laughing, before nibbling on the French waffle she chose.

"Nothing," Oddur replies with a smile. He takes a bite of his veggie sandwich and then a sip of warm cappuccino. Lísa ordered a soy latte.

They're sitting on barstools opposite each other at a small round table by the window of Almar Bakery in the town of Hveragerði, one of the best, most splendid bakeries in the country. That morning, when Oddur looked out the window and saw that the weather was almost perfectly summery, he decided that he'd had enough of dark days full of drama and death and that *this* day, there would be light in the darkness that had enclosed his and Lísa's lives the last week or so. He didn't think or say *carpe diem*, but that was exactly what he did.

He borrowed his stepfather's Range Rover and sent Lísa a message, telling her to get ready and pack her swimsuit and a good mood because he was on his way and would accept neither excuses nor refusals. She'd been so confused that she just said okay and did as he asked, *heeded* without thinking about it or having opinions on it. And in retrospect, she found it pleasant, and even sexy, too. Besides, she just would have spent the day pitying herself and worrying.

Oddur drove the two of them out of town. After crossing Hellisheiði Heath under subdued sunshine with lava and moss on both sides, their route lay straight to the Laugaskarð Swimming Pool, the most beautiful in the country. There they relaxed in the steam room and hot tubs and played in the pool, with the blue sky above, the mountain looming over them and the wooded hillsides, the river rushing by and hot springs all around.

They kissed, hugged, lay in each other's arms, and melted into the gurgling water, the steam, and the rays of the autumn sun. For over an hour, they forgot not only time and place but also all the horror, all the death, and all their worries. The past was forgotten, the future didn't exist and everything was intimacy, heat, and gleams in their eyes.

A touch, a kiss, a breath …

Lísa sips her latte, blinks, and looks out the window as if distracted. Oddur feels a sting of anxiety in his stomach because he knows that she has slipped out of the daydream that this trip has been. She's thinking outside the soap bubble they've been floating around in since before noon. In just a moment, she'll say something that will burst the super-delicate bubble and pull them back into chilly gray reality.

"What?" he says softly, because he simply can't wait like this between hope and fear.

"Nothing," she says, smiling apologetically. Then the smile disappears and she looks straight into his eyes. "But have you heard anything more from, you know?"

Oddur shrugs sadly. "No message today. Not yet. But something happened yesterday. I met the person I'm supposed to kill. He contacted me first."

"What?" exclaims Lísa, frightened. "What are you talking about?"

"He didn't know I was supposed to kill him," says Oddur. "But he suspected, correctly, that I was involved in all this insanity. This game or whatever this is that Deathbook is spinning up. He's one of us, that kid. He's already gotten a subject and everything."

"And what?" asks Lísa anxiously. "Is he supposed to kill you?"

Oddur shakes his head. "But he wants me to kill him. He's dying, see. He has cancer and will die anyway. But if I kill him, he'll escape becoming a murderer. And then I'll have done my part."

"But …?" Lísa tries to get a grip on this. "But you won't *escape* at all. You'll kill him, that boy."

"He's dying anyway. He asked me to do it," says Oddur.

"You can't do this. Can you?" asks Lísa in horror.

"I don't know," says Oddur. "But if I do, you'll escape too."

"Me?" asks Lísa, confused. "How so?"

Oddur smiles a crooked smile. "You're his subject, the boy who wants me to kill him. If I don't kill him, he'll have to kill you."

Lísa cries out softly, but clamps her hands over her mouth as she does.

"So …" Oddur shrugs. "I don't have much choice, do I?"

"But …?" Lísa takes a deep breath. "But that doesn't change the fact that I have a subject. And if I don't obey, someone will kill my brother."

"No, not if …" Oddur stops, not knowing exactly what he was going to say. Didn't Haukur mean that the chain would be broken if he died? Yes, he said something along those lines, but would it work? Probably not …

"Who's your subject?" he asks.

Lísa's eyes tear up and she bites her lower lip. "I can't tell you that."

Oddur reaches across the table and grabs her hands, which are icy to the touch. "Is it me? Just tell me like it is."

Lísa starts sobbing, and then nods.

Oddur groans. He suspected this. He feared it. But having it confirmed chills his blood.

"What do we do?" asks Lísa in a choked-up voice. "I'm not going to the police, just so you know. I can't take that chance. If anything happens to my brother, I'll die. I couldn't live with it."

"I have a plan," says Oddur in a strong voice. He himself hardly knows what the plan is. Still, he does know it—deep down. There's only one way out of this diabolical maze.

"You do?" asks Lísa in disbelief.

Oddur nods. He has to protect Lísa. He loves her and can't imagine living without her. "Trust me."

After chatting a little longer with the savings bank manager Ellert over a cup of coffee, Hörður says goodbye and drives his SUV down the hill, through the harbor area and on to the Hyrnan cafeteria and convenience store, where he stops to get gas. Then he sits in his parked car with the engine idling and writes down a few notes in his notepad. He takes the psychologist's bill from the inside pocket of his coat and taps his name into the search box on his phone.

The psychologist's name is Ævar Zöega. He has a master's degree in clinical psychology from a Dutch university, and is a married father of two whose main hobby is hiking in the mountains. This is all stated in an article in the *Morgunblaðið* daily from over a year ago, published on the occasion of Ævar's fortieth birthday.

But the topmost result of the search is a two-year-old TV interview with Ævar in which he discusses the process that people who desire gender reassignment have to go through and the prejudices that these same people experience in society, as well as from health professionals. The interview is part of the television news magazine *Kastljós's* coverage of the issue, which was only then seeing the light of day.

Hörður grunts, as he's never fully understood these gay issues. Or are they called *queer* now? He isn't sure, but he misses the good old days when some people were just gays or lesbians and were fine with that. Now it's as if everyone is different, yet no one as different as the next person. People can no longer even be grouped according to their genitals because some are neither male nor female, not a *he* or a *she*, but a *they* or *them*.

A bit further down the list of search results is a TV interview with a young girl who wanted gender-reassignment surgery but was rejected by the system, according to her. The interview is from this past May. The girl wanted to remain anonymous; her face is blurred and her voice is distorted. First, the girl went to a psychologist who helped her with her first steps in the process of gender reassignment. She regularly met with specialists on a public committee that evaluates individuals who want to change their gender. This interview process usually takes six to twelve months, after which time the applicant usually begins hormone therapy, and later the breasts are removed and the genitals changed. But according to the expert committee, this particular girl supposedly didn't meet the conditions necessary for green-lighting hormone therapy.

She was rejected.

"I got the hormones myself; that in itself wasn't a problem," the girl says in the interview, in a distorted male voice. She sounds very bitter, and doesn't seem to be well balanced. *"But if I want to change myself completely, I've to go to Thailand or something. Maybe I will, maybe not. But until then, I'm just a trans woman, not a man. I'm just some freak because that stupid committee failed me on my psychological evaluation."*

"Interesting," mutters the red-haired giant after scrolling quickly through the interviews and glancing over the search engine's main results. Then he enters the psychologist's name in the search window on the *ja.is* app to see where he works, which turns out to be at the Álftamýri Street medical center. He knows the center well because he sometimes goes to a chiropractor there, a spirited Irishman who expertly cracks his back and neck.

Hörður tries calling Rut Ellertsdóttir's cell-phone number but she doesn't answer; it just rings out. He sends her a text message, giving her his name and number and asking her to call at the first opportunity.

The photo that Ellert gave him of his daughter is in the inside pocket of his coat. Hörður takes out the photo and regards it. They're actually both in it, the twin sisters Áslaug and Rut—as different-looking as day and night. They're sitting on a bench in a small park in the summertime, smiling at the person taking the photo. In fact, it's more like Rut is making a face. She's dark-complexioned, and has an intelligent but depressed look about her. Her hair is like that of a wild child, tousled and wooly, and her skin is quite bad. Áslaug, on the other hand, has flowing golden hair and an angelic smile on her face. She reminds Hörður of Laura Palmer, the girl who was found murdered on the TV show *Twin Peaks*. He opens his pocketknife and cuts the photo in half, thus separating the sisters. He sticks the half with Rut back in his pocket, and the other half in his notepad.

Before setting off for Reykjavík, Hörður calls Axel, who answers at the third ring through the hands-free system.

"Yes?"

"I've just finished up here in Borgarnes," says the policeman as he drives out onto the Borgarfjörður bridge.

"*Was your trip a success?*"

"I believe so," says Hörður. "But it remains to be seen. Everything calm in the City of Fear?"

"*Fortunately, yes. It appears that the young folk are taking the informal curfew seriously, at least most of them. Last night was very quiet, at least. So quiet that the restaurant and bar owners downtown are complaining to the media. I also understand from our colleagues in the Intelligence Unit that Oddur and Lísa stayed home last night.*"

"Good to know," says Hörður. "We certainly can use a little peace and quiet to work. Tell me, would it be a problem adding one more of those surveillance cameras? An eye or whatever it's called."

"*Not particularly. What are you thinking?*"

"It's the bank manager's daughter," replies the red-haired giant. "Rut Ellertsdóttir. I need to reach her, talk to her. She's an important witness, or even more than that. But she doesn't answer her phone and may not even live where her father thinks she does. I've got to find her. Even if only to cross her off our list of suspects."

"*I understand. But if you don't know where she lives, how can we shadow her?*"

"Well, it would only be to rule out her living in her uncle's apartment," says Hörður.

"*Where's that?*"

Hörður gives him the address on Drápuhlíð Street.

"*I'll see what I can do.*"

"Thanks," says Hörður. "I'll bring you a photo of the girl. Or should I take it straight to the Intelligence Unit?"

"*Just let me have the photo; I'll scan it and send it on. Was there anything else?*"

"Yes, maybe." Hörður clears his throat. "How difficult is it to access data on psychologists' clients?"

"Very difficult. It requires a very well-founded court order. Why?"

"It's the same girl, the bank-manager's daughter," Hörður answers. "I'm really curious about her. If I don't get hold of her soon, we'll have to take action. Put out a wanted notice for her, get a warrant to search the apartment at Drápuhlíð, and so on."

"Do you think she's dangerous? Violent?"

"I don't know what to think," says Hörður. "But as I said, I want to talk to her, first and foremost. I don't like having such a joker … out there somewhere."

"Joker?"

"A wild card," explains the red-haired giant.

"Agreed."

"We'll be in touch about this."

"Roger."

Hörður drives at over a hundred kph along the foot of Mount Hafnarfjall. In the rear-view mirror is clear, sunny weather, and ahead is a thick cloud bank, like a black wall. Suddenly, the temperature drops and hail hits the windshield with loud pops.

Oddur drives Lísa home. The two of them had been mainly silent on the way back from Hveragerði. As much as it had been a relief to get out of the constrictive capital, it was difficult to return to the chaos, fear, and anxiety permeating what used to be their grayish everyday lives.

"Thanks for today," says Lísa. "It was wonderful."

"It was my pleasure," says Oddur.

"Talk to you later," says Lísa, kissing him on the cheek before opening the car door. It's windy, and the sky is black and restless.

"Yes, of course," says Oddur. He tries to smile reassuringly but doubts that he's managed it.

She gives him a quick smile in return, then steps out of the car and shuts the door behind her. Oddur drives off; she watches the car disappear around the next turn. She'd felt good after their swim, but now it's as if she's made of lead and everything is dark, heavy, and miserable—hopeless.

Lísa takes a deep breath, pulls herself together, and walks in through the door of her parents' house.

"I'm home!" she calls out as cheerily as she can.

"Good to know, dear," her mother calls back, probably from the kitchen. Judging by the smell, she has banana bread in the oven.

Lísa loves freshly baked banana bread, yet the sweet aroma makes her a bit nauseated. She doesn't feel well at all, that's just how it is. She starts taking out her swimsuit to hang to dry and plans to lie down for a while, but stops when she notices that the house is strangely quiet. Usually, her brother is making some sort of racket, either by himself or with those idiots he calls his friends. They play computer games, laugh and talk so loud that it's abnormal.

Lísa goes and peeks into his room, but there's not a soul in that messy, smelly place. She hurries to the kitchen, where her mother is looking in the oven.

"Where's Lárus?" Lísa asks in a flustered tone.

"He went swimming with the boys," her mother replies. "Why?"

"Swimming? At what pool?" Lísa asks frantically. "With what boys? How did they go? When are they coming back?"

Her mother laughs nervously. "What's gotten into you? He's with his friends; they rode their bikes. Then they're going to spend the night at Baldur's."

"Spend the night?" asks Lísa. She's so upset that she can barely breathe. "Who's Baldur? What's going on? I mean, can you go pick him up? He's not going to spend the night somewhere else!"

"Lísa, dear, what's going on?" her mother asks worriedly.

"Going on? Going on?" cries Lísa. "Don't you know that a murderer's on the loose? Don't you know that two boys have been killed? Patrekur was my boyfriend, I knew Bragi, and, and, and …"

She blinks, catches her breath, and begins swaying.

"Lísa!" Her mother just manages to grab her before she collapses to the floor. "Lísa, dear! Is everything …?"

Half an hour later, Lísa is lying under a duvet, staring at the ceiling. Through a haze, she can smell burned banana bread. The curtains are drawn over the window in her room, and the door is half open. Out in the hallway, her mother is speaking to paramedics in a low voice, yet loud enough for Lísa to hear every word.

"There's no need to admit her," says one of the paramedics. "She just had a panic attack, which explains her hyperventilation and fainting. We gave her a sedative. She just needs a little peace and quiet to recover."

"I see," says her mother. "I just didn't know what was going on. But of course she's under a lot of pressure and such. She knew the boys who were murdered. But …"

Lísa pulls the duvet up over her head so that she can't hear what her mother is saying. It's humiliating enough that she called the Emergency Number. What if someone hears about this?

Her mouth is dry and she feels numb and confused. The drug they injected her with makes everything seem distant and muffled, as if she's submerged in some sort of painkiller syrup. She's still anxious, still scared, but it's not as real, not as *close.* More like a memory of fear.

Lísa unlocks her phone. She can barely focus her eyes and her fingers feel fat and numb, but finally she manages to send a message to Oddur.

Do what you have to do. Save my brother. I don't care if I die. I can't let anything happen to him. If it does, I'll kill myself …

THE CITY OF FEAR

Autumn
Third Murder

Outside, an icy rain is falling in the pitch-darkness. Around midday, a sharp western squall hit, bringing hail, but then the wind died down almost as quickly as it arrived, and the hail changed into sleet that melted just as fast and turned into heavy rain.

It's half past ten at night.

Oddur sneaks out through the greenhouse. He told his foster-parents that he was going to watch a show on his computer before going to bed, but then put on a hooded sweatshirt and an old leather jacket with ribbed cuffs and waited for his opportunity to slip out unnoticed. His heart is beating fast and he has a sour taste in his mouth, so stressed and nervous that he can barely think clearly.

Between six and seven o'clock, he'd been in contact with that damn Deathbook. And apparently, the time has come. He has to kill his target before midnight—*or else*. But it will be easy, says Deathbook. All he has to do is follow instructions.

Oddur seizes the opportunity and runs across Suðurgata Road. The rain pours down and forms cold streams. His sneakers are already soaked, as are the hood of his sweat-shirt and the legs of his jeans. He runs past and between houses. He's on his way to the Vatnsmýri neighborhood, to a construction site where a broad, spacious apartment block for students is being built. The building isn't yet at lockup stage; it's just a three-story concrete box that's barely distinguishable from the rain and evening darkness. Enclosing it is a wire-mesh fence, with a gate that allows easy access.

Avoiding muddy puddles, Oddur quickly crosses the gravel lot and finally takes shelter by the cab of a tall crane. He pulls out his phone and opens the messaging app. A new message awaits him.

East of the building is a green trash dumpster. On its eastern side are two openings with black covers. Behind one of the covers is a green bag.

Oddur sticks his phone back in his pocket and peers through the rain. He sees the green dumpster and jogs over to it, to the side facing away from the building. He slides one of the black plastic covers open and peeks into the dumpster, which is full of wood scraps and darkness. He feels around, but finds nothing apart from some boards with nails in them. He opens the other cover and immediately sees the bag, which turns out to be an army-green shoulder bag with a wide strap. He opens it, and inside, finds an unwieldy, white pistol made of plastic and a GoPro camera that can be strapped to one's head.

"Fuck," says Oddur, practically paralyzed with stress. He hangs the bag on his shoulder and sends a message back.

Found the bag. What now?

The reply comes immediately.

Go into the building, the entrance to the left. Turn on the camera and strap it to your head. Cock the gun by pulling the elastic band up into the notch, and hold it carefully. Go down the corridor and turn right into a longer one. The subject will be waiting there. Move closer, don't hesitate, aim and pull the trigger. Go back the same way, put the camera and the gun back in the bag, and put the bag where it was in the dumpster. If you obey all of these instructions, you'll be free.

Free, right … Oddur swallows. He reads the messages again. Then he sticks his phone in his pocket and walks over to the building. He strides over puddles as the cold rain hits him. He's numb and weak; his ears are buzzing and his teeth chattering. He feels as if he's dreaming, as if this isn't happening. But it *is* happening. He's a sleepwalker in a nightmare that's a merciless reality.

The entrance on the left side is like the toothless maw of a blind monster—the lightless, sinister new building swallows him in one bite, as effortless as a giant shark devouring herring. Oddur finds himself in a short but wide corridor that's as cold as a refrigerator and smells of concrete. He squats, opens the bag again, and takes the camera from it. The lens is like a black eye, but he doesn't see a microphone. He turns it on; a soft beep is heard and a powerful *LED* light comes on above the lens.

What if someone sees the light?

Oddur puts the camera on his head and takes care not to let it shine toward the doorway. How does such a camera work? Does the camera itself record footage, or is it connected to a smartphone? He guesses the latter, which presumably means that Deathbook is close, maybe even monitoring his every move.

He pushes aside the thought, shines the light into the bag, and takes the gun from it. It's surprisingly light but is awkward to hold, and is rather slippery to the touch. He stands up, examines the gun carefully, pulls an elastic band onto a kind of notch, and feels the trigger cock.

Oddur takes a deep breath, then sets off for his fateful rendezvous. He walks deeper into the building's darkness and turns right, where a long corridor takes over from the short, wide one. His footsteps are amplified in the empty building, like a muffled drum beat. His heart is beating differently, faster and deeper. He's halfway down the corridor but hasn't yet seen or heard any sign of the *subject*.

He stops, feeling so stressed that he can barely breathe, let alone walk. It's as if his legs have turned into lifeless concrete. He listens to his heart beating and his own breaths, shallow and jerky. The light illuminates the corridor's gray concrete wall.

"Are you there?" Oddur asks in a sharp voice. The question bounces like a ball off the cold walls.

A swishing sound is heard; light footsteps. Then Haukur steps out of one of the rooms and into the corridor. Thirty meters separate them; maybe less. At first, Oddur is relieved, but then despair pours over him.

"I can't do this."

"No bullshit," says Haukur. "You have to do this. We have to do this. We have no choice."

"Maybe," Oddur mutters. He takes a deep breath, trying to relax his tense nerves. But he's so upset that his entire body is trembling. "How? Why are you here? I mean, how did Deathbook get you to come here? Who were you supposed to meet?"

Haukur smiles apologetically. "Everyone has their hidden sides. I came to buy something from someone I don't know. I even brought the money with me."

"I see," says Oddur.

"Just aim at me and shoot," Haukur says in a hollow voice. "Let's get it over with."

"But …?"

"But nothing!" Haukur says so loudly that his childish voice cracks as if he's going to cry. "You've got a camera on your head, you idiot! We're being watched, don't you get it? Shoot, man!"

Oddur is taken aback at this unexpected fit of anger. He's so startled that for a second, he forgets how stressed he is. Before he knows it, he has raised the gun and aimed it at the slender boy, whose eyes open wide behind his round glasses, like a deer in the headlights.

Then he pulls the trigger. *BAM!*

The blow is enormous, and the report so loud that Oddur loses his hearing for a few seconds. The gun kicked so hard that it nearly hit his face. Smoke gushed from it and a strong smell of burned powder tickles his nose.

Oddur lets the gun sink, blinks a couple of times, and stares through the thin smoke remaining. In the strong beam of light, he sees Haukur lying face-down on the hard stone floor. He was thrown backward, turned and landed on his stomach with one hand under him and one leg, bent, out to the side.

"*Shit,*" Oddur whispers, and then he takes a few steps backward before turning and speeding back toward the exit. The beam of light waves back and forth like a sword in the hands of a warrior. He doesn't slow down until he sets eyes on the green shoulder bag lying like a rag on the floor where he left it.

He sticks the gun into the bag, then rips off the camera, shuts it off, puts it on top of the gun, and closes the bag. Done, it's done. He did it, the nightmare is over.

Or what?

Oddur wanders out of the empty building like a drunken man. With the cold rain hitting him, he walks straight over to the trash dumpster without worrying about stepping in any puddles or not. He puts the bag back in its place, not daring otherwise. He's surrounded by darkness and pouring rain, but there's probably *someone* watching his every move. Somewhere there are eyes in the night, the staring, soulless eyes of a bloodthirsty monster that calls itself Deathbook.

"The book of the dead," Oddur mutters through his chattering teeth as he leaves the construction site. He envisions dusty old books full of obscure symbols, horrors, and evil intentions. A notorious sorcerer's screed that contains centuries-old spells and can both trap innocent souls in its slimy web and wake the dead from their long sleep. A diabolical book, bound in human skin and written with blood by the Prince of Darkness himself …

Oddur walks toward the university campus. He's pale and stiff, his eyes buggy. His hair is wet, his jacket is wet, and his jeans are pasted to his thighs. His shoes are sopping with puddle water, his body is trembling, and he moves like a zombie. But he feels neither the wetness or the cold. He has just killed a person and feels as if he himself is dead, as if he's trapped in a bad dream from which he'll never wake up.

But he has a plan. It may not be a good plan, but since he doesn't have much to work with, he's got to roll with it and hope for the best. He finds shelter under the awning in front of the entrance to Oddi, the sharp-cornered, white-painted building of the Department of Social Sciences at the University of Iceland. Once there, he sniffs rainwater into his nose, fishes his cell phone from his jacket pocket, wipes it off with trembling fingers, and finally taps in the number from a soggy business card.

It rings several times before a deep, gruff male voice answers.

"Yes?"

"I killed someone," Oddur stammers, and then he gasps and bursts into tears.

Hörður Grímsson is restless. He's investigating two brutal murders but isn't even close to arresting the murderer. At least not *close enough.* Still, he has the feeling that he's on the right track, but because the feeling is *vague,* he can't feel calm; instead, it's as if this quasi-feeling is crawling over him like a bug, biting him and drawing blood here and there, irritating his skin and making him itch. Because of his, it's impossible for him to stay for long at his workplace on Hverfisgata Street, much less at home in the arms of Bíbí. Which is exactly why he's sitting at this moment in his parked, idling SUV, staring out of the rain-soaked windshield at everything and nothing while his thoughts rush in circles inside his head, like a big group of kids on a sugar high.

It's four minutes to eleven on a Saturday night.

Hörður sighs as he tries to get comfortable in his soft seat, wishing at the same time that everything in his life would fall back into place again, even if only for a few days. He loves working on exciting cases, but this double murder investigation is starting to take its toll on him. He has slept little, eaten little, and is on the verge of a nervous breakdown, so worried is he about the state of the case and his future in the department. What if a third murder is committed? And/or he's unable to track down the murderer? What will the media say then? The public? The public prosecutor? The Alþingi? He can't think these thoughts to the end without envisioning Axel M. Axelsson humiliated to the point of resignation, and himself demoted—or on the dole. And to add insult to injury, he couldn't even take comfort in the arms of his beloved with a clear conscience because he'd cheated on her. He'd even considered leaving her! No, he would be too ashamed. A single smile or hug from Bíbí would crush his heart of stone. And actually, he doesn't have a heart of stone, but the tiny heart of a child who's terrified of everything and everyone.

"You're a big darned clown," Hörður says to himself, like a disappointed parent to an idiotic kid. And he is an idiot, after all. Whatever the outcome of the murder investigation, he's got to forgive himself for cheating on Bíbí and try to bury it deep within the darkness of his soul. Because he's neither ready to confess his mistake to Bíbí nor to let it ruin their relationship. He can't imagine living without her. He knows that now. It's actually the only thing he knows for certain. But can he forgive himself? He isn't sure.

The heavy autumn rain pounds on the car roof, runs in uneven stripes down the windows, forms streams at the curb and flows into the nearest drain. Hörður looks yet again at his watch. Two minutes to eleven. How long is he going to be here? He parked his SUV on Drápuhlíð Street, one house down from the one where Rut is supposed to be living. He has turned off any and all lights and sits there watching the house, which is almost invisible in the darkness and rain. But lights are on behind some of the windows, as well as above the door. The top floor, however, is pitch black.

The red-haired giant is hungry. He'd brought a thermos of coffee with him, a sandwich and a chocolate bar, but fini-shed it all long ago. He'd decided to watch the house until midnight, but might only last until half past eleven. As far as he's aware, the Intelligence Unit has put an *eye* on the house, although he doesn't know this for certain, or where the tiny camera might be hidden. But he decided to keep an eye on the place himself. Not least because he felt like he had to do something. Doing nothing can really stretch the nerves.

Hörður tries to ignore his hunger and relax. He lets his mind wander over the events of the past few days—allowing his memory to run like a dog to and fro over time, dash between places in the archives of his memory and sniff, scratch, and snoop at will. His visit to the savings bank manager, Ellert, comes quickly to his mind. He imagines the interior of the man's house, the pictures on the walls, the bills he looked through and …

The policeman starts when his cell phone rings through the SUV's sound system. He vaguely recalls the number, but is unable to connect it to a name or face before he answers. But it's a number that he has called before, of that he's certain.

"Yes?"

"I killed someone." The voice belongs to a young man who sounds extremely upset. In other words, he could be telling the truth.

Hörður straightens up. In the same breath, a light appears in his side-view mirror and loud pops assail his ears. Someone is driving down the street on a small motorcycle. "Wait, wait! Who is this?"

"Oddur. I shot him, but only because I had to. You've got to …!"

"Wait!" says Hörður for the third time. He's having a hard time hearing the person on the phone, as someone is driving a scooter, a so-called Vespa, past his SUV. On the Vespa sits a rain-drenched, dark-clad girl with a small backpack and wearing a white helmet. Peeking out from under the helmet are light locks of hair that are pasted to the shoulders and sleeves of the girl's jacket. "Where are you?"

"In front of Oddi, at the university. It's a white building, at the end of…"

"I know where Oddi is," says Hörður as he watches the girl park the Vespa in front of the house where Rut supposedly lives. She shuts off the scooter, steps from it and removes her helmet. He can't see her face, but watches her walk up to the house and disappear into it. It's probably the blonde girl that the woman with the dog said sometimes visited the student on the top floor. "Wait there, don't move, don't make any more calls and don't talk to anyone—I'm on my way."

"I promise. Just be quick."

Hörður hangs up, then calls Axel before turning on his headlights and driving off.

"Yes?"

"The third murder has probably been committed," says Hörður agitatedly. He lowers the side window, then reaches down to the floor behind the passenger seat and grabs a blue beacon light with a magnet on the bottom, switches it on and mounts it on the roof of the car. He's done this so many times before that he hardly needs to take his eyes off the road as he does.

"What the hell!"

"But this time I think we've got the culprit." Hörður drives like a madman through the residential area up to Bústaðavegur Road, where he turns west. The engine growls loudly, the rainwater gushes in all directions, and the tires screech at every turn.

"We do?"

"He himself called, the murderer," says Hörður. "Oddur Bjarnason, the third friend. He was with Patrekur and Bragi at the party in Borgarnes. It's all coming together, I think."

Axel sighs into the phone. *"I truly hope so."*

"I'm on my way to the west side of town, to the university," says Hörður. "Call for the forensics team, an ambulance, and the medical examiner. I'll give a more precise location by radio as soon as I know it."

"Roger! Over and out."

"Finally, finally," hisses Hörður after old Steppenwolf hangs up. He tears at over a hundred kph along Bústaðavegur, past the fire station, runs a red light at the intersection at Skógarhlíð and heads down a curved off-ramp toward the West Side. He's tense but also relieved, since the case seems to be getting clearer now.

Oddur, huh? he thinks to himself. He *knew* the boy was hiding something from him. But he can't say he expected this. He can't really see this neat, well-raised young man as a cold-blooded murderer.

But … The red-haired giant shrugs his shoulders. Nothing is out of the question when it comes to crime and love.

The rain pours down, forming a curtain of water. Oddur is so cold that he's afraid he'll lose consciousness. But maybe it's just because he's so upset. He crouches under the awning of the Department of Social Sciences and waits for the policeman, the big one in the leather coat. He'd promised Lísa that he wouldn't go to the police, but he can't see any other way now. He's done what he needed to do. Since Haukur is dead, he can't kill Lísa. She's safe. That's the only thing that matters right now.

When the loud noise of a car engine breaks the silence and a blue flashing light illuminates the falling rain, Oddur knows that his wait is over. A black Ford Explorer comes tearing into the parking lot in front of Oddi; the driver brakes hard and takes the light off the car's roof before stepping out onto the slippery wet asphalt. It's the red-haired giant. With pursed lips and a focused gleam in his emerald eyes, he stamps toward Oddur.

"You've come," says Oddur in a tremulous voice. "As I said, I killed someone. But I was forced to, you've got to believe me! It was Deathbook—it threatened to …!"

"Shut up, boy!" growls Hörður. Did he say Deathbook? "I'll take a statement from you afterward. Where's the deceased?"

"In the new building just over there, on Sæmundargata Street," Oddur answers dejectedly.

"Who is it?" asks Hörður.

"His name is Haukur," Oddur answers with great effort. "Or it was. Haukur Hansson."

Hörður is stunned. The skinny boy with round glasses? "How did you kill him?"

"I shot him," says Oddur in a weak voice.

"Come on, show me," says Hörður gruffly, before pushing Oddur out from under the shelter of the awning toward his SUV, whose engine is purring in neutral. He opens the back door and shuts it as soon as Oddur has climbed in. Then he gets behind the wheel and drives off.

Hörður gets on the radio, which is tuned to a closed channel and has a specific call sign. "It's the building under construction on Sæmundargata. The new student apartments."

"Copy that," someone replies.

Oddur leans forward in the back seat and points out the windshield. "You can turn there, onto the gravel lot. There's an open gate that ..."

He stops when the red-haired giant looks over his shoulder and gives him the evil eye.

"Take it easy, pal," says Hörður. "Any tricks, and I'll cut off your head, gut you, fillet and salt you—understand?"

"Yes, I ..." Oddur stops talking, straightens up, and hardly dares to breathe.

Hörður drives onto the construction site, switches on his brights, and looks in all directions. "Where exactly?"

Oddur clears his throat. "It's the entrance there, down at the other end. But the gun and the camera are in the trash dumpster there."

"Camera?" exclaims Hörður. He drives farther down the lot and parks the SUV halfway between the dumpster and the entrance that Oddur pointed out. He leaves enough room on both sides for the other cars that are on their way.

"One of those GoPro cameras," Oddur answers. "I had it on my head and recorded everything. I had to do it."

"Very well," says Hörður, who has no idea what the boy is talking about. "We'll fill in the blanks later. Come with me."

Hörður leaves the engine running and the headlights on. Taking a long flashlight with him, he steps out onto the wet, muddy gravel lot and opens the back door.

Oddur's face pales. "Do I have to?"

"If you've killed someone," says Hörður coldly, "then you must be able to look at the body, right?"

Oddur swallows, then pulls himself together and leaves the warmth and safety of the SUV.

"Go on, show me," says Hörður. He pushes the boy lightly, making him lead the way. As the rain pours down on him, Oddur strides over the puddles, gradually approaching the dark entrance for the second time in a short time. If he felt bad when he entered the empty and cold building with a loaded gun, he feels ten times worse now, when he knows what awaits him at the end of the long corridor.

Hörður turns on the flashlight and shines it into the empty building. "Don't touch anything and don't try anything. Where's the body?"

Oddur points randomly into the darkness. "Next corridor to the right. He's there."

"Get moving, then!" Hörður pushes the boy, who stumbles off. They come to the long corridor, turn into it and go on, deeper into the concrete maze. Their footsteps echo in a peculiar rhythm. Oddur takes short, quick steps with his head lowered, worried about seeing the bloody corpse. The policeman takes longer and heavier steps, shining his light at the wall as they go.

"Where?" Hörður asks impatiently.

Oddur hesitates, then looks up. He gapes in amazement. The corridor is empty. There's no corpse—nothing. "But …?"

They're back out in the rain. Hörður's face is like a thundercloud. He's shut off the flashlight and is poking Oddur in the back with it. He drives the boy like a calf over the mud toward the green trash dumpster.

"I don't know where he is now, but he was there!" wails Oddur. "I shot him, I swear!"

"Shut up, boy, and show me where this blessed gun is," growls the red-haired giant.

"Here." Oddur walks around the dumpster, intending to slide the black cover open.

"Don't touch it, idiot!" Hörður practically shoves Oddur aside. He doesn't expect to find anything in the dumpster, but procedure is procedure. He puts on disposable rubber gloves before sliding the cover back.

"It's in a kind of green shoulder bag," mutters Oddur, who is sopping wet and has started shivering again.

Hörður shines the flashlight into the dumpster and immediately sees the bag. He clicks his tongue in surprise. "I'll be damned."

He clamps the flashlight tightly under his right cheek, reaches into the dumpster and carefully opens the bag with his latex-covered fingers. Inside the bag is a kind of gun, which looks to him as if it's homemade. The barrel is black on the inside and he detects a faint smell of powder.

"Bingo," he whispers.

"Isn't it there?" Oddur asks from behind him.

Hörður turns around, sniffs a raindrop up his nose, and sticks the flashlight into the side pocket of his sopping-wet coat. Then he swings his handcuffs forward with a well-practiced movement. "Oddur Bjarnason. You're under arrest, under suspicion of having killed Patrekur Jónsson and Bragi Unnsteinsson and possibly a third individual earlier tonight."

"But …?" Before Oddur knows it, the red-haired giant has pulled his hands behind his back and put him in handcuffs.

"But nothing," says Hörður firmly. No sooner has he handcuffed the youth than a number of flashing lights

illuminate the rain, the darkness, and the stony-gray building. Two police cars, an ambulance, and an unmarked
car belonging to Forensics stream onto the lot. Bringing
up the rear of the caravan is Axel M. Axelsson's silver
Mercedes-Benz SUV. The medical examiner is the only
one yet to show up.

"You wait in the car, and then we'll talk at the station,"
Hörður says to Oddur before helping him up onto the
back seat of the black SUV. Oddur's expression is distant;
he looks helpless and shattered, but is at least out of the
rain.

The first person Hörður meets is Jenný from Forensics.
She's wearing a clear plastic jacket with a hood over plain
work clothes. Uniformed police officers take up positions
beside their cars and wait for further instructions.

"What do we have here?" Jenný asks, going straight to
the point, and without any expression but professional
concentration. She clearly knows how to separate her work
from her private life.

"The boy I just arrested has confessed to murder,"
said the red-haired giant as he brushes a wet lock of
hair from his face. "Oddur Bjarnason. He said that the
body was in the long corridor on the right when going in
through that entrance there. But there's no body. In the
dumpster, though, is some kind of gun that I believe is the
murder weapon we've been looking for. The boy said he
used it earlier, when he shot his alleged victim—Haukur
Hansson."

Jenný nods. "We'll check out the gun and the corridor
where the body's supposed to be. And I guess I'll ask the
officers to search the rest of the building."

"That sounds sensible," says Hörður.

"I'll let you know as soon as we find something," says Jenný, before smiling faintly. "I expect we'll all meet up tomorrow morning, at the latest."

"Great," says Hörður. Jenný goes and talks to her men, who split up, while Hörður goes to speak to Axel, who is stepping between mud puddles in his English leather shoes and holding a large umbrella over his head.

"What's the situation?" asks Steppenwolf.

Hörður sighs heavily. "I've arrested the boy. He's confessed to a murder, but it seems that the body has disappeared. If there was any body. I don't know entirely what to think."

"No body?" asks Axel in surprise.

Hörður shrugs. "But the murder weapon has probably been found. The gun that was used to murder Patrekur and Bragi. That's something, anyway."

"Yes, that's something," mutters Axel, who clearly expected better news.

"I'm bringing the boy to the station to take a statement from him," says Hörður. "Then I'll fill you in better."

Axel looks out from under his umbrella, up into the black night sky. "This has got to stop. This has simply got to stop."

Hörður nods, but says nothing. He doesn't really know if his boss is talking about the rain or the wave of murders.

"You've dried out, I see," says Hörður as he sits down at the metal table in the Swimming Pool, the interrogation room of the Criminal Investigation Department. He lays a couple of things on the table: his handwritten notes and a small box containing Oddur Bjarnason's personal belongings—house keys, cell phone, and credit card. Oddur is sitting opposite him, with damp, tousled hair and wearing borrowed clothes, dark blue sweatpants, and a gray cotton sweater marked with the logo of the Police Association.

Oddur nods, and then coughs. The handcuffs have been removed, but he is so pale and miserable-looking that it's as if he has all the worries of the world on his shoulders.

Hörður looks at his watch. It's past midnight, he's tired, and the detainee seems exhausted, if not actually feverish. But he has to take an initial statement from the boy before proceeding; anything else would be untenable.

"Let's start with this," says the policeman, before stating the place and time into a digital voice recorder, as well as the name and address of the detainee. "You called me and said you'd killed someone—Haukur Hansson, right?"

Oddur coughs. "Yes."

"No body was found, but we'll deal with that later," says Hörður wearily. "You confessed to a murder. Why did you kill this person?"

"I had to," says Oddur in a hollow voice. "Deathbook ordered me to do it."

Hörður knits his brow. "Deathbook?"

Oddur nods. "It's a page on Facebook, a kind of 'like page'—Deathbook. I got a request from a friend to like the page. Then I started getting messages from it. It asked me to put someone on a death list. You know, who you would want out of your life, something like that. I don't quite remember how it was worded. But in the end, I chose Bragi, even though I thought it was just nonsense, some stupid game. But then Bragi was killed, and after that I was given a subject. I was supposed to kill someone; otherwise Lísa

would be killed. That's how it works. You get your wish fulfilled, but in return, you have fulfill someone else's wish, or
someone close to you dies."

"Hm, so Lísa is Lísa Kristjánsdóttir, or what?" asks
Hörður, who doesn't quite understand what he's hearing,
but notes it all down immediately.

"Yes, that's why I did as I was told," says Oddur. "To save
Lísa. I didn't know this Haukur at all, but ..."

"Wait a minute," says Hörður, interrupting Oddur.
"Let's just go back a bit. What friend asked you to *like* this
page?"

"It was a girl, Sunna Sæmundsdóttir," Oddur answers.
"But it was probably a fake profile. You know, not a real person, but a made-up account."

"Okay," Hörður mutters as he makes a note of this.
"Here, can you show it to me on your phone? This page."

"Yes, of course," says Oddur.

Hörður hands him his phone, and they both lean
over the table. "Still, make sure not to delete anything or
something like that. I'm watching you."

Oddur nods. He unlocks the phone, opens Facebook
and enters "Deathbook" in the search box. But nothing
comes up.

"Strange," says Oddur, fidgeting in his seat, as if he doesn't feel well. "But the messages from Deathbook must still
be here."

He closes Facebook and opens Messenger, then starts as
if having been jolted with electricity.

"What?" asks Hörður, who is paying attention both to
the screen and the reactions of the detainee.

"The messages should be at the top of the list, but ..."
Oddur points to the top line of the messaging app. There

stands the name *Áslaug*, and next to it is a small circular picture, a so-called chat head, of a smiling blonde whom Hörður recognizes immediately. It's one of the twin sisters from Borgarnes, the daughter of Ellert the savings bank manager.

"But what?" Hörður asks cautiously.

Oddur taps the chat head and the entire conversation opens. "These are the messages from Deathbook! But ...? Why is ...? Everything has changed! The name and the picture. Why Áslaug? She isn't connected to this, is she? Not unless ...?"

"Not unless what?" Hörður sees that the messages are connected to this alleged murder. On the screen are instructions for the messages' recipient on getting the gun from a green trash dumpster, and so on.

"The picture was of a skull, on a black background," says Oddur. "The page itself was all very black, you know, deathly. Lots of skulls and the Grim Reaper and all sorts of *dark memes* and such."

"And you liked it?" asks Hörður. He actually isn't as surprised or shocked as he pretends to be. He would no doubt have liked such a thing when he was eighteen. But there was no *Internet* then, maybe thankfully.

"I'm going to check one thing," mutters Oddur. He clicks on the chat head, and a kind of information page about the person opens. At the top is the picture, and below it are a few options. Oddur chooses the option to view the person's profile on Facebook, but instead of it opening there, a pale gray, dreary screen appears along with the message *Unable to load page.*

Oddur coughs into his clenched fist, then points at the screen. "Look, the page has been deleted."

"When was the last time you talked to Áslaug?" asks Hörður. He takes the phone from Oddur and puts it back in the box.

"The night of the party," says Oddur. "Why?"

Hörður regards the boy for a few moments. He seems to be telling the truth. But he also looks ill. His eyes are watery, he's red around the nose and he coughs now and then.

"Áslaug is dead," says the policeman.

"What?" Oddur is clearly stunned. It's as if he's been slapped. "What do you mean, dead? What ...? When ...?"

Oddur's reaction seems genuine. He's obviously shaken. The red-haired giant can't help but feel sorry for this boy. Of course, he did confess to a murder, but since no body was found, it might be a bit harsh putting him in custody. Or what? Hörður is startled out of these speculations when his cell phone rings. He grunts, looks at the screen, and sees that it's Jenný. Feeling somewhat flustered, he has to take a deep breath before answering.

"Yes?"

"Sorry for the inconvenience. You're probably in the middle of your questioning?"

"In fact, I am," says Hörður, without taking his eyes off of Oddur, who mutters incomprehensibly to himself and stares into space.

"Just as I thought. But this can't wait."

"Oh?"

"As you know, we were investigating Bragi's computer and phone. We tried to find out who it was that lured him to Sævarhöfði, but didn't get anywhere. Other communications of his were neglected, including those with Oddur Bjarnason. But they may matter now."

"Tell me what you've got," says Hörður. He glances inquiringly at Oddur, who looks away, furtively. Or is it desperately?

"On Wednesday evening, Bragi sent Oddur a photo. The photo was probably taken in Ibiza, where they were on vacation, those friends. The picture shows Oddur in bed with a girl, two actually. They're all naked and having fun, if you know what I mean."

"And what?" asks Hörður, who knows *very well* what she means.

"The photo is accompanied by a message from Bragi, threatening to send it to Lísa if Oddur doesn't stop seeing her. And with that, Oddur has a motive for killing Bragi, doesn't he?"

"That could be," says Hörður. "Have you examined the alleged murder weapon?"

"No, but all the analytical work will hopefully be completed before our meeting tomorrow morning. It would help us to have Oddur's phone and computer as soon as possible."

"I'll get the phone to you, in any case. There are particular messages on it that I'd like to ask you to take a closer look at," says Hörður. "See you in the morning."

"Sounds good."

Hörður hangs up and puts the phone back in his pocket.

"What was that?" Oddur asks anxiously.

"Nothing you need to know about at the moment. But that's enough for tonight," says the red-haired giant. "I'm going to ask a doctor to have a look at you. Then you should try to get some rest, and we'll talk again in the morning."

"You said Áslaug was dead?" Oddur is clearly extremely distraught, and/or is feeling feverish. "What happened? And when?"

"We'll talk more about all of this in the morning," says Hörður dryly.

"All right," Oddur whimpers. "Are you going to bring me home or …?"

Hörður shakes his head. "You're sleeping here, my boy. You confessed to a murder and we're allowed to hold suspects for twenty-four hours before they're released or brought before a judge."

He says this with a bad taste in his mouth, as the cells at the Hverfisgata Street station are terribly uncomfortable. Each is basically just a small, cold stone box with a strong steel door, a hard bed, and a thin mattress. The night will no doubt be difficult for the boy.

"But …?" Oddur is on the verge of tears.

"A gun was found," says Hörður. "And you admitted to firing it. The gun is being examined, fingerprints taken from it and so on. As things stand now, we can't allow you to leave here. Many questions remain unanswered."

"I understand," whispers Oddur.

"You're allowed one phone call," says Hörður in a fatherly tone. "For example, it wouldn't be a bad idea contacting a lawyer."

Oddur nods. "Maybe tomorrow, huh? Will you let Albert and Jónína know that I'm here?"

"I'll do that," says Hörður.

SUNDAY

"Seven is a lucky number," says Axel M. Axelsson with the conviction of a preacher. "This is our seventh morning meeting, if I'm not mistaken, and God grant it will be the last … knock on wood."

He knocks three times on the long table with his bent index finger.

"Amen," mutters Hörður, while Jený and Benedikt content themselves with saying "mm-hmm" and nodding their heads in agreement.

It's eight o'clock on Sunday morning and the atmosphere in the operations room is tense, which the attendees know very well can be both a good and a bad sign. The case is either about to be wrapped up, or it's taking a new and unexpected turn for the worse. The only thing that's certain is that *something* is going on—the atmosphere, in any case, is ominous, as if a storm is in the offing.

"What a strange set of circumstances last night," says Axel. "The third murder turned out to be some sort of hoax, yet a suspect is in custody and the alleged murder weapon is being analyzed. Maybe you should start, Jený."

Benedikt raises his hand. "Just one thing first, if I may."

"You may," says Axel.

"Thanks, I'll be quick." Benedikt unfolds a memo. "A call was made to the Emergency Number last night, a minute and a half before Oddur called Hörður. The caller didn't give a name, but it sounded like a woman. This woman said she lived on Eggertsgata Street. She said she heard shots and saw flashes of light from the new building to the north of her street. Then she thought she saw someone poking around at a nearby trash dumpster."

"What was the number she dialed from?" asks Axel.

"It turned out to be of a cell phone that had been missing for more than a week," says Benedikt. "It belonged to a teenager at Hagaskóli Middle School, but the number was registered to his mother. The phone has been switched off ever since it was used to call the Emergency Number."

"Strange," says Hörður.

"The murderer?" Jenný asks.

Hörður nods. "Not out of the question."

"Thanks, Benedikt," says Axel, before asking Jenný for her report.

Jenný clears her throat. "Let's start with the gun, which turned out to be a homemade plastic gun, .44 caliber. The material in it is so-called ABS plastic, the same as in Lego bricks. It's a common type of plastic, used quite a bit for 3D printing. I believe the gun was printed in such a device. We *haven't confirmed* that this is the murder weapon we were looking for, as we don't have a bullet fired from it. So it's probably not the gun that was used to kill Patrekur and Bragi, but naturally, that can't be ruled out."

"But the fact that we found the gun must be considered significant," says Benedikt. Axel and Hörður agree with him.

"But this wasn't the gun that disappeared," says Axel. "The Smith & Wesson belonging to Police Chief Andrés."

"Which weakens the Borgarnes connection," Hörður admits. Axel agrees.

"But where's the police chief's gun?" Benedikt asks.

"Good question," mutters Hörður.

"Except," says Jenný. "On the plastic gun we found only Oddur Bjarnason's fingerprints, which fits in with his account of last night's events. In the gun was an empty cartridge, and its barrel was black with soot and damaged by heat. In other words, the gun had been fired, which also confirms Oddur's statement. No body was found, as you know, no blood or other evidence of a violent crime, but traces of gunpowder were found in the corridor where Oddur said he'd shot a young man, as well as on Oddur's clothes and on the fingers of his right hand. We have no reason to doubt his story, except for the body of a victim not being found."

Axel nods. "Thank you, Jenný. We'll go into more detail about the body later. Hörður, how is the detainee doing?"

"He was extremely shaken last night, but he was also wet and cold," says Hörður. "I had a doctor examine him and it appears that stress did a number on him; he had a fever and a bad cold—a sinus infection. The doctor prescribed antibiotics and painkillers, as well as cough syrup. In other words, Oddur isn't entirely healthy, but he isn't so sick that it's a cause for concern. He confessed to a murder, but was as surprised as all of us when no body was found. I didn't really think I could keep him in custody, but as has been stated, his fingerprints are on the weapon, which could possibly be the gun with which his friends were killed, and it also appears that Bragi threatened him, which gives him a motive to have killed Bragi—sort of."

"Sort of?" asks Axel in surprise.

Hörður shrugs. "Bragi threatened to wreck Oddur's relationship with Lísa Kristjánsdóttir. That hardly seems to be a reason for murder now, does it?"

"Maybe not," says Axel. "But this wouldn't be the first time something like that has happened. But what's your opinion on what happened last night? And by that I mean the body that disappeared—if there ever was anybody to begin with. "

"There is no Haukur Hansson," says Hörður. "I've actually talked to the boy whom Oddur says he killed. His name may be Haukur, but he's definitely not a Hansson. There are only two people with that name; one is about ninety years old, and the other is five."

"This patronymic was often given to fatherless boys in the old days," says Axel. "Hansson means 'his son.' Jenný, will you start?"

"Of course," Jenný replies. "But before I get to the body, I need to share some new information that will change some aspects of the big picture, if not everything."

"Well?" says Axel, both hopeful and prepared for disappointment. Hörður is all eyes and ears.

"As we were finishing up at the scene yesterday, we found something that we'd all overlooked," says Jenný in her deep voice. "Someone had attached a spy camera to a construction crane on the site. A small, battery-powered camera with night vision and Wi-Fi. Whoever it was that attached the camera there was able to monitor our every movement at the scene via a computer or phone."

"What the hell!" says Axel.

Hörður knits his brow, as always when he sinks deeply into thought.

"Do you think the camera was connected to a wireless network?" asks Benedikt. "Because if so, can't we find out to which computer or phone? Aren't such things traceable?"

Jenný shrugs. "Yes and no. The camera has 4G, but also Bluetooth. If it was connected to a cell phone via Bluetooth, that can't be traced, any more than radio waves. Not to mention if the phone was stolen or a disposable one. And as for the camera itself, it's possible to order the same from foreign websites quite cheaply."

"The person who set up the camera may have been the same one who called the Emergency Number," says Benedikt. "The person in question wanted to get the police to come and then monitor their work through the security camera."

"He wanted Oddur to be arrested?" Jený suggests.

Hörður nods, as it's difficult to conclude anything else.

"But what would that person learn from the recordings?" asks Axel.

"One thing and another," Hörður says. "For example, that the police aren't only on the trail of whoever's behind this wave of murders, but also have the murder weapon in their hands and a suspect in custody, Oddur Bjarnason. The big question is this: is this information useful to that person or not?"

"Go on," says Axel.

Hörður clears his throat. "We can make three fairly credible conjectures at this stage. The first is that Oddur is the murderer, but is trying to make it look as if he's a puppet of some unknown individual. In this scenario, it's Oddur who had the ecstasy tablets that killed Eva Andrésdóttir, making him responsible for her death. Patrekur and Bragi knew it, but no one else. That gave them control over him, and they may have used the information against him or threatened to spill the beans in order to clear their own consciences. So he decided to get them out of the way and put on a huge show to hide his path, creating pages and fake characters on Facebook. As has been pointed out, the murder weapon is homemade, which means that anyone could have made it, right?"

Benedikt shrugs. "All it needed was a 3D printer and software, I think?"

"I buy this hypothesis completely," says Jenný.

"But you don't believe it yourself, do you?" Axel asks the red-haired giant.

"That's neither here nor there, for now," says Hörður. "Conjecture number two postulates that this Haukur Hansson is the perpetrator. Oddur and I have both talked to that boy who calls himself Haukur, but I don't know anything about him and Oddur says he doesn't know him. He told Oddur that he was from Borgarnes, that he'd been at the party this past summer and that I'd questioned him as a witness after the murder of Patrekur. The last bit is a lie, but what if the rest is true? What if this Haukur is from Borgarnes and wants revenge for the death of Eva Andrésdóttir? He could be her friend, classmate, or cousin. One thing is certain, and that's that this punk has been snooping around me and this investigation from the beginning."

"Very interesting," says Axel heavily. "We need to find out who he is. You don't have a photo of him?"

"No, sorry," says Hörður. "But he's definitely recognizable. It would be very easy to describe him to a sketch artist."

"The person we're looking for has done his homework well," says Jenný. "This communication via Facebook and other text messages reveal that and prove that the person in question knows the people he's bullying and how to handle them. He's no amateur or idiot. He made preparations for weeks or months. Created at least two fake Facebook profiles and one Facebook page, in addition to which, the person in question got hold of a disposable cell phone and a spy camera, as well as a 3D printer. If I were to imagine what sort of person this perpetrator is, I would in fact guess a seclusive young male with whom no one is acquainted or knows anything about. It would be a textbook example."

"I agree," says Axel. "We've *got* to find this boy. He *must* not remain on the loose."

"You're right," says Hörður. "Yet the biggest question in this particular hypothesis is this: has this Haukur gotten his revenge or not? If he was avenging Eva's death, shouldn't he have killed Oddur instead of asking Oddur to kill him?"

"You've got a point there," Axel mutters after a moment.

"And maybe there was a blank in the gun?" Hörður adds. "Did Haukur stage his death? Did he want Oddur to think that he'd killed him? Maybe, but why, then? Oddur said he'd been wearing a GoPro camera on his head. A camera that was in the bag with the gun. He said he put both back in the bag, but there was no camera there when I opened it. Someone took it."

"What was the purpose of that GoPro camera?" Benedikt asks.

"I don't know," replies Hörður. "But I'll try to find out."

"Maybe there was never any camera?" Jenný suggests.

Hörður shrugs. "Which means that Oddur is lying."

"Those are good and valid questions, Hörður," says Axel. "And they kind of kick the supports out from under hypothesis number two, don't they?"

"They don't strengthen it, that much is certain," says Hörður.

Jenný heaves a sigh. "But you've got a third theory, or what?"

Hörður nods. "It has to do with a person about whom we know, except for *where* she is. I'm talking about Rut Ellertsdóttir, Eva's cousin. She's been more or less confined to a wheelchair in recent years due to a nervous breakdown or some sort of mental collapse in the wake of her mother's suicide. In other words, her disability is psychological and not physical—and in any case, she's no longer confined to the wheelchair. She was at home when the party was held in the summer, but didn't give a statement because she was stuck on the upper floor of the house and therefore didn't personally attend the party, and didn't see what went on on the lower floor. But I feel it fairly certain that the murders of Patrekur and Bragi are connected to what happened in Borgarnes that fateful evening. I sent you all a summary of those events yesterday morning, if I remember correctly."

Axel, Jenný, and Benedikt nod in confirmation.

"I haven't been able to find Rut yet, nor to reach her by phone, which both bothers me and makes me very suspicious," says Hörður. "Why doesn't she want to be contacted? Why is she hiding? What I do know is that Rut is seeing a psychologist, and is probably struggling with mental illness."

"Isn't everyone seeing a psychologist these days?" Jenný asks.

"Mental illness doesn't mean a propensity for violence," Benedikt adds.

"Let Hörður finish," says Axel.

"Thanks," mutters the red-haired giant. "Rut is listed as living in her uncle's top-floor apartment on Drápuhlíð Street, but doesn't appear to live there. A neighbor claims that there's a boy living there, a student. Rut is enrolled at Hamrahlíð Junior College, but has hardly ever shown up for class this autumn. Her father never hears from her and she never goes home to the west, as far as I understand. Where is she? And what does she do?"

"Good question," says Axel.

"But if Rut is the perpetrator," says Jený, "how is she connected to this Haukur? And why didn't they kill Oddur? Why this drama? Why is this 'murder' not a murder but something else entirely?"

"I don't know," says Hörður with a sigh.

"But what do you want to do?" asks Axel.

Hörður clears his throat. "I want us to put out a wanted notice for Rut. I want to get into that apartment on Drápuhlíð, if not with the owner's permission, then with a warrant. I'm going to track down the psychologist. I also want us to have a sketch drawn of Haukur Hansson, and put out a wanted notice for him as well. I'll question Oddur again, dig deeper if I can, after we're done here. I'll also have a better talk with Ellert, Rut's father."

"Very well," says Axel after thinking things over for a moment. "Let's do this."

"Do you think that others are in danger?" asks Benedikt. "Or has revenge been taken, so to speak?"

"Lísa was threatened too, wasn't she?" Jený asks. "That was why Oddur thought he had to kill this Haukur. To save Lísa, right?"

Hörður thinks over her questions. "Since this case is almost certainly connected with what happened in Borgarnes, I believe that there's little or no chance that anyone else is in danger. Patrekur and Bragi are dead and Oddur is in custody. Lísa is connected to the case indirectly, and she was probably threatened only to get to Oddur. I'll contact Lísa today, but I don't think she or anyone else is in any danger. And besides, the gun is in our hands."

Axel nods. "I believe that Hörður is on the right track in all of this."

The red-haired giant blushes with pride. But at the same time, he feels that he doesn't deserve any praise. Not yet, at least.

"There's just one thing I don't understand," says Jenný.

"What's that?" asks Axel.

"Why wasn't Oddur killed?" she asks.

Hörður takes a deep breath. "This is bothering me too, but not much—not at the moment. It's a good question. And I'm going to find out the answer. But number one, two, and three is to find the perpetrator—the murderer of Patrekur and Bragi."

"Right," Axel says emphatically.

Jenný grins coldly. "Oddur's fingerprints are on the gun. Maybe he's the culprit, but has been deceiving us the entire time—and is still deceiving us!"

"Maybe," Hörður mutters, while doubts about everything he's thought, said, and done flow unhindered into his bloodstream.

They're sitting together in the Swimming Pool for the fourth time, Hörður Grímsson and Oddur Bjarnason. The former is no longer sure that the answers he's looking for are to be found in Borgarnes. But at the same time, he can't stop thinking about the *town by the bridge*, as the locals call it. The latter is pale-skinned and watery-eyed, red around the nose and hoarse from his cold. He looks as if he slept both little and badly—and has been crying a lot, for a long time.

"You didn't kill anyone, did you?" Hörður asks gravely.

Oddur shakes his head.

"Tell me about the messages," says Hörður. "From this Deadbook. Was that its name?"

"Deathbook—it was called Deathbook," Oddur replies.

"When did it start?" asks Hörður. "And how many people got messages from it?"

"I only know about myself and Lísa, but I'm sure there were others," says Oddur. He then tells the story in as much detail as he can. He explains the events of the past week as they appear to him. Tells about the creepy Facebook game that starts as a kind of mordant joke but turns into a deadly game of tag in which participants are forced to kill each other according to a system that's both simple and ruthless.

"The only way to get out of it seems to be to kill someone," Oddur says in a hollow voice. "But that's not enough, because someone may have himself as a subject and …"

With a hopeless expression, Oddur throws up his hands.

Hörður finishes noting down the main points, then takes a deep breath through his nose. "You said that you and Lísa had been sent videos of the murders. A kind of confirmation of the killing."

Oddur nods. "She of the murder of Bragi, I of the murder of Patrekur. You could watch it once, and then it was gone. It was on a website that's been taken down."

"You didn't see her video?" asks Hörður.

Oddur shakes his head. "But it was probably a recording from a GoPro camera like the one I was sent, recorded with the same camera that I had on my head. And now the person who put Haukur on the death list has no doubt received the video that shows someone shooting him."

"Right," mutters Hörður as he thinks about it all. So it is a game, as he suspected—if a game it could be called. But who runs the game, and what is its purpose?

"Is Áslaug really dead?" Oddur asks suddenly. "How can that be?"

Hörður grunts. He feels for this boy. But he can't let his emotions affect his work.

"Let's start at the beginning," says the red-haired giant. "Let's start with the party in Borgarnes. And now I want to hear the truth. For example, whose ecstasy pills were they?"

Oddur clears his throat. "They were Bragi's."

"Keep going," says Hörður.

Oddur recounts the events of that fateful evening, telling the policeman the truth. He speaks slowly and omits nothing. Hörður listens, nods, and makes various notes in his notepad.

"I left her there on the bridge," says Oddur. "She didn't want to go back with me. And I haven't seen her since. When I get back to the house, there's a big commotion. Eva is unconscious in the kitchen and ..."

His voice breaks. Oddur coughs and takes a drink of water from the glass that Hörður brought him before the questioning started.

"I know what happened next," says Hörður. "It's in the reports. Unless they're not telling the whole truth?"

Oddur shakes his head. Then he tells Hörður how Bragi signaled to him to get rid of the box holding the pills. He said that he put it in the trash bin in the driveway.

"Did anyone see you put it there?" asks Hörður.

"I don't think so," says Oddur. "But someone took it, didn't they? That must have been what happened, right?"

"It seems so," mutters Hörður, distracted. He's looking for a dangerous murderer. But he isn't looking for him out on the streets, but inside his own head, in the dense jungle that has grown there during the investigation of this case. He's an explorer in the innermost darkness of the human soul, with logic and intuition as his weapons. And he travels ever farther, ever deeper …

"But Áslaug?" Oddur asks in a broken voice. "What happened to her?"

Hörður sighs. "She drowned in Brákarsund. She probably jumped off the bridge. Suicide. I'm sorry."

Oddur's face pales.

When Lísa opens her eyes, she realizes that she's probably managed to get some sleep, even if not very well or for very long—fragments of countless nightmares float around in her mind; her duvet is moist with sweat, her mouth is dry, and she has a bad headache and rapid heartbeat. The curtains are drawn and the air inside her room is heavy and stale. On her nightstand is a half-empty glass of water and a pack of anti-anxiety tablets. She washes one down and hopes it works quickly and effectively.

Wearing her nightgown, she goes to the kitchen. Her mother is there seasoning a leg of lamb, which is doubtless for dinner. The wall clock reads ten-thirty. Lísa sits down at the kitchen table and looks around, half asleep and half stiff.

"How are you, my love?" her mother asks cheerfully.

"I …" Her voice breaks. Lísa clears her throat, and then quickly changes the subject. "Where are the boys?"

She really can't stand it when her mother talks about Lísa's father and brother as *the boys*. It's just so cringing and un-feministic. As if they're some cool guys who are always doing something macho and exciting, while the mom waits at home with cakes and food for them.

"Your dad went golfing after it stopped raining," says her mother. "Lárus went up to Borgarnes with his friend Palli and his father. The basketball tournament is today."

Lísa stiffens. Her heart begins beating faster; her mouth goes dry and her anxiety ramps up. "Where did he go? With whom? What did you say?"

"Oh, the basketball tournament," her mother says without looking up. "It's what he was selling the toilet paper for. They decided not to splurge on a bus, but just carpool. He went with Palli's dad."

"Borgarnes," says Lísa to herself. Where the party was. Where the girl died. They went there together: Patrekur, Bragi, and Oddur. Bragi brought ecstasy pills with him; everyone knows that. And the girl took too many. That Eva. And now Patrekur and Bragi are dead. Only Oddur is left.

And she's supposed to kill him …

"Is everything okay?" asks her mother. "You look like you've seen a ghost!"

"Yes, I …" Lísa blinks a couple of times. "Can we go get Lárus? Can we go now and …?"

She stops when she hears her phone ringing. It's still on the nightstand in her room, ringing over and over.

"Lísa dear, what are you saying?" her mother asks worriedly.

"My phone," Lísa says. She gets to her feet, nearly losing her balance due to the sedative effects of the anti-anxiety drug, and then hurries to her room and answers the phone. "Yes, hello?"

"Lísa Kristjánsdóttir?"

Still feeling dizzy, she sits down on the edge of the bed. "Yes?"

"This is Hörður Grímsson from the Criminal Investigation Department of the Reykjavík Police. We chatted the other day."

"Yes?" asks Lísa, half paralyzed with anxiety.

"I don't know if you're aware of it, but Oddur Bjarnason is in custody. He's told me about this person who's been sending you messages. The one calling himself Deathbook."

"Oh?" Lísa tries to digest what the policeman is saying. "Where is Oddur, did you say?"

"He's here at the Hverfisgata Street station. You don't need to worry about him."

"No?" asks Lísa.

"No, this case is hopefully being wrapped up. But I would like to have your phone examined, and your computer if you've used it in these interactions. By that I mean those messages, from this particular person."

Lísa swallows. "But this isn't over. Oddur is still alive. I've been threatened. My brother has been threatened with death. And he's in Borgarnes!"

"Your brother's in Borgarnes?"

"Yes! At some basketball tournament." Lísa is on the verge of tears. "Can't you have him picked up? If anything happens to him, I'll …!"

Lísa gets a lump in her throat. From the vestibule comes the cheerful ringing of the doorbell. She hears her mother go to the door.

"I'll ask the police in Borgarnes to be on the alert. But you don't need to worry. All you have to do is bring your phone and computer to me here at the station. Can you do that?"

"Yes," whimpers Lísa. "If you promise that nothing will happen to my brother."

"I promise."

"Okay." Lísa hangs up. Then she goes straight onto Messenger to see if there are any new messages from Deathbook. Which turns out not to be the case. She can't even find Deathbook.

Is the nightmare really over?

She shakes out two anti-anxiety tablets and swallows them with warm water.

"Lísa, dear?"

She looks up. Her mother is standing in the doorway, holding a package in brown wrapping paper.

"Someone brought this for you."

Lísa takes the package, which is both small and light. "Who?"

Her mother shrugs. "A blonde girl. She was on a little motorcycle. One of your friends?"

"Yes," says Lísa, just to say something. Her mother returns to the kitchen, but Lísa sits back down on the edge of the bed and tears open the package. She has a bad feeling about this. Beneath the brown paper is a plastic bag wrapped around three things—a newspaper clipping, white tablets in a small plastic bag, and a typewritten letter. The letter is to her. It contains detailed instructions.

Lísa bites her lower lip and rocks in place as she reads the letter. What she reads causes her physical discomfort—a headache, numbness, and nausea. She should call the policeman back immediately—the red-haired giant who said he had Oddur in custody. But she doesn't dare, because the letter writer warns her of the consequences if she disobeys him in any way.

But what she is being asked to do is just so horrible that she can't imagine carrying it out.

But does she have a choice?

"Oh, God," whimpers Lísa. She takes her phone and, with trembling fingers, taps in a number. But it's not the number of the policeman, but rather, the priest who spoke so beautifully about Patrekur at the memorial service at HJC.

Lísa gets up and circles the room. She presses the phone to her ear, wipes away tears from the corners of her eyes and looks at that cursed letter as the phone rings at the other end.

The letter is signed by Deathbook.

Hörður is sitting at his work station in the Cave, with his computer on, trying to ignore the pain in his lower back and the muscle strain in his shoulders and neck. He's in need of a warm bath and a change of clothes; he's hungry, tired, and glassy from cup after cup of coffee. His desk is covered with memos and reports. But the chaos in the real world is in no way comparable to that inside his head, it being of a cosmic magnitude. He feels like he needs to be in at least five places at once, and at the same time, to be doing a million different things. But he can of course only do one thing at a time.

He heaves a sigh, lifts the receiver of his office phone, dials 0 for an outside line and punches in the number of Ellert, the savings bank manager, who answers after a few rings.

"This is Hörður Grímsson, police detective," says the red-haired giant.

"I recognized the number." The bank manager's voice is lifeless and flat, as if coming from a machine rather than a body of flesh and blood.

"Have you heard from your daughter?" Hörður asks directly.

"No."

"When did you hear from her last?" As Hörður waits for an answer, he hears Ellert's breathing. So he must be of flesh and blood after all.

"It's been more than a week. Maybe ten days."

"I see," says Hörður. "But the thing is, I need to talk to her. It's important. So important that we'll be putting out a wanted notice for her."

"A wanted notice?"

"Yes, on the radio and then on television if necessary," says Hörður. "If that doesn't work, we'll be forced to issue an arrest warrant."

"What has she done?"

Hörður sighs. "We don't know. Maybe nothing, but maybe she's involved in the case I'm investigating. But first and foremost, I think she knows something."

"I see."

"Tell me, does she have a friend or cousin of a similar age?" asks Hörður. "I'm also looking for a short, skinny boy. With a shaved head and round glasses. He says he has cancer, but it isn't necessarily true."

"The description doesn't ring any bells."

"What about a blonde girlfriend or cousin?" asks Hörður. "Slender, long hair. Drives around on a scooter, one of those Vespas."

"Rut doesn't have any friends, to my knowledge," Ellert says after a short silence. His voice is so sad and hopeless that it's depressing just hearing it.

"Well then," says Hörður. "But you know where to find me if you remember anything or have something to tell me."

"Yes."

"And keep your phone close," says Hörður gruffly. "I may need to speak to you again today."

After hanging up, Hörður gets to his feet, stretches a little, and then goes and knocks on the door of the department head.

"Come in!" barks Axel M. Axelsson from inside the office.

"Just to keep you informed," says the red-haired giant as he walks into the air-conditioned room.

"Something new?" asks Axel.

"Not really," Hörður answers. "Ellert hasn't heard from his daughter in about ten days. Which forces us to put out a wanted notice for her. I called Police Chief Andrés, and he gave me permission to enter the apartment on Drápuhlíð."

"Good to know," says Axel. "So they're being cooperative, the brothers?"

Hörður nods. "Up until now. But neither of them recognized the boy who said his name was Haukur or of the blonde girl who called me from the bakery at Suðurver—not from the descriptions."

"I see. What about the boy, Oddur Bjarnason?" asks Axel. "How is he?"

Hörður shrugs. "He's doing well, given the circumstances. He has a cold and is in custody on suspicion of having killed two of his friends. Naturally, he isn't exactly a barrel of laughs. But they're keeping a close eye on him down there."

"Yes," mutters Axel. "But then what? Could he be guilty? And he staged that play last night to mislead us?"

"I can't rule it out," says Hörður. "He's contacted a lawyer, a friend of the family. The lawyer wants to be present when and if I talk to Oddur again, and also if we request that he be kept in custody."

"Which we'll do?" asks Axel.

Hörður nods. "If nothing new comes out before midnight today that demonstrates his innocence, we can hardly release him. His fingerprints are on the murder weapon and his alibi is weak. He could have killed his friends."

Hörður Grímsson is standing slouched on the narrow staircase in front of the door of the top-floor apartment on Drápuhlíð while the locksmith does his work. The detective uses the time to put on disposable latex gloves and a hairnet.

"Got it," says the professional, as the lock clicks open.

"Thanks." Hörður steps over the threshold, while the locksmith packs his gear and leaves.

The apartment has around fifty square meters of floor space, but since its ceiling is sloping, those square meters can't be used to their full advantage. The ceiling constricts the apartment on all sides and makes it difficult for the red-haired giant to walk around in it, except right in the middle where the ceiling is highest. The first thing he notices is a marked absence. He sees no shoes and no coats, and in the bathroom there are no toiletries other than a roll of toilet paper. On the sink, however, is a smudge that might be from mascara or something similar—he's seen similar smudges at his own place, after Bíbí, the woman he's living with, *puts on a face*, as she calls it.

The apartment feels empty, as if no one lives in it. There's a single bed in the bedroom, but it has only a mattress, no duvet or pillow. Hörður kneels down and peeks under the bed, but sees only dust and fluff. He does, however, spot a long, blonde hair hanging on the side of the spring mattress.

He removes the hair with a pair of tweezers and sticks it in a small envelope.

There are no dirty dishes in the kitchen and the refrigerator is empty, apart from an old, nearly empty bottle of ketchup and one onion that has begun to sprout. In the room that could be called a living room are an old sofa, a matching chair, and a teak desk. On top of the desk is a stylish electronic device that Hörður doesn't recognize at first. The device is box-shaped, the size of an oven, and mainly empty. It is in fact a box. The box can be opened, and inside it is a complex electrical apparatus that can be moved to and fro. A white plastic cord runs from a spool on the outside of the box to the interior apparatus. The spool and cord remind Hörður of the handline reels used on small boats. The cord is like fishing line, only thicker and softer.

Hörður takes a photo of the device with his phone and sends it to Jenný. Then he opens the desk's drawers. In one of them are two pairs of pliers: needle-nose and classic pincers. He examines the pliers carefully, and finds subtle traces of metal on their teeth. He sticks each pair into its own plastic bag, which he zips shut.

He takes a deep breath, then calls Jenný. He's still half devastated after sleeping with and being rejected by her, but since they're working together on this case, he has to push all his emotions aside.

"Hi."

"Hello," says Hörður. "Did you see the picture I sent you?"

"Yes, it's a 3D printer. The gun we found was made in such a printer. At Drápuhlíð?"

"That's right," says Hörður. He looks in amazement at what's apparently a 3D printer, and can't for the life of him imagine how firearms can be conjured from such an apparatus.

"Is there no computer connected to it?"

"No, there's nothing else here, really," says Hörður. "But I've found two pliers with traces of metal on them and one hair—long and blonde. I'll get them to the forensics lab."

"Great. Then we'll be in touch."

"Yep," says Hörður. He hangs up and sticks his phone in his pocket. His hands are trembling, his heart is beating fast, and his mouth is dry. That deep-voiced giantess still has a grip on him. If she told him to jump off a cliff, he probably wouldn't hesitate.

Oddur might as well be underground, in a dungeon deep beneath a medieval castle made of hewn rock. All that's missing is dampness, cockroaches, and rats. The walls are blue-gray and absorb the faint light that slips through the thick plastic protecting the bulb from damage. The thick paint is riddled with obscene drawings, names, dates, threats, and pornography, scratched there by previous detainees. The door is made of thick steel and has a narrow peephole. In one corner is a disgusting steel toilet with neither a seat nor a lid. He's sitting on his cell's hard bunk with a woolen blanket over his shoulders, rocking forward and back. He's congested, with a cold, a fever, a bad headache, and a dry cough. The cell is very small and confined and seems to become even more confined with each passing minute. And every single minute in this black hole is an eternity of confinement and discomfort.

He called a lawyer, an acquaintance of Dr. Albert's, who advised him not to talk to the police any more, at least not unless he was present. He said he would come and be there when and if Oddur was brought before a judge. He also said that a prosecutor could *probably* have him remanded in custody, but they would have to wait and find out. Then he would be sent east to Litla-Hraun Prison, to the remand unit there. To Oddur, it sounded like a death sentence. Litla-Hraun is a big, disgusting prison far out in the countryside, full of rapists, drug dealers, hatchet men, and murderers. Inmates there have committed suicide or been killed by other inmates. Finally, the lawyer gave Oddur a bit of an earful for calling the police *following the incident*, as he put it. Oddur interpreted the rebuke to mean that he'd practically dug his own grave by confessing to the murder of Haukur, even though no body had been found. Maybe he'd misunderstood the lawyer's words or misheard something, as he thought he heard a gust of wind over his cell phone and then a clicking sound, as if someone were hitting golf balls. But whether …

Oddur starts when the door of his prison cell is unlocked with accompanying clangs and clanks, before the heavy steel door is opened outward and a uniformed police officer appears in the doorway. It's the same officer who brought him a glass of water and antibiotics about an hour ago—sixty eternities. Oddur stares at him with a quizzical expression that's combined with terror and faint hope.

"Someone is here to see you," says the officer. "If you want to meet him, that is."

In the same breath, another man steps into the narrow field of vision. An elderly man wearing a trench coat and a clerical collar. It's the priest who eulogized Patrekur in HJC's auditorium the previous Wednesday, which, in Oddur's mind, might as well have been in the last century or a previous life.

"Reverend Árni Sigfússon," says the officer.

Oddur sighs. He's so lonely that he could cry, and has also cried so much that he feels as if he's empty inside. Making it worse, though, is that he can't imagine opening up to someone he doesn't know. Especially an old priest who will no doubt go on about the power of prayer and how much Jesus loves him. "Thanks, but I'm tired now and am going to …"

He stops when he sets eyes on what the priest is holding in his veiny hands. It's neither a Bible nor a cross, but a YooHoo bear that he's seen countless times before—the bear that Lísa always has hanging on her school bag. The one she hides her weed in.

Did she send the priest to him?

"Yeah, all right," he says hurriedly. "But not for very long."

The officer nods, then lets Reverend Árni into the cell and shuts the door behind him. The lock clicks coldly shut.

"May I?" Reverend Árni points at the sparse bunk, and then sits down next to the prisoner. The priest smiles in a fatherly manner but it's as if he doesn't know what he's going to say, which is a definite relief for Oddur.

"How are you doing?" he asks after a short silence.

Oddur doesn't take his eyes off the bear that the man of God rolls between his fingers and seems to have forgotten. "Did Lísa send you to me?"

Reverend Árni nods. "She came to see me. She told me that you were being held here and were doubtless feeling awful. She wasn't feeling so well herself, to be honest. And yes, that's right—she asked me to bring you this poor little thing."

The priest hands Oddur the bear. He takes it, and, immediately pressing its stomach lightly, feels that there's something inside it, something other than the joints that Lísa usually keeps in it. He can tell that there's paper in there, as well as something hard that moves to and fro between his fingers.

"Is there anything you'd like to tell me?" asks Reverend Árni.

Oddur shakes his head.

"No?"

Oddur clears his throat. "Listen, I don't want to be rude or anything. But I'm kind of under the weather and I think I just need to go to bed. But thanks for coming. It was nice of you to come see me, and to bring me the bear."

"No problem, my friend. God grant you peace." Reverend Árni pats him lightly on the back, then gets up and knocks on the door.

As soon as the priest is gone and Oddur is alone in the cell again, he unzips the zipper on the back of the bear and removes the contents of the secret compartment from it. It turns out to be a folded newspaper clipping and a plastic bag with white pills in it, probably around thirty of them.

What is this?

Oddur unfolds the clipping, and a small, folded piece of paper falls in his lap. He lets it be for the moment, instead turning his attention to the newspaper clipping, which turns out to be an obituary from the *Morgunblaðið* daily. It's as if the blood freezes in Oddur's veins; his eyes fill with tears and he goes numb from head to toe. The obituary is for Áslaug Ellertsdóttir. The date of her death is given as July 10, and she was buried a week later, while Oddur, Patrekur, and

Bragi were drunk in Ibiza. In the accompanying photo, she's sixteen years old, in the bloom of life and beaming.

"Oh, God …" Oddur whimpers. Wiping warm tears from his cheeks, he reads the obituary. It's written by her sister Rut, and every single word is heavy with sorrow and remorse—and anger. She weaves the story of the Irish slave Þorgerður Brák into the short but fateful life of her sister and soulmate …

… It was the villain Skallagrímur who threw a heavy rock at his son's nurse, hitting her between his shoulders and sinking her in the dark sea, murdering her in cold blood. We know who killed Þorgerður Brák, and we remember her tragic death and keep her name alive. But just as the innocent slave was murdered, someone cast a rock at my beloved sister and hit her in the heart, causing her to lose hold of her lifeline, fall and sink into the dark sea within her. It wasn't a real rock but was heavy enough to kill, because words certainly hurt. And the one who threw that rock, who spoke those words, doesn't deserve to live.

My beloved sister! As soon as I …

Oddur can't read any more. He feels as if he could vomit. The words hit him like poison arrows. They pour over him like ice-cold, suffocating darkness … like a rain of heavy rocks.

He puts down the obituary and unfolds the piece of paper that fell into his lap. It's a printout of a message.

You can end this. Or continue the game. It's your choice.
D.

End this? Oddur lifts the bag of pills. Oh, of course. The pills are for him. Are they sleeping pills?

Probably.

Enough to kill him?

Probably.

"Oh, Lísa!" Oddur fights back tears. She says she loves him, but then sends him this. She wants him to take his own life. Otherwise, her brother will die. Is he surprised? Did he think the nightmare was over?

No.

He foresaw it all, more or less. He knew that it would end somehow like this.

FOURTH MURDER

Hörður Grímsson is sitting in front of his desktop computer; he opens the browser and navigates to the country's main news outlets. The announcement that Axel sent to the media half an hour or so ago is already being published. *The police in Reykjavík have issued a wanted notice for two young people.* Two photos accompany the headline: the one of Rut that Hörður got from her father, and a sketch of Haukur Hansson based on Hörður's description of him. *Those who have any information about Rut and Haukur's whereabouts are asked to contact the police.* Axel and Hörður decided not to issue a notice for the blonde girl on the Vespa, as information about her was both scarce and rather general, but requested that all police officers on duty in the capital area keep on the alert for her. Shortly after the announcement's release, Viktoría, the reporter with *DV*, called Hörður. Recognizing the number, he didn't answer.

When the red-haired giant's cell phone rings, he closes his browser. At first, he thinks it's the reporter again, but then sees that it's Jenný. He takes a deep breath before answering.

"Yes?"

"We have the preliminary results of our analysis of the objects you removed from Drápuhlíð."

"Well?" says Hörður. Jenný has seldom sounded as dry and professional, for which he is truly grateful.

"The metal residue scraped off the pliers is lead, on the one hand, and a copper alloy on the other."

Hörður blinks several times as his brain quickly processes this information. "As if from a bullet and cartridge?"

"That's what I thought."

"Was someone disassembling a bullet?" asks Hörður. He imagines a cartridge being held in place with one pair of pliers while the bullet is turned out of it with another.

"Possibly. And then there's the hair."

"Yes?"

"It was easy. 100 percent nylon."

"Nylon?" exclaims Hörður. "Is it from a wig or …?"

"I would think so."

"Okay," Hörður mutters distractedly.

"Any new developments?" asks Jenný. Her professional tone has given way to a warmer, deeper voice.

"No, not as such …" mutters Hörður. "Listen, thanks for this information. I'll contact you if there's anything else."

"Please do."

Hörður hangs up, and then immediately enters another number that he knows by heart. After four rings, the savings bank manager answers.

"Ellert here."

"Have you heard anything?" Hörður asks unceremoniously. He gets up from his work station, grabs his cup, and walks over to the coffee corner. But there's no coffee ready, as he's the only one working in the Cave at the moment and hadn't thought about making any.

"No, nothing."

Hörður strides out of the Cave and into the corridor, with his phone to his ear and the empty coffee cup in his left hand. "We've issued a wanted notice for her, as you may know. Have you seen it?"

"Yes."

Since Hörður is talking on his cell phone, he decides to takes the stairs instead of the elevator to the fourth floor. The phone connection isn't always the best in the elevator. He's on his way up to the cafeteria, where there's almost always coffee to be had. "You're not familiar with the boy in the sketch?"

"No."

"Well then," says Hörður. It isn't exactly fun talking to the bank manager, who becomes more unsociable with every conversation and will no doubt end up as a driftwood log in a suit. "But I have a few questions."

"I'll answer them if I can."

"I'm counting on it," says Hörður as he enters the cafeteria, which is large and spacious, but completely unoccupied at the moment. It's Sunday, of course, and most of the desk cops are off. But the big coffee machine, which grinds premium coffee for every cup, is on.

The red-haired giant puts his cup on a stand beneath the machine's nozzle and selects black coffee. Then he steps slightly to the side while the machine is working, as it's quite noisy. "Question number one. Do the sisters own, or have they owned, a small motorcycle, a kind of Vespa?"

"Yes, or … the Vespa was Áslaug's. She got it in the spring. I think it's here in the garage. Why do you ask?"

"I need to know if the Vespa is in the garage or not," says Hörður irritably. He lifts his coffee cup and takes a sip.

"I'll go check. Hold on."

"I'm not going far," mutters Hörður. He walks over to the windows, which face south. It's fairly bright outside, but the sky is a cold blue, with winter being right around the corner.

Hörður takes another sip of his coffee, which is hot and strong; just the way he likes it. He looks out the big windows at everything and nothing. Here he stood last Monday, watching Oddur and Haukur conversing. Just now, some bum is roaming where they'd been standing talking; otherwise, there are few people out and about. But then an older man in a trench coat appears. He steps onto the sidewalk in front of the police station, as if coming out of it. Hörður feels as if he recognizes the man, who is gray-haired and has a dignified air.

Isn't that …? Yes; it looks to Hörður as if it's Reverend Árni Sigfússon, the priest who handled the memorial services at HJC. Was he at the police station? Doing what? On a Sunday of all …

Hörður stiffens when a black haze begins flickering behind the priest—it's a shadow that shrinks back and hesitates, until finally gliding nearer to the police station and either dissolving or disappearing into the building.

"Oddur," groans the red-haired giant. He puts down his coffee cup, storms toward the exit and presses the red button on his phone before entering a number from memory. It's the number of the telephone *down in the cells*, as is said at the station—at the guard post at the end of the custody corridor. There's always someone on duty if anyone is being held in custody at the station.

With his phone pressed to his ear, Hörður rushes down the corridor and presses the button for the elevator. Finally, someone answers.

"Guard post."

"This is Hörður from CID," says the red-haired giant. "Was anyone with Oddur Bjarnason?"

"Yes, a priest. But he's gone. He didn't stop long."

"Did Oddur ask for him, or ...?" Hörður pounds on the elevator button in the hope that the elevator will come sooner, go faster.

"No, the priest just came on his own."

"You weren't supposed to let anyone in!" growls Hörður. "Did he bring anything with him?"

"No ... or ... he had a teddy bear or something."

"Go and open the cell ... now!" shouts Hörður, before hanging up and dialing 1-1-2. In the same breath, the elevator door opens and he steps into it and presses the down button.

"Emergency Number. Can I help you?"

"This is the police station on Hverfisgata," says Hörður as the elevator door closes. The elevator jerks into motion and starts to descend. "You need to send an ambulance right away! It's best for the paramedics to use the back entrance. The patient is in a holding cell in the custody corridor. I don't know his condition at the moment, but I expect the worst. Do you copy?"

No response.

"Hello?" Hörður shouts into the phone, but the line is dead. "Fuck!"

The elevator opens, and he rushes out and runs to the custody corridor, where he finds the door to cell number one. When Hörður reaches it, he sees that the officer on duty has started CPR on Oddur, who's lying unconscious on the floor, dark blue and stiff, with frothy saliva at the corners of his mouth.

"Keep going, don't give up!" Hörður shouts at the policeman, before dialing the Emergency Number again. On the cell's bunk is a stuffed bear with an open back. Next to it is a newspaper clipping, a slip of paper, and an empty plastic bag.

"Emergency Number, can I help you?"

Hörður looks at the officer, who stops doing compressions on Oddur's chest, throws up his hands, and moans miserably. He has clearly given up, as the prisoner is displaying no vital signs.

"I can't believe that I let the girl play me like that," says Reverend Árni Sigfússon. He's sitting at the kitchen table at his home, more or less in shock. "She seemed terribly worried about the boy, and I felt for her—and for him, of course. But she wanted to kill him? Why in the world?"

"It's a long and complicated story," says Hörður. After contacting the priest by phone, he went to his house to take a statement from him. He could have summoned the old man to the station, but didn't want to impose that task on him.

"I expect she's in custody?" asks the reverend.

"Yes and no," mutters Hörður. "Lísa is in the emergency room of the Psychiatric Ward of the National Hospital, after suffering some sort of nervous breakdown. She was given sedatives and will be in the care of professionals until she's fit to speak with others again."

"I feel very bad about this," says Reverend Árni. "I made a mistake. If there's anything I can do to make up for it, please let me know."

"It was the officer on duty who made a mistake, not you," says Hörður. "Firstly, he shouldn't have let any uninvited visitors visit the detainee, and secondly, he should have searched anyone who came to talk to him."

"I see," mumbles the priests, as shamefaced as a child.

"But you can actually do me a little favor," says Hörður, after a short reflection. "It's a rather strange favor, and not quite according to the book—neither mine nor yours, which is why I'd fully understand if you say no."

"Anything!" says Reverend Árni, with the desperation of a man who wants only to be able to make amends for his crime.

It's ten o'clock in the evening, and pitch-dark outside. Hörður is sitting at the wheel of his SUV, which is parked in an empty lot in front of the medical center on Safamýri Street, and speaking to Axel through the hands-free system. The building's windows are dark, as it's closed on Sundays.

"I've already issued an arrest warrant. The Drápuhlíð house is under surveillance. But no one has seen Rut. Where is she keeping herself?"

"Good question," replies Hörður. "But there was a charge from a hotel on Ármúli Street to a credit-card account at the address of Ellert, the bank manager. Maybe he stays there when he comes to the city. But maybe his daughter is staying there? We should look into that possibility."

"Absolutely. But she would hardly be there under her real name, would she?"

"Difficult to say," says Hörður. "But if she doesn't want to be found, she's hardly going to pay with a credit card, come to think of it. She could be in any hotel or guesthouse."

"Exactly. She could also be at someone else's house."

"Yes, yes," mutters Hörður.

"We still don't know anything about this Haukur or the blonde girl. Partners in crime, it seems. Could it be that Lísa Kristjánsdóttir is the girl on the Vespa?"

Hörður sighs heavily. "Maybe. But I don't think so."

"We've got to find these kids. Where are they from?"

Hörður opens his eyes wide. "Where are they from?"

"Oh, my head isn't really clear; I haven't slept much and am pretty tired. Where are they, I meant to say."

Hörður sees a sedan being driven into the parking lot. It's a Volvo station wagon. "I think the psychologist is here."

"Then let me know what comes out of your conversation. You're perfectly free to lean on him a bit, within reasonable limits. Just remember what I said, huh?"

"I'll remember," says Hörður. "We'll talk later. I'd like to ask you about something. Just a little scenario that I'm thinking about … staging, actually."

"Staging?"

Hörður shuts off his car's engine. The driver of the Volvo has parked it and stepped out onto the parking lot. "I think I know how we can lure Rut out of hiding. I've spoken to the principal of HJC, and Reverend Árni is going to help. Don't give out any information and don't speak to the media without talking to me first."

"The principal? The priest? What are you talking about?"

"It could be called … a performance," says Hörður hesitantly, knowing that the word will jolt his boss.

"A performance?" exclaims Axel.

"We'll talk more later, I've got to go now," says Hörður as he pulls the key from the ignition.

"Why did you want to meet me here?" asks the psychologist Ævar Zöega as he unlocks the door of his office, which is toward the far end of a corridor on the second floor of the medical center. He and Hörður Grímsson had greeted each other on the sidewalk outside, and then the psychologist had let the red-haired giant in through the staff entrance to the building, entered a code to disconnect the security system, and switched on the lights in the corridors. "You could have stopped by my place. I could also just have come to station. Still, it would have been easiest just talking on the phone."

"Everything's a mess down at the station," lies Hörður. "I didn't want to charge into your home, and this is too sensitive a matter to discuss over the phone."

"I understand," says Ævar, who no doubt knows that the policeman is lying. He switches on the light in his office and invites Hörður in. "But if you think I'm going to let you into my files without a warrant, you can just forget about it."

Hörður looks around the room: a typical psychologist's office. A desk, filing cabinets, a sofa and armchair. A low table, upon which are a box of tissues and a vase of flowers. A cheap, framed painting on the wall and a depressing fern near the window. "As you know, a warrant is often gotten after the fact. Through the years, the police have been able to rely on the cooperation of specialists in town, especially if human lives are thought to be in danger."

Ævar signals to Hörður to take a seat on the sofa, which he does. The psychologist himself sits down in the armchair. He's on his home turf and clearly intends to take advantage of that fact. He crosses his legs, clasps his hands, and looks condescendingly at the policeman. "And is that the case? Are human lives in danger?"

"Definitely," says Hörður. He's wearing his coat, unbuttoned, and sits spread-legged. "Murders have been committed and the murderer is still at large. We don't even know if the perpetrator is working alone or has accomplices. The situation is both uncertain and uncomfortable, to say the least."

"And what?" asks the psychologist. "You have a suspect and that person is a patient of mine? Or do you just need a general expert opinion?"

Hörður changes position on the sofa, making a squeaky, crinkly noise as his coat rubs against the leather upholstery. "I'm looking for a specific person. And need to know more about her."

"You've put out a notice for Rut Ellertsdóttir," says the psychologist. "It was in the news earlier. You're welcome to get to the point right away."

"Of course," mutters Hörður. "I …" He stops when his phone starts ringing. He curses under his breath, fishes out his phone, looks at the screen and frowns. Then he turns down the ring-tone volume and sticks the phone back in his pocket. "Excuse me. Just the woman I live with. Probably just wants to know when I'll be home."

"Interesting." Ævar Zöega tilts his head, smiles faintly, and regards the policeman as if he were seeing a rare animal for the first time.

"What?" Hörður asks suspiciously.

"Nothing," says the psychologist. "But it's said that a picture says more than a thousand words. The same can be said for body language and facial expressions."

Hörður grunts. "So what? Yes, I'm looking for Rut, and have some questions about her and her background. She's a bit of a mystery, so it's important for us in the department to …"

Ævar opens his eyes wide and holds out the palm of his right hand, like a teacher silencing noisy students. "I'm going to stop you right there—sorry. But since I'll possibly be testifying in court if your suspicions are substantiated, it's very important that this conversation of ours be within the framework in which I work, and that our two testimonies about what we say here don't undermine my credibility as a clinical expert whom patients can trust."

"What the hell are you talking about?" growls Hörður.

"We can't name any names; can't talk about flesh-and-blood individuals," says the psychologist. "But we can talk about imaginary cases and/or various symptoms of illnesses."

"I didn't come here to play games," Hörður snaps. "Either help me in good faith or …!"

Ævar holds out his palm again, silencing the red-haired giant. "You're looking for a murderer, are you? Tell me something about this person. You've got a suspect in your sights, right?"

Hörður grunts again; this psychologist gets on his most sensitive nerves. He feels like slapping this arrogant prick. But he decides to keep himself in check and play along with the intellectual. "The suspect is a girl of sixteen. She lost her mother a few years ago, and her twin sister two or so months ago. They both committed suicide. The suspect is mentally ill and vengeful. She was confined to a wheelchair for a while, but the paralysis was psychological in nature; the result of a nervous breakdown, as far as I understand. I really don't know any more."

"You say she's mentally ill," says Ævar. "What do you think is wrong with her?"

Hörður grunts. "Isn't that something you would know better than I?"

Ævar shrugs. "I want to hear your opinion."

Hörður snorts in frustration. "What else, then?. She's very angry. But also smart. It's a dangerous combination. I would guess that she's basically depressed and world-weary."

"Who isn't depressed?" asks the psychologist, with a smile.

Apparently not you, Hörður thinks contemptuously as he stares angrily at this healthy, tidy man who doesn't seem to have suffered so much as a scratch or bruise in his vacuum-packed, uneventful life, much less suffered any major trauma.

"But you're right," Ævar continues. "Depression often turns into anger, and world-weariness is certainly a side effect of depression. A world-weary person doesn't really want to live; he longs either for relief or death, and when relief seems out of reach, death is often what he chooses. A person in such a state of mind has no respect for life, neither his own life nor that of others. Which makes it easy for that person to kill."

Hörður is relieved. That was exactly what he meant.

"But world-weariness is only the beginning," says the psychologist. "There could be many more things afflicting the suspect."

"Okay," mutters Hörður, who reads between the lines that there *definitely* more things afflicting Rut Ellertsdóttir. "Like what?"

Ævar shrugs. "What do you think?"

Hörður grits his teeth in anger. He doesn't want to be, and can't be, wasting time with this blather. "I don't know, damn it! It could be schizophrenia or a personality disorder, psychopathy or something worse. The girl is nuts; that much is for sure!"

The psychologist nods. "You're still on the right track. This could very well be a so-called borderline personality disorder. Which doesn't rule out psychopathy. People with this disorder teeter on the borders of normalcy and psychosis, which is where the term comes from: borderliners. Such people are vain, easily offended, and often end up clashing with their immediate circle and their loved ones. They live in a black-and-white world and divide other people into two groups, friends and enemies. Their moods can be extreme, and fluctuate between extreme happiness and rage. In a psychotic state, these people can hear voices, experience hallucinations, and display various other serious psychiatric symptoms."

Hörður listens and nods, as he likes what he hears—this all sounds very believable and could without a doubt be a description of a mentally disturbed murderer. But he's not only looking for a murderer, he's also trying to expose a well-organized, well-thought-out phenomenon that calls itself Deathbook and hides behind a digital veil, and could be either a small cell of malicious young people or something bigger and more dangerous, even a foreign association of nihilists or who knows what. "What about collaboration? This imaginary girl of ours could have accomplices. Is it easy for these borderliners to work with others?"

Ævar looks up and to the side as he thinks this over. "Crazy people can certainly be charming, and as a result, it's relatively easy to take control of weak-minded individuals who are captivated by their persuasive power. Collaboration, no—but coercion, oppression, and domination, yes."

"I see," mutters Hörður. He views this Haukur in the same light: as a submissive follower rather than a collaborator. The boy doesn't seem to have much to him.

The psychologist clears his throat. "But what's afflicting this girl that you're looking for might be more than a literal personality disorder. Her *dilemma* goes deeper; her psychology is complex and reaches quite wide—into other *areas*, so to speak."

"Is that so?" says Hörður, but more out of a mixture of impatience and interest than irritation, because he senses a change in the words and demeanor of the psychologist. He seems to be easing up on the brakes and expressing himself intuitively, even passionately. Maybe he's envisioning a doctoral dissertation on this patient?

"But let's talk a bit about you first, Hörður," says Ævar Zöega, placing his left hand under his chin. "You interest me. Tell me, how long have you had a live-in partner?"

Hörður scoffs. "None of that! I'm not here to play any games, but to expose other people's games. Dangerous games that have cost lives. Either you cooperate fully, or you'll have me to deal with!"

The psychologist doesn't let the red-haired giant throw him off. "I'd guess a few years; three at most. Tell me, do you love your partner?"

"Listen now!" Hörður replies angrily.

"Do you two have children?" asks Ævar.

Hörður reddens with anger but manages to control his temper before saying or doing anything he'll regret. Yet he can't restrain himself completely. "You're a real shitty piece of work. Yes, I love my partner. No, we don't have any children. But we're trying. Or … she, um …"

He stops, curses under his breath, and rolls his shoulders moodily.

"She wants a baby but you're not so sure?" the psychologist guesses. "Maybe you don't want to have a child but don't dare or don't want to tell her because you don't want to lose her or disappoint her."

Hörður gapes in amazement.

With a sarcastic expression, Ævar shrugs. "You wouldn't be the only one. *Nobody* is unique, really."

"Maybe not," says Hörður.

"You reacted strangely when she called just now, the woman you live with," says the psychologist. "It was as if you had something on your conscience. I might have been imagining it. But you looked like a kid who runs into a shopkeeper he's stolen from."

Hörður's face turns bright red. "If you don't mind, I'd like to finish discussing what I came here to discuss."

"You cheated on her?" Ævar asks gently.

"You're on thin ice," growls Hörður. "*Very* thin ice."

"I'll tell you one more thing about the girl you're looking for," says the psychologist. "But first I want you to answer one question. You say you love your partner. The woman you live with, the woman who wants to have a baby with you. But you cheat on her. Why?"

Hörður's temper flares, his whole body stiffens, and he instinctively clenches his fists. "Watch what you say, or I'll pummel you. I swear."

Ævar doesn't show the slightest sign of fear. "Maybe it was just weakness of the flesh. Momentary madness. It's happened before. Maybe you've fallen for another woman, but I doubt it. But maybe you have self-destructive tendencies. Maybe you've never been happier, but deep down feel as if you don't deserve it. Maybe you don't believe in happiness. Maybe you want to ruin your own life because you're more familiar with disappointment and hopelessness than happiness, and we tend to choose what we know over what's best for us. But what do I know?"

"Maybe, maybe, maybe," Hörður mutters irritably. His heart is pounding and he's so hot that he's sweating. Every single word of the psychologist's soliloquy echoes like gunshots in his mind.

Self-destructive tendencies

The bastard really hit the nail on the head there, the red-haired giant must admit.

"But we were talking about the girl," Ævar says suddenly.

"Yes," says Hörður, hoarsely. He breathes lighter, relieved as hell to be out of the psychologist's spotlight.

"The root of all her problems may perhaps not lie in her mind or her heart," says Ævar sagely.

Hörður digests this. "If we admit that mental illness is a disease of the brain and that evil resides in the heart, then there aren't many spiritual places left in the blessed human body. In fact, the heart is just a muscle, biologically speaking. So all of our problems should originate in the brain, right?"

"Whether the heart is just a muscle or an underestimated sense, even the abode of the soul, it's an eternal source of questions and disputes, among artists and philosophers as much as psychiatrists and psychologists—but we'll let this all be for now," says Ævar wryly. "After all, scientists haven't yet found evidence of the existence of what we call the soul, have they."

"That's right," mutters Hörður, who has actually thought a great deal about the heart, the soul, and eternity without ever having come to any definite conclusions. He's generally of the opinion that the soul is fiction and that everyone's life ends when the heart stops beating. But sometimes he believes in the existence of the soul and life beyond the sensory world, a kind of eternity in the spiritual cathedral of the universe.

But that's probably just wishful thinking …

"But our self-image is more than just thoughts, memories, and emotions, isn't it?" asks the psychologist.

Hörður nods to encourage the psychologist to continue. He isn't directly listening, but waiting for Ævar to stop this endless rigamarole and get to the heart of the matter. But of course he is still listening, sort of indirectly and with one ear. The words flow through his brain and become electrical signals that rush along channels and kindle thoughts, retrieve memories, connect, analyze, and …

Suddenly, a light comes on in the policeman's mind. He experiences a mild, pleasant electric shock in his cerebral cortex, his eyes open wide, and he straightens up and gapes in amazement. Yes, of course! That's what he means! He's a specialist in that field, after all—how couldn't he have realized this before?

Hörður laughs, and the psychologist gives him a wry, triumphant smile.

"Where are they from," says the red-haired giant, as he thinks of Haukur Hansson and the blonde girl on the Vespa. Axel M. Axelsson had misspoken, but at the same time pointed Hörður in the right direction. He just hadn't realized it then.

Now he knows not only *who* they are, but what matters most. *Where* they're from.

MONDAY

The morning is gray and cold. It had rained during the night, and the ponderous clouds still spit out a drop or two. The soil is drenched, the streets and sidewalks are wet, and there are puddles and little streams all over the place.

Hamrahlíð Junior College looms against the dark-gray sky like a butte of black rock. Lights shine softly behind the curtains of just a few windows, the parking lots are mostly empty, and only a few souls are out and about in the vicinity of the school—a rain-soaked student or two vanishes in through a strip of light in the butte, like an elf on his way to a secret gathering. The school's normal activities have all been disrupted this Monday; all classes are canceled due to the horrific events that have recently shaken not only this educational institution but also the entire community. Yet a memorial service for Oddur Bjarnason will be held in the auditorium at nine o'clock. This is why the building is open and partially lit.

Axel M. Axelsson drives his Mercedes-Benz SUV into the parking lot in front of the building and parks it as far from the entrance as possible, so as to attract the least attention. He looks at his Rolex; it's seven minutes to nine. The car's engine idles with a low murmur. Axel taps his fingers on the leather-clad steering wheel. He's far from calm and is still skeptical that it was the right decision for him to give

Hörður Grímsson a green light for this unconventional operation, which he actually called a *performance*. But the red-haired giant had made a fairly convincing case for why it should go ahead, in addition to the fact that he was well-prepared, having planned out the operation carefully. But the detective hadn't given much advance notice, and there was a lot that needed to work right in order for them to pull off this *performance*.

Axel had tried to calm and mislead the media by means of silence, half-truths, and a slew of lies. That actually only got them more excited, which is why there are police officers in unmarked cars at all the intersections around Hamrahlíð. Their job is to keep the members of the media away from the scene, should they get or have gotten wind of what's going on—or at least delay them for as long as possible. Axel had had to get the principal of HJC and the school's teachers on board with the Criminal Investigation Department, as well as Oddur Bjarnason's foster parents and a few others. What is worrying old Steppenwolf most is whether Hörður might have overlooked something important in the preparation of the operation—something that could possibly endanger the lives and limbs of the innocent students in the auditorium. The thought is uncomfortable, to put it mildly.

If one student gets so much as a scratch on his forehead, heads will roll at the Hverfisgata Street station, and the head of the CID will be the first one of all. And if any more students lose their lives—and that in the middle of a police operation—the matter will be investigated by independent parties and serious charges will be brought as a result. Then he and Hörður could even end up behind bars.

Axel sweats at the thought. Then he shakes his head as if to push these thoughts aside. He mustn't think such things.

His blood pressure is high enough, but his stomach ulcer has been slowly mending—at the moment. No, he's got to believe and trust. Hörður is no fool; maybe a little careless, but …

Steppenwolf heaves a sigh. It's too late to call it off, anyway. Isn't it? He looks again at his watch. Three minutes to nine. Yes. He'd better get a move on; the service is about to begin. He grabs the key to shut off his car, but stops when his phone starts ringing. It's Jenný from Forensics.

"Yes?"

"Are you inside?"

"No, but I …"

Jenný interrupts him. *"I just finished analyzing the plastic gun, and there's something you need to know."*

Axel's stomach tightens. "Tell me."

Jenný takes a deep breath, then tells him the results of the analysis in short, quick sentences.

Axel feels a chill. "Have you passed on this information to Hörður?"

"I tried to call but he didn't answer. He probably has his phone on silent. But I also sent him a message before I called you."

"Damn it!" hisses Axel. He hangs up, shuts off the engine and puts on his black fedora hat as he steps out onto the wet asphalt. Dressed in polished English leather shoes, a black suit and vest under a black cashmere coat, a white shirt and black silk tie, he heads toward the school's entrance. Steppenwolf's coat bulges slightly at his right hip, from the revolver that he stuck in the holster on his belt before leaving his office.

Again, Axel looks at his watch. He just hopes he isn't too late. That Hörður got the message and will call the whole thing off.

Backstage in the auditorium, Hörður paces the floor with a scowl and a distant look in his eyes. He is *leading the devil by the reins*, as people used to say of those who walked with their hands clasped behind their backs. In his mind, he goes over an imaginary checklist and tries to convince himself that he's well prepared, ready for anything, and has taken precautions against everything imaginable and unimaginable. As far as he can tell, he's done so, but at the same time, he naturally has doubts about his own capabilities and the benevolence of the Lady Luck of the universe.

The back room of the auditorium is fairly spacious; it has three long tables and plenty of chairs, a coat hanger, a large mirror, a kitchenette, and a small toilet. The principal and the five teachers who will take part in the memorial service are sitting together at one table, chatting in low tones and sipping coffee. Hörður didn't eat breakfast, and is so stressed that he feels queasy. He tries breathing deeply and regularly, relaxing his tense muscles, and calming his mind.

Hörður doubtless feels like an actor a few minutes before a premiere, since he's about to step on stage and address an audience. The thought alone makes him feel slightly dizzy. Not only does he have stage fright, he's also worried that something will go wrong, with awful consequences. Not only awful for him and his department, but for …

He starts from his heavy thoughts when an aggressive buzz catches his attention. Is his phone …? He hurries over to the coat rack, where his leather coat is hanging. He fishes the phone out of its inner pocket and looks at the screen. Two missed calls from Jenný and one message.

What now? Hörður sweats with anxiety as he unlocks the phone and opens the messaging app. In the same breath, the principal and the teachers get to their feet. Their chairs scrape the floor, and the hair rises on the back of Hörður's neck as he reads the message from Jenný.

Analysis on plastic gun completed. A BULLET WAS NEVER FIRED from it.

Hörður feels doubts and worries stream like a paralyzing poison into his bloodstream. The gun was never fired. What does that mean? That Patrekur and Bragi *weren't* murdered with it? Most likely. But since one gun could be printed, then …

The principal clears his throat. "Shouldn't we go out on stage? It's nearly nine …"

"I'm coming," mutters Hörður. He taps in a question in reply to Jenný's message.

Weren't other guns just printed, then?

He presses send, and then puts the phone back in his coat pocket. Was that a smart question or not? It probably isn't possible to fire such a plastic gun more than once or twice. They couldn't withstand the heat. So the murderer most likely printed a new gun for each murder. But …

Time is running out; he can't be wasting it on such speculation. He decides to stand by his decision and finish what he's started. Who knows, maybe the culprit will fall into the trap and the case will be closed within the next few minutes.

That would be great, the policeman thinks as he secretly crosses himself.

"After you." The principal opens the side door and lets Hörður and the teachers ahead of him out of the back room and onto the lit stage. The policeman takes a deep breath. It's time; now there's no turning back.

But why was there no bullet in the gun when Oddur fired at Haukur? thinks the red-haired giant as he squints in the glare of the spotlights directed at the auditorium's stage. He follows the teachers to a row of chairs on the right side of the stage and sits down next to one of them. On a small table are glasses and a pitcher of water. He fills one glass.

Hörður's forehead is beaded with sweat and his heart is racing. He'd thought out the alleged murder of Haukur Hansson and come to a fairly clear conclusion on it—but he can't for the life of him recall his conclusion as he sits there like a doomed man on the stage in front of the audience, awaiting his turn.

The principal walks straight to the podium, politely clears his throat and then welcomes the students—the few who are scattered around the large auditorium. There's a slight crackle from the microphone and the principal's low-key voice sounds throughout the hall, like a prayer reading in a cathedral.

Hörður tries to swallow, but his mouth is so dry that it hurts. The plastic gun never fired a bullet? What makes this so important? Is he overlooking something?

Axel M. Axelsson hurries down an empty corridor of Hamrahlíð Junior College. He looks again at his gold watch. It's one minute to nine. He sees two students go through the door of the auditorium, but otherwise, the school appears empty. But Axel knows better. He slows down a bit, then whistles softly and looks in all directions. At first, nothing happens, but then faint footsteps and a slight rustling are heard. Before Steppenwolf knows it, he's surrounded by gray-clad SWAT team members wearing ski masks and bulletproof vests, all armed to the teeth. They had concealed themselves in nearby classrooms under stairs, behind partitions, and on the upper floor of the building. The commander of the gray wolves steps over to speak to the head of the CID.

"Be ready," Axel whispers. "But don't enter the auditorium until I give you the signal. I'll sit near the exit and knock on the door when and *if* we need you. Keep in mind that there are about twenty students in the auditorium, and at the moment, we don't know which of them is or are suspected of murder—if any of them. Understood?"

"*Capeesh,*" says the commander in a raspy voice, before signaling to his men to keep a low profile but be ready at the same time. Focus shines from the eyes behind the masks.

"God be with us," mutters Axel. He takes off his hat, opens the door to the auditorium, and slips in. He finds a seat near the door and sits down gently. The auditorium is dark and nearly empty, but he does see the shapes of students here and there, generally two or three together. The stage, on the other hand, is lit. At the front of is a podium, a large framed photo of Oddur Bjarnason with a mourning ribbon across one corner, and a splendid flower bouquet in a vase. The principal is addressing the audience and behind him, seen from the audience's left, the teachers sit in a row, along with red-haired, black-clad giant.

Axel opens his eyes wide. Is that really …?

Detective Hörður Grímsson has combed his shoulder-length hair carefully and put it in a ponytail at the back of his neck. In doing so, the policeman's facial features and general appearance have changed. His eyes look larger and his mouth wider, his cheekbones are prominent and the same may be said of his ears, which have been covered by his coarse mop of hair ever since the red-haired giant started working at the Criminal Investigation Department. But it's not just the slicked-down hair that catches Steppenwolf's attention; it looks to him as if Hörður Grímsson is wearing a snow-white clerical collar and a black shirt, which is carefully tucked into his trousers.

"I'll be damned …" Axel whispers to himself as the principal finishes his speech.

It's time …

Hörður feels peculiar, as if he's ill or dreaming. He hears that the principal has finished his short introduction and sees that he's leaving the podium. They catch each other's eye, and for a moment it's as if the policeman doesn't know that it's his turn, that it's he who should stand up and walk to the podium and not someone else. But then he blinks his sea-green eyes, jerks into motion, lifts his glass of water, and gets up from his chair in all his glory. The lights are blinding; he can hear his heart pumping fast and smells the heavy, sickly-sweet odor of the bouquet.

Hörður puts down his glass and grabs the edges of the podium with both hands, like a ship captain trying to keep his balance on the bridge as he steers his vessel through heavy seas. He looks out into the dark auditorium and tries to count those present, take note of where they're sitting, and preferably distinguish them. The school sent an e-mail to twenty randomly selected students, as well as Rut Ellertsdóttir. It isn't certain that everyone who received the e-mail is present, nor is it out of the question that the information about the memorial service was shared and that there are more than twenty-one people there, but at a glance, it appears to the policeman that the audience numbers twenty, not counting the man in the overcoat in the back row.

Is Axel here to keep watch on him? So it seems.

Hörður wipes the hot sweat from his forehead. How long has he been standing at the podium without uttering a word? Five seconds? Ten? Longer? The silence is paralyzing at first, and then the audience starts to get restless. One teacher coughs; another fidgets. A few whispers are heard from the audience.

Hörður clears his throat. He'd put together some lines in his mind, decided to a certain extent what he was going to say and in what order, but as he stands there in the spotlight like a petrified troll, he can't for his little life remember a single word of it.

"Dear teachers and students," he says in a serious, breaking voice. "Thank you for being here today. We're gathered to talk about Oddur Bjarnason … to *remember* him."

He runs his eyes regularly over the auditorium, memorizing where the students are sitting, how many are sitting together and which are sitting alone, while at the same time trying to group them by gender and appearance. Three images flicker through his mind at the same time—the photograph of Rut, Haukur's face, and a vague image of a blonde girl with exaggerated makeup. He tries to match these images to the faces in the auditorium, but they're obscured by darkness, while he himself is half-blinded by the light coming from above.

"As your principal mentioned, Reverend Árni couldn't be with you today, but I'm filling that void, so to speak." Hörður forces a quick smile before becoming serious again. He still has his mind on the message from Jenný. Suddenly, the wheels start spinning, and he breaks into a sweat when he realizes what it is about the plastic gun that doesn't make sense. It can hold only one bullet, but Bragi was shot twice.

Either the murderer reloaded the plastic gun and shot the victim a second time, or he or she used a revolver. Which means that that person still has a revolver: the six-shooter that disappeared from the drawer of the police chief in Borgarnes.

Hörður coughs from stress. "But before I begin, I would like to ask you to do one thing. We're going to look inward today, to be alone with ourselves as we unite in grief and remember a beloved classmate, individual, and friend. That is why I would like to ask those of you who are sitting next to someone to move three seats away from that person, and you who are sitting directly behind someone to move two rows back."

A grumble runs through the auditorium, but then a few students shrug their shoulders, and before long all do as the giant priest has asked them. Before a minute has passed, the audience members have spread out around the hall.

Hörður nods, as if to express his approval. If the murderer is among the students, he isn't sitting close enough to anyone that he can quickly take the person hostage, should everything go wrong. "Thank you for doing that. The next thing I'm going to ask you to do is keep calm and sit tight in your seats, no matter what anyone says or what happens."

The students become a bit fidgety at these words, but no one says anything because they can't whisper or speak in low tones to a seatmate anymore, what with everyone sitting alone and half-abandoned in the empty auditorium.

Hörður closely monitors every movement in the hall without staring or focusing too long on the same spot, while trying at the same time to see the students' faces better in the hope of spotting a suspicious person—one or more. But the darkness isn't helping, and students of junior-college age look terribly similar. He can, however, see that there are eight boys and eleven girls. A total of nineteen students. There are four girls with long blonde hair and two short-haired boys with glasses.

"Some of you may have realized that not everything here is as it seems," says the red-haired giant as he fiddles with the clerical collar that Reverend Árni loaned him. The collar is rather small and narrows slightly at the neck. "There are so few of you here today because you're the only ones who received the e-mail from the school. And I'm not a priest, but a police detective. Pastoral care is not my field; I was given the task of finding a murderer on the loose. The person who has the lives of your schoolmates on his or her conscience."

In the auditorium, one or two girls gasp for breath, but otherwise a pin could be heard dropping.

"If anyone among you doesn't have a clear conscience," says Hörður in a deep voice, "I would like to ask that person to surrender … or else to take it nice and easy. It's too late to escape or put up any resistance. I'm not the only policeman here. The game is over."

Hörður pauses for dramatic effect. He looks intently over the auditorium without seeing anything unexpected or suspicious. Of course, it's not out of the question that the murderer isn't there. But the policeman finds that unlikely.

The room is restless.

"Stay seated; keep calm," says Hörður in a fatherly tone. He looks at a blonde-haired girl sitting in the middle of the auditorium. She glances back at him before lowering her gaze. "I know that these situations are both uncomfortable and unfair. But you're in no danger, and this will be over before you know it. Until then, remain calmly where you are."

Hörður wipes beads of sweat from his forehead. But are they really in no danger? Not entirely, that's for sure. He clears his throat before continuing. "This all started with the murder of your classmate Patrekur. He was lured to Heiðmörk, where he was shot at close range. A brutal murder, resembling an execution. The person who lured Patrekur there was clearly a close acquaintance of his, because he knew that Patrekur had certain photos in his possession—photos that he offered to buy. The murderer left a clue at the scene: a small box connected to a certain party in Borgarnes at which a young girl died from ingesting dangerous drugs. Was the murderer trying to tell us something? Was he taking revenge for the girl's death? So it seemed. But the murderer could also have been misleading the police."

Hörður blinks when drops of sweat trickle into his eyes. He tries to slow down his racing heartbeat by taking a deep breath, and then continues. "One murder is one murder too many. Not to mention when a young man in the prime of his life is shot in the head and left in his own blood. Then Bragi was murdered, turning a difficult investigation into a sheer nightmare. What the hell was going on? There were still few clues, except those left for the police. And it appeared that there was a direct connection between these atrocities and the death of the girl in Borgarnes. The girl's father was registered as owning a handgun of the same caliber as the weapon with which the boys were shot—a gun that turned out to be missing. But since the girl's relatives and friends all had alibis, the search for the perpetrator continued, without result. But someone had taken the gun. And by this point, only one of the three friends from Reykjavík who had been to the party in Borgarnes on the tenth of July was alive. Oddur Bjarnason."

Hörður pauses briefly, takes a drink of water, and looks over the auditorium again without seeing anything suspicious or unusual. The students sit stiffly in their seats and glance suspiciously at each other as they stare at the fake priest at the podium. Then he goes on. "At the same time as this is all happening, while the police are investigating two brutal murders and two young men lie cold in the morgue, other, even stranger things are happening in the parallel universe commonly called social media. Days or weeks before the killings began, several young people received friend requests on Facebook, requests that they accepted since it appeared that their schoolmates were sending them—faces and/or names that seemed familiar, without the receiver of the messages directly knowing them. After accepting the requests, these same kids received requests to *like* a certain page on Facebook, or whatever it is you do there, but that page had a highly gloomy appearance and was called Deathbook. You can forget about searching for it now; it's gone."

Hörður takes another drink of water to moisten his dry throat. "Then the kids began to get messages from that Deathbook. It seemed to be some sort of game. It asked those who *liked* it to put someone on a death list. If you wanted someone to die, who would that person be—something along those lines. And the question was asked until the person named a name. One girl named Patrekur, one boy named Bragi—and so on. After Patrekur was murdered, the girl who named him was sent a video. It was a recording of Patrekur's murder, taken with a so-called GoPro camera that was probably strapped on the murderer's head."

Someone in the room gasps.

"That's not all," Hörður says gravely. "The girl then got a new message from Deathbook. Since her wish had been fulfilled, it was her turn. Now she was supposed to kill a person that someone else had put on their death list. She was sent a name, what Deathbook called a *subject,* and was given a deadline to commit the murder. If she didn't do as she was told or go to the police, a certain loved one of hers would be killed. It was made clear to the kids that this was a kind of killing game, if a game it should be called. Those who took the bait were trapped in the web that Deathbook had spun."

Hörður looks intently into the auditorium, as if to challenge the culprit to give him- or herself up. But no such thing happens. The students, however, are agitated, feeling frightened and maybe starting to fear for their own safety. "We at the police didn't know anything about Deathbook or this game—this chain letter of death. We were investigating a difficult murder case and the investigation was going slowly, although I always had the feeling that we were on the right track. But it was always as if we couldn't see the forest for the trees. To add insult to injury, persons to whom there was more than met the eye began to appear. I saw and spoke to a slender boy who said his name was Haukur, and a gabby girl called me and introduced herself as Áslaug. According to her, she and Haukur were students at HJC and worked together on the editorial board of the school newspaper. That turned out to be a lie. But these kids were certainly real. A witness described Áslaug to me. She was said to have long platinum-blonde hair and quite exaggerated makeup. Haukur has cropped hair and round glasses. These kids are real, yet they don't seem to exist anywhere."

Hörður watches the students, who look around fearfully. No one in the auditorium has cropped hair, but one of the boys is wearing round glasses. The four blonde girls look stressed as can be. They're aware that the vague description of Áslaug could apply to them and find it uncomfortable, understandably. But only two of them have completely platinum-blonde hair, and one of them has a noticeable tan. The other is the one in the middle of the auditorium. She's sitting straight-backed, has loose hair, is wearing a dark raincoat and has a purse or shoulder bag in her lap. And she's the only student there currently looking at the red-haired giant and not at the others in the audience.

"Then it was Oddur's turn," says Hörður loud and clear, recapturing the attention of the students, who then settle down a little. "It was he who put Bragi on the death list. And after Bragi was murdered, he got a message from Deathbook. He was given the name of a person he was to kill. The name was Haukur Hansson. If he didn't obey, his girlfriend Lísa would be killed next. But then something unexpected happens. This Haukur Hansson contacts Oddur. Haukur is also tangled in Deathbook's web. His subject is Lísa, Oddur's girlfriend. But he doesn't want to kill her. On the contrary, he wants Oddur to kill him. He's dying of cancer anyway, according to him. And since Oddur is supposed to kill Haukur anyway, he agrees to do as Haukur asks. By doing so, these two intend to break the spell of Deathbook. Yet Oddur realizes that it won't quite work out. He himself may escape, but Lísa won't. Even if Haukur doesn't kill Lísa, that doesn't mean that someone else won't be assigned the task. That's why he decides to give himself up and lay his cards on the table, in the hope that the police can find the culprit and thus break the vicious circle."

Hörður takes a sip of water. The auditorium is silent. He has the undivided attention of the students, who drink in the story. "But then things get complicated. Oddur says that he shot Haukur, but the body isn't found. He also claims to have had a GoPro camera on his head and recorded the murder. The plastic gun he used is found where he discarded it, but not the camera. The recording from it is then presumably sent to the person who put Haukur on the death list, in confirmation and as a warning—this is what will happen to you if you don't listen."

Hörður throws up his hands.

"So that's how it works, right? The murderer isn't one, but many. They're controlled remotely by this abominable Deathbook, which arranges the murders, provides the weapon, and has the murderer in question record the horrific act. One murder calls for another. And the nightmare continues. How many people are tangled in this horrendous web? Who comes up with and organizes such a monstrosity? One person or more? Domestic or foreign? And what's the point of all this, if any?"

The policeman looks inquiringly over the auditorium. "Isn't the murderer going to answer?"

Once again, a murmur passes through the audience.

"Why should the culprit be among us here today?" Hörður asks solemnly, before answering the question himself. "Yes, to get closure. The term 'closure' was originally used for the payment of a debt—a settlement, but is also used for conclusions. This memorial service is a confirmation of Oddur Bjarnason's death. It's the period at the end of his existence. By holding this service, we're commemorating this good young man, as well as *concluding* his life here at this school. My theory is this: Oddur's death was the original and probably the *only* goal of the person who murdered his friends, Patrekur and Bragi, in cold blood. And not only that, but Oddur had to die by his own hand, which he did. This memorial service is the culmination of bloody revenge. That's why I'm convinced that the culprit is here."

Hörður looks over the audience. At the stiff bodies and pale faces. One girl suppresses a cry, another whimpers, and some glance around in despair.

One of the boys raises his hand and asks in a broken voice. "Can't the rest of us go?"

Others seem paralyzed.

Hörður shakes his head. "The last few days have passed so slowly that I feel as if it's been ten years since the murder investigation began, not ten days. Or has it just been nine? I'm not sure anymore. But I know that this is all coming to a close. The end is near. I've been wandering in a maze, a haunted house—in an abandoned castle with long corridors, countless rooms, dungeons, and long, winding passageways. I've been looking for a boy with cropped hair and round glasses and a blonde girl who drives around on a mini-motorcycle, but first and foremost, I've been looking for a depressed, seclusive person with dark, tousled hair and a stubby nose. She's a student here at HJC, but you've never seen her. She lives in a top-floor apartment in the Hlíðar district, yet she's never seen coming there or going. Her mother committed suicide and her father was broken and distant. A cousin of hers died from a drug overdose, and her twin sister took her own life that same day. She's paralyzed, but not, and it was she who stole the gun from the locked drawer at her uncle's house. Her name is Rut Ellertsdóttir, but she doesn't want to go by it. She's a girl, but not. She's a boy, but not."

Hörður blinks his eyes before directing them at the blonde girl sitting in the middle of the auditorium. "And she's with us here today."

The girl doesn't move, but it looks to him as if she stiffens slightly and her cheeks redden a bit.

They look each other in the eye.

"There was an interview with you on TV this spring," says Hörður, with a serious expression. "Your face was blurred, you didn't appear under your own name, and your voice was altered. But it was you. Or should I say *you two?* Because you're not just the wanted Rut. You're also Haukur Hansson. And you're also the girl who has shown up here today, the one with the platinum-blonde hair who says her name is Áslaug, which was your sister's name. That artificial Barbie is the girl you never were; Haukur Hansson is the boy you want to be. But you're neither. Where do these characters come from? From inside your head, out of the dense, dark forest of pain and a broken self-image. As you yourself said, you're a freak. A mentally disturbed freak driven by self-hatred and a thirst for revenge."

"Shut up!" the girl barks as she abruptly jumps to her feet. She points accusingly at the policeman and stares at him with sparks of fire in her eyes. "What right do you have to judge me? You're incompetent and stupid. You tried to stop me, but you couldn't. You lost, but I won. It's you who's the freak, not me!"

Finally! Hörður thinks. He's relieved, but is far from calm. He has managed to trap Rut. But he hasn't arrested her yet, only cornered her. She's dressed in a dark blue or black raincoat and is wearing a soft shoulder bag. The bag hangs below her waist on the right side; its strap crosses her chest and lies over her left shoulder.

"You're not the only one who can play games," says Hörður. He tries to speak calmly and deliberately, despite the pounding of his heart. "This service here, for example, is just a play I've staged solely to lure you out of hiding. As I said earlier, Oddur's death was the original and only purpose of this entire horror. I realized that after he took all the sleeping pills you had Lísa bring to him. But your plan has failed, because Oddur isn't dead. His life certainly hung in the balance and he's still in intensive care, but they've managed to save him."

"No!" cries Rut as she tears off her wig. Underneath, her hair is cropped—only the round glasses and a slight theatrical flair are needed to turn her into Haukur Hansson.

A wave of fear sweeps through the auditorium; the other eighteen students are terribly agitated and clearly want to escape this awkward situation as quickly as they can.

Hörður stiffens up, as Rut's reaction is even more violent than he expected. When he sees her stick her right hand into her shoulder bag, he feels almost sick, because if what he said is true, that it was she who stole Police Chief Andrés's gun, then she still has it in her possession.

"Easy," says the red-haired giant, but he stops when he catches a movement out of the corner of his eye, toward the back of the auditorium. It's Axel M. Axelsson. He has stood up in readiness to knock on the closed door.

What is he doing …?

"Stop! Don't …!" Hörður yells. Axel freezes mid-movement. But Rut doesn't. She looks quickly over her shoulder, then turns around halfway while raising a large handgun. It's an old Smith & Wesson six-shooter, leaden-colored and unwieldy. A big, heavy gun that uses .44 caliber bullets and has already killed two people.

"Don't move, old man!" screams Rut. She points the gun at Axel, who has also pulled out his revolver. Steppenwolf's weapon is a .38 caliber Ruger, black, with a short barrel.

"Drop the weapon!" Axel shouts back. He aims his small gun at the girl with the big gun and waits for her next move.

There's a sharp bang as one of the SWAT-team members kicks the door open. The teachers start in their seats, Hörður's face pales, while the students scream, throw themselves onto the floor, and cover their eyes or ears. The gray-clad SWAT team bursts into the auditorium, kneels here and there and aims automatic assault rifles at the short-haired girl in the raincoat who's brandishing the revolver. She, however, doesn't give up, but just grits her teeth and stares menacingly at the highly trained tactical forces without lowering the barrel of her weapon.

Axel M. Axelsson can hardly believe this is happening. He stands there between the rows of seats, his legs spread wide, aiming his revolver at a young girl holding a weapon that could easily kill an elephant. Steppenwolf's coat is unbuttoned and his hat is on the floor at his feet. Axel looks almost exactly like a burned-out detective in a black-and-white Hollywood movie. But unlike a character in a movie, he's actually in mortal danger. If the girl shoots and hits him, he's pretty much dead, even if it's in the thigh or arm. .44 caliber bullets can easily tear people's limbs off of them, leaving holes and gashes that drain the body of blood in a matter of minutes.

How did it end up like this? He had just sat down in the back of the auditorium and laid low while Hörður let loose. In fact, he'd half-forgotten both time and place, as if he were at a conference or lecture, because he found it so interesting listening to the red-haired giant trace his path through the murder investigation, gradually narrowing the circle while moving farther away from the hard-boiled world of facts and scientific investigation into the sick, complex mind of the alleged murderer, and finally exposing that person in a dramatic way. He carried out that blessed performance of his like a true professional—and toward the end, like a magician, as those present were left breathless when he pulled the villain out his hat like a rabbit.

But then Axel had woken in alarm from a bad dream. Hörður was no magician; the performance was part of a murder investigation, and not a show by any means, and the villain who was pulled into the light was as far from being a cute rabbit as possible. Before old Steppenwolf knew it, he found himself facing a terribly dangerous, unpredictable murderer who was capable of anything, including shooting him straight in the head or the heart.

He'd only been planning to knock on the door—to give the SWAT team the green light to enter. But the girl had been on the alert, and was quicker to react than any predator. He himself had reacted fairly quickly, pulling his Ruger in flash from its holster.

But in retrospect, it was probably a mistake. The girl holding that big gun in both hands doesn't appear to be the type to obey orders or take threats lightly. Her eyes are as dark as night, but at the same time shoot sparks that could ignite a fire. Then the SWAT team had burst in and made the flammable situation even worse. The atmosphere in the auditorium was like a powder keg about to explode.

"Drop the gun or we'll shoot!" shouts the commander of the gray wolves. Metallic clicks are heard as the SWAT team members take the safeties off their rifles.

"Shut up!" the girl shouts in return as she pulls back the hammer of her six-shooter.

"Nothing drastic!" yells Axel, his voice hoarse from stress. He sees the teachers fleeing out a side door of the stage. He also sees Hörður step out from behind the podium and walk to the front of the stage, to the audience's right. He opens his arms and raises his hands high, like a true preacher.

"Silence in the room!" thunders the red-haired giant. He's holding something in his right hand. His fist is clenched around something, but Axel doesn't know what it is.

Hörður doesn't like this at all. The school's auditorium is a scene of chaos and confusion; it's all headed for a shootout that will doubtless claim lives. Axel is aiming a gun at Rut, whose weapon is pointed at old Steppenwolf. Hörður knows that Axel is a good shot, but if Rut shoots first and hits her target, it's uncertain whether the head of the CID will stand up again. However, the chances of Rut surviving the next few minutes are much lower than for the others in the room. Aiming at her are seven or eight automatic weapons, all in the hands of men who won't hesitate to fire or who miss their target when and if they pull the trigger.

To call the situation flammable would be an understatement.

Hörður tries to think both fast and clearly. He instinctively pats his belt and trouser pockets, but he doesn't even have handcuffs or pepper spray, let alone a baton or firearm—not even a pocketknife. But there's something hard in his right trouser pocket.

Is that …?

He sticks his hand in his pocket and grabs a smooth rock the size of a walnut. It's the rock he took from the school project in Rut's room in the house of the savings bank manager in Borgarnes—the *boulder* that the villain Skallagrímur was about to throw at the bondwoman Þorgerður Brák.

"Silence in the room!" To Hörður's considerable surprise, his order has the desired effect. The shouting and screaming stop, no one moves, and all eyes are on the red-haired giant. But the gun's muzzles are still raised, fingertips are tickling the triggers, and the threat is the same as before. Hörður nods curtly, as if to thank his audience for their attention, and then tries to think of his next words, his next *move*, as he takes one more step forward.

"No one needs to die here and now," Hörður calls over the room. Looking at everyone and no one, he acts completely calm even though he's about to have a heart attack from stress, holding his hands up so that those present see that he poses no threat. "No one needs to pull the trigger; there's no need to fire a shot. There are innocent people in here. No one will die here today—*everyone* will walk out of here. Believe me."

"If anyone so much as breathes, I'll shoot the old man," Rut growls. She's still aiming at Axel, who's head is beaded with sweat. He's still aiming at her, as well.

"You there at the back," says Hörður. He looks at the commander of the SWAT team, a robust-looking man of around forty. "Lower your weapons and put the safeties on. Your presence here isn't helping."

"Not a chance," replies the commander, who knows he doesn't need to heed the detective.

"Do as he asks you," Axel then says.

The commander hesitates, then signals his men to pull back. They put the safeties back on their guns and lower them.

"Thanks," says Hörður. He's relieved, but something's still bothering him. Something vague that flickers like a will-o'-the-wisp behind his consciousness. But he can't grasp what it is and tries to push the feeling aside.

"Rut," he says. "Aim the gun at me. You have no quarrel with this man."

"He's pointing his gun at me," Rut hisses.

"Axel, put your gun down," says Hörður. He knows very well that he's taking a huge risk. But this performance was his idea, and the thought of Axel losing his life because of him is almost unbearable.

"But …!" Axel grits his teeth. Then he decides to do as Hörður says. He lowers his gun, bends down, and lays it on the floor.

As Axel rises again with empty hands, Rut turns back around and aims the murder weapon at Hörður, who suddenly realizes what it was that was gnawing at his hindbrain. It's the memory of the shadow he saw at the memorial service for Patrekur—the shadow of death that appeared on stage exactly where he's standing now.

Was it a harbinger of Bragi Unnsteinsson's death? Or a harbinger of his own death? Hörður doesn't know the answer, and doesn't want to know it. All he knows is that hesitating amounts to losing, so he shouts at the top of lungs as he throws the rock at the girl with the big gun.

Rut pulls the trigger. *BAM!*

Axel lays his small gun on the floor between the rows of seats and straightens up again. He sees Rut turn quickly with her six-shooter raised, and at the same time, Hörður reacts, letting loose with a deep-voiced cry and throwing something forcefully toward the seats, like a black-clad baseball player.

Rut fires—the loud report echoes through the room, smoke erupts, and Hörður's head pitches as he loses his balance. A second later, something hard hits the girl's forehead with a loud pop, and she groans loudly.

"No!" cries Axel, throwing up his hands. He sees Hörður Grímsson jerk backward and fall to the floor. At the same moment, the girl collapses, as if someone had opened a trapdoor beneath her.

SWAT team members jump on the unconscious girl, but Axel runs toward the stage, where the red-haired giant lies unmoving. Steppenwolf saw something hit the policeman's head and tear through it like a piece of fruit. He knows it was a bullet, but he neither can nor wants to think that thought to its end.

No, no, no!

Not Hörður, not him, of all people!

TUESDAY

Axel M. Axelsson smiles apologetically as he puts the bouquet he brought in a vase, then evens out the spaces between the colorful, fragrant flowers before throwing the packaging in a trash can by the window. "I know you're not much of a one for flowers. But my wife insisted that I bring you something, a kind of token of gratitude for saving my life. And since I know you don't care much for candy, either, the flowers won. They liven up the room, don't you think?"

"You could have brought me whiskey," mutters Hörður. He props himself on his elbow in his bed in a white-painted, sterile room in the recovery ward at the National Hospital in Fossvogur. He's wearing a colorless, ugly hospital gown and has thick bandages around his head. He's never been paler; his eyes are swimming in a morphine haze, his lips are dry and cracked, and his arms are like lifeless wooden posts. He's weak and fuzzyheaded, bruised here and there, and has an IV in his arm.

He'd been rushed to hospital after being shot by Rut, unconscious and with a fractured skull. The bullet hit him in the right temple, tore through the skin and fractured the bone halfway to the back of his head, without, however, splitting or penetrating it. In fact, the lead skipped off his head, with tremendous force and at a tremendous speed.

The red-haired giant went straight into a CT scan and then to the operating table, where the fracture was repaired and the wound closed.

"They say you'll recover fully," says Axel. He takes off his hat and sits down on a chair for visitors next to the bed. "But you'll have a handsome scar; it's unavoidable. It could have been worse."

"Yes, yes," mutters Hörður, with a slightly sheepish expression. He doesn't feel as if he's saved anyone's life. On the contrary, he feels as if he endangered the lives and limbs of everyone in the auditorium with that prank of his. He should have known that Rut would be armed.

"None of that now," Axel says as he pats the red-haired giant's forearm in a fatherly manner. "I know you blame yourself for what went wrong yesterday morning. But I want you to know that I don't see it that way, and I also want you to know that there will be no repercussions because of what happened."

"No?" Hörður asks in disbelief, having heard tell of critical voices among the parents of the students who were in the auditorium. If there was anything to what Bíbí heard from the news about the matter, there was talk of legal action and sky-high damage payments.

Axel shakes his head. "I just came from a meeting with the parents of the kids who were there. I explained everything carefully to them and dissuaded them from taking us to court. Their kids were certainly there under false premises, having been sent an e-mail asking them to attend a memorial service that was a fabrication, and so on. But it was done out of sheer necessity on the one hand, and with very good intentions on the other. The police had been under a lot of pressure to complete their investigation of this case and arrest the murderer, not least from the afore-mentioned parents. To ensure a speedy and successful con-clusion, the decision was made to set a trap for the culprit. Due to the nature of the case, it was impossible to do so without lying to a few people, and so on. But no one could foresee that the arrest would be made in the way it actually was, with guns being waved and shots fired. As insurance companies would no doubt do under the same circumstan-ces, I referred to the circumstances as a *force majeure*, a series of unexpected events that no one could have actually foreseen. None of the students was injured, thanks to the professional response of the police officers on the scene. The murder investigation has been concluded and the police are grateful for and proud of the students' partici-pation and conduct, and a ceremony will be held to honor them especially for these things, and so on and so forth."

Hörður is very relieved to hear this. "Well played, old man—very well played. So we'll both be keeping our jobs, or what?"

"Of course," Axel declares with conviction. Hörður smi-les faintly, as he knows very well that it could hardly be any closer of a call. Steppenwolf had just barely managed to save them.

"Where's the girl?" Hörður then asks.

"She's in custody, and is undergoing a psychiatric eva-luation," Axel answers. "I guess she'll end up in the psychia-tric ward? I highly doubt she'll be deemed compos mentis. At least she seems to be far from sound-minded."

Hörður agrees. When he thinks of Rut, he doesn't imagine a body or a face, but a vague haze that revolves around a mesmerizing voice that fluctuates between being a sickly-sweet song and toxic bitterness. "She hardly knows who she is, the poor thing. Or *what* she is. She's certainly dangerous, both to herself and to others, but she needs help, first and foremost."

"And she'll get that help, if she *wants* it, nota bene," says Axel, and at the same moment, his phone starts buzzing in the pocket of his wool coat. "She was the one who murdered Patrekur and Bragi, wasn't she?"

"Yes," mutters Hörður. "That's how it looks."

Steppenwolf taps his fingers on his thighs, then stands and puts on his hat. "I really can't be staying. I have a lot of work to get done. But I'll try to stop by again tonight or tomorrow."

"It was good to see you." Hörður squeezes out a smile, then sighs, shuts his bloodshot eyes and falls fast asleep.

I got the hormones myself; that in itself was no problem, the shadow whispers in Hörður's ear. But if I want to change myself completely, I have to go to Thailand or something. Maybe I will, maybe not. But until then, I'm just a shadow, not a person of flesh and blood. I'm just some freak because that stupid committee failed me on my psychological evaluation.

A freak that crawls into your head and eats your brain, lays eggs in your heart and lets the maggots hollow you out from the inside until there's nothing left but crumbling skin that turns to dust and blows away on the wind …

When Hörður stirs, it's evening. The ward is almost dead silent; the room's lights are off, but moonlight seeps through the white blinds in the window. He clears his throat, blinks several times, and waves his hands in the air as he tries to get his bearings, not remembering at first where he is or why he's there. Then he stiffens and goes numb from head to toe, because someone is in the room with him. At the foot of his bed stands a white-clad, pale being, staring at him. But who or *what* it is, he doesn't know.

Is it a ghost?

Hörður gasps and sits up halfway. But then he realizes who's standing there and relaxes a little.

"You scared me half to death," he says, his voice hoarse from his drug-saturated sleep and the stress of recent days.

"Sorry," says Oddur. He's wearing a long gown marked with the logo of the hospital laundry room, with bags under his eyes and sunken cheeks. "I heard that you were in the room next door. But I wasn't able to come see you before. And then I didn't want to wake you. So …"

"No problem," mutters Hörður, before gesturing to the boy to sit down in the visitor's chair. "How are you otherwise?"

"Just so-so," Oddur replies. He takes a seat and squeezes out half a smile. The boy has clearly been shaken badly, and his childish face is marked with strain. He'll probably get back to normal, though; more or less.

"It could be worse," says Hörður, just to say something.

"Yes, yes," says Oddur. "Do you happen to know how Lísa is doing?"

"Yes and no," Hörður answers. "She's recovering, I understand. She's in the outpatient ward and is on some medication. She'll make a full recovery … hopefully. Are you going to visit her or …?"

Oddur shrugs. "Maybe. Or no, probably not. I still love her, I think, but … I don't know if I can understand what she did or forgive for it."

"No, I can see that," mutters Hörður. He's incredibly relieved that the boy survived his suicide attempt. But it was a very close call. After reconnecting with the Emergency Number, he was given important instructions that undoubtedly saved him. Among other things, he was asked if there was a defibrillator handy at the police station, which there was—as he knew—but he hadn't remembered it in the heat of the moment. The device had proven to be very easy to use and within two minutes, it had restarted the young man's heart.

What a relief that had been …

"Thank you for saving my life," Oddur whispers, as if he knew what the policeman was thinking.

"My pleasure," says Hörður, moved by the boy's words. The flowers that Axel brought Hörður are all hanging their heads in the vase on a small table by the headboard, like mourners at a funeral. It's as if they're sad about all the bad things that have happened in the preceding days.

Hörður suddenly realizes what a long trail Rut Ellertsdóttir has left behind her. It's a dark, bloodthirsty trail of death, sorrow and destruction—a trail of anger, violence, disappointment, and broken hearts.

But it all started when a young man snapped a string in the heart of a sensitive teenage girl.

"But you don't still want to die, do you?" he asks hesitantly.

Oddur shrugs, looking distracted and sad. "I don't know. No, I guess not. But I felt as if I had to die. Or that I didn't deserve to live, rather. I blamed myself for Áslaug's death—rightly so. And that's why …"

He stops, heaves a sigh, and shrugs again.

Hörður shakes his head. "Her death wasn't your fault. Relationships end every day. But people don't take their own lives every day because of broken hearts. Or, maybe …

I don't know, and anyway, *that's* not what matters. We aren't responsible for the well-being or lives of other adults; that's just how it is."

"Yeah, yeah," says Oddur, misery incarnate.

"Time heals all wounds," says Hörður. He tries to sound positive and reassuring, which isn't easy because he doesn't believe these words himself. "Or so it's said. Maybe it's right, maybe not. All I know is that life goes on. But that doesn't mean it will get better."

Oddur smiles faintly, and at the same time gets a little gleam in his eyes. "You're not very good at this, are you? Psychotherapy and all that."

Hörður laughs out loud. "I guess not."

"Still," says Oddur with a grin. "It's really nice talking to you, see."

"Is it?" says Hörður, breathing a little lighter.

"The thing is, I don't feel too well … because of what happened with Áslaug," says Oddur, in a tone both sad and sincere. "So … if you have any advice or anything, it would be appreciated."

"Well, no … I don't know," mutters Hörður, looking embarrassed. He nearly adds, *it's not as if I'm your dad or anything*, when he remembers that the boy was an orphan and raised by a childless middle-aged couple who could almost be his grandparents.

"No big deal," says Oddur, clearly disappointed at the answer he was given.

"But I can try, if you want," Hörður splutters, feeling terribly guilty.

Oddur is all eyes and ears.

"Let's see …" Hörður clears his throat. "Of course, I haven't exactly been in your shoes. But not so long ago, my aunt died. She was murdered, in fact, but that's a different story. In other words, she died unexpectedly, and long before her time, and her death weighed heavily on me because I felt guilty about something that I'm not going to go into here. But there were certain things that I wanted to talk with her about and apologize for. But, you know, she was dead and buried, so it was too late or do or say anything."

"And what did you do then?" Oddur asks eagerly.

Borg in Mýrar

*Winter
Closure*

The first snow of the winter had fallen during the calm, frosty night—a nippy breath from the icy expanses of the universe. The morning is like a still image, a postcard—a living photograph frozen in time. The movements, life, and colors of summer had gradually mellowed with the advent of autumn, faded and thinned and turned to nothing. Then winter came and stopped the decline with a cold kiss; it wraps everything in a white, crackling linen and transforms ever-moving nature into a splendid death mask of marble.

Oddur drives over the Borgarfjörður bridge, with the ice-covered Hvítá river on the right and the dark gray fjord on the other, as well as Brákarey Island. Behind him rises Hafnarfjall Mountain garbed in white; ahead is the town at the end of the bridge, then western Iceland, from where you can drive north, to the Westfjords or out to Snæfellsnes. But Oddur isn't making a long trip. He drives straight through the town and the roundabout at its other end, out onto Vesturlandvegur Highway. He passes Loftorka, a large plant that produces precast concrete walls and pipes, and then takes a quick right onto a gravel road that leads to the historic farm and church estate of Borg, the home of the settler Skallagrímur Kveldúlfsson. At the lightly wooded site are a small, white-painted wooden church and an old churchyard.

Gravel and ice crunch beneath the rental car's tires. Oddur could have borrowed his stepfather's Range Rover, but he didn't want anyone to know about this trip of his. He's doing this for himself, and on his own terms. He parks the car in the parking lot in front of the church, next to a stacked-stone wall that separates the parking lot and the churchyard. He shuts off the engine, takes a few deep breaths. Then he opens the door to the cold air, taking with him the flower bouquet that was lying in the passenger seat. It consists of sixteen red roses.

Oddur walks slowly along the wall, through its gate, and finally into the churchyard, which is both unostentatious and peaceful, not least under the newly fallen snow. The sky is clear and blue; the air is completely still, and every footstep breaks the tranquility with a scrunch reminiscent of the sounds made by a wooden ship rocking on heavy waves. Oddur is wearing a coat over his black suit, no hat, and ankle-high leather shoes. His breaths visible, he stands there for a moment looking this way and that. But he sees no recent grave, the snow having erased all signs of activity. As death makes all men equal, so the snow evens out the difference between old and new, living and dead.

Oddur shivers from the cold. He turns up the collar of his coat, walks slowly around the churchyard and tries to read the headstones and crosses. When he finds what he's looking for, he's relieved at first, but then his stomach tightens, his knees go weak and his mouth dry. They're resting side by side, mother and daughter. Áslaug and her mother. To both sides are reserved grave spaces. Presumably one for the savings bank manager, another for Rut.

What now?

Oddur stands there staring; his heart is beating fast and he has a lump in his throat. Why is he so stressed? It's not as if anyone's watching him. Or listening.

Áslaug is dead. Everyone here is dead and has been for a long time. Some for hundreds of years. This is a place of memories. Oddur is the only one here drawing breath. A visitor from the world of the living. An intruder in the land of the dead.

Shouldn't he just lay the flowers on the grave? Or is he supposed to make the sign of the cross first?

Or …? Oddur looks around. There's no one around. He's alone. Yet not. Rushing through his mind are images of the girl who was his girlfriend for a time; memories, smiles, and countless words and phrases. Kisses, touches, looks. His heart pounds; in it, a fire burns—a fire of remorse, shame, and guilt, combined with love, warmth, and bitter regret.

"I …" Oddur stops when his voice breaks. What was he going to say? He isn't sure, but …

Suddenly, his emotions overwhelm him. He falls to his knees, which hit the hard ground sharply. His eyes fill with warm tears, his throat tightens, he gasps through sobs. He lays the flowers carefully on the grave—one rose for each year that she lived.

"Forgive me," Oddur groans through tears. The tears fall down his cheeks, his nose is stuffy, and his whole body trembles. He cries hard and loudly, like a little child—like a broken man. "Forgive me, dearest Áslaug."

His tears are warm, clear, and cleansing.

DEATHBOOK

Autumn
A New Game

Hákon unlocks his cell phone and decides to give his social media apps a once-over before switching off the phone and going to sleep. Or, it's not like he really decides; it's more of an involuntary habit—or a bad habit, rather. Sometimes, it's as if his phone controls his life, and not the other way around. But anyway … someone has added him on Facebook. It's a girl. Björk Björgvinsdóttir, dark haired and very good looking. Hákon is relieved, because it's been quite some time since any girl added him on social media. In the spring, he'd actually been accused of rape, because of which, he had a bad name. He hadn't even been charged; a girl on Twitter just accused him of sleeping with her *without consent*. He hardly remembered sleeping with her, but is at least 80 percent certain he didn't do anything wrong. But not many people were willing to listen to his side of the story; instead, he was basically slaughtered online. For a few weeks, his life was pure hell, but that period seems to be over—thankfully.

He looks through the profile of the girl who added him, clicks on *see more about Björk.* She went to Hagaskóli Middle School and is now at the Commercial College of Iceland. She seems familiar, but still, he can't quite place her. But since she's at the Commercial College like him and so good looking and all that, he accepts her request.

Hákon makes his usual app circuit—Instagram, Twitter, Snapchat—and sees nothing exciting—but first and foremost, nothing bad about himself. What a relief! He takes another look at Facebook, where he has a few notifications. Someone commented on a post on some page that he once liked; a few events that his friends clicked "interested" in are starting soon, and so on, and his newest friend, Björk Björgvinsdóttir, invites him to like a page called Deathbook—neither more nor less.

Hákon frowns. A year ago, a mentally ill girl killed two guys at HJC, and as far as he recalls, she used a "like page" called Deathbook to fuck with them and others. She'd created some sort of game in which the participants could have a chosen enemy killed, but then had to kill a stranger in return. Incredibly sick!

"Strange," Hákon says to himself. That page still exists? He's too curious not to do anything, so he likes the page and opens it. Deathbook appears to live up to its name. It looks to him like a gloomy place, with extremely dark images—ghosts, zombies, leafless trees, crows, the moon in clouds, and the Grim Reaper. The profile picture is of a sinister skull with a hood on its head. Next to it is the name of the page. Below it is the following identifier:

Local Service—663 followers

@NewDeathbook

"What is this?" mutters Hákon. He sees that quite a few Commercial College students have already liked the page. Maybe this is just some Commercial College fad that he hasn't heard of. That wouldn't surprise him.

In a dark basement room, the screen of a stolen laptop illuminates a ghostly face. Pale fingers move like spider legs over the keyboard and the screen displays a list of nearby wireless networks, all password-secured. Low clicks are heard as the fingertips dance over the keys. A program is launched—a hack that unlocks the selected wireless network. In a few seconds, the computer is connected to the Internet. The fingers dance; the Thor browser is opened, then Facebook, and finally the Deathbook subpage.

The page's administrator cracks the knuckles of his bony fingers before opening Messenger, writing messages to several people and immediately pressing *send*. A new game has begun …

THE END?

About the Author

The Dark Prince of Nordic Noir: Stefán Máni was raised in the rural fishing village Ólafsvík, on the Snaefellsnes peninsula in western Iceland. At the age of twenty-six, he put all his belongings in an old car and moved to the capital city of Reykjavík to publish his first book. For the first ten years as a writer, he was working full or half time as a construction worker, a dishwasher, in a printing press and in a home for the insane. His first major success, at home and abroad, was the haunting thriller *The Ship*. Since then, he has been writing the hugely popular Grímsson detective series, along with occasional thrillers and other work. In 2012 the movie *Black's Game* premiered, based on his bestselling thriller by the same title. The movie is the second most popular and second highest grossing film in Icelandic history.

About the Publisher

This book is published on behalf of the author by the Ethan Ellenberg Literary Agency.

https://ethanellenberg.com

Email: agent@ethanellenberg.com

Facebook: https://www.facebook.com/EthanEllenberg LiteraryAgency/

www.ingramcontent.com/pod-product-compliance
Lightning Source LLC
Chambersburg PA
CBHW060618100726
47907CB00006B/1677